The Music Book

EDWARD GLOVER

Gilbert

with best wishes

from Shirley [illegible]

x

Published by Edward Glover

ISBN: 978-0-9929551-0-6

CONTENTS

EDWARD GLOVER

FOREWORD

Some years ago, in Berlin, my wife and I acquired two eighteenth-century paintings.

One was a portrait of Frederick the Great of Prussia, painted when he was comparatively young by a known artist. The other was a picture of an unknown, well-dressed, good-looking, middle-aged man, possibly Prussian, painted by an unknown artist – apparently in 1765, according to a faded handwritten label on the back of the frame. Still in Berlin, I found, in the city's well-known flea market (while rummaging through some 1938 German army call-up papers from the eve of the Munich conference), an original British passport personally issued, in October 1853, by the then Foreign Secretary to Robert Whitfield, his wife and son to travel to the European mainland. On the back of the passport are the stamps of some of the German states the family visited.

Towards the end of 2011 I decided to write a fictional story linking the two pictures and the passport. The result is the tale you are about to read. Two of the characters are actual, well-known historical figures – Frederick the Great, a proponent of enlightened despotism, and Louis XV of France. There are incidental references to some other historical personalities who actually lived at the time and who have helped to provide the necessary backdrop to the story. The remaining characters – and of course the words spoken by the monarchs and the two documents written by Frederick – are merely a fiction of my imagination, created during the long and pernicious Norfolk winter of 2011–12. The time span of the story – 1764 to 1766 – was arbitrarily set by the barely visible date on the back of the portrait of the unknown man. But what is indisputable is the passport Robert Whitfield received some eighty-seven years later to travel on the continent of Europe. Whether a member of an earlier generation of the Whitfield family made a similar journey across Europe almost a century before will remain a matter of conjecture. I have simply used an author's licence to recount such an event.

* * * * *

I wish to thank warmly several people for their crucial assistance and advice as I wrote my book: first, Jenny Langford, a close friend and history freak like me, who kindly read countless early drafts and who helped with some of the initial research; Odile Castro, a dear French friend, who with her sister, Marie-Claire, helped me to envisage the characters who appear in the book in Paris; and Peter Stanford, the journalist and broadcaster and another good friend, who, despite other pressing commitments, patiently read a later draft and who provided some much-appreciated advice on style and final touches to the book.

I would also like to thank equally warmly three special friends and colleagues: first, Tony Burgess-Webb, for his support, encouragement and media-related advice, despite his many other commitments; Michael Woods, for his legal advice and unstinting patience; and Professor Ingrid Stahmer, a close friend for many years and formerly deputy governing mayor of Berlin, from whom I acquired the portrait of Frederick the Great as well as her infectious interest in eighteenth-century German history. My gratitude also goes to two other dear and long-standing friends in Berlin whom I have known since 1985, Bianca and Jurgen Freymuth-Brumby, who helped to inspire my fascination with Berlin and its history, who provided useful information about roads and transport at the time in which the story is set, and who with great patience helped to check the manuscript for factual accuracy and authenticity.

Before the story begins, I wish to acknowledge my deep debt to Sue Tyley, my most patient and highly professional copy-editor. So generous in her time, she checked the final draft for spelling, punctuation, style and storyline. My warm thanks also go to Niall Cook, who designed the book cover, prepared the text for eBook publication and gave other much-valued assistance.

I should also like to acknowledge and thank Lucy Inglis, whose recent and most enjoyable book *Georgian London: Into the Streets* has been an extremely helpful source of information and facts about mid eighteenth-century London; and the excellent exhibition *Georgians Revealed* at the British Library, which shone a clear and fascinating light on the life, style, attitudes and culture of this important period in British history.

My thanks also go to Alison Conway, whose book *The Protestant Whore: Courtesan Narrative and Religious Controversy in England, 1680–*1750 provided most helpful background to attitudes to prostitution during that period, and to the late Nancy Mitford, whose book *Frederick the Great*, first published in 1970, is an immensely readable and colourful account of the life of the Prussian king.

In addition, I extend my warmest thanks to Colin Crane and his assistant, Neil Austin, at Paris Print, my local printers in Norfolk, for making countless copies of re-writes and for helping me in other ways towards the final version of this book.

I also wish to acknowledge three houses that have made a deep impression on me and which helped to inspire my depiction of Meltwater Hall: first, the Casa de Pilatos in Seville (particularly the seventeenth-century upper rooms and their contents); second, Anglesey Abbey in Cambridgeshire (for its configuration and furniture); and my own house in Norfolk.

I would also like to thank my daughters, Caroline and Charlie, and my sons, Rupert and Crispin, for their own deeply appreciated encouragement of my efforts to complete the story. After a lifetime in the British diplomatic service writing briefs and reports, turning my hand to writing an eighteenth-century fiction was not easy. But I was determined to try. They urged me not to give up.

Last and above all my deepest and most special thanks go to my wife, Audrey, who constantly inspired me to keep going and complete the story during the dark and cold months in Norfolk this year and the winter before.

In conclusion I dedicate this story, spanning certain places to which diplomacy and family life have taken me, to Audrey,

Caroline, Charlie, Rupert and Crispin; and of course to Berlin, where my wife and I were stationed from 1985 to 1989 and where the germ of this story was sown without my knowing it at the time.

Edward Glover
Norfolk
March 2014

DRAMATIS PERSONAE

England

Sir Robert Whitfield, Master of Meltwater Hall and its estate
Lady Thérèse Whitfield, Sir Robert's wife
George Whitfield, their son
Arabella Whitfield, their daughter
Lady Barbara Ward, Sir Robert's mistress
John Bolton, an agent in England of King Frederick II of Prussia
Mrs Hallam, proprietress of an establishment in Chesterfield Street, Mayfair
Mrs Rathbone, proprietress of an establishment in Shepherd Street, Mayfair

Prussia

King Frederick II of Prussia
Colonel Carl Manfred von Deppe, formerly of the King's Life Hussars and now Master of the Herzberg estate
The stranger, a most secret agent of King Frederick II

France

Maria Louisa de Vervins, sister of Colonel Carl Manfred von Deppe and wife of Captain Etienne de Vervins
Captain Etienne de Vervins, aide de camp to the General commanding King Louis XV's Royal Guard, Paris
Marie-Aurore de Vervins, the young daughter of Captain and Madame de Vervins
General de la Rivière, General commanding King Louis XV's Royal Guard
Louis XV, Versailles and Paris
Madame Victoire de la Rivière, the General's wife
Sophie de la Rivière, the General's daughter

EDWARD GLOVER

PROLOGUE

Two items were consigned for sale at a leading international auctioneer in London on Tuesday, 23 October 2012. The principal one was an eighteenth-century music book; the other a nineteenth-century British passport (very different to the modern passport, though some of the wording is similar to that found in the inside cover of a modern British travel document). While the old passport bore little comparison in value to the book, the items were linked historically. They were listed as Lots 242 and 243 in a general auction of music, continental books and manuscripts. That morning in London there was the usual auction room bidding activity from specialist British dealers, but the book and the passport had also aroused the interest of private bidders, notably one in Germany. After their formal description, the auction of the two lots began.

* * * * *

Exactly 159 years earlier, on 3 October 1853, at the Foreign Office in London's Whitehall, not far from Mayfair, George William Frederick, Earl of Clarendon, Her Majesty's Principal Secretary of State for Foreign Affairs, personally signed a passport issued in the name of Robert Whitfield, so he, his wife and son could travel on the Continent.

Two weeks later Robert, his wife, Emily, and his young son, Charles, departed from Dover by boat for France to trace the journey of Arabella Whitfield, his forebear, who had left the same port for Calais and beyond eighty-eight years before, on Monday, 2 December 1765.

Robert Whitfield and his family were following the steps of a remarkable young woman who, forced by family circumstance, had decided at the age of twenty-two to turn her back on privilege and comfort because of her insistence that she should not be treated as someone else's chattel. Defying the social conventions of her time, she wished to be personally responsible for her own fate in life, whatever the cost. The actions she took in fulfilment of her ideals, and the events that ensued, changed the fortunes of two families – her own in England and that of another in Prussia. Those fortunes would be inextricably linked until finally broken in the mud of Flanders in the Great War of 1914–18.

As the cross-channel boat slipped its moorings on that sunlit autumn morning, Robert Whitfield sat back and undid the satin ribbon securing the brown leather-bound music book, embossed on the front with the initials *AW*, that had belonged to his ancestor. Carefully reopening the album he leafed through the sheets of neatly transcribed but fading musical scores, including transcriptions of compositions by Johann Sebastian Bach, Handel and Telemann.

It was an exquisite book, but battered. Some of the stitching on the spine was beginning to come apart. Many of the pages – some sewn to the binding and some loose – were dated prior to 1765 and, like the book's cover, bore the initials *AW*. They were well-thumbed. Towards the back of the album there were some less familiar musical transcriptions, dated 1766. One was dedicated to "My beloved Carl Manfred". In the margin of another was a small pen sketch of an evidently large house, beneath which was written the name Herzberg. On yet another there was a charming small drawing of a large and imposing tree with two people sitting beneath it and a glimpse of the same house behind. The remaining pages, each containing a few bars of music, were – with the exception of one – all undated and written in a different hand, though most likely a woman's. Some appeared to be snatches of musical scores for children. The only date visible amongst them was 1769.

Robert Whitfield had examined the book several times before, but this time, as he closed it, a small slip of folded paper fell from the inside flap of the rear cover binding. He gently opened it. In small and fine handwriting similar to that elsewhere in the book were written the now much-faded words, "I will do what people want but only as I want it to be." He wondered what had prompted the writer to write those words. He hoped his journey would explain.

PART ONE: DESCENT INTO THE UNDERWORLD

CHAPTER 1

Retribution, Solitude and Dancing

Saturday, 24 November 1764

Though it was late autumn and a bitter easterly wind blew across the wide north-German plain, King Frederick of Prussia was still at his much-loved summer palace of Sanssouci in Potsdam. Just returned from another inspection of the construction of his new palace (the Neues Palais) nearby, he sat alone in the library. The building work seemed to be taking longer than ever. Once again he had chided the architect for the delay in completion. Despite more assurances that the palace would be finished on time and on budget, the King complained that he was not convinced and once again threatened serious consequences if the building was not more advanced by the time of his next inspection. As he left, he mumbled – loudly enough to be heard – that a spell in jail might help to concentrate the architect's priorities.

Seated before the fire, eating a fine meal – dressed for once not in his usual simple military uniform and boots but in white breeches and a red waistcoat under a blue frock coat he had not worn for several years – he reflected on another year of success and setback in his lifelong policy to extend Prussia's borders. He was getting old – his bones ached – and once again he had been thwarted in some of his plans by the treachery of so-called friends and the scheming of enemies. But there could be no going back on his grand plan to expand Prussia, however long it took. He knew there was more war to come and that he would probably die in his military boots. In the meantime, while there was a lull on the battlefield, he would intensify his undercover activities to pick off some of those who had betrayed him – he never forgot old scores – or who stood in his way. But those he could really trust to help him achieve success were fast diminishing in number.

He still could not bring himself to admit that he had been largely responsible for steadily driving friends and advisers away. The inner circle around him had become smaller by the year. He was conscious – from listening at keyholes – that there was backstairs gossip about his vindictiveness and sometimes odd behaviour. To everyone he cut a solitary and unloved figure. But the King dismissed the chatter. He was who he was. He could not change now. People would just have to accept him. He would press on regardless. That was the way it had always been and it would have to remain so. Of all those around him, he knew there was still one man, who lived in the shadows, who was intensely loyal. He could entrust him with any task, however difficult, costly and bloody it might be. So great was his trust, he would place his life in this man's hands, but his only.

The King drank some wine. He pondered his options in the year ahead: Russia to the east, France to the west and Austria to the south. And apart from these pressing affairs of state and the intricacies of military strategy, there was one particular personal score that had remained outstanding for many years. Now, new information had come into his hands, which at last provided an opportunity to close the matter to his private satisfaction – to deliver retribution. In doing so, he would finally discharge a solemn promise he had made to a dear friend many years before. It was time for revenge. He pulled the bell rope to summon the man in the shadows to receive his instruction, knowing he would ensure that the necessary action would be taken without delay.

A short while later, a tall, thin man entered. He bowed to the King.

Frederick handed him a piece of paper on which he had scrawled a name.

"Find him and do what is necessary."

He then handed the man a second piece of paper on which was written another name.

"Arrange for this man to be present when you do so. I have my reasons for wanting him there. Make sure he comes to no harm. And I want to see him before he leaves on this mission."

"Yes, Your Majesty," the man from the shadows replied. "It may take time to do what you ask, but it will be done."

"No matter," replied Frederick. "Now be gone."

As the man returned to the shadows, the King considered his instruction. Why exact vengeance after so many years had passed? Why not let matters rest? Yet he had always believed promises should be kept. Keeping a promise was a sign of a man's strength of will. And this had been a most solemn promise. Besides, as he had long been convinced, every man has a wild beast within him. And this beast could not be constrained. He would not change his mind.

* * * * *

That same evening, a day's ride away from Potsdam, another solitary man sat pensively warming himself in front of the fire in his library. He had spent most of the day in the saddle, touring his large estate at Herzberg. Carl Manfred von Deppe leaned back and reflected on times past and to come.

It had been a good twelve months on the estate. Further improvements to the land had been made, income was increasing, and he was now admired by his tenants and fellow landowners for what he had achieved in recent years. But, despite frequent social gatherings and occasional visits to Berlin on business, he remained unmarried. Now aged forty-one, he contemplated the prospect of spending the remainder of his life alone. None of the women to whom he had been introduced of late, or whom he had met on the dance floor – daughters of fellow landowners, or those with whom he had danced at the King's palace in Berlin – aroused his physical or intellectual interest. Many were plain; many were empty-headed; and many would almost certainly spend his hard-earned money to show off their finery in evenings of mindless chatter. A soldier by background, he believed that it was better to remain single than suffer such a fate.

There was, however, one task he still had to complete, and that was to renew contact with his sister, who had eloped to France several years before and who, according to her last letter, now lived in Paris. She had written to him multiple times in the past, but he had not been a good correspondent and consequently she had given up trying to keep in touch. He should go to Paris before long to see her, and to find out if her marriage had provided an heir to whom he could entrust Herzberg. He vowed not to let another year slip by without finding time to travel. As soon as winter was past and spring was firmly in its place, he would make every effort to go to France. He had to find her.

* * * * *

Far away at Meltwater Hall in England on that same evening, and despite an early snowfall, Sir Robert and Lady Whitfield's guests began to arrive at six o'clock for dinner and dancing – or "north Norfolk's French soirée", as it was described locally.

The Whitfield family had lived at Meltwater in Norfolk for several generations. As a result of the family's continuing accumulation of wealth through the export of corn and the consequent expansion of the estate, which in turn helped to increase rent income from tenant farmers and others who worked and lived on it, Meltwater had gradually become an island of some substance and influence in the county – though certainly not yet on a par with the aristocratic Holkham or Houghton estates.

The estate stood in more than 1,200 acres of rich, low-level farmland sloping gently upwards towards a pleasing, undulating line of soft hills overlooking the sea. Comprised of red brick with some flint in the Norfolk style, the imposing house had been rebuilt and expanded towards the end of the seventeenth century, replacing an earlier and more modest building from later Tudor times. It was broad-fronted, but thin in depth. The rear of the house faced due south. Its long patio provided shelter from the northerly wind, allowing the family to enjoy the benefit of spring warmth and autumn sunsets for longer than others. Beyond the patio was an expansive garden, comprising lawn but with elegant and well-maintained herbaceous borders, sloping up towards the orchard and farmland beyond. To one side of the house, beyond a low wall and hidden by trees, were cottages for the staff of ten who served the family and the house. There was also an extensive kitchen garden. It was a pleasant and comfortable house, but always undergoing change. Sir Robert had never-ending plans to extend the house even further as his increasing income permitted.

That evening a steady stream of carriages turned from the road – leading from the market town of Freshchester in the west – to enter the grounds of Meltwater Hall through the large open gates and up the long driveway, flanked by flares, towards the distant house. The driveway was bordered on both sides by lawns, particularly striking in the summer, and enclosed by shoulder-high red-brick walls. But now the lawns and the top of the walls were covered in snow several inches thick. The flickering flares, reflected in the snow, created a theatrical effect and heightened the expectations of those arriving. Nearer the house, the guests passed through even larger wrought-iron gates, cast at the local foundry, to enter a grand gravel forecourt.

The carriages drew up one by one outside the grand front porch, thought to be the last remains of an Augustinian monastery that had stood there until the Reformation. Above the entrance was the Whitfield coat of arms, illuminated by a large lantern, reminding everyone – if that were necessary – whose house it now was.

For what had become a prestigious annual event, Sir Robert and Lady Whitfield had invited more than seventy guests from amongst the great, the good and the socially promising of north Norfolk. The much-sought-after invitations had been sent out a month before; recipients of the invitation cards noticed that they were printed on expensive stationery. Prior gossip concluded that this year's event was to be even bigger than the previous year. The steady flow of smart carriages into the forecourt underlined that this was indeed to be an impressive evening. There was much excitement among the occupants as they descended from their conveyances. It was evidently going to be a highly exclusive occasion.

Sir Robert regarded the party as another opportunity to show off proudly the latest architectural additions and embellishments to Meltwater, to enhance further his presence in the county and, of course, we must not forget, to advance his parliamentary ambitions. But most of all it was an evening for Sir Robert and Lady Whitfield to draw attention to their daughter, Arabella, now of highly marriageable age and an asset in the building of family alliances, and for their son, George, to spot a possible wife. It was time for him to make a suitable match and so settle down as the future heir to the estate.

But the Whitfields were not alone in these ambitions. Indeed, all those invited saw the occasion as a time to have fun, to socialise, and for sons and daughters, conscious of the need to find potential marriage partners, to socialise and flirt. This was the one evening to make their mark. And for older guests it was, naturally, a chance to see who had not been invited or who had been asked for the first time and for mothers to push their daughters. The whole evening would quiver with intense sexual and social frisson – a display of human nature at its best and its worst.

On arrival there was much laughter as guests shed their cloaks and coats and took off their outside shoes to put on dancing pumps. In preparation for the evening, all those invited, particularly the young, had sought extra dance lessons to ensure that they would not commit any faux pas on the dance floor and would be familiar with the latest steps. Everyone knew that the ability to dance well on such an occasion was crucial – an important key to romantic success, particularly as the dancing would mimic the rites of courtship as it had always done down the ages. Clumsiness could be social suicide but dazzling dance steps might secure someone's destiny.

Once all the guests had arrived, been warmly greeted by Sir Robert and Lady Whitfield and served their first drinks, the hubbub of laughter and gossip in the Long Gallery was broken by the announcement of the first dance. This was a minuet, to be danced by the host and hostess, in accordance with the ritual of formal dancing at court. Lady Whitfield, tightly corseted, wore a sumptuous ball gown with a pointed stomacher and hooped skirt to make her waist appear even smaller. Sir Robert concealed his plumper figure behind a long blue cutaway jacket worn over a yellow waistcoat and white breeches. For him this minuet would be a severe test of his dancing skill and, conscious that his wife's technique was superior to his, he had (unknown to her) briefly enlisted the services of a dancing master in London to make sure he would survive the scrutiny of his guests. There was a rousing cheer as the two took to the floor and an even greater cheer as they finished, so opening the way for the guests to take to the floor themselves.

Furnished with chairs, mirrors and small tapestries placed against the long north-facing wall, the Long Gallery, which was essentially a wide corridor off which doors opened into the various main rooms of the house, was an attractive and light place to keep cool in the summer. But in the winter months, it served as a barrier against the cold wind blowing off the North Sea two or three miles beyond the end of the long driveway. For an evening such as this it was an ideal place to dance and to keep warm. With the close proximity of bodies, the energetic dancing and a multitude of candles – the array of tall beeswax tapers a clear indication that the evening was going to be a long one – the cold outside was soon forgotten.

Arabella Whitfield's music teacher had assembled a small but lively orchestra from Norwich and her dancing master stood poised to help lead the dancers in their steps. Those ready to dance formed lines, men facing women. The music teacher raised his baton and the terpsichorean festivities began in earnest. Arabella's first partner was Mr Charles Barrow, whose father was a landowner from the eastern part of the county. Handsome but somewhat shy, he greatly admired Arabella because of her beauty and grace and her slim figure, revealed by the fact that she chose not to wear a hoop under her skirt. But he found her intellect and feisty character daunting. She liked him, found him a good dance partner and was attracted by his good looks, but was deterred by his lack of knowledge of the wider world. Moreover, he was certainly not championed by her father who, although beaming with pride that evening, was disappointed that the highly eligible Lord Henry Simon had been unable to accept the invitation to Meltwater. Lord Henry's family had great wealth, owned a substantial amount of land in Dorset and occupied a seat in the House of Lords. The charming but diffident Charles Barrow bore little comparison.

Arabella's second partner was Mr Quintin Hines. He was a more flamboyant young man and a close friend of her brother, George. He lived in London but his family owned land in the southern part of the county and, like Sir Robert Whitfield, his father, Sir James Hines, had significant additional business interests, the income of which was largely derived from the Americas.

"Miss Whitfield," he said as they danced, "you are truly an accomplished dancer. Your steps match your wit."

"You flatter me, Mr Hines."

"I would like us to spend more time together so we can become better acquainted. Perhaps you might come and stay with my aunt in London? I am sure she would love to meet you."

"Mr Hines, I thank you for your kind invitation, but with the roads as bad as they are I am not sure this is the best of times to make long journeys. I am certain you can use your time in London – in the company of my brother, no doubt – to play cards and to enjoy the company of other young women with whom I believe you and he already spend considerable time."

"I think you must be mistaken, Miss Whitfield."

"I do not think so, Mr Hines. Some may think the women in this county backward but we are remarkably well informed. It is on that basis we can judge a man's true character and intentions."

"Miss Whitfield, I see I must work harder to dispel your misconceptions."

"I fear you will have to work very hard to do so," replied Arabella.

Other young men pressed Arabella to dance and she accepted every invitation. But none of her partners really gained her close attention, despite the intervention of her mother to urge her to dance more than twice with Mr Lovegrove and Mr Thomas Hill, both of whom Sir Robert also considered possible suitors for his daughter. In Arabella's judgement, all were either unconvincing or flawed. None measured up to the ideal husband she had long had in mind and none inspired any feeling of sexual attraction within her. None made her heart beat faster.

By contrast, her brother, George, in his new tailored jacket and tight-fitting breeches, was greatly enjoying himself. He had already drunk several cups of punch by the time of the second dance, so fuelling his energy on the dance floor. He paid special attention to two young women, Miss Sophie Skipworth and Miss Alexandra Sproule. Both wore more closely fitted dresses – low cut around the bodice and less full below the waist so as to hint at their figures beneath – as, like Arabella, the old and unflattering style of panniers, hoops and stomachers were not for them. Their respective mothers ensured that their daughters were barely off the dance floor and were as near as possible to George Whitfield, if not dancing with him.

After almost two hours of drinking and dancing, food was served in the dining room. There was a rich array of meats, including pork, lamb, partridge pie, liver and bacon, as well as cheeses, fruit, blancmanges, biscuits, gateaux, jellies and ice creams which it had taken the staff at Meltwater many days to prepare.

With its simple setting, the dining room was probably the oldest part of the house – Meltwater's architectural core. It had a substantial hooded fireplace, above which was a large painted wooden statue of an ascending angel, possibly from the Rhineland, of which Arabella was particularly fond, especially at Christmas time when its raised right hand held a big candle lit on Christmas Day. In the fireplace was a great bronze salamander, which Lady Whitfield had brought from Paris. She prized it because in medieval times a salamander was thought to be invulnerable to fire and therefore an antidote to flames. She would sometimes remind her husband, when he questioned its prominence in the house, that the salamander had been the symbol of the early sixteenth-century French king Francis I and was to be seen on the chimney pieces of his chateaux at Fontainebleau and more widely in the Loire valley, where Lady Whitfield's family owned land. Sir Robert remained unimpressed. The large oak refectory table was of the year 1641 and possibly had once been used as a head table in a monastery or castle, as reflected in the elaborate carving down one side. On the walls hung family portraits, including a striking picture of Lady Whitfield, painted by a talented French artist to mark her marriage to Sir Robert. Meals were taken here every day.

That evening there was clearly not enough space for everyone to sit around the dining table, though Sir Robert artfully managed to arrange it that his most important guests sat there, especially those he felt would advance his political ambitions. The rest of his guests served themselves buffet style and either returned to the Long Gallery to be close at hand when the dancing resumed or sat in the living room, adjacent to the dining room.

With oak beams, oak-panelled walls and stone-mullioned

windows, the living room was large and imposing yet comfortable. The centrepiece was a late seventeenth-century stone fireplace to which had been added a decorative overmantel. There were numerous carpets of Indian origin on the floor, extensively covering large black and white tiles beneath. On three walls more pictures of previous Whitfields had been hung. On the south-facing fourth wall was to be found a tapestry telling one part of the story of the lion and the unicorn. Upon the top of cupboards and sideboards were sculptures of various animals to be found in Norfolk at that time. The chairs favoured ease over style. Lady Whitfield would have preferred more artistic ornamentation in the living room, but her husband had driven a hard bargain on what he thought the balance should be between his masculine country-based tastes and those of his wife.

Near to the fire was a beautiful walnut table with rounded ends. This was Lady Whitfield's elegant needlework table, with a bin underneath in which she stored her wool and canvases. Its frequent use was evidence that Lady Whitfield was as committed to her creative hobby as her friends were – needlework and embroidery were particularly popular with the upper classes in society, and nowhere more so than in the neighbourhood of north Norfolk – though her efforts to engage Arabella in the activity had largely been unsuccessful. So it was not surprising that several of the older ladies that evening, not invited to sit at the dining table, sat around the needlework table to discuss the latest designs and stitches and, of course, to gossip.

Arabella and her close friend, Miss Lucy Fitch, whom she had known since childhood, crept away to the Oak Room, a formal title earned by its dark oak panelling on all four walls. It was really the drawing room, where the family would warm up after a day out in the depth of the bitter Norfolk winter, or to which they would retreat, even in the summer, after dinner, which was usually eaten around five o'clock. The furniture and the plasterwork ceiling reflected Sir Robert's like of the Stuart period; in the central panel he had not unsurprisingly inserted his coat of arms. The pictures on the walls were either of animals or English pastoral scenes. The fireplace was less elaborate than the one in the living room but still substantial. It was here that the family enjoyed musical evenings, with Lady Whitfield and Arabella performing on the decorated harpsichord, often delving into Arabella's treasured keyboard notebook for inspiration.

For half an hour or so, Arabella and Lucy giggled in private as they discussed the dress of the ladies, in particular the rather excessive application of rouge amongst the older women, some of the more outlandish wigs and hair styles, and which ladies had finally had to concede their age by moving into lace bonnets. Just as Arabella was about to play the harpsichord, she and Lucy heard guests running as the cry went up that dancing had resumed.

As they emerged from the Oak Room, Lady Whitfield appeared.

"Arabella, I have been searching for you everywhere. You should be helping to look after our guests, not gossiping in private," she gently reproved with a smile. "Take Lucy back to the Gallery at once. Shortly, they will be dancing a cotillon."

Lady Whitfield had introduced the French country dance at last year's ball and everyone was waiting eagerly to see who could best execute the simple but energetic moves while keeping up with the lively music.

As Lucy ran ahead to be one of the first in line to dance, Lady Whitfield whispered to Arabella, "Your father wants you to partner Mr Hines again. The young man apparently has good prospects and is therefore a possible suitor. And I think he is keen on you."

"Mama, he may be keen on me but I do not like him. He has a bad reputation in London, which is not surprising, given that he mixes with my brother. When will my father accept that I will choose who I will marry, not him?"

"Hush, my girl, and hurry along."

As they re-entered the gallery, Sir Robert was standing impatiently with Mr Hines.

"This young gentleman has been waiting for you. He would like to partner you in the cotillon and I have accepted on your behalf."

"Surely, Papa, it is a woman's prerogative to decide her own dance partner."

Her father bit his tongue, choosing not to reply.

Mr Hines placed his arm around Arabella's waist to guide her to their position on the dance floor, near pride of place adjacent to the orchestra, which was naturally taken by Sir Robert and Lady Whitfield. Arabella shuddered at the gesture and quickly moved his arm away.

By late evening liberal volumes had been drunk and there was much laughter. The dancing had become even more boisterous. Arabella decided that it was time for her and her mother to display a French dance that they had learnt from Arabella's dancing master.

"Monsieur Kunzl," cried Arabella, "give us the music of Monsieur Moderne, if you please."

He raised his baton and the band played a branle de Bourgogne. Mother and daughter performed the intricate steps to music once played at the court of the Dukes of Burgundy. The guests stood enraptured. Then the music quickened once more as the band played a branle gay nouveau. Lady Whitfield and Arabella invited everyone to join them, forming two circles. The slow measures brought the opposite sexes into close proximity – beating heart to beating heart.

"Who was Monsieur Moderne?" a breathless Lucy Fitch asked Arabella afterwards.

"He was an Italian music publisher in the first half of the sixteenth century who lived in France. My mother was given several sheets of his music, which I now have in my music book. It so pleases Mama and me to dance such courtly steps. And it is such fun to get everyone to dance with elegance and enthusiasm. I can see the exertion has brought a flush to your cheeks. And, Lucy, I noticed how Mr Lovegrove put his arm round your waist and looked into your eyes!"

Lucy giggled and blushed.

At eleven o'clock, the carriages gathered in an ordered line on the gravel forecourt, while inside the candles in the Gallery were burning low in their holders. The withdrawal of further alcohol was an additional indication that it was time for the guests to leave.

"Before you go," called out Arabella, "let us do one last dance! My dancing master will lead the way to the music of Monsieur Rameau, composer to His Majesty the King of France."

With that, the weary band struck up once more and played the throbbing pulses of *Les Sauvages* from Rameau's opera *Les Indes Galantes*. The guests, in two lines, man facing woman, stamped their feet to the beats and, following the example of the dancing master, performed ritual-like arm movements. They then joined together to dance in a giddy circle before repeating the stamping steps over again, this time performing chicken-like arm movements. By the end of the dance no one could stop laughing. What fun it had all been.

Happy guests, some light-headed from too much rum and the younger ones breathless – or *essoufflés*, as Lady Whitfield remarked in French – from repeated dancing, put on their cloaks and outside shoes, said farewell to their hosts and clambered into their carriages. The Meltwater end-of-year soirée had ended. Whether any matches had been made remained to be seen. Sir Robert and Lady Whitfield, together with George and Arabella, retired to the library to allow the staff to begin clearing away before the candles finally burnt out.

Smaller than the other rooms but lighter because of the wallpaper that had been applied the previous year, the library had an intimacy and natural warmth that Arabella much enjoyed. Although its windows were, like the other rooms, traditional in their mullioned style and it had a ceiling of interspersed oak beams, the room was more modern in design and comfort; that is to say, more eighteenth century than the rather austere seventeenth-century dining room. There was a large silver chandelier dating from the early eighteenth century. The writing desk was walnut and only recently acquired; the library table was oak and significantly older though still simple in style. The floor was also oak, covered with patterned carpet squares.

Over the marble fireplace hung a large picture of the Cathedral of Notre Dame, which Lady Whitfield had brought from France as a further reminder of Paris and of her religious faith, which she had to shield carefully in a country that still harboured anti-Catholic sentiment even though James II had fled the throne of England more than seventy years before. Sir Robert tolerated the picture's position; it was one battle of the furnishings he had not won. To one end of the mantelpiece was an early sixteenth-century cedarwood figure of St Florian, alleged to have been a Roman soldier who saved an entire city from burning with a single bucket of water. The statue bore a happy smile which Arabella often reciprocated.

There were many books, contained in floor-to-ceiling shelves – a mixture: some rarer volumes, some bought by Sir Robert on his Grand Tour, some his wife had brought from France from her father's prized collection, and some that Arabella had persuaded her mother to buy for her. Arabella liked to sit alone in this room beside the fire, reading and at the same time listening to the clock ticking remorselessly through each hour of the day.

Now it was Sir Robert who sat comfortably beside the fire, drinking a glass of port.

"Thérèse, I congratulate you. That was truly an excellent party. Well done to you and the staff. Everyone seemed to enjoy themselves. My rum and wine stocks have certainly taken a knock. I will need to organise replenishment on my next visit to London. I thought Lady Poole and Lady Mander were most charming, but their husbands drank too much. Arabella, Mr Hines is clearly keen to see more of you. I will see what I can do to make that happen. And George, you appeared to have a good time. Miss Sproule seemed to have caught your particular attention."

Before either her mother or her brother could respond, Arabella retorted, "I do not like Mr Hines and I doubt if I ever will. He is fine with words but beneath that froth hides a less likeable character."

"Arabella," replied her father, "we will discuss Mr Hines – and indeed another young man I should like you to meet – at a more civilised hour. All I wish to say now is that you cannot continue refusing to marry those who clearly wish to be your husband. The final decision rests with me, not with you."

As Sir Robert stood to refill his wine glass, Lady Whitfield looked at Arabella and put her finger to her lips in an attempt to stop her daughter from responding.

Arabella ignored her. Standing up to take her leave of her mother and father, she retorted, "Both of you should put my happiness above that of others in deciding whom I should marry. I wish to share my life with a man in whom I can place my trust, whom I respect and who will treat me as his equal. I do not want a marriage that is a charade such as the one you and Mama have."

With that she left the library to go to her room, leaving her father enraged by her remark and her mother deeply shocked.

Arabella's bedroom was noticeably feminine, as bedrooms should be. It had a small four-poster bed with a low canopy, a gift from her mother, in which Arabella had slept since she was a child. Its canopy and accompanying curtains had a pretty motif pattern, designed in Paris. The kneehole dressing table was inlaid with ivory and possibly came from India, while the bow-fronted chest of drawers was of English origin. There were many candleholders, and on a winter's night such as that evening, the burning candles, along with the fireplace, which was often in use to fend off the intense cold outside, gave the room a deeply intimate and reassuring atmosphere. On the wall hung small pictures of coastal scenes from England and France, and a painting of Arabella at the age of twelve. This was her private world, to which she would escape to be on her own, particularly when the fire was lit, as it was every day between late September and the beginning of May.

Arabella undressed for bed, brushed her hair and then sat for a short while in front of the fire to which Mary, her maid, had added more wood. She looked into the flames, recalling the evening just past and the steadily growing pressure from her father to marry. But there was a corresponding resistance to his unending blandishments within her, getting stronger by the day. She was determined not to give in. She wanted to marry, but she also wanted a relationship of true reciprocity – a relationship of equals.

She went across to the dressing table and took from the lower drawer a small sheet of paper on which she wrote, *I will do what people want but only as I want it to be.* She then placed the slip of paper inside the back of her treasured music book, which lay on the bedside table, and blew out the candles.

Her mother had given her the book on her seventeenth birthday, to coincide with the acquisition of a new harpsichord for Meltwater. It was skilfully bound in hand-tooled leather, with her initials embossed on the front cover. It had become a source of strength and inspiration. The sheets of music inside were well-thumbed. Of all her possessions, this book was closest to her heart and therefore she took it everywhere with her. Each musical composition inside told a separate story, like the chapters of a book. It and its owner had become inseparable.

As the fire crackled, Arabella lay awake in bed pondering how to resolve her predicament. How could she do her duty as her father's daughter but resist his almost tyrannical approach to the choice of her marriage partner? While she wished to follow in her mother's footsteps of virtue and integrity, Arabella's strong character and her instinct convinced her it was just and necessary to insist on what she perceived as her right to be solely responsible for her choice of husband. However much she thought about it, there appeared to be no solution to the present impasse. Her father expected her to submit. She was determined not to do so. She was still awake when she heard her parents come to bed in the adjacent room.

Their bedroom, as you might expect, was on a grander scale. The four-poster bed made a strong statement. The game-bird chintz, used on both the bed and the curtains, ensured a rural setting. The pervading style of the room was more masculine than feminine, but as Sir Robert was spending increasing amounts of time in London, Lady Whitfield had deftly begun to dilute its effect by quietly adding more objects in keeping with her French birth and femininity. Next to the bedroom was a much smaller room, used as a bathroom, the main feature of which was a large hip bath in which Lady Whitfield luxuriated in her husband's absence. Hot water was pumped up from the kitchen below.

Despite the thick wall between the two rooms, Arabella could hear her father loudly insisting that she would not dissuade him from his intentions. She would marry in 1765 and it would be a choice between Lord Henry Simon and Mr Quintin Hines. Both men were excellent suitors and both would make good alliances for the future well-being of the Whitfield family. Despite his wife's protestations, inaudible to Arabella but evident, Sir Robert made clear there was no going back on his decision.

* * * * *

Three entirely unconnected people went to bed that night – King Frederick of Prussia in Potsdam, Carl Manfred von Deppe in Herzberg and Arabella Whitfield in England. None realised that when the King had pulled the bell rope to summon his most trusted servant he had set in motion a series of events which, in the year ahead, would bring them together. The single thread of those events would be betrayal and the profound consequences it would incur.

CHAPTER 2

Meltwater

Tuesday, 5 February 1765

By February the soirée, Christmas and the New Year had long faded into the background of winter life at Meltwater. The façade the family presented to all outsiders was one of continued equanimity, but it was not so beneath the surface.

Early that February morning, Arabella opened the door of the drawing room. Leaning against a chair in the corner was a painting she had not seen before – a portrait, of a man she did not recognise. She was surprised to see it there. The unexpected rarely happened in Meltwater's ordered seasons and daily routine.

The painting of the unknown man had appeared at the house while Arabella and her mother had been in Norwich for three days, during a brief lull in the weather, to choose some dress fabric from a recently arrived French merchant and to buy new winter bonnets in the latest de rigueur designs. According to the butler, Gregson, it had arrived from London in a consignment of furniture that her father had arranged to be sent to Norfolk in order to make space for some new furnishings in his and Lady Whitfield's Westminster town house. Gregson had directed that the painting be placed in the Oak Room to await Sir Robert's further instructions on his own return from London.

Arabella looked at the picture. She wondered where it had come from. Who was the sitter? It was certainly no one she recognised. When had it been painted? The portrait did not appear old, but the paint was not fresh. She peered at the picture more closely.

There was no background landscape or adornment to provide an obvious clue as to the identity of the man or his surroundings. She pondered whether the sitter's posture indicated a proud and successful man, as the size, rich colours and elaborate gold frame of the picture suggested. What had he done in life to inspire the artist to paint such an evidently fine image? Did his expensive-looking red jacket and embroidered blue waistcoat suggest a particular social position or achievement based on inherited wealth? Had he a kind heart? A young woman like Arabella, contemplating the prospect of marriage, was frequently occupied with the appearance of men; her mother had once said that it was possible to tell much about a man from his dress and demeanour, though she subsequently confessed she had been wrong in her estimation of her husband. Arabella reflected on whether the man in the picture was married and, if so, to whom? And, if he were married, did he have a mistress, as many men did, including within her own family, or was he a loyal and loving husband? If he were not married, how could that be? Was it because he had been seduced by wealth, good living, fame and power and therefore been indifferent or unresponsive to a woman's affection?

Arabella turned to gaze into the flames of the strongly burning fire on that cold but sunlit morning, as though they might reveal the answers to her questions. They did not. She looked again at the picture to study closely the sitter's eyes, now in some shadow as the shaft of sunlight through the mullioned window had moved towards another corner of the room. They were soft and warm. Again she asked herself who this man was. What future lay ahead of him, assuming of course he were still alive?

Intrigued by the portrait, about which her mother also had no information, Arabella returned later in the day to look at it again. She was sure the sitter was not English. Though she had no strong grounds for believing this was the case, the unusual cut and style of his jacket and waistcoat, and even his posture, which was somewhat different from the English portraits she had seen in the houses of her mother's friends, convinced her this was so. More to the point, she could not imagine why her father would want a picture that had no apparent connection to his family, unless of course this was a painting of a distant ancestor, or even Lord Henry Simon, though Lord Henry would be considerably younger than the man portrayed. Or was this another potential suitor? She would have to await Sir Robert's return for an answer.

She chided herself. How silly it was to speculate about the painting. After all, it was only a picture of an unknown man. But her curiosity reminded her of the ever more pressing question she was constantly asking herself as she looked towards the eventual arrival of spring. Was she going to marry this year? If so, who would be her husband? Would her choice prevail over her father's?

She knew what others, particularly her father, expected her to do – to marry someone with good prospects without delay, to stay at home, to have children and to read and sew. But those were the expectations of others, not hers. She asked herself repeatedly – as she had done after last November's dance – what was it she wanted to achieve by resisting her father? With whom did she really wish to share her life? If she had the freedom to choose, how sure could she be that she would indeed find enduring love and respect? Or would it still be a life of disappointment and unhappiness, as her mother's had been?

To the close observer, Meltwater was an unhappy household, but outwardly it was a bastion of comfort, privilege, style and wealth of which there was much local social envy.

At the family's pinnacle was Arabella's father – a baronet and a substantial Norfolk landowner – one of whose ancestors had with foresight purchased one of the two hundred baronetcies sold by James 1 to raise money to pay for an army in Ireland.

Of medium height with a fleshy face, overweight, vicious in temper and oblivious to the concerns and feelings of others, he was committed solely to personal enrichment and the enhancement of his Meltwater estate. Some of Sir Robert's earlier business dealings had been dubious, involving in particular some questionable corn sales aimed at avoiding excise in collusion with equally unscrupulous merchants. Occasionally, in the past, he had burnt his fingers in price speculation. Indeed, on one or two occasions he had been perilously close to overreaching himself, with catastrophic consequences. But though he was never able to get back what he had lost, his financial luck never seemed to run out.

In recent years he had become more astute, vigilant and controlling, and, moreover, had made sure he had nothing to do with the considerable amount of smuggling along the coast, though he was well aware of its existence, and indeed extent, and occasionally sorely tempted to take advantage. The north Norfolk coast was regarded as one of the more lawless parts of England and it was hard for anyone living there to be unaware of the degree to which contraband was traded. But Sir Robert conveniently turned a blind eye. If he ignored what others were up to, there was less likelihood they would question his own business dealings. The family name had to remain unsmirched.

Money aside, his veins, like those of his equally grasping father, Sir William, had long been drained of scruples. Instead of flowing with blood, they throbbed with intense and unalloyed political ambition, even more important to him than his wealth. He bullied people to get what he wanted.

If there was any pleasurable diversion from his ambitions and financial trickery, it was not his wife but his mistress in London, Lady Barbara Ward, a frequent visitor to the Whitfield town house in Westminster. Their relationship thrived on their joint scheming and on her mopping his brow whenever he arrived in the capital.

Arabella's mother, Thérèse de Miron, was French and Catholic. Tall and born into a wealthy landed family south of Paris, she had met Robert Whitfield while he was on his Grand Tour of Europe. Although much struck by her looks, he had married her not so much for love but for her substantial dowry and the eventual prospect of land ownership in France. Once upon a time a vivacious and intelligent society beauty, Lady Thérèse had had her spirit dimmed by years of English provincial life and the confines of what had become a loveless marriage to the boorish Sir Robert. While she enjoyed the fruits of her husband's wealth, she had become in the somewhat unfair opinion of county gossips a rather dull provincial landowner's wife, no longer the assertive and captivating woman she had been in the past.

Yet she still retained her penchant for French style in her taste in clothes (with the emphasis on the décolleté) and a reputation for flashes of Gallic furnishing, which her husband tolerated in several rooms at Meltwater. Moreover, beneath a veneer of rural equanimity and a resigned toleration of her husband's insufferable behaviour, there lay still a feminine coquettish spark, strongly reflected in her daughter, Arabella, and frequently displayed in their lively French conversation, often interspersed with giggles as light-hearted secrets were passed to one another across the harpsichord keyboard when they played together.

George, Arabella's brother, aged twenty-four, was predictably cast in his father's image. Not particularly handsome, he had little care for the annual farming calendar at Meltwater and showed an equal lack of interest in most of its social activities. He resisted all attempts by his mother to turn him into an accomplished violin player. He yearned for the day when he would inherit the estate from his father and have access to limitless money. Until then he was determined to pursue his indulgent interests elsewhere, satisfied that his father would always ensure the provision of adequate funds to allow him to do so. The bleak Norfolk winters and the isolation of the county from London society (that is to say, his version of London society) led him, much to his mother's distress and his father's displeasure, to stay almost permanently amongst his friends in the capital.

His parents frequently encouraged him to spend more time in Norwich. He resisted. Despite the city's many attractions and its relative sophistication, which some said was on a par with London, it was for George a poor substitute for the capital. He enjoyed being perceived as a young blade (many said a roué was a more accurate description), since he carried no sword. He was certainly a man about town, drinking and card-playing at his club, a new establishment in Pall Mall; and, when not playing cards, he was often (it was rumoured) to be found in a woman's bed, so following, in that regard, in the unworthy footsteps of his father, who had been a womaniser before marrying and indeed since.

Living such a life in London inevitably cost money. To accommodate his lifestyle and to pay his accumulating debts, George Whitfield naturally regarded his father as his personal banker. This was not always easy to achieve. His London expenditure was a noticeable and sometimes unpluggable leak in the family's financial balance sheet. Every now and then a large debt would place an added and occasionally significant strain on the family's access to cash and lead to fierce paternal remonstrations. In those circumstances, George would point out that his debts were modest compared to the sums his father lavished on Lady Barbara, his mistress in London, and on the Whitfield Westminster town house (a fact Sir Robert tried to conceal from his wife and daughter). Most of all, George's debts and his frivolous activities added to the existing marital difficulties between Sir Robert and Lady Whitfield, often seen in Lady Whitfield's Gallic outbursts when she berated her husband for tolerating his son's wastrel tendencies. Sir Robert simply shrugged his shoulders. He was confident that in due course George would rise to his responsibilities, particularly when he married.

In keeping with the old adage "like father, like son", George had a mean, quarrelsome and unforgiving streak in his character. His paternally acquired disdain of others was mirrored by the profound dislike and mistrust others had for him, beyond his close circle of friends. He had already, unknown to his parents, won one duel arising from a disputed game of cards. His so far nimble agility in the art of survival and easy access to his father's money enabled him to escape unscathed from his scrapes, misdeeds and, most importantly, his debts.

At the age of twenty-two, the tall and willowy Arabella Whitfield was, in sharp contrast to her brother, strong-willed, well-read, a gifted harpsichordist (like her mother) and provocatively attractive, with an open face, large green eyes and long naturally dark hair, worn either pinned up or, more often, tied loosely back with ribbon. Many in the county deemed Arabella even more beautiful than her mother had been in her earlier years, particularly as she eschewed the rouge and heavy make-up that other women used, often to the long-term detriment of their complexion.

The stylish, quick-witted and charismatically French Arabella entranced her dancing master, Monsieur Augustin Noverre. Noverre's father, Jean-Georges, had brought his ballet company to England from France in 1755, bringing too his ambitions for ballet as an important expressive theatre art. Indeed, he had written down his ideas in his *Lettres sur la danse et sur les ballets.* Augustin had later left London for Norwich on account of debts and, following in his father's footsteps, had established his own ballet company, producing ballets as passionate as his father's. Augustin liked to think Lady Whitfield was his unofficial patron, not least because of her financial generosity, her own French passion, which suddenly ignited in his presence, and, of course, because of her beautiful and equally passionate daughter.

The young and exuberant Noverre sought every opportunity to be in Arabella's presence at Meltwater, multiplying her dancing lessons, much to the amusement of both her and her mother. Indeed, he often dreamt of the "*charmante*" Arabella joining his ballet company, though he knew this would never happen. To Arabella, extra dancing lessons meant more laughter in Monsieur Noverre's infectious presence as they tried the latest dances, more time for conversation in French, and, of course, yet more opportunities for her to tease and indeed occasionally flirt with her tutor.

And then there was Herr Kunzl, her more serious and much older music teacher, originally from Brandenburg. He had been an acquaintance of the late Mr Handel in London. He said he had even met the famous Johann Sebastian Bach. Though stiff compared to the flirtatious Augustin Noverre, Kunzl was an accomplished keyboard player and singer. His visits to Meltwater from Norwich were less frequent than Noverre's, as he spent significant time during "the season" in London, with his quartet, playing at soirées hosted by the nobility. But when he returned to the county he welcomed the opportunity to come often to Meltwater, to improve still further Arabella's proficiency at the keyboard. Over the years he had enhanced her mother's skills, but he considered the young Arabella an even better player. Moreover, he greatly praised her soprano voice and enjoyed teaching her to sing a wide selection of arias he regularly brought back from London.

It was Herr Kunzl who had helped Arabella's mother to assemble the keyboard book, dedicated to Arabella, that she had given her on her seventeenth birthday. The book was bound in handsome brown leather, containing green parchment pages, and was tied by red satin ribbon. It contained a variety of musical pieces, including some preludes and fugues as well as transcriptions, so claimed Kunzl, of some of Bach's keyboard exercises for his second wife, Anna Magdalena. And amongst the loose-leaf music in the book were songs and arias from Mr

Handel's operas, and even compositions from Georg Philipp Telemann, whose music Lady Whitfield had heard performed in earlier years in London and before that in Paris, when Telemann had visited in 1737; plus, of course, other compositions from France.

The music book had quickly become a rich collection of musical treats, to which Arabella and Lady Whitfield had pleasure in adding between Herr Kunzl's visits. While Noverre called Arabella his *petit rossignol* – his little nightingale – the more serious Kunzl described Arabella as Meltwater's *Kapellmeisterin* – its court musician. She was amused by these titles, but particularly touched that Herr Kunzl should think she was sufficiently talented to warrant the title he'd accorded her – similar to that once supposedly applied by the great Mr Bach to Anna Magdalena before their marriage.

With two accomplished keyboard players in the house, there was no shortage of music after supper at Meltwater. Invitations to friends and acquaintances to dine at the house became much sought after, often more for the musical delights than for the quality of the food served at table. Indeed, Arabella's fame as a keyboard player and singer was beginning to become well known in the county.

Alongside her love of dancing and music, Arabella took much comfort from her mother's strong Catholic faith – in contrast to her brother. An elderly priest, Father James, came regularly but unobtrusively to Meltwater, to give communion in a small chapel that Arabella's mother had created on her arrival at the Hall. Catholics were still deeply distrusted, even after all the years that had elapsed since the deposition of James II and the defeat of the Young Pretender, Charles Edward Stuart.

The chapel was used only by Lady Whitfield and her daughter. Her son, George, was non-practising and Sir Robert remained committed to the Church of England (or so he said, which was hard to believe given his frequent non-attendance at the parish church except on high days and holidays). There was red carpet on the floor. A small oak table, covered with white linen, served as an altar on which stood a silver crucifix and two silver candlesticks, given to Lady Whitfield by her priest in France on her departure for "godless" England. In an alcove behind was an almost life-size wooden statue of the Virgin and Child, carved in France in the early sixteenth century, which Lady Whitfield had also brought from her parents' house at the time of her marriage. Facing the altar above the entrance to the chapel was a carved figure of St John the Baptist, pointing towards the Virgin and Child.

Arabella's future had increasingly occupied her thoughts in the early weeks of 1765. A witness to her father's abominable and palpable disdain for her mother, she had long resolved to avoid the same fate of an empty marriage starved of affection and mutual respect. Partly on that account and partly because of what she had read about her historical heroines, Margaret, Duchess of Newcastle, and the famed Elizabeth Dysart, she remained strongly opposed to her father's insistence that he should choose her husband, and she said so every time the subject arose. While Sir Robert saw her as an attractive catch, a strong asset in building new family alliances, in Arabella's mind that made her nothing more than a chattel.

She had strong ideals and stubbornness inherited from her mother and reflected in her Catholic faith. She wanted a different match – one solely of her own choosing. Though her aim was, of course, the prospect of lasting domestic comfort and wealth to which she was accustomed, she wanted most of all, from whomever she married, the respect and honesty to which she believed she was entitled. Her father could not understand her wish to attain equal recognition – to exercise personal choice – in a still repressive male-dominated society where love was more likely to be considered a "sickness of woes" than pleasure and mutual trust.

Arabella was also fired in her opinion of her gender's rights by her admiration for the freedom in marriage enjoyed a hundred years before by her two heroines. She wanted a "companiate" marriage, as they had enjoyed. Though she aspired strongly to such noble aims, her father's relentless insistence on selecting her husband was wearing down her ambition for equality of choice, much to her deepening frustration and steadily growing anger. Her dream of emulating her historical heroines seemed doomed to failure.

While Arabella had once confided to her mother, after her eighteenth birthday, that she had indeed encountered some likeable young men on visits to Norwich – in her mother's company, to buy fabrics and hats and to take tea with some of her mother's pleasant but often uninspiring rural friends – none had remotely resembled her ideal of a husband; nor had those she'd met on her more infrequent trips to London. Moreover, even if some had been moderately pleasing, as one or two had been, none had the financial prospects her father insisted upon. Her dowry, he planned, would be designed to lead to the eventual acquisition of greater wealth, not to support a penniless young man, however likeable and well-intentioned he might be, title or no title.

Arabella knew she led an enjoyable and privileged life within Meltwater's physical boundaries. But as an intensive reader of books and as a keen observer while on her coach rides in the county, she recognised that beyond those boundaries, beyond the walls of the house, the world seemed to be changing. There were still, of course, the bleaker aspects of life, evident in the communities near to Meltwater – death in childbirth, infant mortality and above all the scourge of smallpox, which had no respect for age or class. From time to time she would go with her mother to visit some of the nearby villages to distribute food to the poor and to discuss with earnest local reformers ideas for improving education in local schools. Despite their Catholic faith, to which they did not wish to draw attention, mother and daughter would join parishioners in Meltwater parish church for the Christmas and Easter festivals and often went to evening prayer, particularly when Sir Robert was absent.

They also enjoyed participating in occasional musical evenings at the church. One such evening was the annual celebration of St Cecilia's Day in November. During the fifteenth century the image had emerged of St Cecilia, an early Christian martyr, as a singer and player of the organ, an instrument she is supposed to have invented. Since then the saint had gradually been adopted throughout Europe as the heavenly patron of music.

Invited, with others, to perform on one occasion, Arabella chose to sing an aria in praise of the organ from Handel's *Ode for St Cecilia's Day*.

But oh! What art can teach?
What human voice can reach

The sacred organ's praise?
Notes inspiring holy love,
Notes that wing their heav'nly ways
To join the choirs above.

As Arabella sang, the rector, the Reverend John Blackett, a grumpy man with a tiresome wife, closed his eyes, dreaming he was listening to an angel in heaven. When Arabella finished, to unexpected wide applause, Mrs Blackett nudged her husband from his reverie. He turned to look at her. He was not in heaven.

From all these encounters, Arabella was not only deeply conscious of the poverty around her, and its contrast with her privileged existence; she had also become increasingly aware of the contribution that women, whatever their social position, made to daily life in the nearby communities, often without reward or respect.

Yet at the same time, from her visits to Norwich and to nearby Freshchester with her mother, Arabella was able to see signs of the improving and expanding social activities that were taking place in the county, at least amongst those better off. Entertaining and visiting one another was becoming a strong and indeed increasing feature of county life, together with a growing interest in music, literature and drama, often performed at assembly rooms and inns in all but the smallest of communities. People were becoming less tied to where they lived and, moreover, more open-minded. It was also evident that progress in science, the advancement of machinery and improvements in farming, and, indeed, the building of better roads, were slowly beginning to transform the county. All this encouraged Arabella to believe that, at a time of perceptible social change, she was right to stick to her beliefs and, accordingly, argue her point of view.

While the exterior of the Hall may not have been architecturally striking compared to other houses in Norfolk – nor Sir Robert the most likeable host – its interior was still impressive and many sought opportunities to come and enjoy its comfort and hospitality and, of course, to be able to say afterwards that they had been to Meltwater Hall. But the opportunities for Arabella to share her enlightened opinions with those who came were few and far between. Predictably, everyone deferred to Sir Robert, who disliked the prospect of change. He found it unsettling and intended to do all that he could to keep it from his door. Those around the dining table nodded in agreement. Inwardly, the silent Arabella seethed.

In good weather there was an even greater flow of admiring visitors to the house, either ladies to have tea and to gossip with Lady Whitfield, or those who came to dine with the Whitfields when Sir Robert was not in London – and, of course, to hear Arabella sing and play the harpsichord. Or there was the occasional game of cards, such as quadrille. Dinner-party conversation might be conventional, often farm related and occasionally frivolous, but rarely featured artistic or intellectual content. There was similarly little informed debate or discussion of key events in London or Europe; the latter was too far away. Sir Robert's patronising view was that women were rarely interested in such matters. It was the invitation to the Hall that mattered, to have attentive faces around his dining table and to hear Arabella perform.

If social change such as Arabella had detected was in the air, winters in Norfolk were not part of it. They remained bleak and bone-chilling and visitors were few. It was therefore no surprise that at the beginning of 1765 there was once again dismal grey weather and bitter cold, intensified by the unceasing north wind blowing across the marshes from the dark and remorseless sea beyond. The first snow on the eve of last November's party had never gone. It would be some months before the roads would once again allow comfortable journeys to Norwich or, indeed, to London, and so improve for Arabella the prospect of possible escape from her rural isolation at Meltwater.

Until then she considered herself almost a captive of the largely silent house, apart of course from the moments when she was able to ride by herself along the seashore – hitching her skirts and riding astride. But at least for the present, with Meltwater effectively cut off by the winter from the outside world, it would be more difficult for her father to pursue his misguided and increasingly tiresome efforts to find a suitable husband for her by bringing suitors to stay at the Hall.

Moreover, with the weather now so harsh and the stream of visitors since the party in November virtually stopped, Arabella was even more reliant on her mother's company, which of course she deeply valued. Monsieur Noverre had managed to pay one visit since Christmas, but Herr Kunzl had not yet made his first. Arabella missed them both because being with either of them was a joy, not least because the conversation was almost always in French. But even occasional linguistic enjoyment offered little of the solace she was seeking.

Despite the weather and the family stresses and strains, the house went about its daily winter routine, with the Whitfields served by a staff of twelve. At the top of the pyramid was George Gregson, the butler, ultimately in charge of ensuring that Meltwater Hall's daily routine flowed without any interruption. Next to him, one step down in the hierarchy, was Mrs Langley, the housekeeper, who supervised Martha, Mary, Sukey, Ruth and John, the footman. Mary was young and, as she had shown particular promise, had become maid to Arabella. In addition, there was Hannah, maid to Lady Whitfield, and Betty, the cook. Samuel was valet to Sir Robert (and to George Whitfield on the infrequent occasions he was at home) and there were two coachmen, Jewkes and the under-coachman, Henry. Above this domestic-staff menagerie there floated, in retirement, Sarah Bayley, who had been wet nurse to George and Arabella. No one had the heart to send her away, and Sarah would have repelled any attempt to do so.

The Whitfields' outwardly idyllic family landscape – their most comfortable lifestyle – did nothing to assuage Arabella's growing frustration. The longer she stayed at home, the more likely, she felt, she would eventually succumb to her father's pressure. But if she gave in, by marrying Mr Hines or Lord Simon, she knew she would be another man's chattel for life. She wished to marry neither. To avoid a sentence of lifelong imprisonment in a loveless marriage, to make her own choice, she had to escape from the confines of Meltwater. She longed to be kissed, to be undressed by a man she loved, and for him to give her the physical pleasure she desired, though she was unsure exactly what such pleasure entailed. She could only deduce its meaning from what she had read and what her mother had told her. Sarah's repeated assurances – and, indeed, her mother's – that all would turn out well in the end cut little ice. They did not understand that Arabella was no longer a child and that, as a young woman, she had an irrepressible will of her own.

Her wish to enjoy the fruits of womanhood seemed as unlikely to be realised as ever as she went to her bedroom that evening, contemplating with dread her father's return to Meltwater from London the next day. He would yet again insist on her marrying before the end of the year. She would yet again refuse. And there would be yet another scene. It would be a small mercy that her brother would not be present, boasting to her of his successes at cards, his club and the thrill of life in London. While he did not speak of his female liaisons, Arabella and her mother were well informed from county gossip that he was often in the company of women, not all of them respectable.

That night a strong and bitter wind blew around the house. The interior draughts tugged at the doors of each room. The only light in Arabella's bedroom after she had blown out the candle by her bedside came from the fire the servant, Martha, had lit earlier to warm the room. As Arabella lay in bed she had a premonition that the wind was a harbinger of a final confrontation with her father. A storm was about to break. She would finally have to decide whether to stand her ground or give in. If she remained resolute, the consequences could be far-reaching. Was she ready to pay the price of ultimate disobedience?

To divert her thoughts, she turned her mind once again to the man in the picture in the Oak Room below. Just who was he? What connection had the picture with her father? Was it intended that the man in the painting should be a suitor? Just who was he?

The next morning, Wednesday, 6 February, the house was awake early as usual. There had been a further light covering of snow overnight. Martha reappeared to rekindle the fire, followed by Mary, who came to lay out the dress that Arabella had chosen to wear the evening before.

Arabella looked across the garden and to the hills beyond. There was a trace of sunlight between the clouds but the day looked distinctly unpromising, with a hint of more snow to come. Mary said the same as she brushed Arabella's hair. Arabella joined her mother for breakfast and afterwards went to the library to read.

It was later in the day when Sir Robert returned from London, having stopped the previous night in Norwich to dine with some friends, to check on his grain accounts with the merchants and to buy some fresh wine to restock Meltwater's cellar. He joined his wife and Arabella in the library for tea. He was in a reasonable mood. London and Norwich had obviously gone well. He said he would have to leave again for the capital soon, but on his return to Norfolk he expected to be accompanied by Lord Henry Simon, who would come to stay for several days. He reminded his wife and daughter that he had first met Lord Simon on an earlier occasion in London, at a dinner party hosted by Lady Esther Hemming. They had subsequently met several times at his club. Sir Robert had decided (without disclosing Lord Simon's well-documented cavorting in London) that he would indeed be an excellent match for Arabella, particularly since his father had strong banking money. As he had previously asserted, it would be a good alliance of two families of substance. The marriage would be worth the dowry he would have to pay. Lord Simon would be able to afford a large house (which Sir Robert already had in mind) close to Meltwater, in which he and Arabella could live in comfort and style until Lord Simon inherited his father's fortune.

Arabella's mother appeared to nod in compliance; there was little else she could do. But Arabella, roused yet again by her father's insensitivity and again unable to bite her tongue, insisted that it was for her to decide who might be her husband, not her father. Besides, Lord Simon was a friend of her brother. This made his credentials questionable without going to the bother of meeting him. Sir Robert responded acidly that it was not for his daughter to consider such matters. He was the best judge of what was right for Meltwater, for his family and for its future well-being. Arabella retorted (with a sharpness bordering on insolence that she later regretted) that he applied one iron rule for her but a supple one for her brother, who was able to do what he wished, despite his unworthy reputation in London. Where was the equality in that?

It was at this point that her brother, George, appeared in the library, having unexpectedly returned home direct from the capital in order to persuade his father to loan him more money to pay some pressing debts, allegedly costs in pursuing a wealthy heiress for her hand in marriage, as Sir Robert had encouraged. Father and son adjourned to the living room to discuss the sum involved.

After dinner that evening, during which the conversation had been dominated by Sir Robert's and George's accounts of their time in London, the family adjourned to the Oak Room to play cards and for Arabella to play the harpsichord at her mother's request. Though she was not in a playing mood, she decided to comply in order to distract her father. It was not until later in the evening, when George rose to cross the room to join Arabella at the keyboard, that he noticed the mysterious portrait in the corner of the room, leaning against the chair. He looked at it intently. His face suddenly turned ashen and, quickly putting down his glass of wine, he rapidly left the room without explanation and went upstairs. Arabella and her mother were puzzled by his behaviour. Sir Robert, reading some documents, had not appeared to notice his son's reaction to the picture, to which he himself had paid scant attention.

The next morning, George left the house early for Freshchester, from where he embarked on the first stage of the coach journey to London. His brief note said that, following his discussion with his father the day before, he had decided to return to the capital in order to settle his bills without further delay. When Arabella returned to the drawing room on her way to breakfast, the picture had gone. Sukey said it had been removed for prompt return to Sir Robert's London agent, who had no doubt sent it to Meltwater by mistake. According to a note, it had been intended for a Mr Bolton.

The atmosphere in the breakfast room that morning was frosty, like the weather outside. Sir Robert was still visibly displeased by the abrupt departure of his son, who had pocketed a banker's draft for £200 from him before he left. His mood at the breakfast table darkened further when, in response to his reminder of the imminent visit of Lord Henry Simon, Arabella repeated her objection to his plan, without even agreeing to at least meeting him. Again, Sir Robert warned her about defying his wishes. And again, Arabella refused to consider anyone not chosen by her.

Sir Robert lost his temper. He rose from the table to confront her. As he did so, Arabella rose too.

"Arabella, you are insolent and muddle-headed. You are twenty-two and it is time decisions were made about your future. Your mother and I refuse to support you in your obstinacy. I am bringing Henry Simon to Meltwater and you will do as you are told. If he asks for your hand, as I believe he will, you will marry him and that is an end to it."

Arabella retorted, "You are a brute and I will not give in to your threats."

Sir Robert came closer to her, his face contorted in rage. "You will, my girl," he shouted.

"No. I will not," responded Arabella, standing her ground.

Sir Robert's voice was a roaring crescendo. "Indeed you will. You will do as I tell you. You have had your way for too long, encouraged by your mother."

"I will not do as you tell me," Arabella replied defiantly, adding, "*Je suis comme je suis*. And if you do not know what that means it is French for I am as I am. I am my mother's daughter in that regard."

Losing all self-control, Sir Robert struck her viciously across her cheek with the back of his hand. Arabella shook with fury.

"I have nothing but contempt for you," she uttered, hardly able to speak so great was her anger at what he had just done.

"Regardless of your silly opinions about equality, you will bend to my will, Arabella, and that is an end to it," Sir Robert countered.

"I most certainly will not, even if it means I have to leave this house," repeated Arabella.

Her eyes were agleam with fire and her cheek still bore the mark of her father's hand. She turned on her heel and rushed upstairs, locking herself in her bedroom. Sir Robert made to go after her but Lady Whitfield held him back.

"Sir Robert, what have you done, you silly man? You must apologise when you and she have calmed down. Leave the subject of her marriage alone for now."

"I will not leave the matter alone," he retorted, "and I will not apologise."

Despite her mother's entreaties through the locked door to allow her in, and Sarah's own intervention, Arabella remained in her bedroom all morning. As she slowly recovered from the shock of her father striking her, her anger transformed into a vow of profound vengeance. Deeply though she loved her mother and her life of comfort, the time had finally come to break free from her father's suffocating control and leave Meltwater.

When she heard her father and mother leave by carriage for a pre-arranged lunch with the Wimpoles, Arabella summoned Mary to help her pack some clothes, her missal and her cherished music notebook. She then asked for one of the estate coaches to be made ready immediately, with instructions that Henry, the under-coachman, should take her without delay to nearby Freshchester.

Sarah came to her room and pleaded with her not to leave. It would all blow over, she insisted.

Arabella replied, "Sarah, I respect your judgement greatly, but it will not blow over. My father has laid siege to me. He will never give up. He will continue his unending efforts to overpower me. I know him too well. I have to leave. I have to defend my integrity. If I do not make a stand now it will be too late."

And so, despite Sarah's tears at the departure of her dear child, Arabella made the final and fateful decision to leave Meltwater Hall, regardless of the possible consequences. On the mantelpiece in the living room she left two letters. The first was to her father. It read:

Dear Papa,

I thank you most warmly for your great kindness and solicitude during my childhood at Meltwater. I look back on my younger years within the walls of this house with much happiness and contentment.

But it is clear from your recent actions, most noticeably this morning, that you cannot accept I am now grown up, no longer a child obliged to follow your instructions in matters of the heart. Ignoring the fact that I am a woman with a dignity of her own, you persist in seeking to reduce me to a chattel on the marriage market and to impose upon me a man I have not chosen for myself. Judging by the stories of Lord Henry's behaviour in London, my wedding night would constitute rape by a man I would not love and who, after having his satisfaction with me, would most likely condemn me to the meaningless compensations of a lifetime of lonely domesticity and fecundity while he sought his pleasures elsewhere. Such an outcome would be a betrayal of all that I wish.

I seek instead the freedom to choose my own husband, which surely is my birthright as a subject of the King. In order to exercise my choice, and to pursue my life as I think best, the time has come for me to leave home. I do so with great sadness but strongly believing this is the step I must now take. I will take care to use wisely the many gifts you have given me.

Do not seek to find me. I will find you when I believe I have found the happiness I desperately seek.
Your daughter,
Arabella

The letter to her mother, written in French, was as follows:

My dearest Mama,

It breaks my heart to write this letter and I know how much pain its contents will cause you. But write in this vein I must.

You have given me so much love and joy since you first held me in your arms. Within the bounds of our Catholic faith, you have taught me the most profound truths about life and the importance of self-respect and respect for others. Though my will has sometimes been weak, I have done my best to follow these necessary obligations. You have also given me great strength of character and an iron determination always to seek to do what is right. I ask you to accept my boundless gratitude for these many gifts.

Drawing on all that I have learnt and inherited from you, I have become adamant that I cannot accept my father's wishes in respect of his plans for my marriage. I must seek the freedom to make my own choice in such a personal matter of the heart, not one fettered by the desires of another for reasons of money and the alliances of land.

I will do everything to uphold the values you have instilled in me. Once I have made my own choices to my satisfaction, I will ask you to come to me without delay. In the meanwhile, I will hold you deeply in my heart and in my thoughts.
From your most affectionate and loving daughter,
Arabella

Wearing a black dress, black overcoat and a black bonnet with a veil, Arabella went downstairs, said goodbye to the staff and climbed into the coach, almost overcome by the emotional weight of what she was doing. Henry, the under-coachman, placed the leather bag containing her few clothes at her feet and closed the door.

Sarah, Mary and George Gregson stood in the porch in tears. Seeing them, Arabella was now in even more profound turmoil. She was leaving behind her mother, her home, her childhood and a life of privilege and comfort. But, despite her anguish, she remained resolute in her mind that she had to leave, to turn her back on Meltwater. She was sure that if she did not do it now her personal cause would be irretrievably lost. Departure was the only action she could take. Almost choking on the words, she told Henry to move off. As the coach turned down the driveway, Arabella dared not look back in case her will crumbled like a sandcastle in an oncoming tide. She drew down her veil to hide her tears. In her hands was her precious music book. She clung to it tightly.

Upon her arrival at the King's Head Inn in Freshchester, Arabella quickly sent Henry on his way. She then enquired about onward travel to Norwich. Luck was in her favour. Though it was market day and the streets were thronged with people, she was immediately able to find a seat on a coach about to leave for the city. From there she might be able to find a "flyer" to take her on to London.

Some three hours later she arrived at the Swan Inn in Norwich, the city she knew well. She imagined her father would be returning from lunch by now and, discovering her departure from Sarah and Gregson, would no doubt shortly set out to find her, beginning in Freshchester. She pleaded with the coaching inn to find a place for her on the next available coach to London. After several hours of waiting – and sleeping fitfully in a dingy upstairs room, fearful of her father banging on the door which she had locked to thwart any unwanted intruders – Arabella managed to secure a place on the first coach very early the following morning. By now she had little money left.

As the London-bound coach left the city limits, she glimpsed Jewkes, driving her father's coach in the opposite direction, towards the Market Place. As she had rightly surmised, Sir Robert and Lady Whitfield, not finding her in Freshchester, had assumed she had sought refuge with one of Lady Whitfield's friends in the city. Her father's rapid appearance in Norwich confirmed Arabella's conviction that he was intent on finding her in order to take her back to Meltwater in time for the planned arrival of Henry Simon.

As she had conjectured on her departure from the Hall, he was resolutely determined to have his way in what he believed were the overriding interests of the family. Arabella calculated that it would take at least one day for him to make contact with all of her mother's friends in Norwich before he realised she had probably gone to London. So she had a good head start on her journey south.

As she sat back in the fast coach to London, squeezed between two elderly ladies and sitting opposite a parson with a squint, Arabella was stunned by the boldness of what she had done: she had run away from Meltwater, abandoned her mother to her father's wrath, and was travelling alone to London without anywhere to stay. And there was the added risk of a young woman travelling alone. Did her audacity represent foolish and selfish pride on her part, or did it reflect her genuine belief that it was right to stand her ground in the face of intolerable and unjustified paternal pressure? Arabella turned the question over and over in her mind, drawing as she did so a little comfort from recalling the opinion of some of her mother's friends that a less formal and more affectionate attitude on the part of parents to their children was emerging in the county. If that were indeed true, it was certainly not evident in her father's approach to her; that enlightenment had not yet embraced Sir Robert. As the coach approached London, Arabella finally resolved, to the point her mind began to ache, that she had been right to take the decision to leave Meltwater.

However, her sense of justification and present resolve did not cause her to underestimate the immense dangers to which she would be exposed in London. She knew from what her father had often said that it was a place of great risk to those not used to the tumult of daily life. Behind the façade of shops and imposing buildings on the main thoroughfares there lurked an unpleasant and frequently sordid underworld whose population included the destitute, professional beggars, pickpockets, thieves and prostitutes. There was money to be made, but often from other people's misery. Her mother had once said to Arabella on one of their infrequent visits to London how important it was for a woman of good repute to avoid eye contact with any man if she did not want to be propositioned.

Despite the frightening risks that lay ahead and the more pressing matter of a lack of money, Arabella kept telling herself that, whatever the possible dangers, she had taken the right step to thwart her father, deeply unsettling though that had been. But her resolve would have to remain firm whatever setbacks she faced. She would repeatedly have to remind herself that she was not a chattel but a human being with the right of personal choice. She had decided to make a stand and stand she would.

On arrival in London late that afternoon, Arabella decided to go immediately to the Hemmings in Westminster, long-standing family friends, particularly of her mother. They were much surprised to see her unannounced on their doorstep, but warmly welcomed her and invited her to stay in their best guest bedroom. She explained to them over supper what had happened. Lord and Lady Hemming appeared sympathetic.

Weary but delighted to have arrived safely in London, Arabella went to bed. But she could not sleep. As she lay awake, she heard her hosts whispering on the landing as they retired to their rooms.

"Thomas, you must send a message to Sir Robert first thing in the morning to tell him that Arabella is here. He and Thérèse will be distraught not knowing where she is. She has always been an independent-minded child, but her family's reputation and her own safety must come before her personal wishes."

Lord Hemming replied, "Esther, I will but we must not tell Arabella."

Overhearing this, Arabella immediately decided that she would have to leave the Hemmings as soon as possible in the morning. But where could she go? Tomorrow would be Saturday and the beginning of the weekend when many places would be closed. Suddenly, she remembered the owner of the coffee house in Piccadilly, Monsieur Auguste Gaillard, whom her mother had always visited on her earlier visits to London. He had entertained her mother, and, indeed, Arabella herself when she was younger, at his house in Brook Street, just along from the house where Mr Handel had lived. Arabella had once overheard acquaintances of her mother speculate that her and Gaillard's intimacy together might have suggested more than a platonic friendship. Whether this was true or not, surely Monsieur Gaillard would help her?

At the first break of light the next morning, Arabella slipped her few belongings into her leather bag and tiptoed downstairs. After a brief and hushed word with the under-servants, she left through the basement door for Brook Street. By the time the Hemmings rose, the bird had flown.

London was grey and bitterly cold on that Saturday morning, 9 February. Arabella knew it was far from safe for a well-dressed young woman to be alone on the streets at such an hour. She hailed a sedan chair and shortly arrived at Gaillard's house. As the Hemmings had been, he was astonished to find Arabella at his door. It took him a minute or two to accept that the tall and attractive young woman before him was Arabella, who had been a child when he had last seen her.

Gaillard invited her to sit in front of a warm fire in his parlour, where she told him of the event that had brought her unexpectedly to London. Her spirit, her striking features and her well-spoken French, uttered with ease, warmed his heart. This vivacious young beauty reminded him of her mother, Thérèse, with whom he had spent many hours in the past recalling Paris and enjoying their more intimate moments.

After listening to her story, Gaillard confessed that unfortunately she could not stay with him. His new companion, who had shared his house since the death of Madame Gaillard two years previously, might become jealous of such an attractive young woman joining his household. More important than that, he suggested, Arabella's mother might soon guess she had sought his help. It would be bad for him and his business to have her father, Sir Robert, threatening to make trouble at the coffee house. Any scene would be best avoided. But he would help her find refuge. He asked Arabella to wait beside the fire until he returned.

First, he went to Piccadilly to ensure the coffee house – still (much to Gaillard's annoyance) known as Mr Jasper's after its previous owner, but (to his pleasure) equally considered one of the more reputable in London – was meeting the early-morning refreshment needs following the city's all-night entertainment. Coffee, tea and chocolate always had to be available and of good quality. His patrons appreciated that. Less was known about some of the other services offered. Then, as he had promised Arabella, before going back to Brook Street, Gaillard made some discreet enquiries as to where she might safely stay for the next few days. He returned with the address of a reputable lodging, recommended by a friend. He believed the lady of the house, with whom he was acquainted, would give Arabella safe shelter for as long as was necessary while she considered her future.

Noticing that after his return Gaillard was regularly looking at the parlour clock, Arabella took this as a sign that she should take her leave. As she rose from her fireside chair, Gaillard said he would have liked her to stay longer, but he had to attend to his lawyer who would shortly arrive with some legal papers to be signed. Arabella assumed he was referring to his companion. Sorry to leave the warmth of his fireplace but thanking Gaillard profusely for his help and his coffee, Arabella said goodbye, extracting a promise that he would not disclose to her family the address he had given her. She slowly descended the staircase to collect her bag.

As she approached the front door, an elderly but sly-looking lady – who, unknown to Arabella, was the eyes and ears of Auguste Gaillard's mistress (indeed it was the mistress's mother) and who had been listening at the door – whispered, "Better not to trust Monsieur's judgement on such matters. What do men like him know? Nowhere is safe for a young woman on her own in London. You are more likely to be safer from your father here." And putting a finger to her lips, she pressed into Arabella's hand a piece of paper with another address written on it.

The old lady summoned a sedan chair and paid the chair men. Arabella thus left Brook Street, not for the address Gaillard had given her but for an address in Chesterfield Street, Mayfair, provided by a devious lady keen to dispose of someone she believed (mistakenly, of course) would be a possible rival to her daughter for Monsieur's roving eye.

Little did Arabella know that on that day she had been maliciously directed towards an establishment in the demi-monde of eighteenth-century London, where the daily trade comprised sexual favours, prostitution and, of course, corruption; a place where young girls like her easily disappeared into a dark swamp. As she rode in the sedan chair towards Chesterfield Street, Arabella was oblivious to this act of betrayal by one woman towards another. Nothing had yet occurred to shake her innocent view that most people were good and could have no grounds for wishing a stranger harm. Fortified by her trust in the goodness of human nature, she was relieved that she had successfully negotiated her first steps in London. Buoyed by her misplaced confidence, she believed she was now about to take yet another step towards exercising her right to choose her husband. She was no longer in thrall to Meltwater.

Neither Arabella nor Auguste Gaillard nor, indeed, the old lady knew that Gaillard had just turned away his daughter. How could they? Lady Whitfield had never disclosed to anyone that he was the father of her beloved child, who was about to slip into a dark pit.

CHAPTER 3

Demi-Monde

Number 35 Chesterfield Street was a large and proud double-fronted house in the upper reach of Mayfair close to the park. Arabella walked up the steps to the imposing black front door. She hesitated. She was about to knock on the door of a house in London about which she knew nothing. Should she do so or should she return to the Hemmings and await her fate? If the latter, there would be only one outcome – to return to Meltwater, however much she might kick and scream. The thought of the punishment she might expect within its walls, as well as being ultimately forced to marry someone she could never love, filled her with dread. To return home was not a prospect she could countenance. All that she possessed in the world at that moment was in the bag at her feet – a few clothes, her missal and her music book. Her purse was almost empty. Having come all this way, it would surely be weak-willed of her not to take the next step. All that she wanted, without effort or reserve, was a once-in-a-lifetime love. That had to remain uppermost in her mind. And if she did not knock she would be homeless on the streets of London. There was therefore no choice. Arabella knocked on the door.

A maid answered. Arabella asked to see Mrs Hallam, the name on the piece of paper the old lady had given her. The maid asked her to wait. After what seemed many minutes, she returned and, having taken Arabella's coat and bag, gestured her to enter the parlour on the right-hand side of an impressive hallway leading to a wide staircase. The room was tastefully furnished with pictures and furniture in the French style. There she came face to face with Mrs Lucy Hallam, a tall grey-haired woman, a faded beauty with a somewhat yellow pallor to her face, though still elegant and well-spoken. Mrs Hallam invited Arabella to sit down. She was immediately struck by the attractive, stylishly dressed and poised young woman, from an evidently wealthy family, sitting in front of her, but who appeared – beneath an outwardly calm demeanour – to be in some emotional distress. Mrs Hallam asked how she might help.

"My name is Arabella Whitfield. I have arrived in London at short notice and those with whom I had planned to stay are not available. A family acquaintance made some enquiries and suggested that you might be able to offer me hospitality for a few days," said Arabella.

Mrs Hallam eyed her closely and, after a long pause, said, "Miss Whitfield, have you run away from home?"

Arabella flushed. "Yes," she admitted, referring to some unspecified difficulties with her father over the matter of marriage.

Mrs Hallam asked, "Have you any money?"

Arabella said she had a little left over from her journey to London, which she hoped would be enough to pay for her short stay in London. In due course she intended to make contact with her mother about her future intentions.

After some reflection, Mrs Hallam said she did have a room to spare and therefore was able to invite Arabella to lodge for a few days, as she had asked.

"Let me show you your room," she said.

Mrs Hallam took Arabella up the wide staircase to the second floor and showed her into a room overlooking the street. It was spacious and had a large bed, a couch, a desk and chair, a wardrobe and a washstand. The furniture and curtains were again in the French style, like some of the bedrooms at Meltwater but distinctly more feminine.

"I hope this is satisfactory," said Mrs Hallam.

Arabella said it was.

After helping Arabella unpack her few belongings, Mrs Hallam suggested that she might wish to rest. At Mrs Hallam's request, and with some disquiet, she handed over her little remaining money to pay for her board and lodging.

As Mrs Hallam left to go downstairs to reflect further on her new guest, Arabella called out, "If anyone comes looking for me, please do not tell them I am here."

"Of course not," replied Mrs Hallam.

Later, the maid who had answered the front door brought Arabella something to eat and drink and lit the fire and candles, as it was a dark and dismal day. After eating a little food, she sat in front of the fire. She began to cry, as she thought again about what she had done: deeply crossed her father, deserted her mother and run away to London. Her mother, her most trusted friend, would be distraught. Moreover, in a show of poor manners, she had left the Hemmings without saying goodbye and thanking them for their hospitality. She had been to see Monsieur Gaillard, who would surely tell her mother she had visited him. Now she had taken refuge in an unknown house. No one, except the old lady at Monsieur Gaillard's, knew where she was and her remaining money had been taken from her. She had effectively disappeared and was at the mercy of Mrs Hallam.

Arabella had put herself in great peril. She was now on her own, far from the sheltered world of Meltwater, the warm comfort of her bedroom and the reassuring words of Sarah, who still liked to read children's stories to her from time to time. Her mother had often told her that London was no place for a young, unmarried girl from the country – it was full of predators, unseen beneath the murky waters of city society. Now Arabella was exposed to this very danger. All she had was her precious music notebook and her missal. She was deeply apprehensive of what might happen but remained determined not to turn back.

She opened the music book and ran her fingers across some of the scores, as though trying to touch her mother's fingers, which had traced the same notes. Placing the book beside her, Arabella knelt by the fire and, opening her missal, she prayed earnestly to the Virgin Mary for forgiveness for what she had done, caused surely by her pride, and asked for protection in the days ahead.

Later she ate a little more. Tired and increasingly frightened as evening approached, Arabella undressed and went to bed. Mrs

Hallam came to see that she was safe. She sat on the edge of the bed holding Arabella's hand for a few minutes, comforting her just as her mother or, sometimes, Sarah used to do. After Mrs Hallam left, Arabella cried herself to sleep. She awoke in the night to hear distant laughter and whispering outside her door. She slipped out of bed to make sure the door was secure. It was. But the key that had been there earlier had disappeared. The door was locked from the outside. She could not escape. Arabella returned to bed and tightly hugged the bedclothes around her.

During the next two days, Arabella hardly left her room, though when no one other than Mrs Hallam was about she quickly visited the library on the floor below to choose another book to bring back to read in front of the fire. The weather outside did not change; it remained grey and bitterly cold. From time to time she saw from her window some younger and older well-dressed ladies appear and disappear during the day and early evening, sometimes on the arm of a man, but no one looked up and saw her. She heard frequent activity and laughter in the house long after dark. It was often the sound of men. She peeked through the curtain to look at the street below. Some were arriving; some were leaving, sometimes in the company of masked ladies. Arabella began to realise the purpose of the house. Her fears deepened even more. Her room was locked from the outside every night after dark. She was a prisoner of the night.

It was on the afternoon of Wednesday, 13 February that Mrs Hallam invited Arabella to take tea with her in the parlour downstairs.

"There has been no post and no visitors for you, my dear, since you arrived, and I am not aware that you have written to your mother. This would suggest that it is most unlikely you will have money to pay for a further week in your room. The money you gave me on your arrival ran out two days ago. Am I right?"

Her face reddening, Arabella replied, "Yes, Mrs Hallam. I have indeed made no contact with my family for the reasons I explained to you on my arrival. And they have made no contact with me."

"I see. As they do not know where you are, that is not surprising," responded Mrs Hallam.

They sat facing each other, not speaking, with only the sound of the ticking clock to keep them company in their silence.

Then Mrs Hallam said, "Miss Whitfield, let me be frank. I understand from my discreet sources of information and other reports that your father is making many efforts to find you. This will be costing him money. That being the case, I think it highly unlikely that he, or indeed Lady Whitfield, would ever provide the money you need to remain in London of your own volition. They clearly prefer to spend money to find you in order that they can take you home."

Tears filled Arabella's eyes.

"Have no fear, dear Miss Whitfield. I too once ran away from home. I will not reveal your identity or your whereabouts to anyone. But the facts are that you cannot stay here indefinitely without paying for your keep."

Arabella recovered her composure and asked how it might be possible to remain for a while longer.

Mrs Hallam replied, choosing her words carefully, "In this house, certain well-born gentlemen of different ages come to seek companionship, comfort and indeed pleasure. Do you think it might be possible for you to help me provide a little of what they want?"

Though Arabella had started to suspect the purpose of 35 Chesterfield Street, she was nonetheless shocked by the words Mrs Hallam had just uttered. Fighting hard to hold back her emotions, she had the urge to flee the room, rush upstairs, collect her belongings and leave the house as quickly as possible. But she remained seated. Her head span as she tried to decide what to do, what to say. If she left, where would she go? She remained even now implacably opposed to returning to Meltwater. And even if she were to do so, she could easily guess the consequences. She had no money of her own to go anywhere else in London. Another solution would be to seek refuge on the streets. But that thought filled her with horror. Recalling stories of the plight of the Edinburgh homeless, she pictured herself at the mercy of thieves and vagabonds, forced to live in foul-smelling cellars full of rats. Recognising the inescapable predicament in which she had placed herself, Arabella had only one option: to stay in Chesterfield Street. She regained her composure and, with her heart beating rapidly, whispered her assent.

Mrs Hallam rose from her chair. She took Arabella gently by the hand and led her upstairs to a locked room on the third floor. She removed a key from her bodice and opened the door. Inside were long rows of well-made dresses, hanging from large hooks on the walls; many were self-evidently stylish and obviously expensive.

"If you are going to be with me for a while, Miss Whitfield, you will need some flattering dresses to wear. You come from a good and, I imagine, wealthy background. I am sure that if you were at home you would wear attractive dresses paid for by your father and mother. You should have the same while you are here. After all, the more attractively dressed you are the more our visitors will like you and indeed the more they will be prepared to pay for the pleasure of your company."

Those words struck terror into Arabella.

Judging her height and slender figure, Mrs Hallam took down two dresses – one of blue velvet with white ribbons and another pink with an abundance of lace. She asked Arabella to try on the blue. She did so and, after helping her with the lacing at the back, Mrs Hallam turned her round to face a mirror in the corner of the room. The dress fitted – and indeed flattered – her well. Her breasts were exposed in a way her mother would never have allowed. Seeing her blush deeply, Mrs Hallam assured Arabella that their exposure was highly fashionable in London and in fact was deemed a sign of great femininity, in contrast to the need to cover an ankle, let alone a leg, in public at all times.

Before asking Arabella to try the pink dress, Mrs Hallam removed Arabella's corset and tightly laced her into another one that was smaller around her waist, which made her breasts even more noticeable. Barely able to breathe because of the constriction, Arabella tried the pink dress, which fitted her equally well. The frill across its bodice was almost low enough to reveal the top of her nipples, and there was a bow conveniently placed below, which, if pulled, would expose even more of her chest.

It was decided that Arabella would take the two dresses to her room for use in the days ahead. Mrs Hallam said both would be worn without panniers or hoops, thus highlighting her slender figure and, of course, making sexual activity easier and more rapid. She said Arabella was free to return to the room later in her stay to choose other dresses.

"This will not work, Mrs Hallam," said Arabella. "My father spends considerable time at his town house in Westminster. Before too long he, his friends – and indeed my brother George, who is always in London to gamble and drink – will discover my whereabouts and they will drag me back to Meltwater to be punished and married to someone I do not love. I could not bear that. I have run away from home. You must understand, I cannot go back. But I am not sure I have the will to do what you are asking me. I have never exposed my body in this way before."

"I understand your fears entirely, though I wish you had told me earlier that your father has a town house in Westminster," said Mrs Hallam. "I would not want your whereabouts to be discovered either. But there is a fashionable solution, which would help to conceal you from those in London who might recognise you," she added. "I propose that you hide your face while you are in the company of others."

She reached for a small box from which she took some pins to fasten Arabella's loose shoulder-length hair into a tight chignon.

"This is what we will do," she said. "They are all the rage."

She pulled down from a shelf a larger box and from it lifted an exquisitely made and elaborate Venetian-style mask, white with an embroidered pattern in silver and edged in black. She gently placed the mask over Arabella's head and face and closed a clasp at the back of her neck, locking it in place. The richly perfumed mask fitted tightly. Once again, she turned Arabella to face the mirror. As it was now quite dark outside, Mrs Hallam lit two candles, so Arabella could see herself better.

She stood transfixed, gazing at herself through the mask, barely breathing. She was no longer Arabella Whitfield of Meltwater Hall. She had become a mysterious young woman in a high-class brothel in London, about to lose her virginity in a way she had never imagined. Her eyes began to fill with tears but they were hidden by the mask. The thought of what she had agreed to do – to join Mrs Hallam's household – filled her with horror. Men touching her body . . . It made her nauseous. But this, it appeared, was the price she would have to pay for her independence. Yet oddly, in her kaleidoscope of emotions, she felt a momentary tingle of excitement at the thought of pretending to be someone else; experiencing in anonymity a different life, to see where it might lead. After all, it would only be for a while, she told herself. Arabella almost giggled for a moment, but then once again plunged back into despair. Her body was about to be used for the pleasure and financial benefit of others. She had read about whores and courtesans. She was about to enter their world. She was filled with terror.

Though Arabella's face was hidden, Mrs Hallam sensed her inner turmoil.

"You do not have to do this," she said. "What I have proposed you can accept or refuse. If you wish to change your mind, we will speak no more of it. I will arrange for you to return to Meltwater at once. But you have said that if you go back you will be harshly punished for running away. I would not want that to happen to you. Of course, you can leave this house and try elsewhere, or take your chance on the streets of London, but they are no place for a beautiful, young and well-educated woman such as you. Or, as I have suggested, you can stay here for a while and see what may unfold. Perhaps this house will lead to the destiny you seek."

Arabella was in torment. She could not decide what to do. Return home and accept her fate, as she had considered doing so often in the past days, or face the unknown. She agonised. Mrs Hallam remained silent. After some minutes, Arabella finally decided.

"My father has behaved like a tyrannical monarch. He should have protected me, a vulnerable woman and his daughter too. He should have allowed me to decide who I marry. As he has done neither of these things, I must protect myself. I will therefore stay for a short while."

Mrs Hallam smiled gently. Her skilful recruitment had worked its magic.

Arabella reached to undo the clasp behind her neck. Mrs Hallam, calling her by her forename for the first time, said, "Dear Arabella, do not remove the mask until tomorrow. Wear it for a while to get used to your mysterious new disguise. The mask is yours to keep. If you treat it well, it will protect you. The clasp is such that only you will be able to open it. I will now take you to your room and there you will stay. Under no circumstances should you attempt to remove your mask until tomorrow morning. Do you understand?"

Arabella nodded. They left the room, Mrs Hallam taking with her the clothes Arabella had brought with her to London, saying she would put them away for safekeeping.

As instructed, Arabella stayed in her room, full of deep apprehension at what was to happen. She tried to read, but in the gathering gloom it was difficult to see the pages through her mask. She sometimes paced around the room and sometimes peered out at the street below from the corner of her window. It was raining. Raindrops chased each other down the window pane, just like the tears on her cheeks behind the mask. Arabella wanted so much to remove it. It was suffocating. But Mrs Hallam had not shown her how to undo the clasp and she dared not break it.

Later in the evening, Mrs Hallam returned to her room.

"There is a young gentleman downstairs whom I have selected to have his pleasure with you. I will shortly bring him to your room."

Arabella clasped Mrs Hallam's hand and cried through her mask, "I have never been with a man before. No man has ever touched me in this way. I do not know what to do. Mrs Hallam, I cannot do this. The thought of a man touching my body repels me. These are not the circumstances in which I ever imagined I would lose my virginity."

Mrs Hallam replied softly, "I repeat what I said earlier. If you do not wish to do this, let me remove your mask and I will show the young man to someone else. But if you wish to stay, then this is what you must do. What is your decision?" Her voice had an edge to it.

Arabella, still in distress, suddenly cried out, "I will stay and do as you ask."

In response, Mrs Hallam explained what would happen. "As this is your first time, his penetration of you will be painful. But once the pain is past, you will no longer be a young girl but a woman – mistress of your own body, ready to experience the pleasure that men can bring to the female sex. As a source of gratification to them, you will soon realise just how much domination you exercise over men because of their addiction – as to a drug – to the delights you can provide. And of course you will be truly free of Meltwater. Nor must you forget that you will enter a world where there is much social and financial gain to be had. You might even acquire a rich patron to advance a career for you on the stage at Drury Lane, and who knows where that might lead? Nell Gwyn was a successful actress who became the mistress of

King Charles. Sophia Baddeley, who began life in similar circumstances to you, is rumoured to appear soon on the stage. Kitty Fisher is said to be earning one hundred guineas a night, and Nelly O'Brien is mistress to members of the aristocracy. You too may expect such a match in due course and to live in a grand house with people to protect you. But let us take one step at a time. I will be nearby should you need help."

Mrs Hallam proceeded to make Arabella ready, removing her corset, loosening her dress and undergarments, applying perfume and preparing the bed. A few minutes later, she ushered in a short, stocky, pale-looking young man, then withdrew. The quality of the young man's clothes indicated his obvious wealth. He revealed he was soon to marry and that, once he had done so, he hoped to continue his free life in London. It would simply be too boring to spend all his time in rural isolation with his new wife away from his friends in the capital.

After finishing the glass of claret he had brought in with him (it was clearly not the first he had drunk that evening), he drew close to Arabella, who sat on the edge of the bed.

"This is exciting. I have never been with a woman whose face I could not see before, but I suppose there is always a first time. Mrs Hallam tells me that you are a virgin. I always relish being the first to breach a young woman's wall. But we had better begin as I have a game of cards at my club later this evening. Besides, I have paid good money for my pleasure with you."

Taking Arabella's hands in his he raised her to her feet and gazed at her, peering closely into her eyes behind the mask. Standing in front of her, he slowly ran his fingers from her throat down to and across the top of her breasts and on to her crutch before turning her round. He asked her name. She did not answer.

"So be it, my nameless, faceless one."

He pulled the bows on the back of her dress. It quickly parted, enabling him to remove it. He then undid her shift, allowing it to fall slowly about her feet. He turned her round, fondled her breasts and then sat her on the end of the bed and removed her stockings. He momentarily placed his fingers on the clasp at the back of her neck but Arabella, scarcely breathing and rigid with fear, quickly pulled his hands back, whispering that the mask could not be removed. He asked Arabella to stand in front of him.

In the candlelight, she stood stripped bare in front of a man for the first time in her life, a man whose hands were about to touch the intimate parts of her body. She started to shake, while desperately fighting back the tears behind her mask. After removing his jacket and waistcoat, pulling down his breeches and putting on his linen condom, the young man, his breath smelling strongly of claret, pushed her roughly back onto the bed, forced her legs apart and began to enjoy the pleasure for which he had paid Mrs Hallam handsomely. There was no gentleness in his appetite and Arabella struggled hard to resist the urge to fight free of his grip. As he repeatedly pressed down on her, she felt herself drowning in a sea of nausea and pain. She repeatedly swallowed back her vomit.

Less than an hour later the young man dressed quickly and left the room, promising to return soon to have more pleasure with her. Arabella sat undressed on the floor in front of the fire, a coverlet pulled tightly around her shoulders. She was still shaking from the shock of what she had just endured – the wretched and violent penetration of her body. She felt sore, desecrated and deeply ashamed of what she had just done. The experience had been sickening and repellent. She looked at the bed. The soiled and blooded sheet was testament to his rape. Arabella felt physically sick and wanted to rip the mask from her face. But if she did so she would have to face herself in the mirror; to see her shame. That would be unbearable. She took a corner of the sheet and rubbed violently between her legs, trying to remove all trace of him. She sobbed quietly.

But as she feverishly turned over in her deeply troubled mind what had happened, she sensed, even at this moment of great darkness and despair, a possible flicker of light, a flicker of hope. Perhaps Mrs Hallam had been right about the aftermath. Though the circumstances of her first sexual experience had been unimaginable in their directness and violence, her "client" had made her a woman, releasing a physical restraint that had bound her hitherto. She was now equal in one respect with her mother. Though she felt every fibre of her body had been stained and her soul burdened with guilt, she kept telling herself over and over that she had taken another step towards her independence, despite the brutality she had experienced.

Mrs Hallam entered the room.

"You did well, Arabella, very well. He was satisfied. Next time I will not be close by, as I believe you are now able to receive visitors on your own, but I will be selective in choosing who comes to see you. A young woman of your education deserves quality."

"Thank you, Mrs Hallam. How long may I stay here?" asked Arabella.

"That is entirely for you to decide," replied Mrs Hallam. "Now, you should sleep."

Arabella tried to undo her mask.

Mrs Hallam knelt down beside her and whispered, "I will show you how to release the clasp in the morning. You can then put the mask away until next time. But you must wear it until tomorrow. It will give you a place of refuge from the truth of the mirror. Go to sleep in your new identity and wake with it. In the morning, we will also discuss your new name."

Arabella asked who the man who had come to her room was. Mrs Hallam replied, "My dear, discretion is so important in these matters. But if it is of any comfort to you, it was Lord Henry Simon."

Arabella audibly gasped and her body shook uncontrollably. Rage poured through her like a torrent of water. She retched. Mrs Hallam asked her what the matter was.

"This was the man," Arabella replied, "that my father had intended I should marry. I have now seen him revealed as the reproachable man I always knew he would be. My decision to leave Meltwater has been vindicated."

Mrs Hallam put her arm round Arabella's shoulders. "That is the way of men," she whispered. "It was ever thus and will always be so."

"But not for me," Arabella cried out defiantly. "My heart rejects the family who could allow their flesh and blood to be abased in such a way. No man will ever have dominion over me, forcing me into such subjugation as I have just experienced in this bed."

Mrs Hallam sought to soothe Arabella, now sobbing. She had seen reactions of this sort amongst her new arrivals before, but the vehemence of Arabella's response surprised her. She assured Arabella that the emotional storm would soon pass.

"My dear, as someone recently wrote, we women have to resign ourselves to the plain fact that young men, strangers to wedded love and domestic comforts, range at large on the common of prostitution."

It was clear from her shaking body and rage that Arabella's emotions were of profound intensity. Looking at her crouched by the fire, Mrs Hallam realised that Arabella was different from the others under her roof. She was young, well-educated, articulate, musical (judging by her music book) and came from an upper-class background. And she had beauty, deep emotions and intelligence. Her introduction into the Chesterfield stable would require care, patience and skill, but Mrs Hallam was convinced that with gentle moulding, good investment and a sensitive selection of clients her new "niece" could go far in the demi-monde.

After re-arranging Arabella's bed and placing some more fuel on the fire, Mrs Hallam quietly left the room. As she did so, she smiled at Arabella and remarked, "You are in the world now, you know."

Arabella made no comment.

Still smiling, Mrs Hallam locked the door behind her. She had acquired a new well-bred girl in her stable of nieces. With careful nurturing she would surely excel. It was all the more essential that her identity should remain hidden.

Once she had put on her nightdress, Arabella again sat in front of the fire, hugging her knees and rocking to and fro. What had she done? What mortal sin had she committed? Nonetheless, though the pain – physical and emotional – from her first client had been unimaginable, Arabella still felt, even now, despite her self-loathing and disgust, that her judgement to turn her back on Meltwater rather than be bullied into marrying the man who had just abused her, reeking of wine and sweat, had been vindicated. She had witnessed a man who would never have loved her had she married him, and who would have slept with others after their marriage.

Fervently wishing to go to sleep to escape from what she had just endured and to forget her guilt, Arabella opened her music book, recalling the words of Semele in Handel's opera *Semele*: "O sleep, why dost thou leave me?" Sleep would surely transport her back to an unblemished world. She tried to sing herself into repose.

But sleep did not come to Arabella. Still, the single candle burning by her bedside kept away the evil spirit of Henry Simon, while the flames of the fire reflected on the ceiling kept her company in her isolation. The sound of people and coaches in the street outside never ceased. All the while, she wrestled with her conscience.

Her mother had told her that a woman's body was sacred. It was her property, her temple, to which she alone held the key. Lord Henry Simon had forcefully penetrated her temple. He had done to her what she had so vehemently forecast he would do if she were to marry him as her father wished. But his violation of her was surely the consequence of her decision – no one else's – to exercise her personal freedom over what to do with her body. She had decided to knock on Mrs Hallam's front door several days before. Twice she had been offered the opportunity to turn back; twice she had assented to stay. While what had happened demonstrated the powerlessness of women in the grip of men, that night, despite the pain and the shame, she was able to convince herself that she had been transformed, by her own hand, into a different being, one better able in the future to dispense and withhold favours as a mysterious masked woman. And her body, though she had allowed it to be compromised, still remained in her possession. Slowly, Meltwater dissolved into the darker recesses of her mind. Though no one knew where she was, she began to feel strangely safe and strong. Despite the affront to her dignity, despite her submission, she had conquered the first step in her personal struggle for emancipation. Finally she fell asleep.

Mrs Hallam woke her the next morning, Thursday, 14 February.

"Arabella, it is time to rise. Let me show you how to release the clasp."

She did so and then gently removed the mask, placing it back in the box on the desk.

Arabella looked at herself in the mirror. Her eyes were puffy and red from crying.

"Tonight," said Mrs Hallam, "I have arranged for us to attend a musical evening – a masked dance, to be held in Soho Square. Many people will be coming and all my ladies will be there. I should like you to join us. By the way," she continued, "early this morning people came to the house to ask if I had seen a missing young girl. It appears they had information from a Piccadilly coffee house that she might be in this area. I said there was no one of that description here, but I am sure they will not give up their search. They will return, I am certain, particularly as I understand your father may now be offering a possible reward for any information that may lead to your whereabouts. In case they come again during the day and you are not in your room, I will provide you with a veil to wear."

Arabella gave a faint smile. "Thank you, Mrs Hallam," she said, "but I would prefer to wear my mask when I am not alone in your house. It would make me feel safer and stronger."

"Arabella, I am pleased to hear that," Mrs Hallam replied. "In the circumstances I believe that would be wise."

Before leaving the room, Mrs Hallam asked Arabella to lie back on the bed and to pull up her nightgown to her waist. "We must protect you as best we can from the risk of bearing a child and from disease," she said. Spreading Arabella's legs apart and peering closely at her genitalia, she commented that Lord Simon had indeed been rough in his penetration. "I will spare you until you heal."

As she straightened Arabella's nightdress, Mrs Hallam said she was keen to avoid pregnancies amongst her charges and accordingly asked Arabella to keep a record of her menstrual pattern and other physiological signs so she could "rest" at the monthly peak of her fertility. Arabella blushed deeply.

"Have you lost blood recently?" she asked.

"Yes, just a few days ago," Arabella replied, unable to look at Mrs Hallam, so embarrassed was she.

"Good," said Mrs Hallam, "then you will be safe for a week or so. The physician, Mr Holland, will come to inspect you from time to time." She added, "As you speak excellent French, I have decided that your name henceforth will be Antoinette Badeau. That is the name I will call you at all times, and the one to which you will answer as long as you are in my care. I hope you like it. I think it suits you, and the men who come here will find it alluring. You should speak French at all times. If you need to speak English, do so with a French accent. Arabella has gone."

Arabella nodded but made no comment. Mrs Hallam left the room.

After dressing and then brushing and pinning up her hair, Arabella once again put on the mask, fixing the clasp in place. She looked at herself in the mirror. A curious sensation passed through her sore body. She felt transformed. She had a new identity and the mask was her new face. As long as she wore it, she would be the mysterious Antoinette Badeau, answerable for her own actions, and not Arabella Whitfield. Arabella would recede into the background, becoming a mere observer, not a participant, in what was about to unfold.

There was a knock at the door and the maid asked Miss Antoinette if she could enter to make up the room.

"You may," replied the voice of Antoinette, speaking English in a delightful and coquettish French accent.

Wearing the pink dress Mrs Hallam had given her the day before, Antoinette left the room to go down stairs. Her new life had started, but for how long she did not know.

That night the masked and mysterious new Antoinette Badeau mingled with other masked women at a soirée at Carlisle House in Soho Square, hosted by Mrs Teresa Cornelys, whose daughter, Sophie, had been fathered by the famous Giacomo Casanova. Parties and balls at Carlisle House were always grand and opulent affairs to which she invited nobility and gentry. Though filled with a deep fear that her identity might be discovered, Arabella – under Mrs Hallam's watchful eye – began to circulate with new confidence. Men approached her, kissing her hand and seeking favours, which were politely declined. Mrs Hallam observed Arabella closely and was soon quietly pleased with the prospects of her new young and unexpected acquisition. She was sure that, with skilful teaching and the provision of expensive clothes, Antoinette Badeau would indeed be a particularly good long-term investment – good for her accounts, that is. Having noticed Arabella's music book, and having in fact leafed through some of its pages when her charge was downstairs, Mrs Hallam decided that her investment should include the provision of a harpsichord.

Arabella was thrilled by its arrival in her bedroom three weeks later. While the pastoral pictures it bore reminded her painfully of Meltwater, at last she could play once more. After indulging herself with some of her favourite pieces, Arabella stopped and pulled a small sheet of paper from her dressing-table drawer. She wrote:

I have now lodged with Mrs Hallam for nearly a month. My room is spacious and comfortable but my life is bleak. I have lost my purity in circumstances I never imagined.

I cannot return home. I feel disgust and loathing. I hide my shame behind a beautiful mask and an assumed name. But my plight is my own fault – whether a consequence of my pride or of true conviction my mind is in such turmoil I cannot decide.

But I am grateful for Mrs H's protection, for fresh clothes and a warm room in which she has kindly placed a harpsichord. Most of all I have my beloved music book to keep me company.

I have chosen my course, set my compass and now I must complete the voyage on which I am embarked. Holy Mary, Mother of God, please protect me.

Dating and then folding the paper, she placed it inside the rear flap of her music book.

It was not long before many sought to enjoy the pleasures of the mysterious masked French woman, whose fame was beginning to circulate by word of mouth amongst the clubs and salons of London, and a little later on printed but discreet lists of courtesans (which were in sharp contrast and markedly superior to Harris's well-known and more regular public lists of common prostitutes to be found in Covent Garden). Greatly valuing her asset, Mrs Hallam closely controlled access to her prized Antoinette. Those allowed to "visit" were quickly seduced by the whisper of her silk, the flutter of her lace and the wisp of a garment that she teasingly used to hide as much as it revealed. The seduction was even more intense on account of the juxtaposition of an exposed slim and beautiful body with an unseen face behind a never-removed mask.

So successful was Antoinette proving to be that some of those whom Mrs Hallam carefully chose to admit to her room soon became addicted to the French woman's "body and her play". Some were mesmerised by the way Antoinette toyed with them; others soon became infatuated by her laughter, her French accent and her repartee, as evidenced by the flowers and gifts left for her, sometimes together with proposals of marriage or "suitable arrangements"; and some were transfixed by making love to a woman whose face was always hidden by a mask. And of course there was handsome payment to Mrs Hallam for Antoinette's services. In her conversations with Arabella, Mrs Hallam chose never to refer to the money she received, sensing that she would not want to know, but from time to time she did leave a little of the proceeds in her room, and when she did, Arabella would swiftly hide it because to her each amount was tainted. But there again, one day it might help to pay for her escape.

As the days and weeks went by, Arabella continued to justify her presence in Chesterfield Street by differentiating – separating – herself from her other identity, Antoinette Badeau. Convincing herself she was just a spectator at a theatre or in a dream, Arabella admired the masked Antoinette – her self-confidence, her coquettishness, her talent for flirtation and her easy laughter. She also admired Antoinette's strong, sensuous and tantalising sexual repertoire, which she used with increasing skill and dexterity to manipulate the men who enjoyed her company. It was the deeply sensual Antoinette, aware of her effect on men, who was often in full control of the sexual needs of her clients. Frequently, she liked to play a game – sometimes giving what was sought, sometimes provocatively denying it and laughing as she did so, amused by the effect her teasing refusal had on those in her bed. She played men just as an angler might play with a fish he has hooked, gently reeling in his catch. On other, quieter occasions, Antoinette would play the harpsichord in her room; sometimes, wearing only her unlaced shift, playing musical treats as her clients sat beside her, mesmerised by the keyboard dexterity of the masked woman, which a few thought surpassed even her accomplishments in bed.

Arabella also observed Antoinette's ingenuity in resisting the unacceptable demands sometimes made of her, though not always with success – on one occasion she was driven to strike the face of a client who had become violent during intercourse. Already inebriated (having eluded Mrs Hallam's close scrutiny of his suitability for her prized niece), he tried after rough foreplay to flip Antoinette onto her front for anal sex. Flushed with profound anger, Antoinette struggled free from his grip, slapped his face (Arabella instantly recalling what her father had done to her) and pushed the drunken man backwards off the bed onto the floor, cursing him in French as she did so.

"You may think I am a French whore, but how you penetrate

me to satisfy your so-called pleasure is for me to decide, not you, you pig. Now get out!"

He lurched towards the door, pulling up his breeches with one hand and scooping up his jacket and wig with the other.

"I won't forget this," he screamed.

Shortly afterwards, Mrs Hallam came to Arabella's room to find out what had happened. Still smarting from the assault, Antoinette retorted, "I am grateful, Mrs Hallam, for the refuge you have given me and I tolerate what you have asked me to do to earn my keep. But what that man tried to do to me was abominable and unnatural. I therefore forcefully rejected him and will do so again, whatever the cost to me or you."

Mrs Hallam looked closely at the masked young woman still quivering with anger as she gathered her shift around her slender body. It was clear Antoinette had identified a limit beyond which she would not be pushed. Mrs Hallam quickly realised that her prized Arabella, hiding behind the mask of Antoinette, was too precious an investment to lose. She would have to ensure this line was never crossed again.

Arabella, as the voyeur, observed that Antoinette, despite her playfulness and strong character, did not draw any real enjoyment from her sensuality and its effect on her "visitors". The respect Antoinette appeared to seek was never available from those who embraced her, however solicitous they might appear to be. The process in which she engaged – or which she tried to manipulate – was merely mechanical. The physical and loving pleasure that Arabella sought for herself was not present in Antoinette's bedroom. Perhaps such pleasure did not exist, Arabella pondered.

Week after week the mask enabled Arabella to delude herself that she was merely an onlooker in the sordid world Antoinette occupied. But late at night in bed, with her mask removed, Antoinette vanished. It was then that Arabella came face to face with her self-deception and the reality that she was compromising her principles and her faith. Alone in the dark she felt imprisoned in a suffocating blackness, locked in an underworld in which there was no light, no way out. But when she woke the next morning, put on the beautiful mask and heard the maid who came to her room greet her with "Good morning, Miss Antoinette," Arabella and her guilt disappeared, replaced by the captivating and light-hearted young French woman.

Though there were occasional uncorroborated reports that her father and brother were still searching for her, by the spring, Arabella (or rather Antoinette) had become sufficiently confident to leave Chesterfield Street in the evening in Mrs Hallam's company, her face concealed either by a veil or her mask; until then, the soirée at Carlisle House had been her only outing. They visited other houses, or went to Drury Lane Theatre, or, more than once, to Ranelagh Pleasure Gardens, where she and Mrs Hallam and some of her other nieces would stroll around the ornamental lake, admire the Chinese Pavilion or sit in the Rotunda where there were private rooms for flirtations and the chance to listen to a variety of music, including some of the latest compositions of the composer Thomas Arne. They even went on one occasion to Bagnigge Wells, once the summer residence of Nell Gywn, but Arabella did not like its tinge of unrespectability.

Some of Mrs Hallam's young nieces sought to become friends of the guarded but coquettish Antoinette, dazzled by her vivacious personality (when it was allowed to shine) and musical knowledge. Though Arabella became increasingly relaxed and confident, she remained vigilant and sometimes withdrawn, much to the disappointment and, indeed, criticism of some of the older women in Mrs Hallam's circle, who regarded her reserve and, more particularly, her refusal to show her face as snobbery. She found this hard to bear, but decided that she would trust no one. Her identity and whereabouts had to remain secure.

Keen to flourish even more publicly her newly acquired prize, one warm spring evening towards the end of May, Mrs Hallam invited Antoinette to join her and others at a concert in Lincoln's Inn. It was a glittering candle-lit occasion, with elegantly dressed ladies, many masked and some in fancy dress, on the arm of handsome men.

Wearing a broad-brimmed hat decorated with ribbons, her mask, a fetching satin gown with a low-cut frilled bodice just covering her nipples and a black choker around her neck, the mysterious young French woman, Antoinette Badeau, turned many heads that night as she took her seat on Mrs Hallam's left, with Mrs Hallam's escort, the ageing Mr James Fortune, on her right. While Ranelagh Pleasure Gardens, which frequently appeared on her list of outings, were colourful and amusing, particularly on evenings of masquerade, Arabella – or Antoinette Badeau, as she continued to insist – was mesmerised by the wealth, elegance and style on show that evening in Lincoln's Inn. She felt she could almost touch the unmistakable current of intense sexual play beneath the surface, the active provocation and the pervading corruption of morals.

There appeared on the platform a young nine-year-old boy, who, together with his sister, began to play the most divine music, including his own composition for four hands. Arabella, the musician, the possessor of her cherished musical notebook, sat enraptured. She looked at the programme. She was listening to Wolfgang Amadeus Mozart and his sister, Nannerl, performing shortly before their departure from London for Paris.

As the notes flowed from the keyboard, Arabella – feeling that she was floating far above the concert-goers in the hall below – suddenly and vividly recalled her mother, the harpsichord at Meltwater, Herr Kunzl and all the events that had passed since she had run away from home. These memories, blended with Mozart's delicate music, caused Arabella immense pain. She sensed Antoinette looking at her, puzzled. Though no one could see them, tears trickled down Arabella's face. She wished that the day would soon come when she could leave Mayfair, discard Antoinette's mask and play music again free from fear – to a man she truly loved and whom she could embrace without disgust. Of course Arabella accepted that, while Mrs Hallam had recruited her, as Antoinette, to the demi-monde to provide services to rich men, she had also saved her from her father and her unhappy existence in Norfolk. But the price she had paid in self-esteem had been costly and profoundly demeaning. The music she heard stirred within her an urgent longing to escape from Chesterfield Street and to continue her search for passionate, free-flowing love, peace of mind and the respect for which she was so desperate.

Before going to bed that night, Arabella wrote on a fresh sheet of paper:

> *I have just returned from Mr Mozart's concert. He was so young, so handsome and so skilled at the keyboard. He even played from memory music that I have in my music book. What an evening of breathtaking light, sound and colour. The Holy Spirit was surely present.*

What a contrast tonight was to my daily existence as Antoinette B – waiting for Mrs H to bring suitable men to my room in return for money. But I thank her for her careful selection, since some of the men I glimpse from my doorway entering other rooms appear repulsive.

Mr Mozart has inspired me to escape. But how can I do so?

Arabella's urge to escape became even greater when she heard the young Mozart again in Thrift Street, Soho in June. With money at low ebb, Wolfgang's father, Leopold, used the evening to present his son and daughter, Nannerl, almost as circus performers, playing music on sight at the request of members of the audience. Prompted by Arabella, Antoinette joined in the fun by passing a note to the young Wolfgang asking him to play from the *Gradus Ad Parnassum*, a treatise on counterpoint, which the Austrian composer Johann Joseph Fux had written in 1725 and which her music teacher, Herr Kunzl, had drawn to her attention in several of her music lessons. Responding eagerly, Mozart laughed out loud and played – without hesitation or slip – part of the *Gradus* for the elegant lady in the mask, adding some ornamental flourishes as he did so. Arabella did not know that Mozart already possessed a copy of the *Gradus*, which he had annotated. She was entranced. She wished to go up on the platform and hug the young boy.

As she returned to Chesterfield Street, Arabella felt a new fire of rage begin to burn fiercely within her. Even more strongly than the previous recital, the elegance and harmony of the music she had heard that night contrasted brutally with the sordid world of sex that she observed and, as Antoinette, experienced every day. The sheer beauty of the music reminded her that she had not been to Mass since she left Meltwater. Not only had she turned her back on her family and her home, she had neglected her Catholic faith. Arabella felt deeply ashamed. She decided that she had to find soon the moment to shatter the defences she had built around herself and to seek to atone for her mortal sin. The walls around her might have protected her from her father but now they had trapped her in a fresh darkness. Antoinette, her other personality, might wish to stay behind these walls but Arabella did not. However, the chance to escape them seemed as remote as ever. Mrs Hallam kept

Antoinette (she never thought of her as Arabella Whitfield) under lock and key. She was too precious an investment to let go.

It was at this point that two people entered Arabella's life at Chesterfield Street. The first was a pretty but frail young woman, Jane Cummings. Though she was well-educated, well-mannered and her company enjoyable, Jane's story was sad. She had been orphaned at the age of five and had gone to live with her aunt and uncle in Somerset. Her kind and generous uncle, paying for her to have a good schooling, died several years later and within a year her aunt had fallen in love with a local textile maker. They married when Jane was twelve and lived happily together as a family until they fell upon hard times and family life began to deteriorate. Her step-uncle became an alcoholic and in due course left home, taking with him what little money he and her aunt still possessed. Though Jane pleaded to stay at home and help her aunt bring in some income, it soon became apparent that, at the age of fifteen, there was no longer a loving home for her. She decided to go to London to seek work as a governess in one of the large houses, but this was not easy and before long she came to the attention of Mrs Hallam who, as Arabella had come to see over the months, was always keen to find new talent to fill her stable of nieces. She put Jane in a smaller room along the same corridor as Arabella.

Jane found her introduction to Mrs Hallam's evening guests difficult to accept and often came to Arabella to seek strength and comfort. Arabella remembered her own early weeks at Chesterfield Street and so did her best to provide the companionship and support that Jane desired. But it was not easy for Jane. She would talk wistfully about her childhood and naturally asked Arabella about hers. Trying hard to make sure she did not let slip her real identity, or lose her French accent, Arabella concocted an imaginary childhood in France and a voyage to England. But as Jane talked about childhood often, it was sometimes difficult for Arabella to remember what she had said previously. On occasions Jane, who was rather inquisitive, questioned apparent inconsistencies in what she told her. This made Arabella cross but she remembered to bite her tongue just in time.

Still terrified of being discovered by her father, Arabella chose to wear her mask whenever she was not alone in the house, even during the day when there were no male visitors. Jane followed her example. But after a while, when they were alone together in each other's room, Jane would remove her mask, brush her hair and apply make-up. She implored Arabella to remove hers. But Arabella refused, insisting that it reflected her French identity, protected her privacy and indeed was her real face. She had decided at the beginning of her stay at Mrs Hallam's that she would never trust anyone – not even Jane. Moreover, when she wore her mask, Arabella was able to convince herself she was Antoinette, a different person who was far removed in temperament, style and beliefs from the young woman of Meltwater Hall. Arabella knew this separation was a fiction, but without maintaining the pretence she found it difficult to accept what she had become: a high-class whore.

The two became firm friends and were often together during the day. But after a while Arabella noticed a subtle change in Jane's demeanour. It became apparent that one particular visitor, John Bellamy, had become smitten with his sexual companion and he soon began to spend two or three evenings a week in Jane's company. Before long they were going to the theatre together. As Jane became increasingly enamoured with Bellamy, the less reliant she became on Arabella during the day. Arabella welcomed this and on the occasions when she and Jane were together she became more circumspect in what she divulged about her own visitors and background. She was only too aware from those who came to see her just how many secrets they disclosed while sharing her perfumed pillow. She soon recognised that the indiscretions and peccadilloes of others could be a powerful tool for social advancement in her new profession. But though Antoinette might be tempted to use such information to her advantage, Arabella was not. She found the thought of blackmail repulsive.

The other person in Arabella's working life was the still-handsome wealthy widower Lord Tumbleton, whose name she recalled her father had mentioned once or twice. In his sixties and somewhat foppish (and heavily made up with a beauty spot), Tumbleton was a kind and gentle person. He was uninterested in intercourse, a relief to Arabella. Instead, he asked to sit beside her while she played the harpsichord for an hour or more, unclothed apart from a silk shawl draped over her shoulders. He particularly liked the masked Antoinette to play from her music book, the leather binding of which she had covered to hide the initials *AW*. Sometimes she chose melancholy songs by Pierre Attaignant, a French music publisher in the first half of the sixteenth century who became royal music printer and librarian, or she played the Bach her music teacher had taught her.

On arrival in her room, Tumbleton would remove his jacket, waistcoat and wig and then undress Arabella. Placing a shawl across her shoulders and slipping her feet into an elegant pair of slippers, each one bearing the letter *A*, he would lead her to the stool and ask her to play on sight from melodies he would bring with him and which he would often sing. Sometimes she would play pieces she knew well from her music book. As Arabella played, Tumbleton would stroke her thigh and occasionally trace the outline of her breast with his index finger. In their early encounters, he begged her to remove her mask, but when she repeatedly refused he soon realised his requests for sight of her face would never be granted.

On other occasions, he would ask her to lie on the bed, with her right thigh draped across her left leg and her left arm across her stomach with the fingers of her left hand touching the lower part of her right breast; her right hand would touch her throat as though she was inclined to remove her mask. Her head would rest on a rich-red silk cushion, which he insisted she should use in this pose. Tumbleton would sit beside the bed, sometimes wearing a cardinal's robe and cap, smoking, drinking wine and reading from Vasari's *Lives of the Painters, Sculptors and Architects*, while his right hand occasionally rested on her left shoulder or touched her left breast. With the room lit by candlelight and Tumbleton displaying all his eccentricity, the scene was like a painting from a Renaissance villa in Florence. Antoinette found the pose amusing; the masked Arabella found it deeply disturbing.

On one occasion, Tumbleton fell deeply asleep. Arabella quietly slipped from the bed and, wrapping her shawl tightly around her, sat at the harpsichord. Opening her music book, she turned the pages until she found a piece of music to match her melancholy. She paused at a Bach sarabande, but selected instead the adagio from Corelli's *Christmas Concerto*, which brought back memories of playing to her mother. As her fingers deftly touched the keyboard in the candlelight, she recalled the first time she had played the piece to her mother. How she wished they were together again. She stopped abruptly. The memory had become too painful.

After a while Arabella became tired of Lord Tumbleton and suggested to Mrs Hallam that she might introduce him to another of her nieces. Mrs Hallam said he had insisted on being with his beautiful Antoinette and he paid well. He became so obsessed with his mysterious young lady that, a few weeks into his patronage of her, he proposed to Mrs Hallam that she release her into his permanent keeping so she could play for him at his home in Chiswick. Indeed, she might also play – fully clothed – to his near neighbour, Lady Barbara Ward, who unbeknownst to him was mistress to Antoinette's real father. He was ready to offer Mrs Hallam a very handsome fee and to provide a life of luxury to his own private harpsichord player and personal beauty, who would be obliged to spend much of her day displaying her beautiful body to him and to those whom he would invite to view her. Arabella was horrified at the proposition, particularly when Mrs Hallam seemed to favour it as offering a lucrative return on her investment. Moreover, she had no wish to meet her father's mistress. But the proposal was abruptly terminated when Lord Tumbleton died suddenly trying to make love to a prostitute in his bed at home, in practice for the eventual arrival of his Antoinette.

Late spring became summer and summer became autumn. Arabella remained at Chesterfield Street under Mrs Hallam's close supervision. She rarely mixed with the other resident women – partly still fearing her real identity might become known, so providing a clue that might be passed in loose-tongued gossip to acquaintances of her family, who were still, it seemed, making efforts to find her; and partly because she perceived herself to be desperately clinging to an ever narrowing ledge overlooking an ever darker Hades below her. She feared that one silly or ill-conceived move would cause her to lose her fragile hold on the rocks to which she was cleaving precariously and tumble deep into the blackness below. If that were to happen, she would never be able to find her way back to the daylight of the world she had left behind.

One Tuesday evening in early October, Arabella was in her room, waiting for Mrs Hallam to tell her whether she would be visited that night. While she (or Antoinette Badeau, as her mind still tried hard to insist, but with diminishing success) had become accustomed to the routine of her courtesan life, the arrival of the darker evenings and colder weather reminded her that she had now been at Chesterfield Street for almost eight months. She began to plan with greater resolution how she might flee Mrs Hallam's control and, if successful in doing so, where she might go. If she did not try to escape soon, her present fate would be truly sealed.

Having adjusted her dress and then her hair, Arabella once again put on her mask, locking the clasp and so becoming Antoinette Badeau. While gazing at herself in the mirror and gently turning from side to side in the candlelight to admire her svelte figure as she had seen Antoinette do often, she suddenly heard a commotion downstairs. There was a pause and then the noise resumed. She was sure she heard the voice of her brother, George, above the din. Arabella froze in terror. She was about to be discovered and dragged back to Meltwater to face the wrath of her father, who would punish her all the more severely once he knew where she had been hiding and discovered the secret life she had been leading as Antoinette.

Mrs Hallam entered her room, greatly flustered, and for the first time in months called her by her real name.

"Arabella, you must hide, my dear, this instant. Mr George Whitfield, your brother, is downstairs, with others. They are drunk and insisting on seeing all the girls in the house so they can choose their menu of entertainment. He must not find you. I fear for your life if he discovers your true identity, and my own reputation will be sullied. Indeed, I may even be arrested for abduction. What a terrible thought! And I will have lost one of my most attractive courtesans. Come with me at once."

Mrs Hallam and Arabella ran along the corridor and up the next flight of stairs to the third floor. Turning left at the top they went along a poorly lit passage, which Arabella had never visited before, until they came to some shelves containing rows of leather-bound books. Mrs Hallam reached under the top shelf and pulled a handle. The panel of books opened. Behind it was a door. She pulled a key from her pocket and opened it. Behind the door was a small enclosed space with a stool in the corner. It reminded Arabella of a priest's hole she had once seen in a Catholic house in Norfolk.

"You must stay here until they have gone," said Mrs Hallam. "Do not make any noise."

Arabella stepped into the tight dark space, gathered the skirt of her dress closely around her ankles and sat on the small stool.

"Please come back for me soon," she whispered earnestly to Mrs Hallam.

"I will," she replied.

The door then shut, the lock turned and she heard the thud of the panel of books being put back into place. Arabella was alone in darkness. She began to panic but realised this would not help. She had to keep her nerve.

Hours seemed to pass; Arabella had no idea of the time. She could not see. She was cold and began to shiver. Finally, she drifted into a fitful sleep but awoke suddenly when she thought she heard the sound of footsteps and muffled voices getting nearer. After a while the footsteps and voices disappeared. There was silence once again. Her fingers touched the walls of her suffocating sanctuary. It was not high enough for her to stand, not long enough to stretch her legs, and there was no room to turn on her stool. There was not even enough space for her to raise her hands to try to undo the clasp at the back of her neck and so release her mask, which had become oppressive in the stifling confines of her hiding place. But, even if she could remove it, she realised that her mask was her last line of defence should someone try to enter the space in which she was trapped.

After what seemed an eternity of time, of drifting in and out of consciousness, Arabella heard the panel of books moving and a key being placed in the door lock. She held her breath and said a prayer and made the sign of the cross while she waited for the door to open. A beam of candlelight entered. It was Mrs Hallam. She reached in and, placing her left hand under Arabella's right arm, helped her to stand.

"Be very quiet," she whispered. "I will help you to your room."

Once inside her bedroom, Arabella asked what time it was.

"It is Wednesday, past four o'clock in the morning. Your foul-mouthed brother and his friends were here for many hours. They have just left, but I think they will be back soon. They said they were most disappointed not to see the French girl in the Venetian mask, about whom they had heard much from Henry Simon and others."

"What am I going to do?" asked Arabella.

"It is unsafe for you to remain here," replied Mrs Hallam. "You should sleep for a while, but after you have rested I will make immediate arrangements for you to move to another house not far from here. I will miss you greatly, but it is for your own safety – unless you wish to return home."

Arabella replied defiantly that she would never do so as long as her brother and father were alive.

"So be it," said Mrs Hallam. "Now, into bed and rest."

Removing her dress and mask, Arabella got into bed and fell into a restless sleep. She had a nightmare. She dreamt she was encased in a tomb, the walls of which were slowly compressing her into an ever narrower space. Every time she managed to break free she fell back into the darkness. The effort to escape became more and more exhausting. She struggled to breathe, pressed harder and harder with her outstretched arms to stop the walls around her getting still closer. There was no escape. She was about to be crushed. She screamed.

At that moment, Arabella woke, her hands and forehead damp with sweat. She could see daylight coming through between the heavy curtains. Mrs Hallam rushed in.

"My dear child, what is the matter?"

"I dreamt I was being crushed in a tomb that was getting smaller and smaller. However hard I pressed against the encroaching sides, I could not escape," said Arabella.

"I am not surprised you had a nightmare," Mrs Hallam replied, "shut in that pitch-black cell for so long. But I had no choice if I was to save you from your malevolent brother."

Mrs Hallam then explained that she had already sent a note to her friend, Mrs Rathbone, in Shepherd Street, asking her to provide shelter to Arabella for a while in case her brother did come back to find the woman in the white and silver Venetian mask and discovered her real identity. Mrs Rathbone had agreed to take her. Within the hour, Arabella would have to leave Chesterfield Street. Mrs Hallam asked her to dress quickly and to pack her things with all speed in her leather bag. She, meanwhile, would attend to further matters towards her safety.

Arabella had scarcely finished packing when Mrs Hallam returned with two of her servants, who carried a trunk; Mrs Hallam herself was carrying a decorated box.

"I do not need a trunk for my clothes," said Arabella after the servants had left.

"The trunk is to convey you from this house," said Mrs Hallam. "A man has been standing outside across the street for some hours, and I have received a note that your brother will return here this evening and demand to have the services of the woman in the Venetian mask, whatever the price charged. I suspect he will try to find out who is behind Antoinette Badeau's mask. For your safety and for the sake of my name, we must convey you out of the house secretly using the doorway at the back and then through the garden and coach house. You must therefore hide in the trunk."

Arabella put her hands to her mouth in horror at the thought of being placed in such a small space only hours after emerging from her tomb upstairs. Mrs Hallam said there was no alternative, unless they were to be discovered. She then handed Arabella the decorated box. Arabella looked inside and saw a Venetian mask even more beautiful than the one she had worn since arriving at Chesterfield Street. Instead of white, it was covered in gold.

"Please take this mask. I will destroy the other. You do not want anyone to recognise you in your new lodgings."

Arabella put on her new mask and gazed at herself in the mirror. It was again heavily perfumed but tighter and still more beguiling than the one before.

"Dearest Arabella," said Mrs Hallam. "The mask you now wear has belonged to me for many years. My lover gave it to me in Venice. He died two years ago and I no longer wish to keep it. It is decorated in real gold. I want you to have it. You have been a good and faithful girl. One day, when it is no longer necessary to be masked because you have found true happiness, I hope that you will keep it to remember our friendship."

Arabella put her arms around Mrs Hallam's neck and began to cry.

"No time for tears, dear child."

Arabella began to unclasp her new mask. There was a noise downstairs.

"There is no time for that. Keep it on," said Mrs Hallam. "Quickly, get into the trunk. Your life is in danger." As she uttered these words she pressed into Arabella's hand a leather pouch.

"Here is some money. It is richly deserved."

Arabella realised that this was a token payment for services performed; a small proportion of the earnings from her prostitution. To her this was yet more tainted money, like the earlier modest payments she had received from Mrs Hallam and which she had hidden at the bottom of a drawer. But in her dire predicament her instinct to survive outweighed her deeply held moral scruples. The money might well help her to escape. She took the pouch.

"Say goodbye to Jane for me," Arabella said.

"Of course I will," replied Mrs Hallam.

After a brief hesitation, Arabella stepped into the softly padded trunk and lay on her side, her knees and hands drawn up under her chin. Hastily, Mrs Hallam placed two dresses over the top of her, with some crinoline and other material, and stowed the decorated box for her new mask at her feet. She then shut the lid of the trunk and locked it.

Arabella could barely move or breathe. Her mask pressed on her face. As in her overnight hiding place, she soon lost all sense of time. It seemed she had waited endlessly before the trunk was suddenly lifted and carried downstairs. It swayed from side to side. Suddenly, it was dropped with a thud onto the floor of a hand-pushed cart. Several – or perhaps seventy – minutes later, the cart, on which the leather bag had also been placed, began to move over cobbles. Arabella had left 35 Chesterfield Street.

By the time the cart eventually stopped and the noise of the streets had receded, Arabella was in great discomfort. She was desperate to get out. She was sure she would soon die of suffocation. She felt the trunk being lifted and again it swayed from side to side as it was carried upstairs. Eventually, it was set down heavily on a carpeted floor.

After an interminable interval during which there was earnest discussion between muffled voices, Arabella heard the sound of the key in the lock. The clothes on top of her were removed and then Mrs Hallam helped her out of the box in which she had been locked for over two hours.

"I am sorry that it took so long, but to follow a direct route would have been too dangerous."

Arabella swayed on her feet as she rubbed her sore and

cramped limbs. Mrs Hallam removed the mask. Turning, Arabella came face to face with an elderly beak-faced woman, to whom she was introduced as Antoinette Badeau.

"Antoinette, this is my dear friend, Mrs Rathbone, who is going to look after you as I have done. I have explained everything to her. She knows what has to be done and the secret to be kept."

With that, Mrs Hallam gathered her cloak about her, pulling the hood over her head, and left the room. Arabella was never to see her again.

Arabella's life in London was about to turn yet another page. She soon realised that she and her sexual services had been sold to Mrs Rathbone.

Later that day, Arabella wrote:

> *Tonight I am in a new place. I realise now I have been sold.*
>
> *Mrs H says Mrs R's establishment will provide all that I need, and my protection. Perhaps that is so. But I must confront Antoinette. It is I who must triumph, not she.*

Arabella did not know that her removal from Chesterfield Street was to take her a step closer towards the denouement of her life's adventure.

CHAPTER 4

The Man in the Upstairs Room

The new lodgings in Shepherd Street at which Arabella arrived on Wednesday, 9 October 1765, were neither as spacious nor as elegant and comfortable as Mrs Hallam's. It soon became evident that the regime was more restrictive and Mrs Rathbone less gracious than Mrs Hallam. The library was smaller, so there were fewer books from which to choose, though the clothes that she could choose to wear were of similar quality and quantity to those in Chesterfield Street. And sadly there was no harpsichord in her room, which meant there was more time for reading and reflection. There was another change of practice, too: unlike Mrs Hallam, Mrs Rathbone referred to Arabella as Antoinette in the presence of visitors, not Mademoiselle Antoinette Badeau. Arabella sensed that Mrs Rathbone was less concerned about her background than her predecessor had been.

Wearing her new mask daily, Arabella continued to observe from afar the power of Antoinette's sensuality, which had been so evident in the scenes she had played for Lord Tumbleton, and the potent effect it had on the smaller and somewhat different circle of men who came to see her at Shepherd Street.

Nudity did not trouble Antoinette. Her long, slim and sculpted body transfixed all those who saw her unclothed. Letting her shift slip theatrically from her slender shoulders to reveal her bare body, and to see the impact this provocation had on her clients, amused Antoinette. These physical encounters emphasised her dominance as an object of intense desire. She acted out her role as a sexual muse with cold-blooded self-discipline. Arabella remained deeply impressed by Antoinette's wilfulness and her capriciousness. And she continued to admire her rock-hard ability to survive; the way she controlled her emotions with an iron grip during displays of her womanhood. Still believing she was only a spectator, Arabella convinced herself she saw merely the actions of another person, not her own. She believed she was bodily disconnected from what was happening far below her, that she was not in any way responsible for Antoinette's sexual ingenuity.

Nonetheless, though this separate woman was able to enact a convincing sexual repertoire, Arabella became increasingly aware – from seeing into Antoinette's mind – how she inwardly loathed the men who came to her room, the men to whom she offered herself. She might perform with allure but their groping and their often wine-soured smell repelled her. Their disloyalty to their wives angered her. Her mask thankfully prevented them from kissing her lips or putting their sex-soaked fingers into her mouth.

But as each passing day shortened, Arabella faced an uncomfortable truth. The wall she had placed in her mind between her and Antoinette was beginning to crumble. With every visitor that entered the bedroom and fondled Antoinette's body, Arabella became aware it was her own breasts that were being touched, not Antoinette's. When Antoinette rebuked an elderly client for being too rough, Arabella suddenly heard her own voice speaking in anger, not Antoinette's. Then one dark day, with rain beating against the window panes, she finally realised that the wall between the two personalities had vanished. Her pretence was no longer tenable. The two different identities had elided into one – into the single person of Arabella. She understood that the past months had been a deception, and felt ashamed of her self-delusion.

The more she pondered this inescapable conclusion over the days and, especially, the nights that followed, the more Arabella realised the absurdity of the illusion to which she had clung from the beginning. She had culpably allowed herself, while pretending to be Antoinette, to become the object of fantasy possession by her clients. She had persuaded herself that it was someone else –

Antoinette – who was enjoying the self-esteem generated by the sexual praise given to her; that it was Antoinette's body, not hers, that was being used for sexual gratification. Alone in her bed and unmasked, Arabella recognised in her miserable loneliness that it was she who was the sexual chattel. It was she who had compromised the fundamental personal principle she had written on the slip of paper in her music book the night before her departure from Meltwater. A separate Antoinette was but a figment of her imagination. As Arabella's conscience forced her to acknowledge this distressing fact, she was wracked by the sense of deep self-degradation she had first experienced at Chesterfield Street. Accepting how weak and stupid she had been, she fell to her knees each night to pray for redemption.

Through bedside prayer, she grasped that she was engaged in a battle of wits with Antoinette Badeau. Antoinette represented carnal evil. Arabella endeavoured to summon the courage to overcome her self-delusion of the past months. The final disappearance of the wall behind which she had been hiding convinced her that, if she found the strength and commitment, she could achieve victory over her adversary. It was she, the responsible, restrained Arabella – the rebel determined to embrace freedom only on her own terms – who would force her foe, Antoinette, to submit.

Acknowledging her betrayal of her principles, Arabella resolved in a last supreme leap of faith and allegiance to break free of the shackles she had allowed others to place on her in the grubby world in which she had been dwelling. It was time to leave. If she did not do so soon, one day she would look at herself in the dressing-table mirror and see that evil had triumphed and that her self-delusion had become reality. Antoinette would have won after all. And if Antoinette won, she – Arabella – would not stay young for ever. Before long she would inevitably slide down the whore's social pecking order, possibly becoming, in the end, one of the common prostitutes of Covent Garden, marked as such by wearing a red headscarf or her skirt hitched up on the left, and living in a seedy backstreet room.

By the beginning of November it was already cold and, with an opportunity to escape yet to materialise, the bleak prospect of Christmas in Shepherd Street began to cross Arabella's mind. She thought of Meltwater on Christmas Day: of the blazing log fire in the dining room; the multitude of candles burning in every room, turning the Hall into a temple of light; the magnificent dishes on the table, the abundance of food; her mother singing French carols and lullabies in the Oak Room while Arabella accompanied her on the harpsichord, and the two of them going to Mass at midnight in the chapel. The thought of her mother not knowing where she was at that special time of the year filled her with great sadness, not least because of the reports she might have received from her husband and son that her precious daughter had fled to the world of the London courtesan. Somehow Arabella had to reassure her mother face to face that she was alive and safe. This would be difficult to do while imprisoned at Shepherd Street. Arabella made up her mind. She would escape before Christmas and make a new beginning.

For much of the remainder of that month, Arabella spent her time in her room, which overlooked the small garden at the back of the house, as Mrs Rathbone encouraged her to do. With continuing disturbances on the streets over the Stamp Act and food shortages, Mrs Rathbone's business declined. Fewer visitors came. But, though times were quieter, Arabella was acutely aware that she was still under Mrs Rathbone's close scrutiny, as one of the most talented assets in her coterie. The quieter period gave her more time to plot her fast-approaching disappearance from Shepherd Street. It also caused her to think of the changing of the seasons in Norfolk.

As each day passed, Arabella saw the leaves on the tree outside her prison window – for prison it seemed – turn from green to brown and then swirl and fall in the chill and gusty wind. At Meltwater the leaves would have gone by now, blown away by the fierce gales off the sea. A small fire was now lit every day in her room. It reminded her that bigger, more warming fires would now be lit daily in every room at Meltwater. She recalled her bedroom at the Hall and how on cold dark nights she loved to pull the curtains round her four-poster bed and dream of another world in which she was a princess carried away by a prince to a magic land.

It was on the afternoon of Tuesday, 19 November, that Mrs Rathbone came once again to see her prized Antoinette in her room. Arabella, who had received few visitors so far that month, was sitting by the fire. An open book rested on her lap as she gazed into the flames, thinking of her mother and Meltwater. Her golden mask lay on the bed ready for use in the evening. Her long, lustrous, well-brushed hair fell about her shoulders and touched the top of her breasts. As she entered the room, Mrs Rathbone, though an embittered woman and dispassionate, successful proprietress of Shepherd Street, was touched by Arabella's beautiful but sad face.

"Antoinette," said Mrs Rathbone, "a special visitor, Monsieur Moreau, is coming to stay with us for a few days. He is French and he will be tired after a long journey from Paris. I do not know exactly how long he will be in London, but I have been asked to arrange for you to visit him in his room while he is here, to make him feel comfortable. He will be in the large room at the front of the house and I have been told he is unlikely to go out as he does not know London. Besides, there are some preparations for his onward journey that will require him to stay inside. Until his arrival you should remain here in your room, as there will be various comings and goings downstairs that need not concern you."

Arabella was intrigued by this request. Usually, her visitors came to her.

"When should I go to him?" she asked.

"I will tell you once I know more precisely what is required of you, and once he has arrived," Mrs Rathbone replied. "What I do know is that he will not have asked for you, or indeed anyone else, so he will not be expecting you – your presence has been requested by a third party. You should therefore go to his room after he has retired for the night. And you should go wearing nothing under your cloak so you can slip easily into his bed. And of course you should wear your mask to hide your identity. I will tell you when he has arrived. Until then you will have no other visitors." With that Mrs Rathbone promptly left the room.

It was several days later, on Saturday, again in the afternoon, that Mrs Rathbone returned, this time finding her charge curled up asleep on her bed, her hair loose, looking almost like a child. Mrs Rathbone sat on the bed and gently touched Arabella's outstretched hand. As she did so, she felt a pang of momentary remorse that she had in effect bought this beautiful girl from her sister-in-trade, Mrs Hallam, and, like her, had made Arabella a source of good income. Surely this young and talented woman deserved better. But running a business left no place for raw emotion or sentimentality. She dismissed the thought from her mind.

"Wake up, Antoinette, Monsieur Moreau has arrived. Please go to his room after midnight. Here is the key to his door in case he locks it. As I have already told you, he will not be expecting you and thus he may be asleep, so please go to him undressed. Give him pleasure and make sure that when he falls asleep afterwards you leave his room quickly. You must be gone before he stirs in the morning. Remember to lock the door when you leave and return the key to me immediately. I have been told that the Monsieur is most important and everything should be as I have described. I will come to your room later tonight to tell you precisely when to go to him. Do you understand what you have to do?"

Arabella nodded, still puzzled by this unusual request.

After eating an early supper, she undressed, washed and applied the remains of the perfume Mrs Hallam had placed in the trunk that had brought her to Shepherd Street. She brushed her hair, pinned it up and put on her mask, fixing the clasp firmly in place. Then she took from the cupboard a long ankle-deep red cloak, placed it around her shoulders and pulled the hood over her head. Drawing the cloak tightly around her naked body, she sat close to the small fire to keep warm. The request she had received was singular. Men always came to her, and knowingly so. This time she would be visiting, in the dark, a man who would not be expecting her. She felt apprehension but also an unfamiliar sense of pleasing anticipation, which she had never experienced before. And this time it would be Arabella, not Antoinette, in attendance. Engaged in what she intuited would be her final struggle with Mademoiselle Badeau, Arabella would be vigilant to ensure that her adversary did not regain the upper hand. She was now responsible for her own actions, no longer hiding behind Antoinette. Arabella moved closer to the fire to await Mrs Rathbone's knock on the door. She watched the flames and the rich red embers below, letting the cloak fall open so she could feel the warmth of the fire on her skin. Arabella sensed the proximity of a new beginning.

A short while later there was a tap on the door. Mrs Rathbone, holding a candle, beckoned Arabella to follow her. Arabella took from the mantelpiece the key Mrs Rathbone had given her earlier and quickly followed in her bare feet, once again drawing the cloak tightly around her. There was some movement on the floor below but the corridor along which they tiptoed was silent. At the end of the corridor, they turned right, going up several stairs to a short landing. Turning to her left, Mrs Rathbone came to a door. She gently turned the handle. It was locked. Passing the candleholder to Arabella in return for the key in Arabella's hand, Mrs Rathbone silently unlocked the door and half opened it before inserting the key into the inside lock. Putting her finger to her lips, Mrs Rathbone gestured Arabella to enter. Taking back the candle, she whispered to Arabella not to forget to return the key.

Arabella crept into the room as the door closed noiselessly behind her. It took several seconds to identify the position of the bed, despite the glow from the fire, which was still alight. Once she had done so, she stole towards the sleeping form of the mysterious Monsieur Moreau. As she reached his bedside, Moreau stirred. Struggling to wake, he moved to raise himself on one elbow to better see the figure standing by him, while trying with the other hand to push back the bedcovers. But instinctively and quickly Arabella leaned across him. Without thinking what she was doing, she gently took his hands and pressed him back onto the pillows, stretching his arms above his head. As she did so, the cloak slipped from her shoulders. Silently, Arabella lowered herself onto him. As his resistance gradually ceased, she released his hands and began to run her fingers across his lips.

Her mind began to play tricks. A voice within her said, "You are Antoinette. Arabella would never do this." Another replied, "No. It is not Antoinette. It is me, Arabella. Antoinette is but a name."

Feeling Moreau begin to harden beneath her, she slowly raised herself and, placing her thighs across his lower body, sat astride him. She began to ease his nightshirt upwards. He made no effort to stop her. He said nothing, nor did she.

Arabella realised that for the very first time and without explanation it was she who was initiating intercourse. She was not watching Antoinette perform. In the preceding months she had dismissed all those who came to see her as visitors of Antoinette. This man seemed to be different. He belonged to her, Arabella, not Antoinette. There was gentleness and softness about him, something she had not encountered before. Arabella quickly became aware of a growing and longing ache within her, a longing she had never felt until now. She slowly eased him into her.

Arabella had never taken such a step before. Nor could she remember Antoinette ever being in such dominant physical control. Ultimately, she had always submitted. As Moreau grew strongly within her, Arabella raised herself upright and drew his hands to cup her breasts. As he held them and touched her nipples, she suddenly began to feel herself slipping out of control, sliding towards the edge of a dark pool. However hard she tried to resist, the edge of the pool came steadily nearer. Suddenly, she lost her grip and fell into the liquid darkness. She felt herself begin to drown. Her lungs bursting for air, she tried to reach up above her as she sank ever deeper. Gasping, she began to shake violently, her body seeming to shatter into pieces as she tried even harder to reach out, to touch a distant light above her head. Suddenly, her inner being seemed to explode and she was impelled upwards towards an intense brightness that engulfed her. As her body finally emerged into a brilliant blue sky, Arabella – not Antoinette – cried out in ecstasy. She sank exhausted onto Moreau. He cried out from the depth of his own pleasure.

She slipped to his side, her hand pressed against his chest. For several minutes they did not speak.

Feeling her face, he whispered in French, "Who are you? Why did you come? Why do you hide behind a mask? I want to see your face and to touch your lips."

"Monsieur, this is not the time to ask. You should sleep now," Arabella replied softly, also in French, as she placed her fingers on his mouth to hush him. She suddenly realised that she was no longer speaking in Antoinette's coquettish style.

Within moments, he had fallen asleep, a hand cupping her breast as they lay together. But Arabella remained awake.

She had come to a strange man's room on instructions to provide a sexual service. She thought it would be Antoinette who would win this battle of wits, who would perform in her usual ice-cold controlled way. Instead, she, Arabella, had taken the step to place a man inside her; he had not forced his way into her. Yes, she had been instructed to give pleasure, but he had entered her because of her sudden inexplicable longing that he should do so.

The consequence had been an orgasm of exquisite intensity, the first she had ever experienced. Her actions, her feelings and his immediate powerful response had unlocked her prison door. She had finally exercised her own prerogative in the control of her conduct. No previous client had ever inspired her, or Antoinette, in this way. Each encounter had been mechanical. But this experience had pierced her inner being.

Arabella touched the face of the man sleeping beside her. She wished she could unclasp her mask and kiss him deeply, but that was not possible. She drifted into drowsiness, forgetting Mrs Rathbone's instruction to leave the room as soon as her client was asleep.

She was woken by a cough in the corridor and then a faint tap on the door. Quickly and silently she slid out of bed, picked up her cloak from the floor and stood for a moment in the first light of day coming through the almost-closed curtains, gazing intently at the handsome man still deeply asleep.

Arabella gasped. The narrow shaft of light now shone on the sleeping figure. Perhaps the light was playing a trick, perhaps it was just her excitable mind, but she thought that the man in the bed, the man who had given her such exquisite pleasure, appeared to bear a striking resemblance to the man in the picture she had seen in the drawing room at Meltwater. Surely she must be wrong.

Suddenly the figure began to stir. Clutching her cloak tightly around her, Arabella quickly opened the door. Mrs Rathbone was waiting outside, already silently mouthing remonstrations about falling asleep in her client's bed. Running to her room and locking the door behind her, Arabella removed her mask, unpinned her hair, put on her nightgown and got into bed, her mind spinning with the image of the face she thought she had seen, almost forgetting the pleasure she had experienced for the first time. She failed to notice that she had dropped in Monsieur Moreau's room the lace handkerchief her mother had given to her, embroidered with the letter *A*.

Before she slept, Arabella wrote on another small sheet of paper:

> *I have been touched by many men since my arrival in London. All of them have been dislikeable, many unpleasant and some loathsome.*

But last night I shared a bed with a man whose face I could not see but with whom I felt immediately at ease. I was drawn ever closer to him by some irresistible power. I wanted to hold him and to feel him inside me. He submitted to me with gentleness and respect. I experienced for the first time in my life a true physical pleasure and comfort. And it was I who made love to the faceless man, not Antoinette.

I now know what I seek. The time has truly come to escape from my prison, sure in the knowledge that what I have been seeking for so long really exists. I am now wholly convinced that if I strive hard enough I will find the happiness and esteem for which I yearn.

Much later on that Sunday, Mrs Rathbone came to tell Arabella that she should return to Moreau's room after midnight. Arabella displayed no emotion, though secretly she was pleased to do so, despite being even more puzzled as to who Moreau really was and why his portrait – if it was his – had been at Meltwater.

She tried to rest. She tried to read. But she could not quell her restlessness. Eventually, it was time to prepare to return to the room at the end of the corridor. After washing and putting on her mask, and again wearing only her cloak, Arabella waited impatiently for Mrs Rathbone's knock on the door. At last it came. Once more, she found herself in Moreau's room. He appeared to be asleep. She moved to his bedside, letting the cloak fall from her bare shoulders as she silently slipped into his bed. As she did so, he startled her. He was awake. She touched his face and felt his smile. He touched her mask.

He made no attempt to push her away. Without speaking, he removed his nightshirt. He then lay down, pulling her onto him. He pushed her thighs apart so that she was kneeling astride him, her upper body upright, as she had been the night before. He cupped her breasts and began to massage her nipples gently with his fingers. She shuddered with pleasure and sensed the same strong pulsating urge of the night before beginning to throb inside her. Her mask was suffocating. Though she longed to spring the clasp and remove it, she knew that she must not, but this did not stop her kissing him on the lips. The lust of the previous night rose uncontrollably inside her. He asked her to put him inside her. Once she had done so they moved together in rhythm. She was soon overwhelmed with even greater ferocity and speed than the first time. As he reached his own climax, she again shook violently, gasping for breath.

Afterwards, with her back pressed against his chest and his arms holding her so tightly she could not move, he repeated his questions: who was she and why was she masked? Arabella gave no reply but squeezed his hands. He soon fell asleep. She listened to the sound of the wind and rain outside, counted the beats of her heart. She felt triumphant and at last deeply needed. Antoinette Badeau had finally vanished. The fiction of two separate identities was entirely gone. Arabella was now the only identity. She had embarked on another part of her long journey but still with no idea of where it would end. Though frightened about what might lie ahead, the time had come to escape from the demi-monde without further delay. She now knew what true pleasure and the possibility of love meant. It existed and she had to find it. She fell asleep, unable and unwilling to break free from Moreau's grip.

She woke suddenly to find Moreau standing beside the bed as he pulled on his shirt. He looked down at her semi-naked body. Without listening to what he was saying, she hurriedly got up, wrapped her cloak around her and quickly went to the door. As she did so, he pressed her lace handkerchief into her hand.

Back in her room, and ignoring Mrs Rathbone's insistent knocking, Arabella sat down on her bed and sobbed, overcome with grief. Full of anguish at leaving behind such unalloyed pleasure and sense of possibility, she was flung back into the despair of her seedy room. Perhaps she could not after all rid herself of the unwanted existence to which she seemed chained. Perhaps she was destined to be Antoinette Badeau for the rest of her life. As a woman, the life of the courtesan was all she knew. Perhaps that was all she was fit for.

No, it was not, she insisted. If she was to experience the sexual satisfaction she had found in the arms of Moreau, her life of self-deception and desolation had to end – now. There had to be no more waking up in the morning finding everything dark and grey. She must wake up to warmth and colour. After hours of talking to herself and a bedside prayer, she made up her mind to escape from Shepherd Street within hours. Though she might risk her life by leaving her present shelter, she had to reach up from the perilous ledge on which she had been balancing for the past ten months and begin her ascent back to the world of light. Moreau had inspired her to take her courage in her hands.

Sitting in front of the fire on that Monday, 25 November 1765, Arabella decided what the first rung on her ladder to freedom would be: to see her mother. It would shortly be the first of December. At the beginning of December her mother always travelled to Norwich, staying for several days to meet her Catholic friends to mark, as they always did, the start of Advent and to buy gifts at the Christmas fair. This would be a dangerous journey for Arabella to make. Not only would she be travelling alone in winter weather; she would be doing so without the safety of her mask, only a veil to hide her face. She might easily be recognised once she got to Norwich. But Arabella was resolute. She wanted her mother to see her, to hold her, but she also wanted to persuade her to accept she would never return to Meltwater while her father was alive. And having not been to Mass for many months, she wished to confess her sins to a priest, to do penance and to take Communion.

Later in the morning Mrs Rathbone came to scold her for not listening for her knock on Moreau's door. She added that it would be unnecessary for her to visit him that evening, as he would be leaving shortly. The news that she would not be expected to go to Moreau that night reinforced Arabella's conviction that her intention to leave was right, though she felt an emptiness at the thought he would not hold her again.

Arabella told Mrs Rathbone that she had been thinking for some time of travelling to Norwich to see her mother, whom she had not seen for nearly a year. Perceiving evident reluctance to let her go, Arabella implored Mrs Rathbone to release her. Mrs Rathbone said that would not be possible. It would soon be Christmas and the New Year season, and she wanted all of her "family" to be available. Moreover, times were hard and that being so, the income Arabella generated was necessary. She suggested that Arabella might travel sometime later, in the months ahead. Arabella pleaded again, but Mrs Rathbone replied, "Antoinette, the answer is no. You must remain, and that is the end of it."

That night Mrs Rathbone kept a close eye on Arabella, though unlike Mrs Hallam she never locked her bedroom door.

After midnight, when the house had become silent, there being few visitors because of the sudden bad weather, Arabella got up and laid on the bed the few clothes of her own that Mrs Hallam had put in her leather bag at the time of her sudden move from Chesterfield Street to Shepherd Street. They included the black dress, veil, hat and coat she had been wearing when she knocked on the door in Mayfair all those months ago, and a simple green dress Mrs Hallam had said she could keep because it matched her eyes. After dressing in the outfit in which she had arrived in London, Arabella quickly packed her few personal toiletries, her own underclothes and stockings and the green dress, on top of which she placed her missal and the music book. She made sure not to take anything Mrs Rathbone could possibly claim belonged to her. Then Arabella counted the small amount of money that Mrs Hallam had given her over their months together. The miserly Mrs Rathbone had given her none. She thought she would have enough money for a sedan chair to Charing Cross and her subsequent coach ride to Norwich. Lastly, she put her gold mask in its box, securing the lid with some ribbon. While it was a reminder of Antoinette, it was too precious to leave behind. Besides, it would be a reminder of her deeply sensual nights with Monsieur Moreau. Wrapped in her black coat, Arabella lay on the bed, hardly daring to sleep.

Once she heard the early movements of the scullery maids after four o'clock, Arabella got up, washed her face and crept downstairs to the kitchen where the cook, Mrs James, also now up, was already preparing breakfast. The two whispered. Mrs James hugged her and, after pressing a large piece of freshly baked bread, wrapped in cloth, into her hand, she unlocked the kitchen door.

Dressed in black with her face hidden by the heavily veiled broad-brimmed hat she had worn to hide her grief at leaving Meltwater almost a year ago, Arabella quickly climbed the steps to the pavement. It was bitterly cold; a deep frost heralded the beginning of a severe winter that would last until February. She looked up at the house. There was no light from any of the upstairs windows. Mrs Rathbone was still in bed. Bracing herself against the sharp and penetrating wind, Arabella walked briskly along the street, carrying her small leather bag and the box containing her mask. Her luck held. She soon found a sedan chair to take her to Charing Cross. And so it was that Arabella absconded from Mrs Rathbone's establishment, determined never to return.

With eyes lowered, she was the first in line to board the next fast coach to Norwich, looking fully the part of a tragic young widow. To her horror, she noticed in the throng of people – of all shapes, sizes, classes and ages, jostling for places on coaches to myriad other destinations – the figure of Jane Cummings, whom she had befriended at Chesterfield Street. Arabella pulled her veil down as far as it would go and turned away. She prayed that Jane would not recognise her. How could she, since Arabella had never removed her mask?

But she suddenly remembered that, late one night, Jane had burst into her room to announce with great happiness that her regular visitor, John Bellamy, had that evening persuaded Mrs Hallam to let him take her to his home for the weekend, so they could spend more time together. Jane said she was sure it was a prelude to her becoming Mrs Bellamy, now that the first Mrs Bellamy had died of consumption. Arabella was getting ready for bed, and had almost removed her mask, as this was the moment of the day, brushing her hair, when she could return to being Arabella rather than Antoinette, and look forward to sleeping without the mask constricting her face. Quickly turning her back, Arabella had refastened the clasp, but she had often wondered whether Jane caught a momentary glimpse of her unconcealed face, reflected in the candlelit mirror. Jane never owned that she had, only remarking that surely, for once, Arabella could speak to her unmasked.

Jane approached Arabella, who was about to mount the step to climb into the Norwich coach, and placed her hand on her arm.

"Please, is this the coach to Newmarket?" she asked. She appeared frightened. "No one seems to know. I must not miss it, as Mr Bellamy has kindly agreed to meet me. Please can you help?"

Arabella turned to look at Jane through her veil. She thought she saw a flicker of recognition on Jane's face, but it quickly disappeared in her anxiety not to miss the early-morning coach to Newmarket.

"No, this is the coach for Norwich. Do you see the man with the red beard over there? He seems to know the direction of each coach. He helped me. I suggest you quickly go and ask him. I am sure he will be able to assist you." As she spoke, Arabella realised that she had inadvertently blurted out her own destination.

"Thank you so much. You have been most kind, Miss . . . ?"

"Miss Blackthorne," replied Arabella, giving the first name that came into her head. "I wish you a safe journey."

"Thank you. And I wish you the same," said Jane as she hurried away.

Arabella felt guilty that she had not said more to her erstwhile friend, but she had no time for such pleasantries at present, nor inclination to reveal any information that might compromise her mission to be reunited with her mother.

Such was her preoccupation with avoiding being recognised by Jane that Arabella had failed to notice who was behind her in the queue to board the Norwich coach. No sooner had she taken her seat than a man in an ankle-length coat and with long unkempt hair climbed into the compartment, followed by another wearing a tricorne and a well-tailored, grey, almost military-style overcoat with polished brass buttons. Beneath the unbuttoned coat there was the glimpse of a red embroidered jacket and beneath that the hint of a blue waistcoat. Arabella looked down, anxious to avoid eye contact, which might lead to unwanted conversation. Curious, she glanced up again and for longer as the coach filled to capacity. She gasped. The man in the grey overcoat sitting opposite her was surely the man in the picture at Meltwater. She could not be certain, but the blue of the waistcoat and the edging of the jacket looked similar to those she had seen in the portrait. She lowered her eyes again, as she dared not look at his face for more than a moment at a time, but after several more stealthy glances she was almost convinced he was the man to whom she had made love in Shepherd Street. Arabella found it difficult to compose herself and she was conscious of a deep blush spreading across her cheeks.

"Is anything the matter?" the unkempt stranger opposite asked her, with a half-smile.

The man beside him looked up and for a long moment gazed intently at her veiled face. He had soft blue eyes and a gentle but sad expression. He glanced at her gloved hand, in which she tightly held a white lace handkerchief.

Putting it away, Arabella replied quietly, "I suddenly remembered that I had forgotten to bring something for my departure. But no matter, it can wait until I return."

The stranger replied, "It will be a long journey to Norwich. If there is any way we can assist you, please let us know."

"Thank you, I will," replied Arabella, looking down once more to avoid the attention of the man in the picture and the mystery he represented.

The carriage at last began its journey. Arabella sat back, her eyes closed. As she pondered her predicament and the likely dangers ahead, she heard the sound of French being spoken, though it was not possible to discern exactly what was being said above the clatter of the carriage wheels. She briefly opened her eyes. The man in the picture was speaking softly to his companion, the long-haired stranger. She had heard the accent – not that of a native French speaker – in the bedroom at Shepherd Street. She was now more than ever convinced that he was indeed the man Mrs Rathbone had said was called Moreau. She closed her eyes again and tried to sleep. But it was a fitful sleep.

Meanwhile, in Shepherd Street, Mrs Rathbone raged about the flight of Antoinette Badeau. Neither Mrs James, the cook, nor the under-maids could account for what had happened, since Antoinette had disappeared early in the morning while they were distracted getting the kitchen ready. Mrs Rathbone said she would take immediate action to seek Antoinette's arrest for the theft of clothes that did not belong to her.

CHAPTER 5

The Search

Sir Robert and Lady Whitfield were shocked to read Arabella's letters on their return to Meltwater Hall after lunching with the Wimpoles. Her father was enraged at what she had done, and her mother was deeply distressed and in tears. Sir Robert summoned the butler, Gregson, for a full explanation, and demanded that Sarah Bayley account for why she had been unable to dissuade Arabella from leaving. After all, she had known Arabella since she was a baby. Gregson said he had done his best to stop her, but it was clear their daughter was determined to leave. He could not override Arabella's instruction to Henry to drive her to Freshchester. Sarah gave a tearful account of her attempt to persuade Arabella not to leave, but her entreaties had not convinced Arabella to reconsider, particularly given her deeply emotional state. Sarah implored Sir Robert not to punish his daughter when she came back, as she surely would once she had had time to consider the gravity of what she had done. Arabella was a loving child and, though headstrong, greatly valued her family. This did not mollify Sir Robert.

Afterwards, in the privacy of the library, Lady Whitfield remonstrated with her husband. His outburst, culminating in his striking Arabella, had been inexcusable, and had caused her to flee the safety and comfort of her home and the love of her mother. Sir

Robert was a bully, and his behaviour towards her and Arabella bordered on the tyrannical. It was now necessary for both of them to make every effort to find their daughter, and to persuade her to return to Meltwater, and to do so in a spirit of forgiveness and understanding, not hostility or recrimination. She insisted that Sir Robert would have to apologise to Arabella for his conduct, and allow her to participate in the choice of her husband.

Though barely able to contain his anger, Sir Robert listened to his wife. His response, however, was uncompromising. He refused to give any undertaking to do what she had asked of him. He would decide later what would be done. The first step was to find Arabella and to bring her home as quickly as possible, to avoid further embarrassment to the family. The second was for her to apologise to him for her high-handed behaviour in leaving Meltwater, so exposing him to ridicule in the county. The third step was to make sure she met Lord Simon and, if he asked her to marry him, to accept.

As Henry had not yet returned from Freshchester with the second coach, Sir Robert and Lady Whitfield decided, after further accusations, to begin the search for Arabella there. Within an hour or so of the Whitfields' return from the Wimpoles', the principal coachman, Jewkes, had changed the horses and Sir Robert and his wife set off at a furious pace. They arrived in Freshchester within two hours, missing Henry on the way; he had made a diversion on his return to the Hall, calling at the blacksmith's to fit one of the horses with a new shoe. They soon established that Arabella was not at either of the town's two coaching inns, but at the second, Sir Robert did manage to elicit a vague description of a veiled young woman who had travelled to Norwich. The description seemed to fit what Sarah and Gregson had said Arabella had been wearing. As it was now getting late in the day and the road to Norwich was difficult in the dark, the Whitfields returned to Meltwater for the night.

Lady Whitfield had many friends in the county. She often invited them to tea or insisted on including them in dinner parties when her husband returned to Meltwater from one of his periodic visits to London (which, if the truth be known, were less about parliamentary business than about spending time with his mistress).

When Sir Robert was away, she welcomed any opportunity to escape the solitude of the estate. Her choice of places to go was limited. She rarely chose London, even though her friends there often pressed her to come. Lady Whitfield had no wish to stay at their town house in Westminster, where she knew her husband often entertained his mistress, Lady Barbara Ward, and her friends. Lady Barbara was no shrinking social violet. She was regarded by some (including, of course, Sir Robert) as a London beauty, though from their two brief encounters Lady Whitfield considered her well past her prime (as women are prone to comment acidly about one another).

With London not an appealing option, Norwich was the next best diversion. Indeed, many considered the city to rival the capital. It had many trees and gardens, and there was an abundance of foodstuffs in the markets: fish from the North Sea was plentiful, and there were always plump ducks, geese and turkeys to buy. The houses in the better parts of Norwich were smartly dressed in stucco. For cultural and social activities, the city offered the New Theatre and the Grand Assembly Rooms, which were often used for balls, concerts, card-playing and dinners. Lady Whitfield had frequently been to the Rooms in the past. Arabella had even danced there once, with Monsieur Noverre's ballet school. And of course Norwich was not exempt from the London craze for pleasure gardens, boasting My Lord's Garden, Moore's Spring Garden and Quantrell's Gardens and another, The Wilderness, which was famous for its breakfast entertainments. Nether Row had become a favourite promenade for the gentry because of its high-quality shops selling luxury goods, such as hats, gloves, leatherware and tea; everybody who was anybody had to be seen on Nether Row, including Lady Whitfield. Highlights for her and Arabella, when they went to the city together, were coffee at the Saunders Coffee and Tea House and a fine dinner at the White Swan Inn, one of the best-known of Norwich's leading coaching inns.

When Lady Whitfield and Arabella went to Norwich to shop for gowns, hats and dressmaking material that they had seen in the catalogues received regularly at Meltwater, they often stayed at Mrs Willoughby's comfortable lodgings. They were close to the Market Place, the centre of the city, thereby making it convenient to walk to see friends, to exchange gossip, to shop, to go to the theatre, to hear music and, of course, for Arabella to have the opportunity to tease and flirt with Monsieur Noverre. In all of these activities Lady Whitfield much enjoyed Arabella's company; her daughter was her one remaining inspiration and solace in the rural life she now led. Norwich was a pleasing diversion from Meltwater with its constant reminder of her husband's betrayal of her love.

Very early the next day, Jewkes took Sir Robert and Lady Whitfield to Norwich. As the coach surged along the road, Lady Whitfield's happy memories of visits to the city were overwhelmed by her deep distress at Arabella's sudden departure.

From Lady Whitfield's rapid enquiries of her friends, it seemed clear that Arabella was not to be found in Norwich. Rather, if the innkeeper's description of a young woman who had boarded the London flyer was correct, she had stayed briefly at the White Swan overnight before taking the coach that very morning. Sir Robert cursed himself for not going to Norwich the evening before. It was evident they would have to find their daughter in the capital. That would not be easy. Moreover, given that her present frame of mind appeared highly disturbed, there was no knowing what precipitate action she might take to put distance between herself and her father. Meanwhile, his wife's friends would be passing the news of Arabella's flight on to their own friends. The cat would be out of the bag. Sir Robert's anger mounted.

Once it was clear there was nothing further to be done in Norwich, Sir Robert and Lady Whitfield headed back to Meltwater, to see if Arabella had had a sudden change of mind and returned there in the meantime. In the privacy of their coach, as the implications of her daughter's actions became more apparent, Lady Whitfield again remonstrated with Sir Robert that his recent behaviour towards Arabella had been intolerable. He could only blame himself for her leaving home. While she conceded that the time had come for Arabella to marry, and that Sir Robert had the right to give his final approval to her intended husband, he had failed badly to understand that his approach to such matters was not at all in keeping with the changing and more compassionate times. Arabella might be headstrong and outspoken – as she herself had once been – but that fact should not deny their daughter the right to express her frank opinion on the matter of marriage. The choice of husband was as much hers as his. If Sir Robert only held his daughter in the same respect as he did his political friends in London, and was as indulgent towards her as he was to their son, the most unfortunate confrontation at Meltwater would have been avoided.

Sir Robert knew his wife was right but could not bring himself to admit it. Used to getting his own way over the years, and obsessed with his campaign to secure a parliamentary seat – and perhaps, in due course, a seat in the government – he had decided that he could not allow his careful plans to be put at risk by his daughter's manifest obstruction of his will – conveniently erasing from his mind the fact that he had physically struck Arabella in front of the servants, so provoking her to leave home. He still insisted to his wife that he was ultimately responsible for the family's destiny and the promotion of Meltwater's interests to secure it. Accordingly, his daughter had to obey him just as she, Lady Whitfield, should comply with his wishes in respect of what he believed was to their best advantage. Despite his wife's spirited intervention, the baronet remained unmoved.

Arabella had not returned. Accordingly, Sir Robert decided to leave immediately for their town house in Westminster, from where he would begin his search for her in London with the help of their son, George, already there. He was determined to find his daughter wherever she might be. It would also provide a timely opportunity to keep a closer eye on George. There was another unspoken motive: his wish to ease his current worries by enjoying the physical company of his mistress, Lady Barbara Ward, whom he knew would be anxiously awaiting his return to the capital. He told Lady Whitfield that he might be gone for some time, such was his determination to find Arabella and so resolve the question of her marriage once and for all.

Sir Robert's departure left Meltwater in disarray. A rural family landscape that had seen years of apparent tranquillity was now exposed to turbulent currents, internal division and local gossip fed by loose talk amongst the servants. What they had witnessed had been repeated elsewhere on the estate and in the surrounding villages within hours. For her part, Lady Whitfield became increasingly distressed by Arabella's flight from the house and frequently burst into tears. Not only was she worried that her daughter had exposed herself to grave danger by travelling alone to London, she had also suddenly lost her intimate companion and her music partner, and, of course, her closest confidante with whom she exchanged women's private concerns and gleeful indiscretions. Future visits to Norwich would not be the same. Her profound anger and bitterness towards her husband for what he had caused were barely concealed. He had revealed his dreadful temper for all to see. That had been unforgivable.

In the servants' quarters, opinion was split. Some, including Gregson, Sarah Bayley and Betty, the cook, believed Arabella should have stayed at Meltwater in order to reach an accommodation with her father. This view was largely special pleading on their part because they found Arabella's humour and laughter a most welcome daily antidote to Sir Robert's often fluctuating moods, many of which were not pleasing to witness. For their part, Mary (maid to Arabella), Sukey and Henry – all younger members of the household staff – believed Sir Robert had placed Arabella in an impossible position and therefore quietly supported her decision to leave. But everyone was agreed that Arabella's disappearance had caused profound unhappiness at the Hall, which they earnestly hoped would soon be dispelled by her return.

Sir Robert was pleased to reach London and the arms of his mistress. He had acquired the Westminster town house, which he regarded as exclusively his, some five years before. It was here that he spent considerable time in the shadow of parliament, hatching various plans that on the face of it seemed to make little progress towards advancing his political career, while keeping in close touch with his bankers and other friends at his club. His liaison with Lady Barbara Ward was the cherry on the London iced cake. He had first met her at a soirée, soon after purchasing the house. Her elderly husband, Sir Peregrine Ward, who had made a fortune through investments in India, was now in his dotage and therefore not often seen during the London season.

Lady Ward was of medium height, somewhat plump and regarded by some as good-looking. Still reasonably young, she was humorous, financially secure and due to inherit – and indeed add to

– the family fortune, as there had been no children of the match, nor of her previous marriage to Sir Dashwood Wentworth, her late first husband. But most of all she was politically well-connected and had become famous in London for her dinners, to which she was able from time to time to invite senior members of the cabinet. Once she had even managed to secure the presence of the young Prince of Wales. To Sir Robert this political entrée was invaluable given the current instability of the government over the Stamp Act and its application to Britain's colonies in the Americas. If there were to be a change of prime minister, Sir Robert desperately wanted to be on the side of the next incumbent, whoever he might be. He believed Lady Ward could be instrumental in making it possible for him to represent the important Freshchester borough, while she, for her part, dreamed of boasting that she had made Sir Robert a member of the government. Last but certainly not least, she still had a strong sexual hunger and therefore liked Sir Robert to be with her as often as possible to satisfy her needs. He was not one to disoblige.

The Whitfield town house in Westminster was in a terrace of similar houses, as Sir Robert was not yet able to afford a large detached property, the like of which was more the preserve of the wealthy nobility. The house, tall rather than wide, was brick-built and flat-fronted, with three floors, not including the basement (where the kitchen and storage area were to be found). There was a small but imposing portico to shield the front door.

The main room on the ground floor was the parlour, where Sir Robert spent most time when he was at home during the day, receiving guests to the house, often for tea or for claret. Such events were an opportunity for him to display his elegant manners and polite conversation – learnt from his wife, though he would never admit it.

Adjacent to the parlour was the dining room, with a table large enough to sit twelve guests. Somewhat sparsely furnished, on the walls were paintings of Norfolk scenes and on the sideboard two wooden sculptures of animals which his wife had dislodged from prominence at Meltwater in favour of some of her French pieces.

On the first floor was the more comfortable drawing room, with well-upholstered chairs he had chosen with Lady Whitfield. Unlike the parlour and dining room, the drawing room had a fitted carpet, a sure indication to his visitors that Sir Robert was up with the latest fashion style and, moreover, had the money to afford such an expensive item. A connecting door led to a small library, where Sir Robert used to have his more intimate conversations, particularly with Lady Barbara. Each of these rooms had good decorative fireplaces where wood was burnt, though coal was now becoming the favoured fuel in the house despite its cost. Beeswax candles were burnt throughout. The most expensive of candles, they were another palpable indication of Sir Robert's financial ability to buy the best in order to impress.

On the second floor were the master bedroom and the principal guest room, the latter used by Lady Ward when she stayed, which was frequently. This was the bed Sir Robert shared with her, leaving the master bedroom unused and cold, like his marriage. On the third floor were three smaller bedrooms, one of which George Whitfield took. The five junior domestic staff (Mrs Brady, the cook, two footmen, Folkes and Denton, and two maids, Tilly and Ruth) slept in tiny rooms carved out of the attic, while the superior housekeeper, Mrs Jones, had her room behind the kitchen. In all, it was a fine and well-run town house. Over the weeks ahead it would become the centre of the effort to find Arabella.

On arrival in London, Sir Robert immediately consulted Lady Ward, who was delighted that her "dearest Robert" was back in town from gloomy Norfolk. Even though she had a fine house of her own to the west of London, in the rural riverside area of Chelsea, she liked being with him as much as possible, since he indulged her expensive tastes; she also liked, as much as he did, being in the midst of parliamentary politics and its manoeuvrings. He then sent a message to his club, asking George to come and see him as quickly as possible.

Lady Ward advised that, as news of Arabella's disappearance – and its provocation – would spread fast in the county, and to his friends and connections well beyond, Sir Robert should speak quickly to his and Lady Whitfield's friends in London to make sure that none was sheltering Arabella – and, of course, to put his side of the story about what had caused her flight.

He started with the Hemmings, in response to their written message that Arabella had stayed with them for one night on her arrival in London. He was irritated that they had not done more to keep hold of her, but was obliged to hide his displeasure with them since Lord Hemming was an acquaintance of some of those upon whose favour the promotion of his career depended.

With Lady Ward's encouragement, he formulated a plausible story to explain why his daughter had suddenly left Meltwater. He explained to Lord and Lady Hemming that, in the past year or so, Arabella's behaviour on the matter of her future had become increasingly irrational, and that he and his wife had found the situation more and more trying. Her impulsive decision to run away from home was the latest manifestation of her volatile state of mind. As they were fond of Arabella, the Hemmings asked Sir Robert whether her account of the dispute with him was true, particularly her claim that he had struck her. Sir Robert, conscious that Lady Hemming may already have repeated his daughter's account to her friends over innumerable cups of tea, admitted that in his exasperation at her refusal to do as she was told he had gently tapped Arabella's face. But it had been in response to an utterly outrageous and unacceptable outburst of disobedience and ungratefulness on her part. Sir Robert insisted that his action bore no comparison to the recent allegation, now a matter of wide gossip in Norfolk, that Mr Farrow, a clergyman, had beaten his wife and kept her short of money. He had done neither of those things – ever. Arabella had lived a gilded life.

Since the more enlightened view of the desirability of a gentler relationship between parents and their children had not yet gained ground in the circles in which Sir Robert moved, his account of what had happened went largely unchallenged by the Hemmings and others. He spun a similar story at his club in Pall Mall. Lady Ward used the same explanation with her own friends, adding that today's children had become too spoilt.

Sir Robert found apparent sympathy, too, when he explained to Lord Henry Simon why he was not yet in a position to confirm when it might be possible for him to visit Meltwater and so lay the basis for an amicable match. There had not been time for a proper discussion with his daughter and, of course, Lady Whitfield. He was confident this would happen in due course. Moreover, his daughter was not currently at home.

Lord Henry appeared quite relaxed at this news. He mused to himself that, if he were to believe the gossip about what had recently happened at Meltwater (he did not disclose to Sir Robert the extent of his information), he had managed a lucky escape from a possible alliance with an unruly young woman. Knowing when it served to be tactful, Lord Henry simply responded that he had pressing business in London, which would keep him fully occupied until the end of the season. He left it to Sir Robert to let him know when it might be appropriate to come to Norfolk. But Sir Robert was shrewd enough to realise that, behind the polite exchange, Lord Henry's marriage to Arabella was fast disappearing as an option. This fact only deepened his anger towards his daughter.

It was Lady Ward who, with Sir Robert's agreement, approached Monsieur Auguste Gaillard, owner of the well-frequented coffee house in Piccadilly, to see whether he might have heard any news of Arabella's whereabouts. They agreed that her approach would have to be managed with some sensitivity given the commercial business transacted there and the establishment's role as a purveyor of tittle-tattle.

Lady Ward had decided to apply to Gaillard because she had resolved, some time ago, to collect information – largely gossip, of course – about Lady Whitfield and her past friendships in London, in the hope that one day some nugget of gold might come into her hands, enabling her to discredit Thérèse Whitfield by pointing the finger at her cruelty – namely, providing insufficient love and comfort to her husband. The acquisition of credible evidence to this effect might finally allow her to persuade Sir Robert to divorce his wife, so opening the way for her, Barbara, to become the new Lady Whitfield and mistress of Meltwater. Given the financial potential of such a combined portfolio of land, money and future prospects, Sir Robert did not discourage such a plan. But he had always said it would have to wait until after his much sought-after election to parliament as the MP for Freshchester.

Like others, Lady Ward had heard rumours – so far unsubstantiated – that early on in her marriage Lady Whitfield may have had an affair with the handsome Monsieur Gaillard, a man well known to enjoy the company of attractive women, particularly those from France, his homeland. It was said that he was not ashamed of his reputation either. Lady Ward therefore wrote to Gaillard, asking whether he would kindly consider sharing with her any news he might receive in the coffee house about the possible whereabouts of Sir Robert's daughter, since such intelligence would ease Sir Robert's growing concern for her safety and perhaps lead to father and daughter being reunited.

Gaillard was wily. He guessed correctly why Lady Ward had written to him in this way. He knew of her reputation as a deadly rumourmonger and that there had been gossip about his various liaisons. Furthermore, he was aware that this gossip had included tales about him and Lady Whitfield. He had always claimed these were untrue. On receiving Lady Ward's letter, Gaillard was therefore much relieved that he had decided not to offer shelter to Arabella when she came to see him.

To clear his name of any suspicions, he replied immediately to Lady Ward, saying that Arabella Whitfield had called on him briefly, shortly after her arrival in London. She had done so because she and her mother had once or twice come together to see him in earlier years to discuss the affairs of France, in which Lady Whitfield had obviously taken great interest. Having not seen her or her mother for several years, he had been taken very much by surprise by Arabella's recent visit. Indeed, he had barely recognised her on his doorstep. He added that during her short visit to his home to take refreshment, she had not explained what had prompted her to come to London, apart from alluding to a family disagreement. She appeared to have plans for her stay in the city about which he had not pressed her. In conclusion, he wrote that, responding to a question from Arabella, he had suggested a place in Mayfair where she might stay in safety, the address of which he had given her and which he was happy to give to Lady Barbara. He had then attended to other affairs, at which point the young lady had left. He had not heard from Miss Whitfield since.

Much to Lady Ward's disappointment, Sir Robert decided to take the contents of Gaillard's letter at face value rather than seek further information. Apart from checking the Mayfair address that Gaillard said he had given to Arabella, to which it transpired she had never gone, and all the family's London acquaintances, he had no wish to enter into any fracas with Gaillard, details of which might swiftly do the rounds in his coffee house and elsewhere.

Lady Barbara speculated that, while Arabella could potentially be anywhere in London, there were grounds for believing she was hiding somewhere in Mayfair, albeit not at the address provided by

Gaillard. Though its character was not as notorious as Covent Garden's, it remained the fact that there was a considerable number of establishments in Mayfair that were part of London's well-known demi-monde and to which homeless young women, even well-educated ones, turned for shelter. If this was where Arabella had gone, it was even more pressing to find her quickly before her name and, more importantly, that of her father were sullied. The last thing Sir Robert needed was for his daughter to become sucked into the world of the courtesan and for this to become public – to the cost of his carefully constructed public reputation and indeed her own. If Arabella really was now in the demi-monde and could not be retrieved, she might well have sealed her fate. She might either disappear for good, possibly under an assumed name, or her discovery and capture would enable her father to have her placed under lock and key in an asylum for not being of sound mind. She would certainly be disinherited.

Thus prompted by his mistress, Sir Robert furthered his enquiries into the possibility that Arabella might be somewhere in Mayfair by asking his son, George, to talk to his friends, to ascertain whether any of them had heard about – or in fact seen – a young lady matching Arabella's description. They were likely to be a good source of information, since, whether married or single, they were frequent visitors to Mayfair, not just to gamble and to drink but to seek the company of women. After all, Sir Robert had done so himself in the past and now of course he had a mistress of his own. Sir Robert spoke of a possible reward if he received good intelligence leading to the discovery of Arabella's whereabouts.

Accordingly, within a few days of Arabella's disappearance, there began a concerted effort by George and his fellow card-playing roués (including, unbeknownst to Sir Robert, Lord Henry Simon) to explore in depth what Mayfair had to offer. The area was popular amongst the better off and titled, as the quality of women men might enjoy there was judged to be higher than in other parts of London. But seeking out who was who was not easy.

First, the establishments in Mayfair were often discreet. The young, the rich and the famous who frequented them had no wish to see their own or their fellow visitors' activities revealed, particularly if a man exposed as a result of enquiries might prove to be the benefactor or patron on whom one was dependent for personal advancement. Second, identifying women was not straightforward given the growing fashion to conceal faces behind masks. Finding out who was behind a mask might prove a deeply embarrassing revelation. After all, a man of substance might seek out the most beguiling masked beauty only to find it was his wife cavorting with a man not her husband just as he was seeking sex with a woman not his wife. Last, no one wanted to gain a reputation for spoiling the allure and excitement of the London demi-monde. It encompassed a far-reaching layer of society, including royal circles, and it generated money and sexual pleasure; any betrayal or compromise of personal secrets, particularly touching what happened in the privacy of a bedroom, might lead to the culprit being blackballed by his gaming partners at his club.

Despite these sensitivities, George and his friends did their best, but could find no one who had seen Arabella in Mayfair. They even tried other, less salubrious areas of London, such as Covent Garden and Bedford Square. Their failure to acquire any reliable information as to her whereabouts did not, of course, completely rule out the possibility that she was under their noses, hiding in plain sight amongst the many young women who came to London to seek their fortune through sexual activity, in the hope – as outlined to Arabella, and constantly exploited, by Mrs Hallam – that this might lead to adoption by a wealthy patron or benefactor, who in turn would provide them with a comfortable life and even, perhaps, a career in the theatre, or open the way to court and the royal bed.

Sir Robert soon realised that unless Arabella was already dead, whether through mishap, her own deliberate act or by someone else's hand, or had fled to France, which he thought unlikely at this stage, it would take more time and money to find her. Discovering where she was would require great patience, like trapping a sly fox at Meltwater. Indeed, he was under no illusion: finding Arabella would be harder than catching a fox. She was stubborn and scheming like her mother. After all, she was half French and he had learnt from personal experience – from his marriage – never to trust a citizen of that country. He also realised that visiting every house in Mayfair and removing the mask of each woman found there would be like looking for a needle in a haystack, and besides, it would be impractical to seek to do so. Nevertheless, Sir Robert encouraged George and his débauché friends to remain vigilant as they went about town, in case they caught any glimpse of Arabella or secured any reliable report that might prove a vital clue to her location.

At the same time, Sir Robert decided to put it about among his friends and political acquaintances that he was now deeply concerned that, because of the length of time she had been missing, Arabella might have been abducted by undesirable people. It was therefore even more imperative to find her, and he confirmed publicly that he was offering a reward for any information leading to her safe return. This new approach was widely reported in London journals and gossip sheets, and indeed beyond the capital. The missing baronet's daughter had become something of a cause célèbre. Sir Robert hoped that these deliberately instigated reports would help to portray him as a caring father, desperately seeking the restoration of his daughter after a most unfortunate dispute about her future. All was forgiven, he made clear. He and Lady Whitfield wanted to see Arabella back in good health at Meltwater as soon as possible.

There was one other, more discreet step Sir Robert took. He decided to solicit the help of some reliable people he knew – amongst the corn merchants he had once used to dispose of the annual Meltwater crop at the best price with minimum payments to the excise men – to see whether they could locate Arabella in Mayfair or elsewhere. He also asked them to arrange similar observation at Dover, just in case she attempted to leave England for Calais or others tried to abduct her in that direction. After all, if these contacts were largely successful in smelling out the proximity of excise men, who were constantly trying to uncover shipments of corn on which duty had not been paid, they might well be successful in finding his daughter. These contacts would cost him money. But a great deal was at stake. Arabella had to be found, however much, or long, it might take.

The news reports, the continuing public speculation about the fate of the baronet's daughter and, of course, the regular visits by George Whitfield and his accomplices, together with ongoing enquiries by Lady Ward amongst her friends, did not go unnoticed by those who ran establishments in Mayfair. In Mrs Hallam's case, she had exercised in the face of this activity even greater care over the choice of those she introduced to her new charge – significantly fewer than she had planned, but enough to produce an adequate return on her investment. This careful approach would help to ensure that the real identity of Antoinette Badeau remained uncompromised. But, as the weeks passed and the fervid speculation did not cease, Mrs Hallam began to realise the necessity of preparing an alternative refuge for Arabella, now discreetly talked about in certain social circles as La Badeau, should her presence in the house become known.

Mrs Hallam still hoped that such a step would be unnecessary. She wanted to keep Arabella in her possession as long as possible, since she was much superior in grace and beauty to her other charges at 35 Chesterfield Street. Though she might at present receive fewer visitors than had been expected, she was young; her long-term financial expectations remained substantial. But Sir Robert Whitfield's shadow seemed to be growing longer by the week.

For Lady Whitfield, the weeks and months following Arabella's disappearance were hard to bear. Her close and trusted companion was no longer at her side. The harpsichord was no longer played and the library was largely unused. She lay awake almost every night wondering where Arabella might be, but increasingly fearing that she might no longer be alive, since she had received no letter or message from her.

Meanwhile, the work of the estate went on regardless. As in previous years, the corn was grown, cultivated and sold. Rents were collected from those who lived on Meltwater's 1,200 acres or in the nearby tied villages, which Sir Robert had been assiduously buying up to increase income.

On his periodic return to Meltwater, Sir Robert made continuing efforts to assist local landholders who might be inclined to vote for him at the next parliamentary election – if, of course, he were selected to stand. Their support would be crucial if the Freshchester constituency was to be bought, which he knew was likely to be the case. He was under no illusion that the price for each vote would be high. Even if it were too high, it still had to be paid.

When Sir Robert was at home, the Whitfields continued to show to the household staff and close friends an outward pleasantness to one another. But no one was fooled. Beneath the thin surface of chilly civility there lay deep hostility between them. Lady Whitfield had still not forgiven her husband for his unwarranted injury to Arabella's self-esteem and her disappearance. As each day passed, her contempt became ever more visceral and therefore harder to conceal. Several times she considered the possibility of returning to France, if only temporarily, but decided this would not be practical. Still hoping that Arabella would return, she concluded that she should remain at Meltwater. Besides, she refused to give her husband any pretext to use her departure from England as grounds for divorce. The thought of the dreadful Lady Barbara Ward taking her place at Meltwater was inconceivable.

All Lady Whitfield could do as each month passed was to receive Catholic Communion in private, to see her friends, especially those in Norwich, and occasionally, as a diversion, to spend money on clothes, though her heart was not really in the buying of new bonnets and dresses, as Arabella was not there to help her choose. Despite Sir Robert's repeated statement that he believed Arabella to be alive and well in Mayfair, and that in due course she would come to light, Lady Whitfield's spirits steadily declined as the days slipped by with still no news of her daughter. Her frame of mind was not helped by her husband's continued threat that, if it were found that their daughter had become a courtesan while in Mayfair, he would immediately disinherit her and banish her from the family. Lady Whitfield could not believe that Arabella would have done such a thing. She could only hope and pray that she was right and he was wrong.

As the year 1765 neared its end and winter began to grip Meltwater and Norfolk, Lady Whitfield accepted an invitation from her friends to travel to Norwich to celebrate Advent. A few days away, staying at Mrs Willoughby's comfortable lodgings, would be a welcome respite from the gloom of the Hall.

Much against her inclination to stay at home waiting for Arabella's knock on the door, Lady Whitfield arrived in Norwich on Monday, 25 November, to spend time with her friends, to join them in looking at the latest fashion arrivals and to celebrate Advent on 1 December in the company of Monsieur Noverre. She hoped that the arrival of Christmas a month later would restore Arabella to Meltwater and so bring about a joyous reunion.

PART TWO: A KING'S COMMAND

CHAPTER 6

Herzberg

28 September 1765

Carl Manfred von Deppe sat in his library, looking out over the extensive garden to the endless flat Prussian plain beyond. The King's letter lay in front of him. The fire flared as dusk fell and the shadows of encroaching winter advanced another day.

Once a royal hunting lodge, the house in which he lived was low in height, lavishly glazed to let in the light – full windows leading to the surrounding garden in the large rooms downstairs, more restricted apertures in the smaller rooms upstairs. The house was well-appointed – comfortable furniture throughout; a big, plentifully stocked library, with a significant collection of books on farming and Prussia, gathered by his father; a morning room to receive guests; a spacious but barely used dining room; a gallery lined with ancestral portraits; a receiving room (once used by a King to receive his visitors); several small side chambers; and a large bedroom, once the royal bedchamber, with a commanding view of the gardens through three double windows. Each room downstairs had visual and atmospheric echoes of the past. But the house was silent.

The familiar voices he had known were gone. His elder brother, Frederick Ludwig, likeable but a compulsive gambler at cards, had died some years previously, in Paris, in mysterious circumstances. It happened shortly after the beginning of his long-sought engagement to Marta von Helmsdorf, the beautiful but headstrong daughter of one of Prussia's richest merchants. His father, Gottfried Johann von Deppe, had never recovered from Frederick's death. His will to live had been further sapped by the death of his wife, Anna Margaret; the elopement to Paris of his daughter, Maria Louisa, with a young French army officer, since when there had been a dwindling correspondence and little news as to her welfare; and the prolonged absence of Carl Manfred on military service. He had drowned in the icy water of the lake near the house. With his father grieving and alone, there had been no figure of authority or energy at Herzberg. The estate had slipped inexorably into disrepair, with steady loss of income.

This was the desolate scene that Carl Manfred saw on his return from Potsdam one cold winter's morning in December 1762: the graves of his father and mother; the unloved house; its neglected garden; and the poorly maintained estate, unproductive and diminished – despite the efforts of the long-serving and faithful agent, Maximilian, to maintain the land that Carl Manfred had inherited. The candlelit sparkle of Herzberg that Carl Manfred recalled from his infrequent visits home in earlier years had gone. In its place, he found furniture beneath grim shrouds and the windows shuttered, allowing little daylight to pierce the gloom of each room. The house seemed to have stopped breathing.

When he entered the long gallery, family portraits from the last eighty years stared silently down at him – pictures of a family who had once been Prussian newcomers, but had since become respected landowners in the neighbourhood. As he walked along the line of pictures, he paused at the portraits of his mother and father, side by side. Next to them was Frederick Ludwig, his brother, and beside him his pretty sister, Maria Louisa, painted to commemorate her thirteenth birthday. And there was his own picture, painted when he was thirty-four, dressed in his red jacket and blue waistcoat. He reflected that he and his sister, a silent, distant absence in Paris, were all that remained of the von Deppe family. On that first day back at Herzberg, it had seemed to him that the family's extinction was but two heartbeats away. The strong easterly wind blowing then had accentuated the impression of a bleak future.

The next three years had passed without particular incident – just prolonged hard work to restore the estate. The only strange event had been the recent unexplained disappearance of his portrait from the gallery. Maximilian said it had vanished one day while Carl Manfred was away, during the visit of an unknown caller. The space on the wall remained empty. A Berlin artist had offered to paint a new portrait of him, but Carl Manfred had declined. He could not be bothered. As a simple soldier he thought it would be vain to sit for a picture that no one else would see. It was better to leave an empty space. If his sister had been blessed with a child in Paris, perhaps its portrait could fill the void.

Carl Manfred rose from his chair to gaze through the library window at the garden and across to the undulating family estate, recalling the effort he had invested since 1762 and the changes he had made. He was tall, well-built, with a straight Prussian spine. He had a cool, unswerving and unsmiling look, which conveyed, correctly, to the observer the impression that he was gruff in manner – a legacy of his military service as an officer in His Majesty's Life Hussars. To those who knew him only slightly – that is, to most – he was rarely off the defensive; civil but unexpansive. His answers to questions were short – often just one sentence. But in private, in the company of those he knew well and trusted, he relaxed and displayed an engaging sense of humour and a sharp intellect. He was finely dressed and conveyed in his manner a measure of outward accomplishment and self-confidence. He was no longer a soldier but a landowner of note.

He turned to look into the fire with its rich tapestry of red and yellow flames, seeing there scenes from his troubled childhood, his escape to Berlin and eventual military service. He had always felt insecure, partly because he had been overshadowed by his brother, and partly because of the financial uncertainties of his early army days, frequently due to the lack of monetary support from his father to help meet his officer obligations. He had trusted few in the army and rarely displayed his emotions, even after a bloody battle. Despite the increasing esteem in which he was held by his fellow officers throughout his career, even after his departure from the Hussars he never opened up to those who sometimes came to Herzberg to see him. He continued to protect his privacy with the same deep commitment he had shown to his career.

His love of King Frederick had been unbounded and often visible. That love remained. Carl Manfred looked at the portrait of the monarch, given to him personally by Frederick himself and which he had hung in pride of place above the library mantelpiece. The picture, painted in 1757, was the familiar side profile of the King, his face turned to the left, regarding the viewer intently. It was a constant reminder of the soldier King, Frederick, his commander-in-chief, alongside whom he had fought and to whom he had always been loyal.

Since Carl Manfred had assumed personal charge of the estate, Herzberg's fortunes had recovered strongly – now prospering from increased income, as the balances in the account books revealed. Though his clothes were rich in colour and of obvious quality, his hands were still somewhat rough from his willing physical contribution to the maintenance of the estate over the last three years. He liked to lead his estate workers just as he had led his men in the army. The rewards of his labour – the silverware on the dining table, the monogrammed glass goblets and the decorative porcelain, together with the quality of food he could now afford – were of sufficient quality for Herzberg to have hosted a brief visit from the King the year before last.

Carl Manfred's future well-being seemed assured. But the respect he had earned from his wealthy neighbours could not hide the emptiness he had felt since that first day as owner of Herzberg. He remained unmarried and without close female companions. He was as uncommitted to a woman now as he had been when he returned home three years before. While some unmarried women had joined the occasional dinner parties he gave for neighbours, and while one or two of those present had clearly set their sights on him, encouraged by their mothers to do so, none had stirred any passion within him. So it remained the case that no woman shared his bed. Indeed, it was hard to remember when he had last unlaced a woman's bodice and kissed her breasts. It was equally hard to see what personal fulfilment lay ahead, other than further toil on the estate. He was unsure whether Herzberg would die with him – the last of the von Deppe family male heirs – or whether there would be another generation to come. But that thought quickly left his mind as he returned to his desk and picked up the King's letter once again, rereading the request to attend upon him at Potsdam regarding a matter of great urgency and secrecy.

CHAPTER 7

The King's Letter

As he rode to Potsdam on the first day of October, Carl Manfred recalled the military career that had brought him to this privileged position of personal service to the King of Prussia. To escape the shadow of his stronger and more flamboyant elder brother, he had gone to Berlin University. After three years of struggling determinedly to complete his law studies, and with no obvious future at Herzberg, he responded to a call to join the army, as Prussia faced yet another campaign against the Austrians. Starting in the King's Life Hussars as a subaltern, Carl Manfred's unfolding and unexpected skill as a soldier, matched by his strong personal commitment, dedication and loyalty to the King, soon became evident. Though shy and uneasy in the company of his fellow junior officers, he was promoted in due course to the rank of captain and later appointed lieutenant colonel in the close group who guarded the King at all times. Like those around him, he had learnt to speak French (the language of the court) and some English, though the King used German with his officers and palace staff. After further steadfast duty and loyalty on the battlefield and consequent promotion to colonel, it was with profound regret and reluctance that the King had agreed to Carl Manfred's honourable discharge in December 1762, to enable him to return to Herzberg following the death of his father. When he bade farewell, Carl

Manfred had pledged that, if ever his support were needed, the King should write to him. He had now done so.

After an overnight stop en route, Carl Manfred reached the King's palace at Potsdam on Wednesday, 2 October 1765. The weather was dry but cold. Though it was comparatively late in the year, the King, then aged fifty-three, was still at his beloved summer palace of Sanssouci rather than in Berlin, keeping a close eye on the building of the Neues Palais. Prussia was still at peace following the end of the Seven Years War against Austria two years before, during which the King had tirelessly fought to extend further the territories that comprised Prussia. More recently, there had been the signature of a defensive alliance with Russia, which guaranteed Prussian control of Silesia in return for the King's support of Russia against Austria and the Ottoman Turks. But in spite of these agreements, the soldier King was restless. More battles loomed in his never-ending effort to expand Prussia into an ever stronger European power.

The King did not receive Carl Manfred until the following day, when he greeted him warmly. As Carl Manfred walked towards him, Frederick seemed more stooped than when he had taken leave of him three years earlier. On closer scrutiny, the King had aged significantly, showing the physical wear and tear of long military campaigning and endless political manoeuvring. But as they began to speak, his iron will was still obvious, his blue eyes ever more penetrating.

Carl Manfred knew that in recent years the King had lost many of his friends, either through death or through desertion as a result of Frederick's increasingly capricious behaviour, which included a tendency to ridicule people upon whom he had previously relied for advice and support. Perhaps it was this diminishing circle of people around him that was responsible for the palpable melancholy Carl Manfred now observed, despite the King's recent strategic successes and the public acclamation they had earned him. And perhaps the loss of valued friends, his advancing physical frailty and his growing tendency to be alone gave him more time to reflect on the earlier personal tragedies in his life, of which there had been many.

Looking into Frederick's eyes, Carl Manfred thought he could see in their depths the savage horror of all those years ago, when the young Crown Prince Frederick had been forced to witness the decapitation of his boyhood friend, Hans Hermann von Katte. The execution had been ordered by his father, Frederick William I, as punishment for von Katte's seeking to flee to England with the Crown Prince to escape royal control. Throughout their association, Carl Manfred had never known the King to speak of this terrible event, nor of the unforgivable mental cruelty his father had inflicted on him. But many said it still haunted him. Carl Manfred knew that the King had found out about his own unhappy childhood at Herzberg and it was possible that, on account of this shared sadness, an invisible unspoken bond had tied them together.

After riding together on two of the King's finest horses to see the construction of the Neues Palais, which had started two years before, and, on their return, walking in a biting wind along the terrace of Sanssouci, the King asked Carl Manfred to join him in the library.

They sat down. In front of the King lay a folded and sealed document alongside a similarly sealed letter and an empty leather despatch case. After putting the documents into the case, he leaned forward and said in a hushed voice, fearing perhaps that he might be overheard, even though they were alone, that he wished Carl Manfred to travel to London, in the utmost secrecy, as his personal courier. Immediately on arrival he was to hand the despatch case to Mr John Bolton in Shepherd Street. He was to remain at Bolton's bidding in England until all necessary action had been taken, in accordance with his instructions. Once Carl Manfred's task was finished, he was to return to Prussia, to deliver his personal report. He hoped that Carl Manfred would seek an audience with him as early as possible in the new year.

The King added that only he, Bolton, Carl Manfred and a fourth person, whose identity he could not at present disclose, knew of the forthcoming journey. Neither its secrecy nor its purpose must be compromised.

Having fastened the buckle of the despatch case, the King handed it to Carl Manfred together with a separate leather pouch, containing, he said, a significant sum of money for the journey ahead. He insisted it was for Carl Manfred to decide which route to take to England – either westwards to Hamburg and then across the North Sea to the east coast of England, or through France to

Calais and then Dover. But whichever way he went he could not be late for his appointment with Bolton in London before Christmas.

Carl Manfred nodded. As the King was speaking, he had already decided to travel to Calais via Paris. He did not enjoy travel by sea, and avoided it except where absolutely necessary. Besides, he wanted to find his sister.

The King took Carl Manfred's hands in his and, fixing him with his piercing blue eyes, spoke with great emphasis.

"Do what you have to do. Do not fail me."

"I will not," replied Carl Manfred. "You have my word."

"Thank you," answered the King. "I know I can trust you. Now, be on your way."

After a final brief exchange of pleasantries, the King wished Carl Manfred a safe journey. The audience had come to an end. The King rose. Carl Manfred stood, bowed deeply to his monarch and left the room.

The die had been cast. As a result of the King's instruction, a man would forfeit his life for a betrayal long ago.

After lodging that night in a nearby hostelry, Carl Manfred set out for Herzberg the next day, to prepare for his immediate departure for England. He would regret leaving the comfort, industry and familiarity of his estate, but would not be sorry to avoid Christmas in a house empty of voices. At the same time, and despite his pride at being asked to act as the King's secret messenger, he was uneasy at what might lie ahead. What had the King ordered?

As Carl Manfred climbed into his carriage to leave Sanssouci and return to his overnight lodgings, he was unaware that someone was watching him carefully from a window. It was the man who had responded when the King pulled the bell rope ten months before; the man who had prepared the mission on which Carl Manfred was now embarked. This man was a deadly snake, which is why Frederick trusted his judgement without reservation.

The documents the King had given to Carl Manfred had taken many months to get ready.

On receipt of the two names from the King, the man in the shadows had set about his work with great diligence and stealth. It had required considerable time – not helped by a bad winter – to establish the exact identity and whereabouts of the man whose name the King had written on the first piece of paper. Frederick was impatient for progress; the man in the shadows assured him he was working hard, together with his agents beyond the boundaries of Prussia, to put the necessary foolproof arrangements in place.

The information the King had acquired about his foe had to be carefully verified and the necessary corroboration obtained. There could be no room for mistakes in such a highly sensitive matter. Too much haste and the chance of political embarrassment to the King would no longer be minimal. Maintaining the safeguards required to ensure that the mission would not be compromised was not easy, especially when the interception of insecure royal communications was a common occurrence. Few were well enough trained in the art of encryption. And even those who were skilled at it could not always be trusted. Spies pleaded loyalty but, as he knew from his own tactics, spies could often be turned. Everyone had a price. In addition, it was necessary to make contact with John Bolton, who, in the King's opinion, had proved himself a firm friend of Prussia and was therefore worthy to be entrusted with such a personal task. The man in the shadows, who had not met Bolton before, could only accept the King's word that this was so.

Once he had checked to his satisfaction the accuracy of the information about the first name he had been given, and Bolton had agreed, in an exchange of secret messages, to play his important part in carrying out the King's wishes, the man in the shadows turned his attention to the name on the second piece of paper, that of Colonel Carl Manfred von Deppe.

He knew of him. Indeed, he had seen him in action in the King's Hussars. Von Deppe had proved he was loyal and discreet, but he had been a solitary man and solitary men sometimes hid secrets that could put their loyalty in jeopardy. Some secrets were so dark as to cause their keepers to become untrustworthy if cornered. So the man in the shadows made the necessary, discreet enquiries and travelled to Herzberg – at a time when, thanks to some of those enquiries, he knew von Deppe would be away – to find out for himself how the man lived and to peer into his background, to see if could uncover any indiscretions.

He was assisted in this regard by Maximilian, the land agent, a slippery individual whom he had once known and helped to escape from a serious misdemeanour. Maximilian therefore owed him a personal favour and now was the time for him to repay it. On the day he intended to visit Herzberg in the absence of von Deppe, the man in the shadows instructed Maximilian to spend time visiting tenants on the estate and to ensure that he was undisturbed by servants. He added that on his return to the house in the evening, Maximilian should ignore the disappearance of any item that might be missing. If he failed to comply, his life would be at grave risk.

The plan worked well. Once Maximilian had mounted his horse, the man in the shadows spent time in Carl Manfred's library, quickly sifting through personal papers and estate accounts. He made a few notes before carefully replacing each document as he had found it. To his relief, the man in the shadows found nothing compromising. His final act at Herzberg was to remove a portrait of von Deppe from the gallery and wrap it carefully, then he left with it for Berlin.

Maximilian soon spotted the missing picture but honoured his word, saying nothing about the visit. When von Deppe challenged him about the disappearance of the portrait, he could offer no explanation, only a grovelling apology for allowing such a theft to take place.

After completing these exhaustive checks, the man in the shadows reported to the King that he was satisfied the impending highly secret affair of state could be conducted safely. Shortly after receiving this assurance, and without saying a further word, the King wrote two documents, one longer than the other. He paused once or twice in the course of writing the second one, gazing out of the window, lost in thought. When both were finished and he had read through them, his lips silently mouthing the words he had written, he personally sealed each document, placing his ring in the wax to reproduce the Prussian double-headed eagle. They were ready for despatch. Then he wrote a personal message to Colonel von Deppe, requesting him to come to Potsdam as soon as possible.

CHAPTER 8

Paris

After leaving Herzberg on Monday, 7 October 1765, Carl Manfred arrived in Paris almost three weeks later, on Friday the 25th. Despite the notoriously poor roads across the German states, it had been an uncharacteristically fast journey, using hired coaches rather than the slower and more cumbersome public diligences. Because of the King's instructions, he knew he could not linger too long in any of the places he stayed. Besides, there was ample money to travel in some comfort. Moreover, he wanted as much time in Paris as possible, to find his sister, Maria Louisa.

He had barely heard from her since her elopement with a handsome young French army officer, Lieutenant Etienne de Vervins, five years ago. De Vervins had accompanied the French ambassador to Berlin for a meeting with King Frederick. Maria Louisa had been in Berlin staying with Carl Manfred at the time, to escape from the monotony of life at Herzberg. She encountered the dashing young officer at a soirée at the King's palace. They met often afterwards, and a month or so later, when the French ambassador left Berlin to report to the French king at Versailles, Maria Louisa eloped with Lieutenant de Vervins, knowing without even asking that her father would have opposed her marriage to a French soldier. Her father had long spoken of his wish to see her marry a wealthy Prussian, whose family owned land twice the size of Herzberg. Such a marriage might one day help enhance the value of Herzberg through the families' alliance. Three months later, Carl Manfred received information that Maria Louisa had married Lieutenant de Vervins. His father was saddened to hear this news. He had loved his daughter deeply, particularly as she had greatly comforted him on the death of his wife.

Having found lodgings in the Place Royale, the next day, Saturday, 26 October, Carl Manfred sought the assistance of the Prussian ambassador in Paris, General Gotthold von Lessing, to find Maria Louisa. He had known the ambassador from his presence at Frederick's court and had written to him the day before his departure from Herzberg. However, as the letter had not yet arrived, the ambassador was surprised to receive a handwritten note from Carl Manfred, asking to see him urgently. He replied immediately, inviting Carl Manfred to come to his residence for supper.

It was an elegant house not far from the Place Royale. In his outward appearance the General had changed little. Tall and ascetic-looking, von Lessing had been one of Frederick's better generals – a clever tactician and a good commander of men on the battlefield. But he had aged considerably since Carl Manfred had last seen him and was showing some signs of deafness in one ear. Over a simple but adequate supper, they recalled past Prussian campaigns and discussed the prospects for enduring peace in Europe – and, of course, the King's remaining territorial ambitions and the risk of them leading to further war. They agreed that the French king and the Russian czarina continued to be Frederick's greatest foes, more so than Poland and Austria. England was vigilant but uncommitted, as always.

Without divulging the purpose of his mission to England, Carl Manfred explained that he wished to find his sister, Maria Louisa. Following the death of his elder brother and father, he now administered the Herzberg estate on his own. He wanted to be reunited with his sister, to exchange news about all that had happened since her departure from Prussia, especially their father's death, and to meet her husband. He could not stay long in Paris due to urgent business in England, but he implored the ambassador's help in finding Maria Louisa without delay.

General von Lessing was deeply touched that Carl Manfred

should confide in him in this way. He remembered him from his army days – a quiet but highly effective officer whom the King clearly admired. But the man seeking his help across the table appeared sadder and more reflective than the officer he had last seen in Berlin.

After they had eaten, the ambassador invited Carl Manfred to fetch his belongings and stay at his residence while he made enquiries about Lieutenant de Vervins. Carl Manfred was delighted to accept after the rigours of his long journey from Herzberg and given his unfamiliarity with Paris.

Later that evening, as he returned to the ambassador's house, he happened to look over his shoulder and thought he saw a shadow in the nearby lamp light. Carl Manfred paused, clutching the leather despatch case the King had given him tightly in his hand. While he waited for the front door to open, the shadow disappeared. Carl Manfred was glad to get to bed that night.

Late on Monday, 28 October, General von Lessing brought news of Lieutenant de Vervins. He was now Captain Etienne de Vervins, aide de camp to General de la Rivière, who was in command of the King's Guard at Versailles. General de la Rivière had fought as a colonel alongside Marshal Prince de Soubise at the Battle of Rossbach in 1757, where King Frederick had defeated the French forces during the Seven Years War. Over dinner, conscious that Carl Manfred had said he needed to leave Paris soon, the ambassador said Frau von Lessing, his wife, had already written to invite Madame de Vervins to call on her at the residence as soon as practicable in order to meet a visitor, whom she might know from the land of her birth. This would give Carl Manfred the opportunity to meet the lady whom he believed was his sister.

Two days later, Madame Maria Louisa de Vervins arrived at the ambassador's residence. Frau von Lessing greeted her warmly – they recalled that they had once met before – and invited her into the library. They chatted for a short while over tea, while Carl Manfred peered through a half-open door at the other end of the room. His heart jumped. It was indeed his sister. Excusing herself from Maria Louisa's presence, Frau von Lessing left the room. As she passed through the doorway, Carl Manfred nodded to her.

With Maria Louisa now alone, Carl Manfred entered the library. She turned to look at him, putting her hand to her mouth in astonishment. As she rose from her chair, she stumbled, as though to faint. Carl Manfred caught her. They hugged each other wordlessly, in tears. After what seemed many minutes of silence, they sat down beside each other, Maria Louisa holding her brother's hand in both her own. Frau von Lessing briefly entered, smiled and then shut the door gently behind her, leaving brother and sister to recount the lost years.

"I have to leave Paris within the next few days on urgent business in England," said Carl Manfred, "but I intend to come back as soon as possible, when I hope we might spend a little more time together before I need to return to Berlin and then Herzberg."

"You must stay as long as you can on your return from England," replied Maria Louisa. "My husband should be back in Paris by Christmas and I would so much like you to meet dear Etienne. But before you leave for England, you must meet my daughter. I am very proud of her."

"Of course," said Carl Manfred. "It would give me the greatest pleasure to meet your daughter – my niece."

The next day, 31 October, shortly before Carl Manfred was due to leave for England, Maria Louisa returned to the ambassador's residence with her daughter.

"This is Marie-Aurore. She is three years old. I am so thrilled you are able to meet her."

The child was enchanting, with blonde hair, her mother's deep-blue eyes and the most exquisite smile.

"You are truly fortunate," said Carl Manfred.

As they talked more about the years they had missed, and he held Marie-Aurore on his lap, he felt deep personal regret that he had not married. He recalled once again the empty rooms at Herzberg and the long absence of a woman in his life. There was little prospect that this would change.

"I will be back soon from what I have to do and we will indeed spend more time together before I return to Prussia. And of course I would like to have the acquaintance of your husband."

"I do not know what it is you have to do in England that seems to weigh heavily on your mind," said Maria Louisa, "but whatever it is, please take care. I wish so much for us to spend time together in the future, to make plans for my daughter and to come and see you at Herzberg."

Holding Maria Louisa's hand and then giving Marie-Aurore one last hug, Carl Manfred said, "I promise I will be back. Having found you I do not wish to lose you again."

As their hands parted, Maria Louisa passed her brother a sheet of notepaper, bearing the crest of the commander of King Louis's personal guard, on which was written her address, number 76 Rue St Louis, and a formal invitation to stay.

"On your return to Paris, whenever that may be and however late the hour, you must come and be our guest. Please promise me you will. If you do not, I will ask my husband Etienne to find and arrest you." She laughed.

"I promise," said Carl Manfred, and bade his sister a sincere auf wiedersehen.

The following day, Carl Manfred took leave of the ambassador and Frau von Lessing and set off for Calais. He was saddened at leaving Maria Louisa and her daughter, and troubled that the night before, as he had looked out of his window before going to bed, he thought he had once again seen a dark shadow moving across the road. The parting from his sister, his prolonged absence from Herzberg and the daily visual reminder of the leather despatch case from the King weighed ever more heavily on his mind.

His sense of foreboding intensified the nearer he got to the French coast. The journey had been slow, taking five days owing to bad weather and dependence on public diligences. The road was badly rutted, adding to the discomfort of riding in foul weather, and there had been an attempted robbery on the way – a not infrequent hazard of coach travel and, on this occasion, easily foiled, but it fuelled his unease nonetheless. Buffeted by rain and wind, Calais seemed a dismal little port, but Carl Manfred was relieved when, at last, he arrived.

After securing lodgings, his next task was to find a boat to take him across the Channel to Dover. In the harbour he found craft large and small, constantly coming and going. The thought of several hours on a boat pushing its way across a dark and turbulent sea filled him with deep gloom and a considerable degree of fear. He had been a soldier and was now a landowner. Going to sea had always been the least pleasure of his life. His apprehension was made worse by the increasing prospect of having to stay in this miserable windswept place, possibly for several days, until the storms eased. Carl Manfred spent over a week in the port, waiting for the weather to improve so that the crossing might be less uncomfortable. He tried to read but his mind would not concentrate.

Finally, having identified a boat willing to take him to Dover at a reasonable price, Carl Manfred plucked up his courage and embarked for England on Sunday, 17 November. It turned out to be a difficult passage. The waves were rough and he was severely seasick as the small boat tossed its way across the Channel. Dulled by illness, he failed to notice a stranger observing him from a distance. It took many miserable hours to reach England, and even then he had to wait before the tide was high enough for the boat to enter harbour. He resisted the inclination to shorten the delay by clambering into a small rowing dinghy, violently pitching in the water below. He had no wish to be plunged into the sea at this point in his journey.

Once ashore, he was faced with the choice of resting in Dover for a day or two to regain his composure, or pressing on to London. Carl Manfred decided on the latter course. His arrival in England had already been much delayed. Now he had landed, it was urgent that he proceed quickly to his next destination to meet the mysterious Mr Bolton and perhaps learn more about what lay behind the mission the King had given him.

Using some of the English he had learnt while in the King's service, and from British mercenaries fighting on the Prussian side, he was able – after a further wait of several hours – to negotiate a seat on a fast coach to London. It was another long, tiring journey and he soon fell asleep, unaware that the stranger from the boat – and the dark shadow from Paris – was already in a coach some distance ahead, preparing to meet him in London.

CHAPTER 9

London

Carl Manfred von Deppe arrived in London at around six o'clock in the evening on Wednesday, 20 November 1765. After weeks of almost continuous travelling he felt fatigued, his bones ached, and still the purpose of his journey, and the contents of the sealed letters from the King in the leather case to which he clung each day, remained a mystery. But now he faced the challenge of finding Shepherd Street in Mayfair and Mr Bolton. Notwithstanding his command of the English language, he feared this would not be easy.

The coach from Dover had delivered him to the Golden Cross Inn, Charing Cross. He stepped down and was immediately surrounded by street vendors and sedan-chair carriers, touting for business. Though it was not raining, the streets were damp and filthy, and full of noise. Maria Louisa had given him a roughly printed map of London, which he had tried to memorise in Calais, but it was still difficult to find his bearings in the dark as he pushed his way through the huge crowd of people – including other new arrivals, similarly disoriented – surging around him. Beggars tried to reach into his pockets. He would have to ask for help.

Just then, someone seized his right arm. Spinning round, thinking he was about to be robbed, he came face to face with a tall, swarthy man with black shoulder-length hair, wearing a long coat down to his ankles. As Carl Manfred struggled to free his arm, his heart hammering, half from anger, half from fear, the man spoke to him in fluent German.

"Welcome to London, Herr von Deppe! I have come to take you to Mr Bolton, who awaits your arrival with great eagerness. Give me your bag and follow me."

Relief and bewilderment ensured his compliance. Still clinging to the leather document case, Carl Manfred followed the long coat and flowing hair through the throng. His guide strode ahead, roughly pushing aside everyone in his way. They turned into a side street, where the stranger almost pushed him into a small black coach before jumping in beside him.

"Move on," cried the stranger in perfect English.

The coach lurched and moved forward.

"Who are you and how do you know who I am?" asked Carl Manfred. In the dim light of the single candle swinging loosely in the greasy lantern, he peered at the man facing him.

"You do not need to know my name," the stranger replied. "In my profession, the less people know about me the better. But I knew it was you long before you disembarked at Dover. I knew you in Paris. Indeed, I knew all about you before your departure from the King's palace of Sanssouci, because it has been my business to follow the progress of your entire journey. With the help of associates you have reached London safely without ever realising I was behind you. As for the attempted robbery, that is just a fact of life on the road, as you will know from your army days. But you would have come to no harm. I would have made sure of that."

He drew a long-bladed knife from inside his coat sleeve, toying with it as though to prove his point.

The horses' hooves clattered on the wet cobbles. With the blinds down, it was difficult for Carl Manfred to see clearly where they were going.

The stranger leaned across and in a menacing tone whispered, "From now on, Herr von Deppe, you will speak only French, and your name while you are here is Monsieur Philippe Moreau. Farmer George may sit comfortably on the English throne but the English are suspicious of us Germans and especially of King Frederick of Prussia. They know little of what we are up to. We are perceived to be continually starting new wars, and in so doing we stir up the French, who do not like the English. So we are not popular in England at present. The English want Europe to be quiet – no one to become too powerful across the Channel."

"But I am sure the French are more unpopular in England than us," interjected Carl Manfred.

"That may indeed be the case, my friend," the stranger quickly responded. "France is England's historical enemy. The English regard the French as deeply untrustworthy, always provoking trouble, interfering in England's business – and of course there are all those unsettled scores from the past. This habitual mistrust now has the whole of Europe as its target, Prussia included. Nevertheless, for the English it is better the French they think they know than the Prussians they don't. Besides, as you well know, the court and men of good birth still speak French – the language of diplomacy. Do you understand?"

Carl Manfred nodded.

Neither spoke during the rest of the journey.

The coach came to an abrupt stop. The stranger swore at the coachman in his perfect English, adding, "If I had my way, your horses would whip you!"

Carl Manfred got out and found himself standing before a large terraced house with a short but steep flight of steps to the front door. There were many windows but, in contrast to the adjacent dwellings, all the curtains were tightly drawn, perhaps indicating matters to hide from passers-by. The street was poorly lit and muddy underfoot. Dark shadows of men and women glided along the road, laughing and jostling.

The front door opened and there appeared in the light of the hallway the silhouette of a short, rotund man, who called out, "Welcome to London, Monsieur Moreau. Do come in. We have been expecting you for some time."

"He is the butler, called Thomas," whispered the stranger behind him.

Carl Manfred went up the steps and entered the house. The stranger followed with his bag.

After taking Carl Manfred's coat, Thomas led him along the well-lit passageway to a door on the left. Carl Manfred half turned, hoping to catch a clearer glimpse of the stranger, but he had disappeared.

Inside the room, he was met by a tall, sturdy but stooping figure with grey hair, standing in front of a well-stoked fire. Speaking French in a clipped tone, and betraying the hint of a Scottish accent, with which Carl Manfred was familiar from his army days, the man said, "Good evening, Herr von Deppe – or Monsieur Moreau, should we say. My name is John Bolton. Please take a seat. It is a pleasure to meet you, particularly as I have heard much about you from our mutual friend in Berlin. You have had a long journey and you must be very tired. I look forward to hearing more about your travels in the morning. Thomas will show you to your room and make sure you have everything you need for a comfortable night's rest, and, of course, something to eat and drink. But before I let you go, I understand you have something for me from His Majesty."

Carl Manfred hesitated, gripping the document case ever more tightly.

"Monsieur Moreau," said Bolton, "I am indeed Mr Bolton, the designated recipient of your letters." He handed Carl Manfred a crumpled travel document bearing the name of Bolton, signed by King Frederick. The date indicated he had been in London for several years. "Please, I wish to have the letters."

Carl Manfred removed the two documents from the despatch case and handed them to his interlocutor. He watched closely as Bolton examined the two seals.

He opened the first letter, which Carl Manfred instantly recognised as being in King Frederick's distinctive scrawling hand. Bolton studied it carefully, rereading it two or three times. After a pause, he broke the second seal. This document appeared to be longer and more formal, in smaller handwriting (but again recognisable as the King's), with a large Prussian crest at the top. As he unfolded it to its full length, a small lock of blond hair fell to the floor. Bolton retrieved it and put it in his pocket. He then slowly read the contents of the document. Reaching the end he paused and looked away in deep thought. The only sound came from the blazing fire. He lifted the second document again, and reread it intently. A smile gradually spread across his face as he refolded both sheets of paper and locked them in a desk drawer. He then turned to Carl Manfred.

"Monsieur Moreau, you have delivered to me two very personal documents from His Majesty. They require the earliest possible action, and you are to play a significant part. As soon as it can be arranged, you will leave London to witness the punishment of a terrible wrong committed against His Majesty the King many years ago. Though some preparations have already been made, our journey will require further careful planning, and great secrecy. Those plans may take a day or two to implement, though I intend we should accomplish our mission as quickly as possible. It is my task to prepare what is required. Your role is to witness its completion and then return to His Majesty to report that his order has been carried out. You will therefore remain here in Shepherd Street while I make the final necessary arrangements. Should you wish, you may take the opportunity to see a little of this great city, enjoy some of its delights. But don't wander too far or you may get lost. And we would not want that to happen. Good night, Moreau. Sleep well."

Tired, road-soiled and deeply puzzled by what Bolton had said, Carl Manfred was pleased to be shown to his bedroom. It was large and well-furnished, with two windows overlooking the street. A fire burned in the fireplace. After eating a piece of pie and some fruit that had been set out on the table, and drinking a glass of good claret, he undressed. Then locking the door and putting the key on the bedside table beside the empty leather case, he got into bed. Though tired, he lay awake for some time, watching the reflection of the flames on the walls of the room. He thought for a moment he could hear a woman's voice, followed by laughter.

He fell asleep exhausted. Later, he awoke to what he thought was a noise outside his bedroom and the scrape of a key finding a lock. He listened but heard nothing more. He felt for the door key on his bedside table. It was still there. He turned over and went back to sleep.

He half stirred when he heard another sound – this time of a door opening. Carl Manfred thought he must be dreaming. He drifted off to sleep again but a few moments later he stirred once more. He saw a shadow moving slowly towards him. Was he dreaming or awake? Half asleep, he attempted to raise himself and to call out, but soft hands swiftly, tenderly pushed him back. The hands then took his forearms. He was purposefully pressed down onto the pillows. A voice whispered in his ear, in French, telling him not to speak. The shadow began to ease into his bed. As it did so, a cloak slipped from its shoulders to the floor.

He could only see the silhouette of a body, blocking the dwindling light from the fire. A woman. Unclothed. And sweetly perfumed. Surely he must be dreaming? The woman ran a finger along his lips. He put his hand to her face but she was masked. She stretched his arms further above his head and then, with her hands in his, slowly lowered herself so as to sit astride him. Her right hand gently pulled his nightshirt up above his thighs. She then took his hands and cupped them to her breasts. They began with her encouragement to move in rhythm. Still unsure whether it was a dream or really happening, he sought to resist, but soon gave up his unconvincing efforts to do so. The years of loneliness slipped away as he embraced the unknown woman and she eased him into her.

Carl Manfred woke with a start. There was much bustle in the house and soon there was a knock on the door. The voice of a maid said she wished to attend to his room at his convenience and to announce that breakfast would be served downstairs shortly. He asked her to return with some hot water. As he rose from his bed, there was no trace of the woman in the night, only a hint of perfume on the pillow next to his. He recalled her body entwined with his. A lace-edged handkerchief lay on the floor. She had obviously not been a dream.

There was no sign of Bolton when Carl Manfred went downstairs. In daylight, the house, which appeared large, was somewhat grubby. The furnishings were faded and there seemed to be a smell of decay. He had breakfast alone. It comprised hot chocolate, bread and some meat pie, served by a pale-faced young girl who looked much older than her likely age. Her fingernails were badly bitten and her hair somewhat unkempt. As he finished eating, a tall, plump, sly-looking woman, with an excessive amount of rouge on her cheeks, appeared. She announced herself as Mrs Rathbone, the lady of the house. She greeted her guest in French and asked if he had a comfortable night. Carl Manfred said yes, declining to mention his late-night visitor just in case he had indeed been mistaken.

From what he had seen and heard so far, he concluded that the house where he was lodging was probably a brothel – though perhaps more upmarket than some he had seen during his military campaigns, when he had gone to round up soldiers missing on the eve of battle. If Bolton wanted to hide his real identity as an agent of the King, he speculated, a brothel was one of the better ways of doing so.

Rising from the table, Carl Manfred asked if Mr Bolton was available. Mrs Rathbone said he had gone out early on business and she did not expect him back for some time.

Carl Manfred decided to go for a walk. The morning was dry and bright but bitterly cold. With a hand-drawn map that Mrs Rathbone had provided, as well as the one Maria Louisa had given him, he proposed to walk from his lodging to find the river. Leaving the house, he walked south east, towards Westminster.

London was big and noisy, hectic with people, coaches, carriages, sedans, and horses, hawkers and vendors. Running footmen barged through the teeming crowds to clear the way for a coach or sedan. There were many imposing buildings. Berlin, which he knew well, did not compare. He walked for an hour, carefully memorising landmarks in order to find his way back to Shepherd Street. Once or twice, he sensed he was being followed, but when he turned round to look there was no obvious pursuer. He eventually found the river and paused for a while, awed by its size, the many boats and the recently completed Westminster Bridge. He then turned and made his way up Whitehall, towards Piccadilly, where he found a coffee house.

The man who greeted him was middle-aged, had a fox-like face and was evidently loquacious. Carl Manfred asked for coffee. The same man brought it to his table and then sat down.

"My name is Auguste Gaillard. I am the owner of this establishment. My grandfather fled to England some eighty years ago, at the time of the Huguenot repression in France. Welcome to London. May I ask your business in England?" he enquired.

"Personal business, Monsieur," replied Carl Manfred.

"And where have you travelled from?" asked Gaillard.

Carl Manfred replied that he had just arrived from France.

Now speaking French, Gaillard asked where he had been in France. Carl Manfred replied that he had been visiting his sister in Paris.

"Judging by your accent, you are not French. Where is your true home?"

Carl Manfred hesitated and then, avoiding a direct answer, replied, "I used to be in the army, so I have been everywhere. But I know Paris well."

"That's my home town, Monsieur! Whereabouts in Paris does your sister live?"

"She lives near the Place Royale."

"And will you be long in London, Monsieur?"

This man was unduly inquisitive and starting to irritate Carl Manfred. He was thinking how best to reply when he sensed someone behind him. He spun round. It was the stranger, who looked at him warningly.

"I am visiting some business acquaintances for a few days. Now my friend has come and I must go."

"I wish you well, Monsieur," said Gaillard. "Come back if you have time to talk about Paris. I am here all the time."

"I will," said Carl Manfred as he hastily finished his coffee. Then he left with the stranger.

They began to walk briskly towards Shepherd Street.

"Be very careful where you go and what you say," the stranger said, in the same menacing tone he had used before. "The task on which we are embarked could end in disaster and you with it, if you are not careful. Go back to Shepherd Street and stay there. Bolton will be ready to travel the day after tomorrow and we will go with him."

The stranger then turned on his heel and disappeared.

By the time Carl Manfred reached Shepherd Street, it was already mid-afternoon. The house was busy. He accepted Mrs Rathbone's invitation to eat almost immediately. The meal completed, there was still no sign of Bolton, but plenty of activity as maids went up and down the stairs and rooms were prepared – fires in each and an abundance of wine.

After another glass of wine in the dining room, Carl Manfred returned to his bedroom to reflect on the day and in particular his encounter with Monsieur Gaillard. He also thought about the night before – with pleasure. There was still a trace of perfume on the pillow. He sat down by the fire and fell asleep. After a while he was woken by the sound of voices and laughter in the next-door room – one man and one woman. He did not know it, but the man was George Whitfield. Soon there were additional but more distant noises as footsteps sounded in the corridor. Carl Manfred locked the door, undressed, got into bed and fell quickly asleep.

It was some hours later that he stirred, conscious of someone near him. A dark figure approached the bed, silhouetted by the remains of the fire and the flicker of a dying candle in its holder on the other side of the room. He attempted to raise himself but, just like the previous night, the figure pressed him back onto the pillows. As he fell back, he recognised the perfume of the night before. The mysterious masked woman had returned. This time he made no attempt to reject her. He wanted her.

She let her cloak drop to the floor and slid silently, unclothed, into his bed. Her left breast brushed his cheek as she did so. A frisson of excitement ran through his body. Without her bidding, he removed his shirt and lay down again. With his encouragement, she sat astride him as she had done the night before. She put her mask to his face as though to kiss him. He felt her breath on his lips. The woman slowly ran her right index finger up and down his body – from his thighs to his lips and back to his thighs. Carl Manfred cupped her small but firm breasts and began to massage gently her hardening nipples. Both bodies became aroused and began to move together in a quickening rhythm.

After a while, she lowered her full length onto his body, placing her thighs between his legs and pinning his wrists above his head with her hands as they continued to move as one. As Carl Manfred hardened, she kissed him repeatedly on the lips through her mask. Then she eased him into her and placed her outstretched arms onto his, their fingers intertwined. He surrendered. She cried out as her body, pressing down on his, shook violently. After her climax, he pulled her down beside him. They fell asleep, he holding her tightly in his arms to prevent her escaping from his bed.

As dawn began to break, he awoke to find the masked woman still asleep beside him. He slipped gently out of bed, put on his shirt and crept across to the other side of the room. He felt for a new candle. Finding one, he put the wick into the embers of the fire. Once it had caught, he took it on tiptoe back to the bed and bent down to look closely at the woman who had shared his bed.

Though she was half covered by the bedsheet, he could see in the candlelight that she was tall, slim and lithe with long elegant legs. As he held out his hand to touch her, hot wax fell onto his fingers. He made a sound as it did so. She woke suddenly. Her skin glowed in the flickering candlelight. Her breasts were exquisite and her eyes glimmered through her richly decorated gold mask, which covered her face and hair completely.

"Who are you?" he asked in French, the language in which she had whispered to him that night and the night before.

The beautiful creature quickly rose from the sheets, putting her right forefinger to his lips to silence him. Slipping off the bed, she stooped to reach for her cloak on the floor. Finding it, she swiftly swirled it over her shoulders and wrapped it around her body. Pulling the hood over her head, she turned to leave the room. He reached out to touch her but she sidestepped his movement and moved quickly towards the door. He tried to stop her but again she eluded his outstretched hand. Then the candle in his fingers went out and the room was dark once more. As the shrouded figure turned the key in the lock and opened the door, he called out, "Will I see you again?" The figure paused, but gave no answer and then left the room, locking the door behind her. The masked woman had gone.

Carl Manfred returned to bed, burying his face in the pillow to capture her fragrance. He had not shared his bed with a woman for many years, and with one who had given him such unalloyed sexual pleasure, never. For two nights, an unknown woman – a woman of the night – had come to his room, despite a locked door. She had brought him profound gratification, shown him rare, tender intimacy, even though it was in a brothel. But if she were a prostitute, she was sophisticated and alluring. On leaving the army he had vowed that he would never again lose himself with a prostitute. But the woman in the mask had given him pure ecstasy for two nights. She was now his secret. He longed to see her face.

He fell asleep. When he woke, after opening the curtain to let in the daylight he once again smelt the pillow. The scent of perfume was still there. He noticed a strand of long black hair that must have escaped from beneath her mask. He wrapped it in a piece of tissue and put it in a corner of his bag.

It was now Monday, 25 November, with still no sign of Bolton. Carl Manfred contemplated another walk, yet hesitated at the thought of a further encounter with the menacing stranger. But used to vigorous exercise at Herzberg, he decided to go out after all. He saw no sign of the stranger, though he sensed he was not far away. On his return to Shepherd Street later, he was advised by Mrs Rathbone that Mr Bolton wished to dine with him shortly.

The two ate together in the same room where Bolton had welcomed him on his arrival in London five days before.

"I trust you have enjoyed your stay in London so far and that Mrs Rathbone has ensured you have everything you require," Bolton said.

Carl Manfred wondered whether "everything" included the unknown woman who had twice entered his room, but he decided to say nothing.

"Since your arrival and my receipt of His Majesty's instructions," Bolton continued, "I have been in touch with contacts outside the capital. There are still one or two final matters to arrange but I have decided that you and our mutual friend should leave London tomorrow morning, to travel to Norwich. I will travel ahead. We may need to stay there for a few days before carrying out the King's orders. Or our business may be completed quickly. We shall see."

Bolton insisted that he was not yet in a position to say more about the mission on which they were engaged, but he hoped it would be possible for Carl Manfred to leave England before Christmas to begin his journey back to Berlin.

"The current English suspicion of France and Prussia has made it necessary for us to be most discreet about our plans for what we are about to do," said Bolton. "I decided for that reason that it was best for us to be here in Shepherd Street, where those who come and go are much more interested in matters of great personal satisfaction and therefore not inclined to ask difficult questions. Those who come here place a high value on hiding their sexual indiscretions from those who should not know or do not need to know. They are more intent on protecting their own secrets than seeking to discover the secrets of others."

Carl Manfred privately shared that opinion, after his encounter with the masked woman.

He asked about Norwich and why it was necessary to go there. Bolton replied that it was England's second-largest city after London. He had been there several years before on other business. It was a beautiful city, full of churches and shops, surrounded by rich, flat, agricultural land, some of which would remind Carl Manfred of Prussia. As for why they needed to go there, he repeated that he could not yet disclose their purpose.

After eating, the two men sat before the fire drinking claret, playing cards and talking about the perils of travelling the roads of Europe. Then, as the clock struck midnight, Bolton said they should retire as they had an early start the next morning.

Carl Manfred returned to his room, more frustrated than ever by his inability to find out exactly why he was in England on royal business when he could be at Herzberg supervising his estate. He packed his belongings ready for an early departure the next morning, locked his door and went to bed.

But he found it difficult to sleep. There were noises from along the corridor and, outside, still the sound of carriages clattering over cobbled streets. And he wished to stay awake, to see if the masked woman would return. Eventually, however, he slept. When he awoke next morning, there was no smell of perfume to record that she had been to him. He felt deep regret, but soon put it out of his mind as he placed the last of his possessions in his bag ready to leave London.

So on the morning of Tuesday, 26 November, Carl Manfred left Mrs Rathbone's house in the company of the stranger. Returning to the point of his arrival, they went immediately to the Golden Cross Inn at Charing Cross. Carl Manfred was unaware that an hour or so before, Arabella Whitfield, the woman who had twice shared his bed, had left the same establishment for the same destination. From now on, the paths of all three would become inextricably linked and would remain so in the weeks ahead.

PART THREE: RETRIBUTION AND SALVATION

CHAPTER 10

Encounters

The following day, Wednesday, 27 November, the London flyer clattered to a halt in the Market Place in Norwich, the city's centre point from which streets, lanes and alleys descended into haphazard loops and webs of dark, winding passageways. The journey had taken many hours. Three people descended stiffly onto the cobbled square: Arabella, the stranger and the man she knew as Moreau. Across the way was the daily market, filled with stalls, vendors and hawkers.

After collecting her bag and still tightly holding her precious box, Arabella looked for a sedan chair to take her to Mrs Willoughby's lodgings in St Giles Street, where, if luck were with her, she believed she might find her mother. As she did so, Moreau and the stranger asked if she needed any assistance. She declined. They took their leave and turned away to walk across the Market Place in another direction. Finding a sedan chair quickly, Arabella sat back, contemplating what she would say to her mother.

* * * * *

Following Arabella's flight, life at Meltwater had been wretched. Lady Whitfield remained distraught. Her daughter, companion and confidante had vanished – there had been no sign of her, nor any contact. She barely spoke to her husband, whom she continued to hold responsible for what had happened. They spent much time apart, she at Meltwater and he at their town house in London, where he was trying, he said, to find his daughter and to repair the damage he claimed her disappearance had done to his political ambitions in Norfolk. He did not, of course, disclose the solace he was enjoying in the arms of his mistress, Lady Barbara Ward. Lady Whitfield's anguish was all the more acute when, from time to time, her husband and her son, George, reported rumours pointing to the probability that Arabella had sought refuge in the demi-monde of Mayfair. She knew that these fresh rumours would already have reached her county friends, given the speed with which sensational gossip spread. But Lady Whitfield still refused to believe that her beautiful daughter, though headstrong, had become mired in London's lecherous swamp.

As the months passed without news of Arabella, Lady Whitfield's despair deepened, compounded by her remorseless hatred of her husband. It was this vile man who had brought calamity to Meltwater. In doing so, he had betrayed both her love and her reputation – not that either meant anything to him. Lady Whitfield longed to escape, to be rid of him. But, as long as her daughter's fate was unknown, she believed she had to stay in the sarcophagus that Meltwater had become, in the fading hope that one day Arabella would return. Like their mistress, the servants, too, lamented the cheerless chill that, in Arabella's absence, now filled the Hall.

It was against this cruel and unforgiving backdrop that Lady Whitfield became increasingly lonely, almost a recluse, deprived of her husband's love, support and respect, and of the company of her beloved daughter, in whom she had seen reflected the once young and lively Thérèse de Miron. But life had to continue, matching the seasons of the year. She did her best to maintain a fragile veneer of stability at Meltwater, if only for the sake of her own sanity, through her now much more limited social life. As autumn wore on, her declining circle of close friends invited her to come once again to Norwich, to celebrate Advent and to spend some time together. And so it was that, as her husband and son were in London, Lady Whitfield reluctantly decided to go to Norwich to escape Meltwater for a few days and to seek some diversion from her unhappiness. Besides, Christmas was coming and, though the prospect depressed her, it was important to mark Advent with Monsieur Noverre. He would help to cheer her, if no one else could. She arrived at Mrs Willoughby's lodgings in Norwich on Monday, 25 November.

Two days later, Lady Whitfield arranged to meet her dearest and most steadfast friends, Lady Mildmay and Mrs Benjamin, in order to dine together at the White Swan on Nether Row and to plan the rest of their stay in Norwich. She was putting on her bonnet when there was a gentle tap on the door and then another.

"Come in," said Lady Whitfield.

The door opened and a veiled woman entered. The two women looked at each other for a moment.

"What is it that you want? Who are you?" said Lady Whitfield.

The veiled woman closed the door. Lady Whitfield looked closely at the figure in black standing before her.

"It is me," said Arabella, gradually lifting her veil, her eyes brimming with tears.

Lady Whitfield gasped, almost fainting, as though she had seen a ghost. Arabella rushed into her mother's arms. Lady Whitfield clasped her daughter, holding her tightly to her. Both cried.

"My darling Arabella, please tell me where you have been all this time. I have been out of my mind with worry. Why did you not write?" she asked.

Arabella did not reply, too overcome with emotion. After holding each other, in tears, for many minutes, enjoying the physical closeness of being together again after such a long separation, they sat down on the bed, holding hands and looking at one another, barely uttering any words. Mother and daughter were reunited.

After Arabella promised not to leave the room until her mother returned from dinner, and her mother promised in turn not to disclose Arabella's arrival to her friends, Lady Whitfield left to keep her engagement with Lady Mildmay and Mrs Benjamin; loath though each was to forfeit the other's company so soon, they agreed it was best, so as not to arouse suspicion. Alone once more, Arabella contemplated how much she should tell her mother of her life in London, but the question was soon pushed aside as she realised the extraordinary danger in which she had placed herself by coming to Norwich. She knew that her reappearance was most unlikely to stay secret. Indeed, it was entirely likely that, despite her promise, her mother would disclose the news of her daughter's reappearance to her friends over dinner. Lady Whitfield had not always been good at keeping confidences. Arabella's fears grew by the hour, since the longer she remained in Norwich, the greater the risk of her whereabouts becoming known to her vengeful father. At the same time, despite the immediate danger of her situation, Arabella could not erase from her mind, however hard she tried, the man in the coach in whose bed she had lain in London and who had given her such deep sensual pleasure.

She lay on the bed at Mrs Willoughby's, her thoughts spinning faster and faster as she pondered her ever worsening predicament. She decided that she could not stay in Norwich beyond the next morning; that she would tell her mother she would never return to Meltwater so long as her father was alive; and that, accordingly, her only option was to return immediately to London. But, if that were her only course, Arabella was determined not to renew her acquaintance with either Mrs Hallam or Mrs Rathbone. This was her chance to make a new beginning and to put the London demi-monde behind her. There had to be another way to gain the freedom she sought. What that way might be she could not at present fathom. As she lay gazing at the ceiling, Arabella's fatigue and anxiety overcame her and she fell asleep.

"My darling child, please wake up," said her mother.

Slowly, Arabella awoke. Sitting together on the bed, with her mother's arm around her, she began to tell her story. She omitted any incriminating or leading details, for fear her mother would be shocked, and, of course, to avoid any disclosure that might possibly, even if inadvertently, reach the ears of her father. He was cunning and would pick up any clue that made it easier for him to find her or damn her further in his eyes and the opinion of his friends. Thus despite many questions from Lady Whitfield about where she had been during the past months, Arabella stuck to the story that she had been in hiding from her father and brother with friends in London and would remain there for the foreseeable future, but she could not reveal where that was. As there could never be any reconciliation with her father, it was essential to protect her whereabouts and identity. She begged her mother to understand. She was sure that before long they would be permanently reunited.

Arabella shared her mother's bed that night. It brought back memories of the many times she had crept into her mother's bed at Meltwater when her father was in London. Then, they had lain awake for hours, talking of France or recalling the French children's stories her mother used to recount when Arabella was much younger. This time, however, Arabella quickly fell asleep in her mother's arms, still exhausted by her flight from Shepherd Street and the long journey to Norwich.

Lady Whitfield lay awake for many hours. She recollected Arabella as a young and high-spirited child at Meltwater. Since running away from the Hall, she had changed. No longer a girl and thinner than before, it was plainly evident that Arabella was now a resolute young woman with dark secrets, and there was the hint – so her mother's intuition detected – of a new sexual self-confidence, which she had clearly acquired in London. Lady Whitfield had lost her daughter – to whom she did not know – but for the moment Arabella was close beside her. She had little doubt, though, that very soon she would lose her again.

The next morning, Arabella told her mother that she would have to return to London. She feared her father would soon find her if she stayed a moment longer in Norwich. Lady Whitfield implored her to remain, and indeed to return with her to Meltwater. But Arabella insisted that the longer she stayed by her mother's side the harder it would be to leave and the greater the risk that her presence would become known to her father. His persistent efforts to find her in London, and what he and his mistress had allegedly said about her, had clearly demonstrated that there would be profound consequences if he ever discovered her. Arabella was adamant that there could never be any reconciliation with her father and, that being so, she would never return to Meltwater while he lived. He would have to die before she ever set foot in that bleak house on the marshes again.

"Dearest Mama," Arabella assured her mother, "nothing has changed. You may think I have let you down. But I believe passionately that women – you and me and indeed all women – should not be viewed as ornaments to society, to be traded in marriage as chattels. Women, whatever their place in this kingdom, deserve the same fundamental rights as men. I may be only one voice, but I wish to be an example others might follow later. You may think this is vanity on my part. It is not. I am absolute in my commitment. I therefore intend to do all I can to ensure that I am not treated as a chattel, as Papa has so dreadfully treated you. I know that he will never change his mind. But neither will I change mine. Because of that, he and I will never be reconciled. Though I seem different now, and my opinions may cause great distress, I pray that you will understand what I am saying. I hold these strong views because you made me what I am. So, Mama, please accept that I must return to London. It cannot be any other way. I could not bear the thought of being dragged back to Meltwater and forced to marry a man I have not chosen of my own free will. That would be to condemn myself to a life of servitude."

Her mother listened to Arabella's words, spoken with a passion she had not heard before. She knew then that there was no longer any prospect of her daughter returning home. But while she now acknowledged she had lost the Arabella she once knew, she admired her daughter's defiant determination to chart a new course in her life. Where it would end she had no idea. But she had to let Arabella go.

"Dearest Arabella, I can see with my own eyes that you are indeed changed. What has happened to you in the past months I do not know and you have decided not to tell me. Be that as it may, I accept that I have lost you – to whom or to what I do not know. You must go. But I beg you never to forget me and to promise that one day you will feel able to be at my side again. I may not be as fluent in words as you, but please believe me when I say that I will always love you. Arabella, you can go on your way in the sure knowledge you will always have my deepest devotion and that you will never leave my thoughts."

The two hugged each other.

"Thank you, Mama," Arabella whispered. "I promise that one day, when I have found happiness, we will be together again."

Growing more tearful at the prospect of being separated from Arabella again, Lady Whitfield fleetingly considered the possibility of fleeing to London with her and taking her to her family in France. But her daughter's words ruled this out. Their parting was inevitable and she had to brace herself to say goodbye.

As Lady Whitfield struggled to compose herself, Mrs Willoughby knocked on the door to give her a message from Sir Robert's coachman. Her husband intended to call for her at five o'clock that afternoon so she could accompany him to dinner with Mr and Mrs Gurney before returning together to Meltwater the next day. Arabella froze at the news that her father may be nearby. She had to leave for London immediately. If she did not, her freedom would be in great danger.

Despite Lady Whitfield's pleadings to stay a little longer, Arabella hastily packed her few things and, after saying a final goodbye to her distraught mother, began to descend the staircase with her bag and the box, not knowing where to go. As she did so, she heard Mrs Willoughby in the hallway below say, "Why, Sir Robert! How good it is to see you. You are early. Lady Whitfield is upstairs with her daughter."

Looking down into the stairwell, Arabella saw her father's hand on the bannister as he began to climb the staircase quickly. In an instant, she swiftly opened a door behind her. She slipped inside the gloomy room and closed the door silently. She slowly turned the key, and then, her body pressed against the door, head tilted to listen more closely, held her breath. She had hidden just in time. She heard her father's footsteps on the landing outside and then on the next flight of stairs.

Arabella suddenly became conscious that someone else was in the room. She span round. Lying on the bed, wrapped in a full-length coat, was a roughly shaven man with long dark hair. He turned to look at her. He was the man she had seen in the carriage with Moreau.

"Madame, may I be of assistance?" he whispered.

Arabella stumbled for words. Deeply flustered, she replied, "I did not wish to be seen by the man who has just gone upstairs," she said.

"Why?" asked the stranger.

"He is my father and I do not want him to find me."

"You clearly cannot stay here," the stranger said. "Do you wish me to help you?"

Arabella, in obvious distress, said yes.

"So be it," said the stranger.

He quickly rose from the bed. She froze in fear as he approached her.

Kissing her hand he said, "Do not be afraid. I will not harm you. I think you were on the coach from London yesterday. You sat opposite us. Am I right?"

"Yes," said Arabella.

At that moment, there was a commotion on the landing and then a rapid banging on the door. The stranger seized Arabella's arm, pulled her across the room, and thrust her behind the thick curtain drawn across the window. On his way to the door he kicked her bag and box out of sight under the bed.

The stranger, looking once more across the room to check that Arabella could not be seen, unlocked and opened the door. Without divulging his name, Sir Robert Whitfield, his face contorted with anger, asked if the stranger had seen a young woman.

"Why should that be the case?" he asked.

Sir Robert attempted to push past him into the room but the stranger barred the way. He told the unwelcome visitor that he had been resting on his bed until he had been disturbed by his pounding on the door. Sir Robert insisted on searching the room. But the stranger said he could not do so and that if he continued to insist he would resist with force. He drew a knife from the sleeve of his coat. Sir Robert retreated hastily but said that he would be back soon with a constable to search for his daughter, whom he believed was hiding somewhere within the building. He turned on his heel and left.

After a pause to make sure Sir Robert had not returned or was listening on the landing, the stranger locked the door and crossed to the curtain. Without disturbing it, he whispered to Arabella, "Not a word, please. Remain where you are without speaking until I say you may move."

After what seemed many minutes, during which the stranger and Arabella could hear raised voices and rapid footsteps on the wooden staircase gradually fade, the stranger drew back the curtain and motioned Arabella to sit down in a chair by the bed.

Looking at her with cold, piercing, blue eyes, he said, "Your father and, I presume, your mother appear to have left. But judging by his demeanour and evident persistence, I am sure your father will be back as he threatened. You cannot stay in these lodgings any longer. What are your intentions?" he asked.

"I wish to return to London as soon as possible," Arabella said, "but until I have the means to pay, I have nowhere to stay."

"This world is full of betrayal, misery, cruelty and despair," the stranger replied. "A young woman should be spared such a fate. If you are prepared to trust me – and I accept that may be hard for you to do, as you have no idea who I am – I will take you to other lodgings where you can stay in safety until tomorrow, when I too will have to return to London. We will then travel together. I assure you that you will come to no harm under my protection."

Arabella looked at the stranger. Menacing though he appeared, she believed she could place her safety in his hands. And if he were returning to London tomorrow, perhaps Moreau would be with him. She longed to see his face again. Besides, the imminent return of her father gave her no other opportunity to escape. So Arabella accepted the stranger's proposal. He was her only hope.

Leaving her alone in the room and directing her to lock the door behind him, the stranger went out. Arabella gazed at him from the window as he left the house. She had just placed her life in the hands of a man she did not know but who evidently knew a man she had already met – intimately – in London. The stranger might lead her to know more about the man she knew only as Moreau.

True to his word, the stranger returned within the hour and, after diverting Mrs Willoughby's attention, he and Arabella, neither with many possessions to carry, left the lodgings in the fast-encroaching dusk. They walked away briskly. As they turned the corner, they heard a coach stop outside the building they had just left. The stranger peered back around the wall of the alley. It was Sir Robert Whitfield, his son, George, and another man, dismounting and running into Mrs Willoughby's lodgings.

"Hurry," said the stranger to Arabella. "We must disappear before they can find us."

After several minutes' walking at an urgent pace, they arrived outside a tall, forbidding building in a narrow alley leading from the top of Upper Goat Lane. The stranger knocked loudly on the front door. Arabella heard the sound of bolts being pulled back. The door opened to reveal a grey-faced elderly woman, her hair tightly drawn back, dressed in black.

"Oh, it's you," she said. "You're early."

The stranger made no response and entered, beckoning Arabella to follow him. The hallway was dark. There was no carpet on the floor and little furniture. Their footsteps echoed as they followed the woman to a room, equally sparsely furnished, at the rear of the house. Arabella felt a chill – one of fear and foreboding rather than cold.

"This young lady needs a room for the night where she is not to be disturbed," said the stranger, speaking in a clipped tone that echoed in the emptiness of the room. "If anyone knocks, asking if a young woman is staying here, say no and then close the door. Is that understood?"

"Yes," replied the woman.

"Good. Then show us the room," demanded the stranger.

As they climbed two flights of stairs, Arabella allowed it was conceivable that the stranger was not English. While he spoke with great clarity and fluency, and had no accent to betray his possible linguistic roots, the curt manner in which he had addressed the lady of the house betrayed the hint of a different country of origin. He was certainly not French, as Arabella knew their culture and style of speaking well. His manner and pattern of speech were more abrupt, staccato, suggesting, perhaps, someone from further east in Europe.

The woman unlocked a door on the second floor to reveal a meagre bedroom. It was cold and gloomy, with a large window that overlooked a small garden and the rear of terraced houses beyond. The stranger asked her to arrange for a fire to be lit as soon as possible, and to bring Arabella some refreshment. With a surly look, the woman nodded and left the room.

The stranger turned to Arabella.

"This house may be bleak but I assure you, Miss Whitfield, you will be safe here until you leave for London tomorrow."

Arabella was taken aback. How did he know her name? Her father had not disclosed his name during their encounter at Mrs Willoughby's house. Perhaps he had discovered her name while he had been staying there.

"And what is your name?" she asked the stranger.

Without answering, he walked quickly to the door and, as he left, he turned. With a trace of a smile, he said, "My name is of no consequence. After the fire is lit and you have taken refreshment, I ask you to lock the door. I will come for you early tomorrow, tapping five times on the door, and together we will leave to catch the coach to London. Until then, be vigilant. Your father is manifestly determined to find you and it appears nothing will deter him from trying to do so."

With that he left the room. But instead of his footsteps going downstairs, Arabella thought she heard him climb the third flight of stairs.

Later that evening, she sat in a chair by the small fire, her spiralling fate preoccupying her mind. She was alone with just a few coins in her purse. Her father, in the same city, had nearly seized her, and her mother was distraught at once more losing touch with her. She was in a dark, inhospitable house, dependent upon a stranger who was possibly from an alien country. What was to become of her? Later, after reading some pages of her Catholic missal, Arabella went to bed, fully dressed. Fearful of the night ahead, she chose not to extinguish the candle and she clung to her music book.

Hours later, after a fitful sleep in the bitterly cold room, she awoke to the sound of footsteps and low voices. The candle by her bedside had burnt out, so the room was in darkness. It was difficult to hear what the distant voices might be saying because of the noise of the wind and rain outside. The footsteps, possibly of two people, came to her door, paused, and then to Arabella's relief walked up the next flight of stairs. She tried to stay awake for the rest of the night, fearing the footsteps might return and an attempt made to enter her room. But, though she thought she heard the sound of voices once more, she slipped back into a sleep full of strange dreams.

On the following morning, Arabella woke with a start at a knock on the door and a woman's voice asking to come in. She got out of bed and unlocked the door. The grey-faced woman entered, carrying a tray with a jug of hot water, a hand towel and a bowl. Arabella said good morning. The woman merely nodded in return. As she left the room she said she would return shortly with some breakfast.

Arabella drew back the curtains. The rain had gone, replaced by a blue sky and sun, though the rays coming through the window carried little warmth. Another day had begun, but she did not know how it would end. At least she knew she would shortly leave Norwich – provided the stranger were true to his word. Her fate rested with the man who had saved her yesterday. There was no going back. The tide was at full flood. She was cut off from the receding world of Meltwater.

* * * * *

As the coach travelled at speed across the flat landscape towards Norwich, Carl Manfred recalled the equally flat lands of Prussia and his estate at Herzberg. The King had sent him on a journey to England, the purpose of which remained unfathomable. Week had followed week, and with the passing of each, Herzberg became ever more distant. The stranger by his side, with his undisclosed identity, had brought added mystery to the venture on which he was embarked.

The only flicker of light in his seemingly endless and bleak journey across Europe was the masked woman who had twice visited his bed in London. She had given him brief but intense happiness. For the time she was with him, he had forgotten his loneliness. But who was she? Why had she come? Was she truly a prostitute? He was sure that was not the case. That she had asked for no money was the least of his reasons for thinking so.

Though she had come in the dark and her face had been hidden, it was evident from his brief glimpse of her half-covered form on the second night in his room that she was young, with a beautiful body, not an older, shop-soiled woman of the night. He had bedded women during his army career. Many had been coarse and well-rehearsed in their sexual repertoire, and he had rarely found enjoyment with any of them. But this woman – whoever she was – had been different. There was something magnetic about her. And though seemingly highly confident in the way she had made love to him, he had detected – looking at her for a moment on that second morning – a definite vulnerability as she lay half exposed between the sheets. Moreover, though he could not be sure, the strength of her sexual climax – almost atavistic in its intensity – suggested that she had received little prior satisfaction of this nature from others in the past. It was also evident from his penetration of her that she had not been widely used. And then there was that unmistakable perfume.

Forcing himself back to the present, Carl Manfred looked around the coach. Beside him, the stranger appeared to be asleep, but his right hand rested on his left sleeve, as though ready to withdraw his long-bladed knife at a moment's notice. On his other side sat a plump middle-aged lady, asleep and breathing heavily. Facing him were a well-dressed elderly man and woman – obviously husband and wife. The man stared out of the window; his wife seemed to be sleeping, but sobbed occasionally behind her firmly closed eyes. What sorrow, he wondered, had touched them? And then, across in the corner, was a tall, veiled woman dressed in black. She appeared to be young. As far as he could judge through the veil, her eyes were closed, but her gloved hands were constantly moving – clasped, unclasped and then clasped again – suggesting nervous apprehension. And beneath her hands, on her lap, lay a box.

Eventually, the coach arrived in Norwich. It was a cold, miserable day and, although the afternoon had not ended, it seemed dusk had already come. Carl Manfred and the stranger disembarked and, after asking if the woman in black required any assistance, which she refused, they walked quickly away from the Market Place. Rather than taking sedans, they continued on foot along winding streets and dark, narrow alleys. It was slow progress. The stones beneath their boots were wet and slippery and it was necessary to avoid the rivulets of human waste trickling down the central gully.

At last, they came to a tall and bleak-looking tenement house. The stranger knocked on the door, which was opened by an elderly grey-haired woman.

She looked at them closely and then said, "He is waiting for you upstairs."

Carl Manfred followed the stranger up three flights of stairs and then along a corridor towards the back of the house. The stranger knocked on the door at the far end and a voice asked them to enter. There, with his back to the fire, was Bolton.

"I welcome you both to Norwich," he said. "Mrs Pratt will return shortly with something to eat, but before she does I wish to tell you that we will make a journey later this evening on the written orders of His Majesty the King, which you, Moreau, brought with you to London."

Bolton finished by saying that, upon completion of their task, Carl Manfred would return to the house for the remainder of the night, pending their departure for London the next day. The stranger's lodgings were nearby. He would proceed there once they had eaten, returning to escort Carl Manfred to their destination. And there Bolton would meet them.

After taking frugal refreshment together, Bolton departed with the stranger. Carl Manfred was left alone. He felt cold. He sat in front of the small fire, trying to warm himself, and once again thinking of his distant home, his past career, Berlin, and of his conversation with the King. As he reflected on times past, he could not imagine what lay ahead in the hours to come. He leaned back in the chair and fell asleep.

CHAPTER 11

Execution

It was after nightfall when Carl Manfred woke. He thought he heard voices below, but they faded. A little while later, there was a knock on the door. He opened it. It was the stranger.

"It is time to go," he said.

They went downstairs and let themselves out through the front door.

"Wait here," said the stranger. "I will be back shortly." He walked quickly down the road.

Carl Manfred sheltered in the doorway. It was cold, wet and dismal. A few people scurried past, heads bent against the wind and rain. It was a truly miserable evening. A coach stopped abruptly in front of the house. The door swung open and the stranger shouted from within.

"Moreau, get in quickly. There is no time to lose."

Carl Manfred clambered inside. He sat opposite the tall, cold-eyed, long-haired stranger, whose name he still did not know. Dressed in his now familiar long dark coat, with the collar turned up, the stranger seemed, in the dim light of the carriage lantern, more unpleasant and wild-looking than ever.

"Where are we going?" asked Carl Manfred.

"As I think you may already have guessed, we are going to kill a man on the King's order," replied the stranger.

Carl Manfred froze in his seat.

"Who?"

"You will find out soon enough. And after tonight your business will be done and you can return to Berlin to report to the King."

The horses' hooves resounded on the wet cobblestones. The stranger closed his eyes, but once again his right hand rested on his left sleeve. In the silence and faint light of the carriage, Carl Manfred recalled the men he had killed on the battlefield during the King's military campaigns. He remembered their screams as he had thrust his sword into their chest. He shuddered at the memories of the blood he had spilt. Now it seemed he was to be an unwilling accomplice to yet more killing. But this time it would be clandestine; it would be cold-blooded judicial murder, with the King implicated for reasons he did not know. He wanted to ask more questions but it was evident from the stranger's reticence that he would receive no answers.

After a few minutes the coach drew to a sharp stop. The stranger cursed, just as he had done in London when the coach stopped abruptly outside the house in Shepherd Street. Perhaps it was the same driver. The stranger got out, beckoning Carl Manfred to follow him. As they walked quickly through the darkness and rain, he saw from the light of the stranger's lantern the outline of a large house ahead, surrounded by trees, almost leafless, swaying violently in the wind. The ground was now soft beneath his feet. They had left the cobblestones of the city behind. He followed the stranger along the pathway to the front of the house. It was a wide, dark and brooding edifice. No lights shone from its windows. They entered through the unlocked door and walked along the main corridor, lit by small candles, towards the back of the house. They then turned left down a smaller corridor until they came to a stout wooden door. The stranger opened it and then almost pushed Carl Manfred down the stone steps on the other side.

"Bolton is waiting for you," he said, and then disappeared.

At the foot of the steps, Carl Manfred found himself in a large, high-ceilinged, dank, foul-smelling stone cellar. As it was dimly lit, it was impossible to judge its full dimensions, but it probably extended the width and depth of the house. There was the sound of running water somewhere close by. It took several more seconds for him to take in the scene before him. Standing by the left-hand wall was Bolton. Beside him, at his feet, was a large lantern. In front of it, a shivering, wretched-looking old man knelt, his arms pinned behind his back and shackles on his ankles, their chain linked to an iron loop in the opposite wall.

"Welcome, Moreau," said Bolton. "I am glad you have arrived to witness the fulfilment of the King's orders."

Carl Manfred said nothing, still absorbing the dreadful tableau before him.

Bolton then turned to the man on his knees in front of him and with deliberate movements unfolded the crested paper that Carl Manfred recognised as one of the documents he had handed over in London. Reading in German, Bolton called out in ringing tones, "You, Thomas Wolff, formerly of service to His Late Majesty Frederick William the First, are hereby charged by His Majesty King Frederick with witting involvement in causing and assisting the unjustified and heinous execution of Hans Hermann von Katte, his loyal friend and confidant, and with conspiracy to cause the death of the future King of Prussia."

He thrust into the man's face the lock of blond hair that had fallen out of the second document he had opened in London.

"Here is a lock of hair of the man you sent unjustly to his death. What do you have to say?"

The man mumbled, shaking with fear.

Bolton continued. "It was you who, with others, informed the late King of the existence of His Majesty's most personal letter to his friend about their intention to travel to England. It was you who, with others, betrayed His Majesty by showing to his father the contents of his letter, and it was you who, with others, encouraged the late King to put the Crown Prince and his friend on trial. By so doing, you committed an act of profound treachery. Such was the gratitude you showed for the friendship the Crown Prince bestowed upon you. You compounded your betrayal by encouraging the late King, at the end of the tribunal, to change the sentence of imprisonment to one of execution. And it was you who, with others, helped to arrange that execution. When the late King died, understanding your complicity in this egregious act of betrayal and the enormity of the crime you had committed, you fled His Majesty's kingdom rather than face justice. After your years in hiding, we have finally found you and now confront you with your disloyalty."

He asked the kneeling figure if he had anything to say. The muttered reply was incoherent. Bolton turned again to the paper in his hand.

"By order of His Majesty King Frederick, you are found guilty of high treason and are hereby sentenced to death for your crimes."

The man looked up at Bolton, his face drained white in the light of the flickering lantern and his eyes filling with tears. Silence fell on the appalling scene in front of Carl Manfred, who could not believe what he was witnessing. A large rat scuttled across the floor.

The old man turned his gaze on Carl Manfred, as though imploring him to save his life. Carl Manfred had often seen that look of terror on the battlefield, seconds before he wielded his sword or lance to despatch a fallen foe. He had been taught that there was no mercy in Frederick's army. A spared enemy could cost you your life in the next battle. So he had learned to show no pity. It was either your opponent's life or yours. Accordingly, if this rule still applied, there could be no mercy for the man in the cellar. The King had given his order; it could not be countermanded. Carl Manfred turned his eyes away from the old man's beseeching face.

He heard the sound of a door opening in a dark recess to his right, behind the staircase he had descended a few minutes before. From the darkness emerged the stranger.

"Executioner, do your work," said Bolton.

The stranger swept back his unbuttoned coat and from his belt drew a long narrow-bladed sword which glinted in the light of the lantern. He stepped forward, close to the victim. Bolton bent and pulled from behind him a large block of wood, which he thrust in front of the condemned man and on which he ordered him to place his neck. The old man struggled, but Bolton forced his head down. He then stepped back. The stranger instantly raised the sword above his shoulders and it flashed down. The head rolled from the body, blood pouring from the neck. Then, after a moment of silence that seemed to Carl Manfred to stop time itself, the stranger dragged the headless corpse to the other end of the cellar. Bolton followed, holding the lantern. He opened a large iron hatch. The stranger hesitated, bending down as though to search the pockets of the dead man.

Bolton shouted, "I have already emptied his pockets. Hurry, man, dispose of the body. We must leave here without delay."

The stranger stood up, about to remonstrate with Bolton. But glancing at Carl Manfred he seemed to think better of it. He grabbed the body by the shoulders and stuffed it through the aperture, from which could be heard the sound of strongly running water. He slammed the hatch shut. Producing a sack from his belt, the stranger then walked across to pick up the victim's head, its features etched with terror. He placed it inside the sack, tied the cord and then carried the bag back to the other end of the cellar, where he opened the door through which he had entered. He slammed the door behind him.

Carl Manfred stood speechless – shocked and transfixed by what he had just witnessed. Unable to move, he found it difficult to comprehend the ferocity of the King's vengeance so many years after the death of his friend von Katte – a vengeance of such depth and depravity that it had led to the brutal execution of an old man in a cellar far away in England.

Bolton turned to Carl Manfred and, without saying a word, shook him and urged him to go back upstairs for immediate departure. There was no sign of the stranger at the front door. The coach had not moved. The driver sat motionless, as though made of stone. Bolton helped Carl Manfred, still reeling from what he had seen, into the carriage, and climbed in behind him. The coach moved off. Neither man spoke. Before long the coach wheels struck the cobbled streets of Norwich.

As the coach stopped outside the bleak tenement building where Carl Manfred had arrived hours before, Bolton looked directly at him and said, "The King's business is done, witnessed by your own eyes. It is now time for you to return to Prussia to tell him so. It is important not to keep him waiting. In the morning, you and I will go our separate ways, never to see each other again. You will leave for London without delay and then for Berlin. Our mutual friend" – he was obviously referring to the stranger – "will help you get safely to France. I will stay in England for a week or so to tidy my affairs before my own departure on other business."

Carl Manfred nodded. He had so many questions but, as with the stranger earlier, he knew it was pointless to ask them, as it was certain no answers would be forthcoming. All he wanted was to leave England as quickly as possible, to try to forget the abomination the King had asked him to watch.

That night Carl Manfred slept fitfully, unable to forget what he had witnessed. The rain lashed against the window. He did not extinguish the candle. He wanted it to burn as long as possible to ward away the dreadful, terror-stricken face of Thomas Wolff. He could not banish it from his mind.

CHAPTER 12

The Pursued

The stranger left the dark house through the garden doorway, with the bag containing the head in one hand and a lantern in the other. His sword was once again in his belt beneath his long coat. He walked across the grass towards the trees beyond. When he reached the first line of trees, he carefully began to count his steps as he paced ahead in a straight line. After walking for several minutes and making a deviation to the left, he paused beneath a large oak tree, against which was propped a shovel. He placed the bag and the lantern on the ground. He then drew his sword and wiped the blade on the top of the bag, before returning it to its sheath beneath his coat.

The stranger took the shovel and quickly dug a deep hole in the soft earth beneath the tree. After hitting the bag heavily with the flat of the shovel to disfigure the features of the face inside, he placed it in the hole, and covered it with soil. He scraped fallen leaves and other debris over the site of his digging. He stood for a few moments in the pouring rain, contemplating the execution. Then, after softly whispering the word "traitor", he picked up the lantern and returned to the house to wait for the return of the coach from Norwich.

As he did so, he reflected that the most devoted acts of deference and duty were by no means confined to rooms at court or fields of battle.

He had long been a secret agent and ruthless killer in the pay of King Frederick. As His Majesty's most clandestine spymaster he had created an intricate network of agents and informers across Europe. Many were held tightly in his grip under threat of exposing their own secrets and peccadilloes. This network, this spider's web, gathered often invaluable information about the King's enemies and their machinations against Prussia, and he used what he learned to counterplot. Ruthless and resourceful, he employed whatever means were necessary to achieve the result he desired, whether blackmail, bribery, deception, torture or judicial killing. His brutal methods of interrogation broke the limbs and spirit of the hardest of men. Those to be killed never heard him come; he always struck at the dead of night. Through these means, and staying always in the shadows, he had uncovered, over the years, many of the secrets of the King's enemies, making him one of the best-informed spymasters in Europe. And he operated without any royal restraint. His instructions were explicit: to reveal the secrets and plans of the King's enemies and opponents, and to devise whatever remedies were necessary to thwart them. He received whatever money was necessary to enable him to do so. But the King had made it clear that he would disavow any action that went wrong. The stranger knew that in such circumstances his life would be sacrificed on the altar of plausible deniability.

The stranger had become an expert killer, trapping and eliminating spies and traitors. Learning his trade and how to survive during solitary years in the grubby backstreets of life, he had no soul, no scruples and no tender heart. He was vicious and uncompromising. What had to be done was done. He knew when his master was pleased with his work, though gratitude was rarely expressed. He did what he did because he loved his King.

The stranger was no lover of women. He was a lover of men, a fact he had discovered at an early age through boyhood affection. Intelligent but poorly educated, he was barely thirteen when, through the good offices of Peter Karl Christoph Keith, he had found employment as a page in the service of King Frederick William. Peter Keith, also a page in the royal household – as was his younger brother, Robert – had become a close confidant of Crown Prince Frederick and, in due course, an infantry officer. Keith later became, after the Crown Prince's accession to the throne, a close and deeply respected confidant of King Frederick.

Under the patronage of Peter Keith, who noticed that the silent young boy had certain skills, the stranger became a member of the Crown Prince's circle, albeit a barely noticed one. Because he moved so silently and unobtrusively about the royal household, he was frequently asked to acquire whatever sensitive information he could learn about those who might betray the young Prince's loyalty to them in return for short-term advancement at his father's court. It was at this time that the stranger had first met John Bolton, who was a friend of Peter Keith. Keith may have liked him; the stranger did not.

Following in the footsteps of Peter Keith, the stranger, too, became a close friend of the Crown Prince. They formed a highly personal bond of trust, despite the enormous social disparity between them, and spent much private time together. The Crown Prince's sister, Wilhelmine, once observed that Peter Keith had served her brother with great devotion, being found often in his presence; so discreet was the stranger that very few were aware of the long hours he enjoyed at the Crown Prince's side.

The necessity to spy on the late King in those far-distant days was pressing. For many years there had been no close relationship between the lively, intellectual Crown Prince, a polymath, and his oppressive father, King Frederick William, obsessed with military matters. It had steadily broken down, becoming a relationship of bitterness and rancour, a clash of uncompromising opposites. To escape his father's increasing tyranny towards him, the Crown Prince had made a secret plan to escape to England with his most intimate friend, Hans Hermann von Katte, and other junior army officers. But before it could be carried out, the plan became known – through a misdirected letter, the contents of which were disclosed to the King.

Frederick and von Katte were arrested and subsequently charged and tried for treason. Both were found guilty and von Katte sentenced to death. The King forced his son to watch the beheading from his prison cell. Frederick was devastated. He vowed he would never forgive the betrayers of his friend for their treachery and would seek his revenge, however long it took. Indeed, it would take thirty-five years.

Peter Keith, warned by the Crown Prince that their plan to

escape to England had been uncovered, fled from court. Unlike Keith's younger brother, Robert, who lost his nerve, the stranger kept his. Though his role in the planned escape was never exposed, and his close association with the Crown Prince was known of by so few, he was condemned to banishment from the royal palace. He travelled widely, a solitary figure living in brothels while honing his skills of deception, intrigue and cruelty, in order one day to wreak his own vengeance on those who had betrayed his beloved Crown Prince.

On the Crown Prince's accession to the Prussian throne, the stranger returned to seek employment with his former master and friend. While King Frederick retained a deep affection for him and saw an urgent need for his skills and unshakeable loyalty, there could be no visible place for him at court. Tongues would wag. Instead, the King asked him to become his most secret eyes and ears outside of the court. While the stranger deeply regretted he would not see the King daily, he felt honoured and gratified to have received a mandate to act as his monarch's most important protector. Following his early success in unearthing plots, intrigue and disloyalty, he proposed to the King that he establish a personal secret service reaching beyond Prussia's borders, about which no one but the King would know, to seek out the King's enemies and, moreover, to track down those still alive who had been responsible for the death of His Majesty's esteemed friend von Katte. The King agreed, urging the stranger to follow the example of Sir Francis Walsingham, spymaster to the English Queen Elizabeth. And so the stranger became the deadly spider at the centre of an ever expanding web shrouded in secrecy and mystery.

As he heard the sound of the coach approaching the house, the stranger touched the sword beneath his coat. A smile of satisfaction crossed his face. His name, though few knew it, was Waldemar Drescher (my "thresher of enemies", the King sometimes called him). Shortly before, in the cellar, he had slain without scruple Thomas Wolff, the last of the betrayers of von Katte and the Crown Prince. His Majesty had at last settled a deep and wounding score, courtesy of his late father's page. And Waldemar, as His Majesty's genius of secrets, had not only claimed another victim for his master; he too had settled a very personal debt. It had been Wolff who had denounced him to the late King as a man of carnal evil, an accusation that had contributed to his banishment from court.

The stranger returned to the tenement house in Norwich to prepare to accompany Colonel von Deppe back to London and then to Dover. He knew it would not be long before the headless body of his victim would be fished from the river by those who sought to make a living from retrieving its daily human detritus. Then investigations into its identity and cause of death would begin. That always happened. Nobody left such matters alone, as he knew from similar deeds elsewhere. The stranger regretted that he had not personally searched Wolff's pockets before shoving the body into the water. He should have ignored Bolton in the cellar and checked for himself to make sure all clues as to his identity had been removed. In his business of personal survival you never relied on the undertakings of others. Trust was of no meaning in his lexicon of life. Assurances from others were worthless. He would assume the worst – that Wolff's identity might become known within twenty-four hours of the time of execution. If he were proved correct, there was little time to lose in leaving Norwich and beginning to cover up any mistakes that might lead to Berlin.

Yet the stranger had an additional matter on his mind – the fate of the young woman he had rescued from her father at Mrs Willoughby's lodgings: Arabella Whitfield, known in London courtesan circles, where her true identity remained concealed, only as the masked Antoinette Badeau. Mrs Willoughby had added Arabella's name to the register of guests as soon as Lady Whitfield excitedly divulged her daughter's presence as she went out to dine with her friends. He had glanced at the open register when Mrs Willoughby was not looking. And he knew from his surveillance of Carl Manfred that she had previously been in the house at Shepherd Street and had twice visited his room. One of the maids had confirmed this in return for money and had even described a glimpse of her without her mask.

The two night-time visits had been at Bolton's instigation. He had been keen to keep von Deppe off the streets while he was in London and, having chosen sexual distraction as a way of doing so, had made arrangements with Mrs Rathbone. But he had not consulted the stranger about his intention. Had he been asked, the stranger would have advised against such a plan. But he now conceded its effectiveness in keeping von Deppe indoors – a necessary measure after the Prussian had nearly given away his real identity in Auguste Gaillard's coffee house. The stranger already knew that Gaillard was a French informant, who regularly passed coffee-house tittle-tattle to his French masters. He had also discovered that Gaillard was acquainted with Bolton, because the latter sometimes went to the coffee house. That made Gaillard potentially troublesome.

Though he had hidden his surprise, the stranger had been taken aback to see the young woman board the same coach for Norwich as they were taking. He was confident von Deppe had not recognised her, but he did not know how long it might be before he would, even though her face had been hidden behind her trademark mask. However, he deduced from Arabella's frequent furtive glances that she had recognised von Deppe, either, perhaps prompted by his attire, from the picture at Meltwater (which he had arranged to send to the Hall months before, in preparation for settling another score), or from their sexual encounter at Shepherd Street.

Seeing Arabella Whitfield in great distress and significant danger, he had gone against his professional instinct and offered her his protection. He had done so because her vulnerability and defiance had reminded him of his own isolation, of the risks he had taken, during his banishment from court. Whatever additional obstacles he might have to overcome, he would honour his promise to accompany her back to London. But there could be significant risk in doing so. Their escape plans could be compromised by Arabella's involvement. Despite that danger, the plans had to be implemented nonetheless, in order to extract von Deppe from England as quickly as possible and secure his own safety.

It was early morning, though still dark, by the time the stranger reached the tenement building. The elderly woman let him in. Without a word, he quietly climbed the staircase to the second floor. He paused outside Arabella's room. Hearing nothing, he climbed the next flight of stairs and walked to the room at the end of the corridor. He slowly turned the handle. The door opened. Von Deppe was asleep in the chair, covered by a blanket, the fire low in the grate. The stranger placed his hand on von Deppe's shoulder and shook him gently. Von Deppe woke with a start and looked up at him.

"We must leave for London within the hour. Pack your things. The housekeeper will bring you something to eat shortly," said the stranger.

Von Deppe started to speak but the stranger put his finger to his own lips to silence him.

"I wish to tell you that we will not be alone on our journey back to London," he continued.

"Bolton?" von Deppe asked.

"No," replied the stranger. "It will be the young lady dressed in black who travelled here in the same coach as us. I rescued her from her father yesterday afternoon. She was badly shaken and I brought her here for safety. She is in a room on the floor below. We will leave together to catch the first coach to London."

"Just who are you?" asked Carl Manfred.

"It is better that you do not know," said the stranger. "But rest assured, I am your protector not your enemy. You must continue to trust me."

With that the stranger left the room.

Less than an hour later, early in the morning of Friday, 29 November, the coach that had taken Carl Manfred and the stranger to the place of execution drew up outside the tenement house. The driver appeared to be the same one that had driven them the night before. Three people quickly got inside: Carl Manfred, Arabella, once again veiled, and the stranger, whose identity was still unknown to the two travelling under his protection.

The carriage moved off towards the White Swan Inn near the Market Place. No one spoke. Arabella was profoundly apprehensive at what might lie ahead and still distressed that she had not said goodbye to her mother. Carl Manfred, though deeply fatigued, could not erase the memory of what he had witnessed the previous night. The stranger, though equally exhausted, was as vigilant as ever. He was determined that they should vanish without trace. Covering their tracks and concealing their identity would not be easy. He was already aware of another coach – black, its blinds down – not far behind theirs. He surmised they were being followed.

It was first light by the time they reached the Market Place. The stranger asked them to stay inside the coach while he went to hire a bigger, faster carriage to take them to London. He was ready to grease palms to ensure he got what he wanted. In his absence, Arabella and Carl Manfred remained silent.

After a few minutes, the coach door suddenly opened and Sir Robert Whitfield cried out triumphantly, "I have got you at last. Get out!" He lunged at Arabella, trying to grab her arm. Arabella cried out, retreating across the seat to the far side of the coach to escape her father's outstretched hand. Carl Manfred, at first taken completely by surprise, leaned forward, half rising, to push the intruder back.

The stranger suddenly appeared behind Sir Robert at the open door, and dragged him back onto the road in an iron grip.

"Come with me, you miserable fellow."

Pulling the knife from his sleeve, he held it at Sir Robert's throat, while his left hand gripped the baronet's wrists behind his back. He propelled the speechless Sir Robert towards the nearby black coach and pushed him in, punching him in the stomach as he did so. Slamming the door shut, he instructed the coachman to leave immediately. To make sure he did, the stranger gave the rump of the horse nearest him a hard slap. The coach clattered off down the street.

With the incident having caused a commotion, there was no longer time to secure a fast carriage for their return to London. The stranger decided instead that they would use the smaller coach that had brought them to the square. He ordered the reluctant driver to reload their small amount of baggage and leave for London without further delay. The man quickly stowed the bags and took his seat, but then seemed to hesitate.

"Go now, if you want to be paid," barked the stranger.

Having seen what had just happened and looking down at the menacing long-haired figure below, the driver flicked his whip over the horses and, as the stranger leapt on board, the coach moved off. No one inside spoke and before long Norwich had faded from the horizon.

Sir Robert Whitfield, enraged at the way he had been publicly humiliated in the Market Place, was already plotting his revenge and a renewed attempt to seize his daughter long before the coach reached London. For his part, the stranger was already planning his own countermeasures.

The small coach made fast progress towards London, despite periodic changes of horses. Insisting that he would require one more change of team to complete the journey, the driver stopped at an inn on the edge of desolate heathland about fifty miles from London. Carl Manfred, Arabella and the stranger disembarked and went inside. The room was long and low-ceilinged, with tables and benches stretching its entire length, about half of which were occupied. There was a large fire at one end, with various pots on the hearth. Seeing that his visitors were well-dressed, the landlord offered them an adjacent smaller room for their sole use. The stranger accepted, pressing some coins into the landlord's hand, so ensuring that they would be left alone and that there would be prompt delivery of some bread, cheese, pie and wine. Carl Manfred offered Arabella, still veiled, a seat by the fire in the small room. He sat opposite her, while the stranger sat to one side of him, looking through the half-opened door at the wider room beyond.

"I hear from my companion that you had a deeply upsetting experience in Norwich yesterday," said Carl Manfred in French. "I am glad he was able to protect you."

"He did indeed save me from my father. It was he who tried to grab me this morning," she replied.

"Our thoughts have kept each of us close company on the journey so far, but since we are travelling companions, may I make your acquaintance?" he asked.

Lifting her veil and looking directly at him, she said, "I am Arabella Whitfield and I wish to thank you again – indeed, both of you – for your protection this morning. I am greatly indebted." Sensing that her distress would soon become evident in tears, she made to lower her veil.

"Please, Madame, let us have the pleasure of seeing your face, even though you are understandably still upset by what happened yesterday and this morning," said Carl Manfred.

Arabella blushed and withdrew her hands from her veil. He looked at her. She lowered her eyes in response.

The woman before Carl Manfred was young, tall, slim and attractive, with thick, dark hair, loosely pinned. She was clearly troubled and nervous. Her eyes were heavy, evidence, he thought, of the shedding of many tears during her brief stay in Norwich. Her black dress and coat drained her of colour. But, despite her obvious anguish, there was an inner magnetism about her. He complimented her on her exquisite French.

"My mother is French," she replied. "We spent a year in Paris when I was younger and we always speak French when we are alone. And you, Monsieur, may I make your acquaintance? Where did you learn to speak excellent French, though I venture to suggest from your slight accent that you are not a native of France?"

Carl Manfred's mouth dried suddenly and he instinctively turned to look to the stranger as though for guidance as to how he should reply. Just then the landlord entered and placed some wine and bread on the table, telling his guests that the coachman would be ready for departure well within the hour. The stranger immediately got up and left the room, promising to return shortly after he had checked that this would indeed be the case. Carl Manfred turned to offer wine to his remaining companion.

With the stranger absent, Arabella summoned her courage and, again looking at Carl Manfred directly, said in French, "It would help me greatly, Monsieur, to know your name. After all, you know mine and indeed you have already become acquainted with my father, Sir Robert Whitfield."

She gazed at him with luminous green eyes and a faint smile, as of a player cornering an opponent's piece on the board in the early stage of a game of chess. Carl Manfred looked at Arabella, knowing that she had deftly manoeuvred him to her advantage. He looked momentarily towards the grate, recalling the warmth of the fire in his library at Herzberg many weeks before. He turned back to Arabella, who was still looking at him intently.

"My name is Carl Manfred von Deppe," he replied finally. "My estate is in Prussia, a full day's ride from Berlin. I was once a soldier but now earn a living from my estate. I am in England on confidential business and, as I believe we Prussians are not popular in your country at present, I decided that it would be best if I travelled under the name of Moreau. My French is better than my English. Please, Miss Whitfield," he added, "I should be most grateful if you would not reveal to my companion that I have disclosed my real identity."

Arabella paused and then replied, "Herr von Deppe, I have learned over the past months to be the keeper of many secrets. Yours will remain safe with me until such time as you tell me I am released from my vow of silence on this matter."

She placed her finger to her lips, just as the masked woman had done when she left his room in Shepherd Street.

"I am most grateful, Madame, for your discretion. As soon as we arrive in London, I intend to leave England for Prussia. Thereafter, you will be freed from your promise. And you, Madame, what of your plans?" he asked.

"Monsieur, I am without hope."

At that moment, the stranger re-entered the room to announce that the coach was ready for departure.

After paying the landlord, the three went out into the courtyard. It was dark and cold and a hard frost was beginning to settle on the flagstones. The breath of the horses wafted upwards into the night air. The stranger led the way, with his right hand resting on the left sleeve of his coat. As the stranger turned to speak to the driver, Carl Manfred opened the coach door and gestured to Arabella to mount the step. He held out his right hand to assist her. She placed her hand in his. He grasped it firmly. Once she had stepped inside he released his hold, but observed she retained his hand for a moment longer, looking at him through her veil as she did so. He thought he saw the glisten of tears. She then released him.

Carl Manfred climbed inside and sat opposite her. In the dim light of the lantern within the coach it was difficult to discern her face. As he gazed at the veiled woman in black, he pondered what had led him to disclose his identity to this beautiful, young but obviously most unhappy woman, pursued by a vengeful father. Though he was still haunted by what he had witnessed the night before in the wet, foul-smelling cellar, she had, in their brief moment of conversation, diverted that memory from his mind and somehow caused him to reveal who he really was. He was pleased he had done so. They now knew each other's name and a little of what had brought them together.

The stranger boarded and sat beside him and the coach gathered speed in the dark, each passenger wrapped in their own unspoken thoughts.

Barely thirty minutes after their departure from the inn, the coach suddenly lurched and stopped. The stranger flung open the door to curse the coachman.

"The road is blocked ahead," the coachman shouted back.

The stranger quickly leapt from the carriage. He saw another coach turned sideways across the highway. Standing in front of it were three masked figures with lanterns. The stranger walked towards them, his right hand resting inside his long coat.

"What do you want?" he asked.

The three men now brandished the pistols they had been using the light of the lanterns to hide.

"We want the girl with whom you are travelling," one of the men replied.

"Get out of the way," replied the stranger as he pulled his sword from beneath his coat. "There is nothing for you."

As the stranger was speaking, Carl Manfred appeared beside him.

"What do they want?" he asked in English.

"They want us to hand over the young lady travelling with us. I have said that is not possible and told them to get out of the way."

Neither side moved.

Arabella stepped forward, having overheard the stranger's reply as she approached from the carriage.

"I will go with them, Messieurs," she said. "I do not know who they are, but I will put my trust in their mercy. It is not right that I should detain you from your destination."

"Madame, please return to the coach and let us resolve this matter in our own way. You are in our safekeeping and that will remain the case. Please, return to the coach at once," said Carl Manfred.

Arabella hesitated.

"Madame, please return to the coach at once," he repeated sharply.

As Arabella turned back, the man in the middle of the three masked men raised his pistol as though to take aim at her. The stranger's sword flashed in the light of the lanterns and the pistol fell to the ground. The man screamed in agony as he clutched his bloodied fingers. A second man took aim but again the sword flashed. The man fell to the ground, clutching his arm. The third masked man dropped his weapon in submission.

The stranger bent down. Pulling the mask from the face of the man with the injured arm, he thrust it towards the uninjured man and told him to apply a tourniquet to his comrade. He then pulled the mask from the man with the injured hand.

"So it is you. I wondered when we would meet. If you cross our path again, I promise I will kill you, something I should have done long ago."

Turning again to the uninjured man, the stranger said, "Turn back and take your friends to a surgeon for treatment. Hurry, man. Get out of our way."

Pulling his two companions to their feet, the uninjured man led them back to their coach. It turned and quickly went back in the direction from which the stranger, Carl Manfred and Arabella had just come.

Looking up at their driver, who seemed dumbstruck by what he had seen, the stranger said, "Get us to London without further delay and, when there, say nothing about this incident. If you do, I will surely find and punish you."

The coach began its final stage to London. The three sat in silence. Arabella was frozen with fear at what she had witnessed. Carl Manfred, seated beside her, looked out of the window into the darkness beyond. Then, turning to the stranger, he asked, "Who was the man you said you recognised?"

The stranger paused and then said in a soft voice, "His name is George Whitfield. I believe he is Miss Whitfield's brother. He is also the man who killed your brother in Paris after a game of cards."

On hearing this, Arabella gasped and began to tremble violently. Carl Manfred looked at the stranger in disbelief.

"Surely you are mistaken," he pressed.

The stranger replied that he was not. "Your brother, Frederick Ludwig, travelled to Paris shortly before his death in pursuit of a certain young lady, who was there with her father. Frederick Ludwig, who, as you are aware, liked to play for high stakes at cards, met George Whitfield, who was staying with his friends. They played cards over several evenings. He lost and his debts mounted. He then began to suspect that Whitfield was cheating, though he could not be sure. The next evening they played again. Your brother's suspicions of Whitfield increased, and there and then he accused him of cheating. Whitfield vigorously denied the accusation and challenged Frederick Ludwig to a duel. They agreed to meet at dawn the next day. But Whitfield and some ruffians accosted your brother the same evening on his way to his lodgings and after further argument Whitfield shot him in cold blood."

"How do you know this?" Carl Manfred asked.

"I know because I saw it all happen – at the game of cards and later in the Rue Croyer."

"Why did you not intervene?" asked Carl Manfred.

"Monsieur, I live in the shadows, where it is my duty to be. I see things but I cannot always intervene in matters that do not directly concern me or my master."

"Who is your master?" asked Carl Manfred.

"We are all but pieces on his chessboard," replied the stranger.

Behind her veil, Arabella was deeply distressed to hear what her brother was alleged to have done. Her turmoil was now even greater. She was in a coach, heading back to London, with two men, both foreigners, whom she knew little about. One had injured two people, including her brother, who was said to have killed Herr von Deppe's brother in Paris. The other had known her intimately, though did not yet recognise her as his masked night-time guest. Her head was spinning. She had no abode in London and was completely severed from her family. Though her companions had saved her from whatever punishment her father had so far planned, her future situation appeared even more hopeless. She dreaded the fate that might now await her if she ever went back to Meltwater – freely or against her will.

Sensing her distress, Carl Manfred placed his hand on her clasped fingers.

"Madame, you must not upset yourself. You are safe with us. My companion and I have to leave England as quickly as possible, since today's events mean even more people will likely be looking for us, including, I venture, your father. However, we will do all that we can to leave you in safe hands. Meanwhile, try to sleep. We will wake you as we near our destination."

Arabella unclasped her fingers and clutched Carl Manfred's hand tightly. She fell asleep without letting go.

In case Arabella should wake and hear them speaking in French, the stranger whispered to Carl Manfred in German. "On our arrival, I will take you to a safe address in London, so you can refresh yourself. But within a day you must be on your way to Dover to catch the first available boat to Calais. Neither you nor I are safe in England. I will follow close behind, once I have completed some unfinished business. We will take the girl with us to the safe house, but she cannot stay there for long. Her father and brother will pursue her relentlessly and us as well. I will try to find her another safe place to stay. We must not forget that others will be after us too. Every day boats go out to pull debris from the river in Norwich. It is almost certain that by now the body of the man we executed will have been fished out of the water. I very much hope that Bolton removed all evidence of identity from the body, but I cannot be sure, as he declined to let me check. I smell possible trickery."

Carl Manfred nodded in assent. A few minutes later, he turned to the stranger. "I propose that Miss Whitfield travels with me to Dover and on to Paris. There she can stay with my sister until other arrangements can be made for her safety."

"I believe such a step would be most unwise," replied the stranger. "What we have done in the King's name already risks being exposed. We do not want to increase that risk unnecessarily. The sooner you are on your way from England to Berlin to give the King the confirmation he is expecting the better. I am sure I can find the girl a secure refuge in London."

Carl Manfred replied, "I wish to take her with me. I have little doubt of the fate that awaits her if she falls into the hands of her father and brother. The safety available in London is nothing compared to the greater comfort and security afforded by Paris. The deviation en route to Berlin will be only temporary."

The two men debated Arabella's fate for some time but Carl Manfred insisted that his mind was made up.

The driver called out that they would be entering London shortly. Carl Manfred withdrew his hand from Arabella's.

"Miss Whitfield, please wake up. We are almost in London."

Arabella adjusted her veil but made no response other than, "Thank you."

"On arrival in London," continued Carl Manfred, "we will go immediately to a safe house pending my departure for France as soon as possible. My companion and I are agreed that it would be best if you were to travel with me as far as Paris, where I will arrange for you to stay with my sister, Madame Maria Louisa de Vervins, and her husband, Captain Etienne de Vervins. Once you are in their safe hands, I will take my leave and proceed on my way. I am sure my sister and her husband will help to find you a place of comfort and safety, and perhaps a new life away from those so set on your destruction."

"I cannot accept your offer," said Arabella. "You and your companion have already done so much for me. I am sure I will find a way to disappear in London, as I have done before."

The stranger countered, "Is that what you really want? To be alone, at great risk and with no prospect of happiness so long as your father and brother are searching the streets of London for you? We have left a trail of blood and they will surely seek revenge. As an alleged accomplice, your life may now be in grave danger."

"Sir, I do not know what to do or where to turn," Arabella replied. "I feel so lost. I have made so many mistakes – and I have no papers, so how can I travel?"

Carl Manfred once again placed his hand on hers and said, "It is decided. You will come with me to Paris. In the meantime, you must place full trust in us. Do exactly as we tell you. I promise no harm will come to you. You can depend on us completely."

Arabella, exhausted, nodded.

Within a short while, in the very early hours of Saturday, 30 November, the coach arrived at Charing Cross. The stranger stepped down and beckoned the driver to dismount. Paying him half the sum due, he asked him to take them immediately to an address north of Tyburn, where he would receive the rest owing to him and they would agree another task for which he would be handsomely paid. The coach turned north. Though it was early in the morning and still dark, London life was already stirring. As they passed Tyburn, the occupants of the coach saw two bodies swaying from the gallows, yet to be cut down from their execution. Arabella shuddered and gripped Carl Manfred's hand. His mouth felt dry as he too contemplated the bodies. His fate, Miss Whitfield's and that of the stranger could well end on the gallows if they were not nimble and expeditious in their plans to leave England. Sir Robert Whitfield and his son remained dangerous pursuers.

A few minutes later, the coach stopped outside a terraced house in elegant Cleveland Square, representative of the latest style of genteel properties being built in the newer residential parts of London. The stranger instructed Arabella and Carl Manfred to go inside. He and the driver removed the few items of baggage, including Arabella's elegant box. As he picked the box up, the lid opened and the stranger caught a glimpse of a beautiful gold mask inside. He quickly snapped the lid shut. The mask confirmed beyond doubt that Arabella Whitfield was indeed the young woman whom Bolton had sent twice to Carl Manfred's room in Shepherd Street.

Re-emerging from the house, the stranger asked the driver to take the horses to a nearby mews, where, from information obtained earlier, he knew there were stables. They travelled together on the front box, without speaking. They entered the stables, where the stable-boy took charge of the horses. After instructing the boy to have fresh horses ready within hours, the stranger invited the driver to accompany him to a nearby tavern, to complete payment for the journey from Norwich and, over some ale, to agree terms for a new journey later that day. As they walked down the street, the stranger said he wished to take a shortcut through a passageway. A few paces into the dimly lit alley, he suddenly turned and, thrusting the driver against the wall, grasped him tightly by the throat.

"I saw you pass information at the coaching inn to the men who blocked our way. I am going to kill you. Treachery carries a high price in my eyes."

Using his left hand to pin the driver against the wall by the neck, with his right the stranger pulled his knife from his coat sleeve and plunged it into the man's chest. The man's eyes bulged and blood trickled from his mouth. Moments later, the body slumped to the ground. The stranger shed no tears. Anyone who crossed him paid with their life.

The stranger quickly rummaged through the driver's pockets, removing the leather money bag he had given him earlier. He pulled the knife from the man's chest, rolled the body onto its back and dragged it by the arms further down the alley until he reached an open drain into which he tipped it. The body made a splash and then sank beneath the water. The stranger turned. He caught a fleeting glimpse of the dark outline of a man standing at the end of the alley in the beam of a street light, looking towards him. He ran to the end of the alley. Scanning left and then right, he saw in the dim street light the shape of a figure walking quickly away. As the figure half turned to look over his shoulder, to check whether he were being pursued, the stranger thought he recognised the face half concealed by the darkness. He did not follow.

The stranger walked briskly back to the house in Cleveland Square that Carl Manfred and Arabella had entered shortly before. It was a safe house, which the stranger had personally selected through his spy network; he had chosen not to reveal it to John Bolton, who had a separate stopping point of his own on Carl Manfred's route out of England. Situated some ten minutes' brisk walk from the gallows at Tyburn, it was a three-storey town house with a basement, recently built in the new Georgian style then flourishing in London. The housekeeper was an elderly widow, Mrs Hobson. Stooped by age but still spry and with a finely chiselled face, she spoke in elegant and concise English, suggesting that it may not have been her native tongue. When the stranger entered the downstairs parlour, she was speaking to Carl Manfred and Arabella. They turned to look at him. His face was etched with fatigue. His clothes were travel-stained. His general appearance was unkempt.

"Your rooms are ready. I will serve breakfast within the hour. You can then tell me how long you intend to stay," said Mrs Hobson with a warm smile.

"Thank you," said the stranger. "In fact, we will leave in less than two hours, as we have much distance to cover."

With that Mrs Hobson showed her guests to their rooms on the second floor. As they went upstairs, the stranger whispered to Carl Manfred that they should meet shortly to discuss the journey ahead.

Within the half hour, the two men gathered in the first-floor drawing room. They spoke in hushed voices.

"We need to get out of London quickly," said the stranger, "and you must be on your way to Berlin as soon as possible. There is blood on our hands and I am sure the girl's father and brother will try their hardest to track us down. The father wants to remove her as an obstacle to his career. The brother will want revenge for what happened on the road last night."

"We will need a coach for our journey," said Carl Manfred.

"That is not a problem," said the stranger. "The coach we used from Norwich is still intact and should serve our purpose."

"But what of the driver?" asked Carl Manfred.

"He has been paid and is now gone, never to return," replied the stranger. "The coach and horses are in a nearby mews. They will provide a fresh driver and a fresh team."

"I must remind you that I promised Miss Whitfield that she could accompany me to Paris," said Carl Manfred. "Do you still object?"

"It was intended that only we should leave England to travel to Berlin," replied the stranger. "Whether she accompanies you or not is a matter for you to decide. But in the present difficult circumstances I agree that it is probably better if she comes with us. Besides, she knows too much about us to leave her behind. I am sure she will suffer an ugly fate if she falls into her father's hands."

The door handle turned and Arabella entered the room. She had changed from her black dress into the green one that Mrs Hallam had given her to take to Shepherd Street. A black shawl lay across her shoulders. Her hair was pinned back from her face but fell loosely at the back of her neck. Her face was pale and she looked tired, her eyes still showing signs of earlier emotion. Both men stood up.

"I wish to thank you both again for your great kindness and protection over the last two days. My life has been most difficult since I ran away from home earlier this year. You will have guessed from what you have seen why I took such a desperate step. I understand you have been in England on important business and that with the approach of Christmas you will wish to be on your way. Please, I insist, do not delay on my account or allow me to stand in the way of your departure. I will go back to my earlier lodgings. I am sure they will allow me to stay there."

As she finished speaking, Arabella's voice began to crack with emotion. She reached inside her sleeve for a handkerchief. Carl Manfred stepped forward and proffered his own.

"You are right, Miss Whitfield," he said. "Our business in England is now complete, and we must be on our way as quickly as possible. However, it is clear that your father – and, indeed, your brother – have a score to settle with you, albeit an unjust and unjustified one, and with us too. They will clearly stop at nothing to do so. For that reason, my friend and I have already firmly resolved to proceed with the plan we proposed last night. You will accompany me to Paris, where you can consider your future in the peace and safety of my sister's house. You would be in mortal danger if you stayed in London. Provided there is no unexpected delay, we will leave for Dover within the next hour or so, if not sooner."

No longer possessing the strength to argue and more afraid than ever of staying in London, even in Shepherd Street as Antoinette Badeau, Arabella replied, "You are most kind, sir." She sat down by the fire, lost in her thoughts.

The stranger said, "That being resolved, I will tell Mrs Hobson of our decision."

Carl Manfred drew up a chair to sit close to the fire. He looked at Arabella. Though tear-stained and fatigued, her face, framed in her long loosely pinned hair, was finely drawn. With striking poise and great elegance of movement, she turned to look at him and gave him a gentle smile. Carl Manfred responded by taking her hand in his and, without thinking, raised it to his lips. He kissed it lightly. As he did so, he felt emotion stirring within him. She looked at him and he at her. They said nothing. Then Arabella gently withdrew her hand and whispered, "Thank you, kind sir."

"I am at your command, Miss Whitfield," he replied.

The stranger re-entered the room, shed of his long coat and with his hair tied back with a black ribbon, and announced that breakfast was ready in the parlour. Carl Manfred and Arabella followed him down the staircase. He offered her his hand, which she took in hers. Their bodies lightly touched as they descended the narrow staircase side by side. At the bottom, she withdrew her hand as he gestured her to walk in front of him along the similarly narrow passage to the parlour. He gazed at her back. There was something erotic about its straightness and the movement of her long dark hair, which floated around her neck. He was more determined than ever that he would escort this young, beautiful but sad woman to Paris, whatever the risk.

After a rapid breakfast, at which she hardly ate, Arabella returned to her room. Her journey from Meltwater had taken a further turn into darkness. There were no longer any familiar landmarks in her life. Dark sky and bleak landscape had merged into one. She was more fearful than ever of what lay ahead and of the fate that awaited her if she fell into her father's hands. There was now no going back. In her mind, she heard one heavy door after another slamming shut behind her. She drew comfort from the proximity of a man whose bed she had shared twice in London. His kiss on her hand in the drawing room and the firmness with which he had held her hand as they descended the staircase reminded her of the way he had held her tightly in his bed and his reluctance to let her go. Arabella accepted that they were in parallel worlds. Despite the way he had looked at her in front of the fire, the prospect of moving from her world to his seemed remote. But she resolved to find a way to bring their two worlds closer together, if only for the duration of the journey to Paris, and so perhaps begin to find the happiness she earnestly sought. Might it be with him? But that was surely a fantasy.

Barely had Arabella sat in a chair and fallen asleep than Mrs Hobson knocked on the door.

"The two gentlemen are downstairs," she said. "They wish to leave for Dover immediately."

Arabella got up hastily and rejoined Carl Manfred and the stranger in the parlour.

"I have reason to think," said the stranger, "from something I saw much earlier this morning that spies may soon become aware of our presence in this area and will organise a search of the neighbourhood to find us. We must leave swiftly before they come knocking on the door of this house."

Arabella turned white with fear.

"Miss Whitfield," continued the stranger in a matter-of-fact tone, "we need to disguise you if we are to leave London safely. I have spoken to Mrs Hobson and she has found some men's clothing for you to wear. Please go and change as quickly as you can, while I go to fetch the carriage."

Before Arabella could respond, Mrs Hobson took her upstairs to another bedroom. On the bed lay a pair of brown leather breeches, some thick white woollen stockings, a white shirt and a black waistcoat, a deep-blue military-style knee-length jacket, a long heavy black coat and a cocked hat.

"These used to belong to my son before he was killed in the wars. They may not fit you well but I trust they will serve their purpose. Let me help you change. But first we will have to make you flat-chested."

Mrs Hobson bound white cloth tightly around Arabella's chest, securing it in place with a strong double knot at the back.

"It is important, my dear, that your breasts do not give you away in your new disguise," she said.

Arabella put on the white shirt and breeches. They were tight, but without restricting movement. Mrs Hobson helped Arabella into the waistcoat and jacket, and then drew her hair back into a tail, which she tied with black ribbon at the nape of her neck. Turning to a cupboard, Mrs Hobson pulled out a pair of high, black leather boots with stacked heels and square toes. Arabella put them on with some effort; they were stiff from lack of use and were obviously meant to be worn by someone with much bigger feet than hers. Removing them she put on an extra pair of stockings. This time the boots fitted better. They were considerably heavier than the ankle-style riding boots she had been used to wearing at Meltwater. Arabella stood up. Mrs Hobson then held out the overcoat for her to try on – it was a little large but it would do – wrapped a black silk scarf around her neck and, lastly, handed her the tricorne.

Arabella looked at herself in the mirror. She was transformed. She bowed deeply to the image in the mirror.

"Miss Whitfield has become Mr Whitfield," remarked Mrs Hobson.

Arabella shuddered at the sound of the name Mr Whitfield.

"Now you must go downstairs and try to eat a morsel more before you leave," said Mrs Hobson.

Helped by Mrs Hobson, Arabella packed her dresses and few belongings, her sigh as she put away her music book unheard by the housekeeper. She made sure her precious box was firmly closed, the ribbon securely tied. Carrying her bag and the box, and already feeling the constraint of the binding around her chest, she returned downstairs. Mrs Hobson followed with the long overcoat. When she entered the parlour, Arabella found only Carl Manfred inside.

He gasped visibly when he saw her. Dressed as a man, her slender figure and height were pleasingly highlighted by the tight-fitting clothes. The boots emphasised her long slim legs. Arabella Whitfield looked even more beautiful and striking than she had the evening before. Carl Manfred stood behind her as he helped her to draw in her chair to sit at the breakfast table, urging her to try to eat a little more. He momentarily brushed her arm with his fingertips as he moved away towards the window to look for the stranger. She wished that he had lingered longer behind her.

Arabella studied him as he gazed out of the window. Tall and handsome (even more so than in his portrait) but with sad eyes, he seemed preoccupied. While he said he was looking out for the return of the coach, his gaze seemed to be more distant, beyond the bounds of Cleveland Square. What was he thinking of? Was he thinking of her? She had twice made love to him, but disguised by Antoinette Badeau's mask. He did not know that the hand he had held last night was the hand that had caressed him days before. As she recalled the intensity of those earlier encounters, she felt her nipples harden beneath their tight binding. She began to blush. Arabella resolved there and then that during the journey to Paris she would find the means to make her affection towards him more evident, in the hope that he might reciprocate. But dressed as a man this would not be easy. What she did not know was that at that very moment she was indeed uppermost in Carl Manfred's mind. He was thinking how much he wanted to kiss her.

A few moments later the coach they had used the day before, but now driven by an elderly wizened coachman, drew up outside the house. The stranger quickly entered and said they had no more time to lose. There was a commotion in the next square as a vigilante crowd went from house to house looking for a woman and two male companions on the grounds of possible attempted murder on the highway and a brutal murder in the neighbourhood. After bundling their baggage into the carriage and saying a hasty farewell to Mrs Hobson, the stranger, Carl Manfred and Arabella – a convincing young man in her boots and greatcoat – climbed inside and the coach moved off. First it turned north and then, after several twists and turns, west, past Tyburn and its gallows – with the bodies still hanging – and after a while headed south towards Dover. The stranger said that it would be necessary to stop at Ashford to relinquish the coach. The remainder of the journey to Dover would be covered on horseback. Their escape from England had begun.

After a stop at a coaching inn to water and briefly rest the horses, they arrived eventually at the Warren Inn in Ashford well after dark. As they stepped from the coach, Arabella observed that it was now much colder than in London and the strong gusts of wind carried snowflakes. She wound her scarf more tightly around her neck, and pulled her long coat tightly around her and her tricorne further down over her face. Carl Manfred stood with her in the courtyard. The stranger pressed several silver pieces into the hand of the coachman who had brought them from London, telling him that his services were no longer needed and that he should immediately go inside and get warm.

The stranger slowly opened the door of the Warren Inn. The room was crowded. He stood in the half-open doorway, quickly scrutinising those inside, while alert for danger and rapid escape. In the corner he noticed a man facing him, leaning across a table talking earnestly to a man whose back was to the door. The latter was difficult to recognise because his coat collar was turned up, but there was something about the hunched figure that reminded the stranger of someone he thought he had seen before. Then, holding a jug in his hand, the man got up to beckon one of the serving women for a refill. As he stood, his coat half slipped from his shoulders. The stranger recognised the large round engraved brass buttons on the coat. He had seen them before. Why was the man with the buttons at the Warren Inn? Was his presence planned or fortuitous? Then he remembered. He had seen similar buttons on the coachman of the Whitfield coach in Norwich.

The stranger decided that it was not safe to enter. They were likely to be spotted and risked being apprehended. He walked quickly round to the stables at the back of the inn and asked one of the local coachmen if there was another inn nearby, since the man they had expected to meet was not inside. It was possible their rendezvous was at another establishment. The coachman said that the two nearest were the Oak, six miles away, or the Flying Swan post-house, ten miles away.

"Can you take three passengers to either?" asked the stranger.

"I am afraid I cannot but I am sure the stable-boy can give you three horses for a small fee."

The stranger paused and, accepting the coachman's advice, went in search of the stable-boy. It was safer to be on their way than risk being seen at the Warren.

"Bring three saddled horses, with side bags and some straps, round to the front as soon as you can," he instructed, placing a silver coin into the boy's hand.

The stranger returned to the courtyard and turning to Carl Manfred and Arabella said, "We cannot enter. I mistrust this place. We could be in danger if we go inside. We will go instead to the Flying Swan, some ten miles away on horseback. The horses are coming in a minute. Miss Whitfield, you can ride, I presume?"

"I can indeed, sir," she replied.

A minute or two later, the stable-boy brought three horses into the courtyard.

"These are the best I have."

"Have you got the straps?" asked the stranger.

"Yes," he replied, pulling them from his coat pocket.

"Which way to the Flying Swan?"

"Turn left outside the yard, follow the road for a mile or so and then take the right-hand fork," answered the boy. "If you prefer the Oak, as it is less far to travel in this weather, you take the left-hand fork."

"We'll go the Oak. Tuppence if you give me your lantern, boy. That's all. You can go now."

The boy handed over the lantern and then ran back towards the stable.

"Quickly, let us mount and be gone," urged the stranger.

Carl Manfred helped Arabella to mount her horse.

"I will sit astride," she said. "I have done so before."

As the words left her mouth, she recalled how she had sat astride Carl Manfred in his bed as he fondled her breasts. She knew she was blushing and was glad he could not see her doing so in the darkness.

"Good heavens, your hands are so cold!" said Carl Manfred. "Please take my gloves." He pulled leather gloves from his coat pocket.

"You are most kind, sir," she said as she put them on. They were warm from the heat of his body.

She watched as the stranger placed her box inside the saddlebag behind her and strapped her leather case onto the saddle. He did the same for Carl Manfred and then for himself. All mounted, they moved forward, with Carl Manfred in front, Arabella behind him and the stranger at the rear.

As the stranger left the yard, he turned back to see a black coach with four horses just entering it. He thought he glimpsed the Whitfield crest beneath the mud on the coach door. The stranger was now sure that their escape route had been compromised. If he was correct, the King had been betrayed once again. Whoever was responsible would suffer the ultimate penalty. He pressed his heels into his horse and slapped its side. Coming abreast of Arabella and then Carl Manfred, he shouted, "I think our presence here may have been discovered. I told the stable-boy we would go to the Oak. But in case he reveals our intention, we will go instead to the Flying Swan, change horses there and proceed without delay to Dover harbour."

He spurred his horse on and took the lead, with Arabella and Carl Manfred at her side following closely behind.

Though it was pitch black and the snow was now falling heavily, making the road treacherous, led by the stranger and his lantern they rode as fast as they could, reaching the Flying Swan Inn in under two hours. It was bitterly cold. After a prior surveillance by the stranger, the three entered. It was nearly midnight and there were few inside. The stranger asked for some bread, cheese and wine and for the fire to be stoked. Once warmed, Carl Manfred and Arabella removed their overcoats. The three said little. After eating, the stranger asked for the use of a room in which to rest until the early morning, when they intended to leave. The landlord offered a small room with a large bed, covered with rough blankets. The stranger said he would remain downstairs by the fire as great vigilance was necessary. Carl Manfred said he would do the same as they had business to discuss. He escorted Arabella to the bedroom, resisting the temptation to offer his arm within sight of the landlord. They entered the room and Carl Manfred closed the door behind them.

"Good night, Miss Whitfield," he said. "I will wake you at four o'clock. By five o'clock we must be on our way, whatever the weather. You have been most brave – both today and yesterday. You have my greatest respect. My companion and I will guard you with great care until you are with my sister in Paris. In the meantime, I fear we may have other difficulties to overcome. We will do everything to protect you from harm. Please be steadfast."

Then placing the candle on a low table beside the door, he gently removed her hat and, placing his hands lightly on her arms, leaned forward and kissed her cheek. He stepped back in obvious embarrassment.

"I apologise, Miss Whitfield. I should not have taken advantage of you. Please forgive me."

He made to leave but she caught his arm. She kissed him on his cheek and then whispered, "I thank you, and your companion, for all that you have done for me. I gladly entrust my life to your hands."

Bowing to her, Carl Manfred turned and left the room.

Arabella sat for a while on the bed. There was no sound other than the snap and hiss of the wood burning in the small fireplace and the wind blowing outside. She got up and pulled back the sacking covering the window. The ground was already well-covered in snow. She lay down on the bed. Her body was aching after the ride from the Warren Inn and a lack of proper sleep for days. The leather breeches were uncomfortable. Her breasts were sore beneath the tight binding. She wished to remove her heavy boots, but decided it was better to leave them on in case rapid departure were needed, so she removed only her jacket. Then lying back down on the bed, she spread her jacket and greatcoat over her and wrapped herself in one of the thick musty blankets. She lay on her side looking at the fire. Though her body was sore and aching, her mind found relief in reflecting that the man she had met in London had kissed her hand and now her cheek, not because she was Antoinette Badeau, the woman in the mask, but because she was Arabella Whitfield. Their parallel worlds had physically touched, if only for a moment. She still faced mortal danger, but Arabella now realised her affection for Carl Manfred von Deppe was possibly the beginning of love. She huddled tighter under the blanket, closed her eyes and placing her hands between her legs to keep warm, rocked herself to sleep thinking of the nights she had lain close to him.

Arabella awoke to a tap on the door. It was Sunday, 1 December 1765 – the first day of Advent. Recollections of Advents past had no time to take hold as she heard Carl Manfred's voice.

"It is time to get up," he called softly. "There is a jug of hot water and a fresh candle outside your door. We must leave as quickly as possible."

Arabella thanked him. She left the bed still huddled in the musty blanket and groped her way across the room guided by the faint candlelight penetrating beneath the door. She slid back the bolt and retrieved the candle, the hot water and a bowl. The room was cold and so was she – cold and stiff. The fire had gone out. She opened the curtain slightly. It was still dark but a bright moon shone from a clear sky, revealing deep snow. After washing her face and hands in the warm water, she retied her hair tightly back in its black ribbon and put on her jacket and then her overcoat, finally winding the black scarf around her neck. The more she moved the tighter the restrictive binding around her chest became. Her boots had become even more uncomfortable. But this was the clothing she knew she would have to wear if she were to escape to Paris.

She joined Carl Manfred and the stranger downstairs. After some beer and a slice of bread and jam, they went outside to saddle, load and mount fresh horses. The landlord encouraged them to stay on account of the weather but the stranger said their urgent business drove them on. Telling him of their intention to ride to Canterbury, in order to mislead anyone who might come asking for their whereabouts, the three riders changed direction out of sight of the inn and set off for Dover. The morning was bitingly cold and fast movement was difficult in the snow. But the stranger urged them on. He knew that their pursuers could be hard on their heels, now they had information about their quarry's destination from a privileged source, as he was sure was the case. Arabella hid her face behind her scarf. After a short break at another coaching inn and a long and arduous climb up the steep hills that encircled Dover, they reached the point where they were able to look down at the harbour. They pressed on, finally arriving in the town, deeply fatigued.

Avoiding the coaching inn on Bolton's list, the stranger led them to another inn further along the seafront. There they dispensed with the horses and proceeded on foot, constantly and deliberately changing direction in case they were followed, until they came to a shabby-looking house behind a warehouse.

"We will be safe here while we wait for a boat," said the stranger.

A shrivelled but sharp-eyed and beak-nosed man answered the door.

"Oh, it's you. Welcome," he said to the stranger. "Come in and warm yourselves by the fire. The young man looks exhausted."

After drinking mulled wine and eating some pie, their spirits were restored.

"We want a boat to France as quickly as possible, tomorrow if not today," said the stranger.

"You may be here for longer. There is a queue of people trying to get to France before Christmas," replied the old man. "The only way to leave quickly is to find a boatman who will take you across at short notice. But that will be expensive."

"That is not a problem," said the stranger. "We cannot wait days. We must leave by tomorrow morning."

At the hint of money to be made, the old man suggested accompanying the stranger to the dockside taverns without delay to find such a boat. Within a few minutes they were gone, leaving Carl Manfred and Arabella sitting in front of the hearth.

"You look exhausted, Miss Whitfield. Come closer to the fire," said Carl Manfred.

"May I sit beside you, sir?"

"Indeed, you may," he replied.

She sat beside him on the settle and placed her head on his shoulder. For a while, both said nothing. They just stared into the flames. A few minutes later, Carl Manfred noticed Arabella had fallen asleep. He placed his right hand over her clasped fingers and continued to gaze into the fire. Outside the wind howled off the sea.

Later that afternoon, the stranger and the old man returned. Hearing them at the front door, Carl Manfred quickly woke Arabella and withdrew his hand from hers. Still half asleep, she returned to her chair.

"We have found a small boat that will take us to Calais at first light, despite the weather," the stranger announced. "But as the tide will be going out there can be no delay in our embarkation. If we are too late, the boat will be stranded and we may have to wait another day. We cannot allow that to happen. The crossing will be rough in the present wind but it is best that we do not linger here. My friend here" – pointing to the old man – "will provide us with some more food. But there will be no chance to sleep in a bed."

After the old man had left the room, the stranger turned to Arabella.

"The excise men are closely examining all activity at the docks. We have papers but you do not. As you cannot remain here, we must hide you in a box for the duration of the crossing to France. There is no alternative. Please come with me."

Arabella and Carl Manfred followed him through the house to an attached warehouse. In a corner were some large empty boxes. The stranger looked appraisingly at Arabella and then pulled a large, long, empty wooden crate into the middle of the floor. He removed the loose lid.

"Get inside and lie on your side," he said to Arabella.

The memory of her journey in the trunk from Mrs Hallam's house to Mrs Rathbone's flooded back. She lay down inside and the lid was put loosely in place. After a few moments, the stranger removed it and Carl Manfred helped her out.

"Good, that is settled," said the stranger. "We will seal you in the box and then take you by cart to the dockside. Whatever you do and however uncomfortable you may be, you must not make a sound. Do you understand?"

Arabella nodded, though inwardly terrified by the prospect of the journey that lay ahead.

The three ate well and slept as best they could near the large fire. The wind continued to blow.

At half past three the following morning, Carl Manfred woke Arabella. She took a jug of hot water to a neighbouring room, where she washed her face and prepared for the ordeal ahead. She felt exhausted. Her feet were painful in her boots and her breasts were now deeply sore from the rigid linen binding that had tightened even further. She returned to join the others, ate some bread and jam, and then, at the stranger's command, they retraced their steps to the warehouse, Arabella clutching the box containing her mask, Carl Manfred carrying her bag.

Still in the middle of the floor, where the stranger had dragged it, the box was ready for her. It had been lined with thick blankets and a small pillow, and two holes had been made at each end, above a leather strap, for ventilation. On the lid of the crate, in strong letters in both English and French, had been written the words: "PORCELAIN FOR HIS MAJESTY KING FREDERICK FROM HIS MAJESTY KING GEORGE. HANDLE WITH GREAT CARE." Nearby were a hammer and nails.

The stranger beckoned her to step inside. Carl Manfred moved forward and took her hand. He squeezed it and raised it to his lips. He looked intensely into her eyes. She looked into his and as she did so her eyes began to fill with tears.

"No time for those," he said. He handed her his handkerchief and placed a finger to her lips.

She stepped into the box. She moved to lie down but the stranger asked her to remain standing. Pulling from his pocket two of the leather straps used to secure the saddlebags on the ride from Ashford, he bound her wrists and then her ankles.

"Is that really necessary?" Carl Manfred asked.

The stranger reproved him.

"We have already been betrayed," he replied sharply. "Moreover, our various enemies are likely to have spies on the waterfront. Our lives depend on this crate not being opened. If the excise men at the harbour, or the boatman, hear one sound or detect the slightest movement inside the box, they will open it and we will all be done for. We will go to the gallows, convicted of spying and attempted murder on the highway. And Miss Whitfield will not escape judicial retribution either. It is thus a matter of life and death – ours– that we get her to Calais in an unopened crate. To make certain that happens, we have to ensure she resists the temptation, however strong, to move or call out. We can, of course, leave Miss Whitfield here, but her father will soon find her. He will either dispose of her or incarcerate her in a lunatic asylum. What is it to be?"

Arabella responded immediately and clearly. "Do whatever is necessary."

Pulling a strip of fabric from his pocket, the stranger gagged her, tying a firm knot at the back of her head. Together, he and Carl Manfred then laid the gagged and bound Arabella onto the thick blankets in the crate, with her legs drawn up beneath her. The stranger placed her box beneath her raised arms and put her leather bag behind her feet. He padded the remaining empty space above and around her with more blankets. Then he placed the lid in position and nailed it down.

Bending to the small ventilation hole at the end of the crate nearest Arabella's head, he said, "Within the hour you will be on your way to the harbour for loading onto the boat. Within twenty-four hours, if all goes well, you will be in Calais. Have faith, Miss Whitfield."

Arabella heard the sound of their footsteps receding. The pencil of light through the hole was extinguished. Now in total darkness, she tried to move but could not. The stranger had done his job well. The gag was tight in her mouth, her wrists and ankles equally firmly bound. Her body was wedged in place by the blanket padding. Her breasts were still painful under the binding. Arabella's fate was sealed in a suffocating box. She fought back the tears, determined to regain her composure. In the months past she had often prayed to escape the perilous world of the courtesan before it was too late. Her flight from Norwich, and now from England, in the company of a man with whom she believed she may have fallen in love, made her unshakeably resolved to stay alive in her coffin during the hazardous journey ahead. She had placed her trust in him. If this cruel imprisonment was the price to pay for liberty and a new life in Paris, she was prepared to suffer it. She was convinced that Carl Manfred von Deppe would not let her die – in the crate or on the gallows. Arabella became drowsy and soon slipped into a world of vivid and flashing incoherent images, some more disturbing than others.

Suddenly she awoke to several voices. The first to speak was the stranger's.

"The tide is about to turn. We must leave immediately for the dockside."

The next to speak was the old man.

"I have been down to the quayside. The boat is ready. It is small but sufficient for your purposes. But the place is heavy with excise men –"

"And," interrupted the stranger, "with thieves, spies and cutthroats looking for spoil. I suspect Whitfield's agents are amongst them, some of whom are able to identify us."

Carl Manfred spoke.

"I agree that we should leave now. Another day spent in England increases the risk of apprehension and my return to Berlin being further delayed. Besides, we cannot keep Miss Whitfield sealed in the box longer than necessary. If we do not hurry, she will die of suffocation."

A few minutes later the three men lifted the crate and carried it a short distance before sliding it onto the back of a cart. They then placed other merchandise on top of and around it. The voices became muted. Then the cart began to move.

It was now six o'clock, with barely a trace of morning light in the dark sky. The old man, with the stranger and Carl Manfred sitting beside him their hats pulled down low over their faces, drove the cart towards the harbour. At the entrance, two men in dirty uniforms gestured the cart to stop.

"What have you got in the back?" one asked.

"Some wool and porcelain from His Majesty King George to His Majesty King Frederick of Prussia," the old man replied.

The stranger passed them a forged document.

"Let us have a look."

"We have no time," the stranger replied. "The tide is on the turn and we must get His Majesty's consignment on the way before Christmas Day."

"What's it worth?" came the response.

Pulling a note from his pocket, the stranger replied, "I am sure His Majesty King George can afford five pounds."

"Why, sir, most generous of His Majesty!" the man replied and waved the cart on.

The cart weaved its way along the cobbled main waterfront, which even at that early hour was beginning to teem with people, commodities, handcarts and sedans. At right angles to the quayside were a multitude of jetties. When they reached the top of the jetty alongside which their hired boat was moored, the old man said he could go no further with his horse. The stranger summoned one of the many men pushing handcarts. The crate and baggage were transferred, and the old man said farewell. Escorted by Carl Manfred and the stranger, the handcart moved off down the narrow jetty.

A few minutes later, near the end of the jetty, they came to a small, double-masted colonial-style schooner of the sort often seen in the Americas. The boat was dirty and old, but appeared seaworthy. The captain was burly with a heavy black beard.

"As we arranged last night," said the stranger, "we are the two passengers with a consignment for France."

The captain grunted and then growled, "Get yourselves and the box on board quickly. If we are not underway in a matter of minutes, we will miss the tide."

After paying the handcart man, the stranger and Carl Manfred lifted the crate and carried it to a thin and precarious plank from the jetty to the boat. With the boat bobbing strongly in the water and the plank unstable, it took several minutes to get the crate safely on board. Indeed, at one point it nearly slipped into the water. Once on board, they carried the crate, as the captain directed, to the fore of the boat just in front of the main mast. The captain's mate then placed some tarpaulin over it before lashing it in place. They returned for their remaining baggage, ferrying some items across the plank, hurling over others.

As the captain cast off, two malicious-looking men ran along the jetty, ordering the captain to stop.

"We need to see what you have on board."

The stranger asked the captain if they were excise men. He replied that they were not. He had never seen them before. The stranger told the captain to move out into the harbour as quickly as possible, promising to pay him extra if he did not turn back. One of the men on the jetty pulled a pistol from his pocket, took aim and fired. The bullet whistled over the boat. The other man then also fired, but as the boat lurched in the swell of the changing tide, that shot also missed. Carl Manfred pulled a pistol from his belt and quickly taking aim, pulled the trigger. One of the two men instinctively ducked, slipping on the icy jetty as he did so, knocking his companion into the water.

The boat picked up the wind in its sails and began to head quickly out of the harbour on the ebbing tide.

"They might have been Whitfield's men," said Carl Manfred.

"Or someone else's," interjected the stranger. "I doubt we have seen the end of them. We will have some scores to settle before long. In the meantime, it is essential that we clear Calais as soon as we dock. I suspect that whoever wishes us dead, including the girl, will follow us quickly to France."

"I agree," said Carl Manfred. He added, "Do we free her from the box when we dock or secrete her in it until we get to Paris?"

"If we can find a coach to ourselves at Calais, we will free her there and she will sit inside with us – in her disguise," replied the stranger. "If we cannot, she will have to remain in the box until Paris."

Carl Manfred said nothing.

It took six hours to cross to Calais in the face of a strong wind. The Channel was turbulent. Arabella smelt the sea and sensed the strong wind buffeting the crate in which she was imprisoned. Though padded with blankets, she was very cold. She was in darkness. In the damp air, her gag and the straps that bound her wrists and ankles grew ever tighter. The pain from the binding around her chest was now intense. She felt nauseous as the small boat pitched and rolled in the waves, but she willed herself not to be sick and risk choking to death on her own vomit. She drifted into semi-consciousness.

When she regained consciousness, she heard the intensifying sound of seagulls and felt less pitching of the boat, indicating surely that they were about to enter harbour. At last she was in France, with the prospect of emerging from her suffocating coffin. Later, she could hear French voices as the boat drew alongside, and instructions for the provision of a cart to take the ship's load to the harbour office. After some minutes, the box was unlashed and the tarpaulin. Then it was lifted up, carried a short distance, and placed on a cart. She heard the stranger instruct the carter to take it to the harbour office. There it was unloaded and lowered carefully to the ground.

"What have you to declare?" she heard a French voice ask.

"A gift of porcelain from His Majesty King George of England to His Majesty King Frederick of Prussia," replied Carl Manfred decisively.

"We should open the box to see if the quality of English porcelain matches the quality of King Louis's. Please show me your papers," demanded an official.

He placed his boot on the lid of the crate, pressing hard down to test its thickness. Arabella froze inside, not even daring to breath.

He looked at the papers, passed them back and said that the

crate would have to be kept in the nearby store overnight, so he could check with his superiors whether any royal excise was liable on the contents. After further discussion, the official instructed Carl Manfred and the stranger to carry the crate to an adjacent warehouse. They placed it on the floor and left the building with the official, who locked the door behind them. He told them to wait until the morning, when they should report back to him. Arabella was once again in darkness and in terror, nearing the end of her endurance of pain and suffocation.

Withdrawing to a nearby tavern, the stranger and Carl Manfred agreed that the official would most likely order the crate to be opened before the morning. It was therefore necessary to retrieve it as quickly as possible and set out for Paris without delay.

Later that evening, they approached some coachmen standing idly by the harbour gate.

"We wish to leave shortly for Paris. Is anyone willing to take us at this hour?"

Several of the coachmen refused, but an older man said he would take them, to earn some extra money for his hungry family at Christmas. The stranger struck a deal with the coachman and promised to be back within the hour.

He and Carl Manfred returned to the harbour office, around which there was still much activity on the quayside. They walked slowly past the building and saw, through the window, the official drinking wine with his colleagues. They then approached the adjacent warehouse where they had placed the box earlier.

There was a guard outside. The stranger was ready to knife him but Carl Manfred stepped forward and said, "I am sent by Captain Etienne de Vervins, on behalf of General de la Rivière, Commander of King Louis's Royal Guard, to remove a consignment of porcelain brought from England today and to take it to Paris for examination."

He produced from his pocket Maria Louisa's note to him on General de la Rivière's crested paper, with her address and greetings from her husband, urging him to stay with them on his return to Paris. He proffered the sheet of paper to the guard, who looked at it cursorily and promptly handed it back, suggesting that he probably could not read, though he would have recognised the royal crest.

The guard produced a key from his pocket and unlocked the warehouse door. The crate had been placed on a long table, ready for examination later. Beside it was an iron bar, obviously intended for prising it open.

"This is the crate," said Carl Manfred in the dim light.

He and the stranger then lifted it off the table. As they did so, the stranger placed the bar on top. They carried the crate out of the warehouse. Carl Manfred instructed the guard to close the door. As the guard turned back to obey, the stranger signalled to Carl Manfred that they should place the box on the ground. After they had done so, he spun round and hit the half-asleep guard, still fiddling with the lock, on the back of the head with the bar. The guard slumped to the ground.

Extracting a small hip flask from a pocket in his overcoat, the stranger sprinkled some brandy over the guard's uniform and mouth to suggest to his superiors that he had been drinking on duty. Then he and Carl Manfred picked up the crate. They kept to the shadows as they passed the harbour office, where there was now the sound of singing. Just before the harbour gate, there was a dark corner, hidden from view. The two men put the crate down. The stranger quickly grabbed the iron bar from inside his coat and prised open the lid. Carl Manfred pulled back the blanket padding. As he did so, he saw sheer terror on Arabella's face. He and the stranger lifted her out of her coffin. The stranger cut the bonds on her wrists and ankles, and Carl Manfred removed her gag.

"Welcome to France, Miss Whitfield!" he said.

Arabella smiled weakly at him and then fainted into his arms.

"Quick," said the stranger. "We have no time to lose."

He passed his flask to Carl Manfred, who unstopped it and pressed it against Arabella's lips.

"Please drink this. We have a coach ready to take us to Paris."

Arabella stirred as the brandy trickled into her mouth. She began to cough. The two men pulled her to her feet. The stranger retrieved her bag and box from the crate. They then carried the semi-conscious Arabella to the carriage.

"Our young friend has had too much to drink. Celebrating Christmas too early!" Carl Manfred said to the coachman.

"Paris, as fast as you can," the stranger called out as he climbed inside.

The carriage leapt forward and soon Calais was behind them. The stranger remained awake, thinking of betrayal and revenge. Carl Manfred sat in silence, looking out into the blackness. The exhausted Arabella sat next to him, her limbs aching from her many hours in the crate, leaning against his shoulder with her hand resting on his arm as she drifted into a deep sleep.

CHAPTER 13

The Pursuers

Brushing his selfishness and insensitive behaviour under the proverbial carpet, Sir Robert remained implacable in his unforgiving attitude towards his daughter for what she had done. He considered Arabella guilty of profound ingratitude for the privileged life he had provided for her at Meltwater. That and her insolent disobedience in recent years, particularly her refusal to do as he had asked in the matter of her marriage, had wounded him – or rather, his sense of self-consequence – greatly. Throughout his life he had always got his way, believing that what he wanted was always in the family's best interests. Arabella, no doubt encouraged by her mother, had been the first to thwart him. By the time she left Meltwater, his dislike of her stubbornness and downright intransigence had become profound. Indeed, he had become vindictive. Her actions had brought shame and notoriety to the family name, and set back his political career. Her behaviour was unforgivable and, assuming she was still alive, she would have to be severely punished if she were ever found.

Sir Robert looked back with pride on his achievements. He had enhanced the value of his estate. His accumulating wealth enabled him to enjoy a comfortable lifestyle, from which his family benefited, and helped to pay for the patronage he required to advance his parliamentary ambitions. He had gradually climbed the social ladder not just in Norfolk but in London, where, thanks to Lady Barbara and her connections, he had gained greater access and the respect he had not enjoyed before. He was proud of the network of influential contacts he had built; indeed, some were now dependent on his own patronage. The more favours he did for others, the more favours others owed him. This hard work was designed to mobilise and increase the support he would need in order to be nominated as the Member of Parliament for Freshchester and, if elected, to earn him, at a later stage, a seat in government. But seeking selection was not easy. There were others in the county wealthier than him who eyed the Freshchester seat and Sir Robert was not to everyone's liking. In pursuing his activities he had trodden on some sensitive toes. On the other hand, his growing wealth did not go unnoticed by his political friends in London, who needed people like Sir Robert to help win arguments and seats at Westminster.

While public interest in Arabella's fate may have waned somewhat, Sir Robert's preoccupation with his daughter showed no signs of abating. Her wilful refusal to marry Lord Henry Simon, her disappearance, the possibility that she was in hiding amid Mayfair's demi-monde or had escaped to France, and, more recently, Lord Henry's not unexpected switch of interest to another possible match, in Shropshire, had severely dented his pride. He was sure, despite the expressions of support and Lady Barbara's interventions, that behind his back his daughter's behaviour remained the talk of the London clubs he frequented and amongst his political friends. He felt certain that what had happened had raised questions – unjustifiably, in his opinion – about his personal judgement and family life. He feared increasingly that, despite the continued promotion of his unchallenged version of what had taken place on that fateful day at Meltwater, his failure to locate Arabella and to bring her to heel, or even to find out what had happened to her, would irretrievably damage his hopes of political preferment. He had to bring the matter to a conclusion soon by whatever means at his disposal. If he found her, he was determined to punish her and be rid of her by marriage to anyone who would now take her. If that were not possible, other solutions might be necessary. Of course, if she were in the demi-monde, it might be better to leave her there in the hope that one of her patrons might marry her.

Accordingly, he intensified his efforts to enlist the help of his contacts, some of whom were decidedly shady, to track her down. He insisted to all those to whom he turned for help that her prolonged disappearance strongly suggested she had been abducted and was being held against her will. It was imperative for his and Lady Whitfield's sanity, and the family's well-being, to establish the facts.

His principal ally in his venture of vengeance was his son. George, unpleasant and deceitful, shared and indeed stoked his father's anger at what had happened. Arabella's flight from Meltwater had deeply distracted Sir Robert. Seeking money from him to ease his debts had become harder. Spending longer in London playing cards, drinking and womanising, he was, it could be said, even more determined than his father to find Arabella – to see her disowned, disinherited and indeed expunged from the family. Her expulsion would mean a larger inheritance of his father's estate for him. In George Whitfield's opinion, Arabella should, if necessary, be sentenced to lifelong incarceration in the madhouse.

Despite continuing enquiries over the months, there was still no sign of Arabella. Neither was there a body to prove that she was dead. The rumour that she was living in Mayfair persisted. George Whitfield and his friends went there regularly to check for her possible presence, but it was more often an excuse to enjoy their pleasure – sex, wine and cards – with whoever was available. They had every encouragement to do so, since the flow of young women to Mayfair, often thought to be of greater quality than those in Bedford Square or Covent Garden, was never-ending. Moreover, the sexual pleasure was all the more piquant because many of those providing favours wore masks to increase their allure and mystery, and to conceal their identity and, possibly, their social background. The fashion for masks was often matched by the men. It led to games of trying to establish who was with whom. But so far Arabella was nowhere to be seen.

Those employed by Sir Robert to observe from a distance remained equally unable to acquire reliable, up-to-date information that might lead to Arabella's whereabouts. Standing around on street corners and looking out for suspicious coaches or recruiting sedan carriers as informants yielded few crumbs, though there were occasional revelations about others that were of personal value to Sir Robert for use as discreet blackmail if the need arose. Some of the intelligence received helped to provide a picture, albeit incomplete, of those amongst the new female arrivals in Mayfair who were quickly increasing in popularity, judged by the frequency with which their services were sought. Anyone inclined to scrutinise this information would find that a certain new arrival, Antoinette Badeau from France, was beginning to attract some highly favourable attention for her elegance, her freshness and for the beautiful mask she wore at all times, even at concerts. She had caught the eye of many at young Mr Mozart's performances earlier in the year. And Lord Henry Simon was believed to have encountered her soon after her arrival in London, though Sir Robert could hardly ask his once prospective son-in-law if that were true.

Partly because she was not always available at her place of abode, 35 Chesterfield Street, Antoinette Badeau had begun to gain a reputation – encouraged by Mrs Hallam, the establishment's proprietress – for exclusiveness, for being highly selective in her choice of client, such as Lord Tumbleton. Antoinette's price was accordingly high and some could not afford it. Mrs Hallam was tight-lipped to all about Antoinette's background. She refused to divulge any details about her provenance. Those who visited Antoinette wondered what face lay behind her mask. If it were as beautiful as her body, she would be destined for rich patronage.

These rumours led Lady Ward to suggest to Sir Robert that perhaps the time had come to find out more about Antoinette Badeau by other means. She would of course not permit him to go in person to Mrs Hallam's, as rumours would soon spread that he was seeking his sexual comforts elsewhere, which would be bad for her long-term plan to persuade Sir Robert to divorce his wife in her favour. Besides, it would be politically indelicate for Sir Robert to be seen at such a place. Instead, Lady Barbara encouraged him to send his son, George, back to 35 Chesterfield Street, armed with sufficient money, to insist on enjoying the pleasure of Mademoiselle Badeau. Once with her, he should find the means to remove her mask and see the face behind it.

Pending a suitable opportunity for George to take action, Lady Ward persuaded Sir Robert to arrange for someone to keep a discreet watch on Mrs Hallam's house, to see who came and went. Such close observation revealed no comings or goings of note, and there was certainly no sign of any woman leaving the house wearing Antoinette Badeau's distinctive mask. Unless she had already moved on, Mademoiselle Badeau must surely still be inside.

George and his friends did not wait long before returning unexpectedly to Chesterfield Street to prevail on Mrs Hallam to make available her full stable for their choice, including the mysterious Miss Badeau. Having already drunk a great deal of wine, they insisted, on their noisy arrival, on immediately getting what they wanted. Mrs Hallam, somewhat flustered, explained that Antoinette Badeau was not available, and a rowdy and disagreeable search proved that to be the case. Though flushed with alcohol, after entering her room George believed that she could not be far away, as the display of personal toiletries suggested recent occupancy. After all, he pointed out to Mrs Hallam, the house had been under watch and no one had seen Mademoiselle Badeau leave. He would therefore return to Chesterfield Street shortly, when he expected to enjoy her favour, however high her price.

Some hours later, George Whitfield did indeed return to Chesterfield Street, demanding to see Antoinette Badeau. Mrs Hallam took him to the room he had searched earlier. In it was a young woman wearing the mask for which Antoinette Badeau had become well known. Mrs Hallam asked her to remove it. The face behind the mask was not that of his sister, Arabella. The young woman quickly replaced the mask and George enjoyed her services for the rest of the evening. He was not entirely impressed by Miss Badeau's sexual skills and thought her French only passable. Mrs Hallam gave a sigh of relief. It had been a close encounter, but thankfully the real Antoinette Badeau was now safely ensconced in Shepherd Street, in the care of her friend, Mrs Rathbone, and hiding behind a different mask.

Following George's behaviour at Mrs Hallam's, which had not endeared him to her clients and which had brought some criticism on the family, Sir Robert's search for his daughter lost momentum. There was still no sign of her in Mayfair and George had proved that it was not Arabella behind La Badeau's mask. Perhaps all those rumours had been wrong. As the autumn advanced, Arabella's fate finally began to fade from public consciousness. Sir Robert began to wonder whether this might not be for the best. Perhaps it was better to forget her and concentrate on finding a suitable match for his son, George. Lady Ward encouraged him in this view.

Another reason for trying to put Arabella out of his mind was that Sir Robert was aware he had spent too much time in London in recent months, searching for his daughter and, of course, enjoying the pleasures of his mistress. During the autumn, he began to return to Meltwater more often, to attend to the affairs of the estate, which he felt he had rather neglected, and to renurture the support of those he was likely to need in the next election. Selection to stand for the Freshchester seat was now more pressing, given the increasing instability of the government over the abolition of the recent and now widely unpopular Stamp Act. This Act had imposed a direct tax, especially on Britain's American colonies, requiring many printed materials to be produced on paper carrying an embossed revenue stamp. Passage of the Act earlier in the year had already caused the resignation of the prime minister, George Grenville, who had been replaced in July by Lord Rockingham. It was paramount that Sir Robert should shore up his efforts to be selected as the next MP for Freshchester. Fresh elections might not be far away.

He also needed to go to Norwich, to talk to the corn merchants and to his bankers. It was imperative that his latest corn crop should earn him the best possible price, so that he could replenish the significant amount of money he had recently spent in London – not just on looking for Arabella, but also on ensuring the Whitfield town house was elegant and up to date in fashionable furnishings, and on spoiling Lady Barbara – and of course to pay for other mounting expenses, including his son's debts and the cost of the continuing search for his daughter.

Sir Robert found Meltwater unrewarding after London. The estate and its neighbouring communities had few attractions of the sort he enjoyed in London. Moreover, he missed the company of his mistress. His wife was but a shadow of her former self. She greatly mourned the absence of Arabella, convinced she had been abducted and was no longer in England but possibly locked in a harem somewhere in the Ottoman territories, if not murdered. Sir Robert's presence at Meltwater led to further scenes between them, with Lady Whitfield still holding him personally responsible for what had happened. Her anger towards him was aggravated by the sure knowledge that he had been spending more time with his mistress in their town house than looking for their daughter. The result was that Sir Robert and Lady Whitfield barely spoke to one another and when they did so it was only to keep up appearances in front of the servants.

Notwithstanding the calamity that had befallen the family, Sir Robert was determined to try to salvage his political ambitions. He therefore insisted that he and his wife should continue to provide entertainment at Meltwater for their friends, in between his periodic visits to London, and should spend more time together visiting those whose support he would need at the next election if he were chosen to represent the borough. Lady Whitfield found this social pretence painful, but obediently did as her husband asked. They agreed, however, that until the matter of Arabella had been resolved there would be no soirée this year.

Lady Whitfield's depressed state of mind worsened as the autumn wore on and the days became shorter. Moreover, the thought of celebrating Christmas at Meltwater with Arabella's whereabouts still unknown filled Lady Whitfield with dread. Christmas had always been such a happy time. But this year there would be no happiness. For Lady Whitfield it would be a time of profound bleakness.

After much heart-searching and under some pressure from her husband (who wanted to spend time with Lady Barbara, who had recently complained about being neglected), Lady Whitfield accepted the invitation from two of her closest friends, Lady Mildmay and Mrs Benjamin, to join them in Norwich, at Mrs Willoughby's lodgings, to mark the start of Advent. This would be a chance to buy something to wear for Christmas from amongst the latest styles in dresses and bonnets, and also perhaps to have some fun with Monsieur Noverre. Lady Mildmay and Mrs Benjamin realised how difficult it continued to be for Lady Whitfield, but they believed it was important she should be with her friends at this time, and maintain her seasonal tradition. Sir Robert said he would join her in Norwich towards the end of her stay, coming direct from London in order to see his bankers and the corn merchants and then accompany his wife back to Meltwater. And so it was that on Monday, 25 November, Lady

Whitfield arrived in Norwich to stay at Mrs Willoughby's lodgings together with Lady Mildmay and Mrs Benjamin, as she had often done with Arabella in the past.

Lady Whitfield was overwhelmed with joy when Arabella unexpectedly came to her room two days later, dressed in black and veiled, directly after her arrival from London. Her beloved daughter was once again in her arms, though much changed – thinner but more transparently beautiful. Arabella declined to join her for dinner at the White Swan with Lady Mildmay and Mrs Benjamin, preferring instead to rest in her mother's room after her long journey. She made her mother promise not to disclose her presence in Norwich but, as Arabella had suspected, Lady Whitfield found it impossible to keep the secret, such was her excitement at her reunion with her daughter. Lady Mildmay and Mrs Benjamin, both sworn not to say a word, immediately told their friends and by early the next morning Sir Robert's principal banker, John Gurney, had heard about it from his wife. News of Arabella's arrival was spreading quickly through the social layers of Norwich.

Meanwhile, Sir Robert had left London earlier than planned and arrived at his club in Norwich on Wednesday, 27 November, accompanied by his son, George, in time to attend dinner the next day with Gurney, Gurney's wife and other guests. He was astonished to receive a report the next morning at his club that his daughter had come to Norwich to be with her mother – the more so as Jewkes, the coachman, had just returned from taking a message to Lady Whitfield at Mrs Willoughby's and had mentioned no such thing. Already planning what to do with Arabella when he got her back to Meltwater, he went immediately to his wife's lodgings, to be greeted by Mrs Willoughby telling him that his daughter was upstairs with Lady Whitfield.

He quickly went upstairs to his wife's room in order to confront Arabella, only to find that she had hurriedly left only seconds before, much to the distress of her mother. He rushed downstairs to catch her, but Mrs Willoughby said his daughter must still be in the building as she had not seen her leave. He went back upstairs and started to check each room, most of which were unoccupied. One, however, was occupied – by a long-haired, sinister-looking man. Sir Robert sought to enter, but the man blocked him, saying he was there on his own. Sir Robert withdrew, but vowed to return, with support, to conduct a thorough search of the lodgings. He had to locate his daughter. She could not slip through his hands.

By the time he returned later in the day, the sinister man had left and there was no sign of Arabella. Lady Whitfield remained in her room, deeply upset by Arabella's sudden departure and wounded by her husband's outrageous allegation that her encounter with Arabella had been planned for some time and that she must have known where her daughter had been hiding since leaving Meltwater. By five o'clock it was apparent that Lady Whitfield was too emotional to attend the Gurney dinner, so Sir Robert attended alone, reporting that his wife was indisposed. He was obliged to confess over dinner that he himself had not yet seen Arabella since her arrival in Norwich, but looked forward to doing so the next day. He said he was relieved that she had resurfaced, but that he still remained in the dark about where she had been for the past months.

Later that evening, before returning to his club, Sir Robert went to Mrs Willoughby's lodgings with his son, George, to see his wife. While he wished to avoid another scene, he wanted to discuss with Lady Whitfield how best to find Arabella before she left the city and to convince their daughter that all was forgiven and that she could return to Meltwater. He found Lady Whitfield inconsolable and uncooperative.

The next morning Sir Robert awoke early at his club. He noticed that a sealed letter had been pushed under the door of his room. He opened it. The unsigned letter stated that there was good reason to think that Arabella Whitfield would be leaving Norwich that morning for London, in the company of two others. It was very much in the mutual interest of Sir Robert and the letter-writer to see that Arabella and those accompanying her were apprehended and made to explain their actions. If it was too late to stop their departure from Norwich, it would be necessary to find them before they arrived back in London.

Sir Robert was mystified by the contents of the letter – in particular, the suggestion that his daughter may be travelling with two others, who had committed deeds that, while unspecified, worryingly warranted explanation. But he decided that the information had the smell of sufficient veracity to require his immediate attention. Accordingly, much to the annoyance of George, who had begun to enjoy himself with two of his friends who also happened to be in Norwich, Sir Robert instructed him to hire a fast coach and leave for London, in case Arabella slipped through their fingers in Norwich. At a suitable point on the route, George, with the help of friends, should check any coach coming from the direction of Norwich to see if Arabella was on board. He suggested that they lie in wait at the last principal coaching inn before London, where most coaches changed their horses. If this plan were to work, he had to leave immediately. For his part, Sir Robert would go at once to the Market Square, to observe whether Arabella was seeking a coach for London there. If he found her, he would not let her get away this time. With much complaining, George followed his father's instructions. After all, he was about to ask him for another sum of money to settle yet another debt.

Later, Sir Robert left in his coach for the Market Square, urging his coachman to hurry. Jewkes replied he could go no faster as there was a smaller, slower private carriage ahead of them. As they entered the square, Sir Robert asked Jewkes to stop in one corner so he could see the other coaches coming and going from the nearby coaching inns. He noticed that the carriage they had been following had stopped. The driver had unloaded the luggage but only one occupant had got out. A man in a long coat was striding across the square towards waiting coaches. It suddenly occurred to him that it could be the hostile man he had encountered in Mrs Willoughby's lodgings.

Sir Robert decided to take a closer look at the carriage that had preceded his into the square. As he approached, he recognised the small leather bag on the ground by the wheel. It had a distinctive letter buckle on it. It was surely Arabella's. He opened the carriage door and there was the unmistakeable figure of his daughter. As he reached inside to seize her, he was grabbed from behind. A man put a knife to this throat and, while pinning his hands behind his back, dragged him back to his coach in front of startled passers-by. He was then pushed inside. He turned to look at his assailant. It was indeed the man he had seen at Mrs Willoughby's the day before. After shouting at the coachman to move off, the man slapped the haunch of one of the horses. The horse and its companion in the traces leapt forward and careered away from

Market Square with Jewkes struggling to bring them under control. Sir Robert was thrown to the floor.

Having failed in his attempt to stop his daughter's departure from the Market Square, in the course of which he had been ignominiously assaulted by the long-haired man, Sir Robert returned immediately to Mrs Willoughby's to tell his wife what had happened and inform her that he intended to set out for London as quickly as possible in pursuit of Arabella. She had been abducted and was now under the control of undesirable men. She had to be rescued. It would therefore be necessary for Lady Whitfield to return to Meltwater alone. Lady Whitfield retorted that, far from being abductors, these men were more likely protecting Arabella from her own father. Sir Robert insisted that her assertion was preposterous. Their daughter had clearly become unbalanced and it was time for drastic action to bring the matter to a close for the sake of the family name.

Deeply shocked by recent events, Lady Whitfield remained in her room at Mrs Willoughby's for the rest of the day. In deeper turmoil than ever about Arabella's sudden departure the previous day, and now sure that her beloved daughter was hiding the truth about what she had been doing in London since first running away, Lady Whitfield was at a loss as to what to do next. She could not decide whether to go to Meltwater or to travel to London to stay at their Westminster town house and risk encountering the dreadful Lady Barbara Ward. For the moment, she resolved to go to Norfolk in case Arabella came to see her again. If that did not happen, she contemplated the possibility of returning to her family home, south of Paris, in order to reflect on what to do in the face of a disintegrating marriage and the fact that her daughter might be in serious trouble because of her association with the men her husband had described. With these questions still unanswered, that evening Lady Whitfield took her leave of Lady Mildmay and Mrs Benjamin and returned to Meltwater early the next morning.

Before leaving Norwich for London later that day, Sir Robert received another unsigned note at his club, suggesting an immediate meeting to discuss how best the writer might be able to help in the apprehension of Arabella and the two people with whom she was believed to be travelling, so that they could face criminal charges of a most serious nature. He was to send his reply through Mrs Willoughby. Sir Robert responded straightaway, writing that he would be ready for such a meeting at the earliest convenient time and suggesting a private room here at his club. As instructed, he despatched Jewkes to Mrs Willoughby's, who arranged for the reply to be delivered immediately by hand. He received a prompt response, proposing that he and the letter-writer should meet at noon at the place Sir Robert had suggested.

Sir Robert, who by now was in a highly excitable state about the implications of the latest letter he had received, met its anonymous writer as agreed. The man was older than Sir Robert had expected. Cultivated, elegantly dressed, well-informed and especially knowledgeable about European affairs, he explained to Sir Robert that the two of them had much in common, which, he said, suggested to him that they might be able to do business together.

The anonymous man explained that, according to his good information, an innocent foreigner, long resident in Norwich, had been summarily executed in the city in great secrecy the night before, on the orders of a foreign power. The perpetrators of the execution were now on their way back to London, prior to leaving England as soon as possible for France. He believed that these two men were travelling with Sir Robert's daughter, who, it appeared, had encountered one of them in London, where she had been living as a courtesan since earlier in the year. The crime that had been committed would cause great embarrassment to the government in London if it became known that a foreign power had sent agents to carry out a hostile act within English jurisdiction. There was an uneasy peace in Europe following the end of the Seven Years War. It was therefore highly desirable that nothing should happen to disturb that peace, especially in respect of relations with France. But perhaps more important for Sir Robert, it would have grave implications for him if his daughter were implicated in some way.

The man without a name finished by saying that it was partly because of Arabella's involvement – most likely unwitting – that he had decided to seek Sir Robert's help in apprehending the two men concerned and handing them over to the authorities in London. If that help were provided, it would of course make it easier for Sir Robert to separate his daughter from them and quietly remove her to a secluded place away from public attention. If Sir Robert felt unable to help, there was a risk that when they were finally apprehended – which the man assured him they would be, it was only a matter of time – Miss Whitfield would be directly implicated in what had happened in Norwich and therefore might be charged as an accessory to a capital crime.

Sir Robert listened without breathing to what had been said about Arabella. The blood drained from his face. His hands trembled. He was sweating and he felt unwell. This terrible information could be catastrophic in its impact on his standing in London and Norfolk, and his political prospects would be irreparably damaged. If what he had just been told was correct, his daughter was not only a courtesan but possibly involved with people alleged to have committed murder. He felt faint. He decided that he had little choice but to accept at face value what he had been told. He believed he had to be complicit in the course of action his interlocutor had proposed in order to avoid Arabella appearing in court.

"May I know your name and the foreign power involved?" he asked.

The anonymous man replied curtly, "No, it is best that you do not know. But please be assured that I am certain the information I have given you is correct. Are you able to help me in this matter? If you are, your involvement in the arrest and conviction of these two men may greatly help your prospective career in parliament, to which I know you attach the greatest importance. But you will undoubtedly wish, as part of the solution, to remove your daughter for her own safety. No one would wish to see such an attractive young woman swing from the gallows."

Sir Robert almost fainted in his chair when he heard this last remark.

"Yes, I will assist," he replied.

"Good," replied the letter-writer. "We have much to do and it may involve foreign travel in the pursuit of the malefactors."

For the next hour the two men sat alone in the privacy of Sir Robert's club, plotting what they would do. Sir Robert disclosed that he had already despatched his son, George, to try, with the help of two friends, to intercept the three miscreants on the road to London. But both men thought this plan was unlikely to succeed. The anonymous letter-writer revealed that one of the men they sought was a former senior military officer and the other a vicious individual who hid in the shadows. They would likely stand a greater measure of success if they were to post lookouts between London and Dover, and at the port itself, from which the two men they were chasing were most likely to leave England. Sir Robert said he had such people already in place, following his earlier instructions to them to look out for any attempt by Arabella to leave England from her hiding place in Mayfair, where, even before the confirmation he had received today, he had believed her to be. The anonymous man said he would see if his friends in London might be able to help. The two men decided that, as there was no time to lose, both of them should leave immediately for London and then Kent, in accordance with their plan.

Within two hours Sir Robert's coach was speeding southwards, stopping at certain inns for fresh horses. It was at one such inn, near London, that they caught up with Sir Robert's son, George, and his two friends, who reported that their effort to stop the coach carrying Arabella and the two men travelling with her had failed. George and one of his supporters had been injured in the fracas. This demonstrated, said the anonymous man, how dangerous the two men on the run were and how important it was to remove Sir Robert's daughter to safety before it was too late. Sir Robert nodded in agreement, though he was becoming deeply concerned about the increasing danger to which he was exposing himself and his family. He was accepting at face value the word of a man he had never met before and who would not disclose his name.

Sir Robert, his son and the anonymous man were joined on the continuing journey south by George's friend, James Danford, nursing the wound he had received in the attempted interception of Arabella's coach. They made such speed to London that they thought they could be close behind the coach carrying Arabella and her two companions. Indeed, on arrival at Charing Cross, they spotted it leaving ahead of them. They followed it as it continued its journey northwards past Tyburn.

It was in the neighbourhood of the gallows that Sir Robert and his accomplices lost track of the coach. His coachman circled the district for a while, searching for it. At one point, Sir Robert, his son and the anonymous man climbed down from the coach for closer scrutiny of a house into which they thought Arabella may have disappeared. But they concluded they were mistaken when a smart coach drew up, from which an elegant couple emerged to enter the house.

A passer-by asked him if he needed any assistance. He declined, but suggested that local people should look out for his daughter and the two dangerous villains who had abducted her and had tried to murder his son. If they found her or knew of her possible whereabouts, he wished to be informed at his house in Westminster. He handed the man a guinea for his services and a card giving his address.

Sir Robert, his son, James Danford and the anonymous man arrived at the Whitfield town house in Westminster. After waking up the servants to provide refreshments, the anonymous man said it was necessary to leave for the Channel coast immediately, as he was of the opinion that the three fugitives, as he now called them, could already be on their way in the direction of Dover to board a boat for France. The nearer they got to the Channel port, the harder it would be for them to hide from the lookout men Sir Robert had already deployed in the harbour.

After only an hour of rest, the four left Westminster for Dover in two coaches. George Whitfield and James Danford went ahead in a lighter and faster coach. Sir Robert travelled some distance behind in the slower and larger black coach, now showing considerable wear and tear, accompanied by the anonymous man, who spent part of the journey asleep. Sir Robert remained awake, continuing to speculate how it was that this man, who declined to divulge his name, could be so sure about the movements of the other coach. Where was this journey leading? How had Arabella become involved? How was it all going to end? Would his career survive? And then there were the competing women in his life – his wife and Barbara Ward. How would that situation be resolved? The stakes were now very high. He sweated.

As both coaches progressed towards the Warren Inn at Ashford, which the anonymous man recommended for changing the horses before the final stage of the route to Dover, it became much colder and the rain began to turn to snow, making the road hard going. James Danford and George Whitfield were therefore relieved to be the first to reach shelter at the coaching inn after such an arduous journey, which had started over two days before in Norwich.

While he and George Whitfield were warming themselves at the Warren Inn, Danford looked up and glimpsed through the half-opened door a somewhat dishevelled figure he thought he recognised from the attempted interception on the road between Norwich and London. Before he could be sure, the figure withdrew, closing the door behind him. He described the man he had briefly observed to Sir Robert and the anonymous man when they arrived at the inn later. They agreed that it was most likely to have been the menacing-looking man whom Sir Robert had first seen at Mrs Willoughby's lodgings. They speculated that, having possibly recognised James Danford, the fugitives would have decided to press on towards Dover. Sir Robert and his party, all fatigued, decided that, because of the rapidly deteriorating weather, the lack of adequately rested horses and their own exhaustion, they would delay their departure until the morning.

The next day was bitterly cold, there was much snow on the ground, and the anonymous man, who still maintained he could not divulge his name, much to Sir Robert's increasing irritation, said he was feeling distinctly unwell. It was therefore not until mid-morning when Sir Robert and his travelling companions finally left the Warren Inn for Dover. Though in normal conditions the distance to Dover from Ashford was a comparatively short ride, it was not until late afternoon that the two coaches finally arrived, in heavy snow, at a private house in Dover recommended by the anonymous man. They were greeted by a man called Philippe Robinet.

In discussion at the house they assumed that Arabella and her travelling companions had also reached Dover, reasoning that the fugitives were unlikely to have let the snow hold them up, given their undoubted determination to leave England as quickly as possible. Based on this assumption, and the information from the anonymous man, they agreed that it was now essential to block any attempt by the fugitives to leave by boat. Robinet said that because of the weather no boats would leave until the next day.

Sir Robert immediately summoned Mr Wakes, his "agent", in order to give him an updated description of the menacing-looking man, his possible male companion (who was well-dressed and had the bearing of a former military man) and his daughter. He instructed Wakes that it was essential to watch the harbour carefully and to report any sighting of the three. If they spotted them, Wakes and his accomplices were to raise the alarm and do their best to delay them from boarding a vessel while awaiting further instructions. They should avoid collusion with the excise men. Wakes left without delay. Sir Robert thought over the instructions he had just given. He was anxious that any apprehension be tactfully managed, so he could derive maximum praise for rescuing his daughter from the hands of two desperate foreigners, arrested on suspicion of murdering an innocent man in England on behalf of a foreign power. Such an outcome would surely earn him much praise and advancement.

With the trap laid, Sir Robert, George, James Danford and the anonymous man stayed as relaxed as they could. Philippe Robinet hovered in the background and arranged refreshments. But there was unease in the group. The anonymous man fidgeted; George was anxious to return to the greater comfort of London, as was his friend, James; while Sir Robert felt deeply isolated from Lady Ward's soothing arms in Westminster and from his distant estate at Meltwater. His attention to the estate had begun to slip to the extent that he had become heavily dependent on others, including Lady Whitfield, for its maintenance. This lack of personal control worried him. He feared that others would change what he thought was best for the estate, with possible adverse financial consequences. But most of all he was concerned that he was now exposed politically. If this long and expensive chase across England were to no avail, or were to go wrong, his political ambitions would end and his public reputation be crushed. He cursed Arabella for bringing him to this pass and cursed himself for ever striking her face. Perhaps his judgement was not infallible after all.

Sir Robert received regular reports from his "spies" on the waterfront. He reminded them again that no decisive action was to be taken without advising him in advance what was proposed. For the rest of the day his lookouts had little to offer before they retreated to the warmth of the town's inns to ward off the intense cold of the night. They did not, therefore, observe the menacing-looking man and his companion on the dockside late at night, talking to sailors about a passage to France.

It was after nine o'clock the next day that Sir Robert received word that two men fitting the descriptions had suddenly appeared at the harbour with a large wooden crate on a horse-drawn cart. They had immediately been challenged by excise men who, after receiving a possible bribe, had let them through onto the waterfront. One of Sir Robert's paid lookouts had run back to his master to report the sighting. His master had in turn quickly run to inform Sir Robert. While this was happening, the crate had been transferred to a handcart and thence quickly taken to the end of a jetty, where it had been loaded onto a small boat ready to sail. Just as the lookouts had run onto the jetty and tried to stop the boat from sailing, the vessel slipped its moorings and sailed out into the harbour, destined almost certainly for France. One of the lookouts had attempted to stop the boat by firing a pistol at those on the deck but he had missed. Then another fired. One of the two men on the boat fired back. No one had been hit, but one of the lookouts had accidentally fallen into the water and was now missing.

Sir Robert was dismayed at this news. Their quarry had escaped again. Their plans had gone badly wrong. His informers had fired shots, which he would have forbidden had he known. The two men they had planned to apprehend and hand over to the authorities had, it seemed, now escaped from England. His daughter remained missing. Was she still in Dover or in London? What was in the crate? Was it Arabella – dead or alive? If dead, what were they going to do with her body? If alive, where were they taking her? Moreover, the fracas at the harbour had resulted in one of the lookouts being reported missing – presumed drowned. And the other lookouts were being questioned by the excise men. But they were unlikely to pursue the matter as they would have no wish to confess to receiving a bribe. He would have to pay the family of the missing man to ensure that news of his involvement in the operation did not leak.

The anonymous man appeared to be deeply disturbed by the news from the waterfront. He insisted that he had provided Sir Robert with invaluable information in his possession and had urged him to be decisive. But because of the cleverness of their opponents and the apparent failure by Sir Robert's paid lookouts to watch the dockside the previous evening, the fugitives had been able to make arrangements for an early-morning escape. Now they were gone. The anonymous man speculated that Sir Robert's daughter was in the crate, though whether dead or alive he could not say.

Sir Robert sat apart to consider what he should do. Was it best to return to London and then to Meltwater, to tell his wife that there was no trace of Arabella despite his frantic efforts to find her? She might have gone back to hide in Mayfair; she might be dead; or she might have been abducted and taken to France and beyond. His wife would be deeply distressed by this news and he could judge what her reaction would be. Her state of mind had become increasingly fragile. After a few months, she might recover – or she might decline further and require seclusion for the rest of her life. That would, of course, allow him to spend more time with Lady Barbara Ward and, as memory of Arabella faded from family and local attention, to resume pursuit of his political career. But that was looking ahead. He had to decide what to do now.

George suggested as an alternative that he or his father – or both of them – should follow the two men to France, in the light of further information from the anonymous man that one of them had family connections in Paris. They might catch up with them there. George had been to Paris several times before with his friends. He knew the city well and he enjoyed its delights. Sir Robert calculated that, by allowing George to go, he could assure Lady Whitfield that the search for their daughter was continuing; and he would win sympathy from their county friends and his political connections in London if he portrayed himself as the dutiful father, persisting with his search for his lost daughter. Indeed, he might even suggest that Lady Whitfield join George in Paris in due course. Once there she might abandon him and not return to England, preferring instead to stay with her family or retreat to a convent to mourn for her daughter.

Sir Robert turned the two possible approaches over and over in his mind – to do nothing or to follow the fugitives to France. Eventually, under pressure from George and with the strong encouragement of the anonymous man, he decided that his son should travel to Paris, to be followed at a later date by his mother, if he could persuade her to go. George tried again to convince his father to accompany him, but Sir Robert declined. He decided that it was better for him to remain in England, to keep abreast of his affairs. However, at the last moment, the anonymous man offered to go with George to Paris.

"I should be gratified if you would do so," said Sir Robert. "But if that is to happen, I must know your true name and the real purpose behind the mission that has brought you from Norwich to Dover and which has involved me to the extent it has. There is much at stake – clearly for you but also for me. Unless you divulge your name, I will not allow George to go further."

The anonymous man pondered the ultimatum. He then replied that he would divulge his identity and purpose. He took Sir Robert and his son to another room where he gave them the information they required. Sir Robert listened intently to what the anonymous man revealed. He felt as though he was wading into ever deeper water. Nonetheless, he believed he owed it to his wife to continue his efforts to find Arabella. He did not wish to run the risk of her saying to their friends in her anguish that her husband had abandoned any remaining attempts to find their daughter. He therefore decided that the new emerging plan should go ahead, despite the self-evident dangers involved in doing so. The anonymous man would go with George to Paris.

Immediately, George Whitfield and the anonymous man, who insisted that his name should remain secret to all except Sir Robert and his son, left Dover for Calais in search of Arabella and those who had been with her on the journey from Norwich to Dover.

For their part, Sir Robert Whitfield and James Danford, who was becoming nervous about his own role in the affair and who wanted to leave the embrace of a family that seemed to be descending into chaos, returned to London as quickly as possible. After a brief stay at his Westminster town house and some comfort and reassurance from Lady Ward, Sir Robert returned to Meltwater to tell his wife – once he had faced the barrage of criticism that had become his usual welcome – that he had reason to believe Arabella had been abducted by two foreigners and was now conceivably in France; and that he had sent George to Paris in pursuit, with the help of a well-informed and experienced man, whose name he could not disclose. In the light of George's forthcoming report about the result of his enquiries in Paris – hopefully with news of Arabella's whereabouts – it might be appropriate for Lady

Whitfield to travel to France to bring her daughter safely back to England. Lady Whitfield said little in response, already exhausted from her earlier recriminations. And so it was that for the first time in many years Christmas was not warmly celebrated at Meltwater. It was a bleak time. And it matched the weather.

For George it was a happier time. He was in France; he was free of his father; and he had a substantial amount of money in his possession to pay for his stay and the expenses he would incur. The anonymous man was now quite unwell and had decided to rest temporarily in Amiens, agreeing that in the meantime George should travel ahead to Paris and stay at the Hostellerie du Marais in the Place Royale, where he would begin to approach certain people for information. The names to approach were on a list the anonymous man had given him. Once the two were together in Paris, they would take whatever action was required in the light of latest reports.

Though conscious of the need to find his sister and to discover the possible whereabouts of the two men they were seeking, George found considerable time for other activities, such as drinking, card-playing and chasing young French tavern girls. Contrary to instructions, he decided not to stay at the Hostellerie du Marais but at the more comfortable Hostellerie du Coq d'Or, closer to the cathedral of Notre Dame. This decision – and his rather clumsy efforts at observation and raucous behaviour – soon attracted the attention of some of the very people he was trying to find.

Despite his ham-fisted approach, George was nonetheless able, before long, to establish that his sister, Arabella, was alive and where she was likely to be found. But the information he wrote down for despatch to his father and to the anonymous man in Amiens, and his request for advice on next steps, did not reach the intended recipients because his letters were intercepted.

The health of the anonymous man, resting at Amiens, remained poor over Christmas and the days that immediately followed. It would not be until the beginning of the New Year that he would be fit enough to travel to Paris. George, awaiting instructions, but often in a drunken stupor, encouraged by new drinking partners, continued to enjoy himself in Paris as the city approached the celebration of Christmas. It was then that he received a letter with a plan.

At Meltwater, meanwhile, the atmosphere was icy. It was all the more testing as there had so far been no word from George in Paris via the long but tenuous line of communication that Sir Robert had put in place for him to use. Lady Whitfield spent much of her time in her bedroom, while Sir Robert sat alone in the library contemplating the tumultuous events in the family's life since February. He noticed that recently there had been less contact from friends and acquaintances in the county, and there was a sullen mood amongst the Meltwater staff, who missed Arabella greatly. In London, Lady Barbara continued to speak strongly on his behalf, reminding everyone that it was Arabella's pride and ingratitude that had caused the problems confronting the Whitfield family.

Sir Robert speculated about the prospects for a satisfactory resolution of all matters in the weeks ahead. He wished to see his daughter return alive, but what had happened would only extend the gulf that already existed between him and Arabella. He had never understood his daughter and probably never would. If she returned safely to Meltwater, there would no longer be any likelihood of a prestigious match for her in the county, as she would be the centre of never-ending gossip about what she had done during her months in hiding in Mayfair. According to his information, she had become a courtesan. If this were indeed true, the family name would be indelibly besmirched. If she were now in France as they thought, it might therefore be better for her to remain there permanently, staying perhaps in the care of Lady Whitfield's family.

But for the present there was little more that could be done. Sir Robert hoped that the onset of another year – 1766 – would bring better prospects, restoring equilibrium to Meltwater and advancing his political ambitions, to which he still remained deeply committed despite all he had been through. The only cheering piece of news was that the lookout who had fallen into the water had been found safe and well. Perhaps that was a sign of better times to come.

CHAPTER 14

Light and Darkness in Paris

After several stops to change the horses, the coach conveying Carl Manfred, the stranger and Arabella arrived in the Place Royale, Paris, on Tuesday, 3 December 1765. The fading sky was still light blue despite the setting sun, but it was bitterly cold and snow crunched underfoot.

The three descended from the coach stiff, dishevelled and travel-weary after their escape from England. Arabella was still dressed in the clothes Mrs Hobson had given her four days before. Though her body ached from the discomfort of wearing them, she was elated to be in Paris, which she had last seen with her mother several years before. The dreadful ordeal of the long journey from Norwich to Dover and her incarceration in the suffocating crate lashed to the schooner's deck was now temporarily forgotten amid the sights and sounds of the city.

Carrying their few possessions they walked to the nearby Hostellerie du Marais. Carl Manfred immediately wrote a note to his sister, Maria Louisa, to say that he had arrived in Paris and wished to see her without delay. He would be accompanied by a friend. He asked a young boy at the hostellerie to run immediately with the message to number 76 Rue St Louis and to await an answer. He then arranged for Arabella to have the use of a room upstairs to change while he and the stranger discussed their next steps in Paris.

Arabella removed her overcoat, jacket, waistcoat and shirt. The fabric binding around her chest had become almost like plaster. She struggled to untie the knot at the back but it was too difficult to unpick with her fingers. She would need the help of a woman to release her from what had become a straightjacket. It proved equally impossible to remove her boots, however hard she struggled to do so. She had no choice but to remain dressed as the young man who had left Mrs Hobson's house in London. So she once again put on her shirt, waistcoat and jacket. Before leaving the room, she brushed her hair and retied it into a tail at the nape of her neck with the black ribbon. About to struggle back into her overcoat, she looked at herself in the mirror. Though she was dishevelled and physically exhausted she was in Paris, in the company of a man with whom she was increasingly convinced she had fallen in love, facing the prospect of a new future. She smiled and admired herself in her tight-fitting clothes. But two thoughts cast a shadow.

Carl Manfred would not be staying in Paris. He had already said he would return to his estate in Prussia – far away from Paris. That great distance would separate her from him and she still did not know whether he had any affection for her. Perhaps his intended short stay in Paris before his departure for Berlin would reveal a sign of his feelings. In case it did not, she decided to try, in a flirtatious way, to test him.

The other shadow was that of her father and brother. Both were no doubt still determined to find her and take her back to England to a fate she could not possibly imagine. It was evident they would not stop their efforts to reclaim her, fuelled by their hatred of her for the damage she had most likely done to her father's political ambitions. The thought also crossed her mind that she might now have become a wanted person because of her involvement with the shooting on the road from Norwich to London. If that were the case, she might well be seized as an accomplice to attempted murder should she return to England. She remembered the bodies hanging from the Tyburn gallows.

So as Arabella descended the stairs her happiness at being in Paris was tempered by growing anxiety about her possible separation from Herr von Deppe and judicial punishment if she returned to England. The struggle for her liberation and personal happiness was far from finished.

While Arabella was upstairs, Carl Manfred turned to the stranger.

"I thank you greatly for your vigilance, courage and ingenuity in securing my and Miss Whitfield's escape from England. I still do not know your name but I am profoundly in your debt. I have resolved to stay in Paris until the end of this month to enjoy the company of my sister and her husband and to ensure that Miss Whitfield recovers from her ordeal. I wish to make sure that she will be in good hands in the future before I depart to report to His Majesty in Berlin. After taking leave of His Majesty, I will return to my estate. You are of course most welcome to lodge at my sister's house."

The stranger paused and then replied with great precision. "I thank you for your offer of lodgings but, as you have come to realise, I live in the shadows. That is the way I go about my business of protecting secrets and that is where I prefer to be. From there I am able to observe my enemies and to take whatever action is necessary to defend my country's paramount interests. That is why I followed you to London from Berlin without your knowledge, why I stood close to you in London and why I had to do what I did in Norwich, in accordance with my explicit instructions. I have no remorse for the man I executed there. His betrayal of His Majesty was immeasurable in its depravity and he rightly paid the supreme penalty. You and I are mere pawns in the King's grand designs. We serve him out of loyalty.

"You should be aware that I already knew of the existence of the Whitfield family long before you left Berlin, on account of George Whitfield's vile murder of your brother in this city. Once I knew His Majesty intended to ask you to attend the execution, I sought to engineer by skilful means the possibility that, while in England, you and I might confront Whitfield so that he could receive retribution from your hand for the act he committed – a cold-blooded and unjustified killing arising from his cheating at cards.

"The need to protect Miss Whitfield from the vengeance of her father was unexpected and has indeed proved a complication. It has increased the risks to our safe return to Prussia. The King's enemies are our enemies. At present there are three. First, the officer in charge at Calais will make haste to seek from the authorities in Paris an explanation of the assault of one of his men and the theft of a crate. Second, Sir Robert Whitfield and his damned son, George, will probably pursue us to Paris, as they will likely have realised by now what was in the sealed crate. And there is another person seeking to do us ill. I suspect I know who he may be.

"Much therefore needs to be resolved to our satisfaction before you can safely report to the King. To help find the answers, I will return to the shadows and observe from there. I know where to find you. If I ask for you, I expect you to come without delay or hesitation. But for our safety and for His Majesty, do not stay in Paris longer than the end of this month."

Carl Manfred had listened intently to the stranger. "I will indeed respond without delay to any message you send," he assured him. "As for the officer in Calais, I will seek the assistance of my brother-in-law, aide de camp to General de la Rivière, commander of King Louis's Guard, to bring the Calais business to a prompt and effective end. I am most grateful for your information about my brother's killer. He must be confronted if he shows his face in Paris and the responsibility for taking action against him must fall to me. As for any others plotting to betray us, I leave resolution of their fate to you."

The stranger rose to leave.

"I still do not know your name," said Carl Manfred.

"That is a matter you do not need to know," the stranger replied as he walked away.

Minutes later Arabella returned.

"I could not change," she whispered to Carl Manfred. "Mrs Hobson has bound me so tightly into my disguise that I need a woman's assistance to undress. I hope your sister will not be horrified when I arrive on her doorstep in these clothes."

Arabella smiled, looking at him in a new, flirtatious way he had not noticed before.

He returned her smile and said, "I am sure she will be delighted to have such a talented and attractive companion with whom to share her wardrobe – or for whom to create a new one – as a most fitting way to mark your new beginning in Paris under her care. You need not worry about that."

He wished to say more to her but as he pondered whether to do so the boy he had sent to his sister's residence returned with a message. In it Maria Louisa had written:

Dearest Carl,

You must both come at once. It is such a joy that you have returned safely to Paris in time to celebrate Christmas. I will send a carriage immediately to the hostellerie. Please bring your companion.

Your most affectionate sister,
Maria Louisa

Less than half an hour later Carl Manfred and Arabella left the Place Royale in a smart black coach bearing the arms of the King's Guard. It was a short distance to the Rue St Louis. Within minutes the carriage entered the gates of number 76. It was a grand building, comprising four sides around a large courtyard. It was here that Captain Etienne de Vervins had comfortable accommodation so he could be close to his commanding officer, General de la Rivière. Through many of the windows shone candlelight. Between some of the windows on the first floor were statues of Greek and Roman antiquity.

Maria Louisa was standing in the main entrance at the top of a wide flight of balustraded stone steps, accompanied by two footmen and her maid. A stable-boy waiting at the foot of the steps ran forward to take hold of the bridle of the horse. Carl Manfred turned to Arabella, who was mesmerised by the beauty and opulence of what she saw.

"Miss Whitfield, please wait here for a moment while I greet my sister."

He stepped down from the coach and walked quickly up the steps in his relief and joy to be reunited with his sister.

"Dearest Carl, welcome back to Paris," said Maria Louisa. "I thank God you are safely returned. My husband is with the General at Versailles today, attending the King, but I expect him home tomorrow. He will be delighted to meet you. I have told him so much about you. You and he will have much about soldiering to discuss."

"Dearest Maria Louisa, I am delighted to be back," replied Carl Manfred. He kissed her on both cheeks. "And how is little Marie-Aurore?" he asked.

"She is well," replied Maria Louisa. "You will be able to see her tomorrow. But where is your companion?"

"Maria, beneath her male disguise my companion is Mademoiselle Arabella Whitfield from England. There is much to tell you this evening, but suffice it for now to say she had to flee from her vengeful and despicable father and from her brother too. A second companion and I helped her to escape, but to do so we disguised her as a man, in the clothes she is still wearing. I hope that it will be possible for one of your servants to help her change into clothing befitting her sex. She has suffered a deeply troubling ordeal, but with rest and care I am sure she will make a swift recovery. If you and your husband agree, I hope you will allow her to join us for the Christmas celebration."

"My dear Carl, I am greatly intrigued by your companion. Of course she must join us, without delay. And we will certainly ensure that she regains and indeed displays her femininity once more. Hurry, do not stand there. Go and get her."

Carl Manfred returned to the carriage, opened the door and helped Arabella to descend. They went up the steps and entered the *grande salle*.

"Maria Louisa, it is my great pleasure to present Mademoiselle Arabella Whitfield."

Arabella removed her hat and, since she was still dressed as a man, bowed.

"Madame de Vervins, it is a great honour to meet you," she said. "I thank you for your hospitality in allowing me to stay for a short while. Your dear brother, Herr von Deppe, and his companion saved my life."

"Dear Mademoiselle Whitfield, I am glad to hear that," replied Maria Louisa. "I would expect nothing less of my brother. It gives us much pleasure to have you join us. And I compliment you on your exquisite French. My maid, Sybille, will now take you to your room so you can rest. She and others will help you to change – unless, of course, you wish to stay as you are!"

"Madame de Vervins, while I recognise the unique role of men in a woman's life, I have no wish to pay them the ultimate compliment of remaining dressed like them," said Arabella.

"Well and rightly spoken, Miss Whitfield. Now off with you and, as a beginning, let us remove this."

Maria Louisa, laughing, pulled at the ribbon that tied back Arabella's hair. Released from confinement, it slowly tumbled in fullness about her face and onto her shoulders.

"Good. And when I next see you I expect to see your rising moons."

With that both women laughed and Arabella, still blushing from Maria Louisa's reference to sight of her breasts, followed the maid upstairs.

Sybille ushered Arabella into a bedroom on the second floor, much larger than her own at Meltwater. There was a large four-poster bed with silk drapes around it; beautiful chairs and a large dressing table; and the windows were covered with silk curtains. The room was embraced in rich candlelight. Adjacent was a smaller room with a large hip bath, decorated on the outside with floral patterns. On a small table beside it were many towels.

Arabella turned to the maid and asked for her assistance in undressing.

Sybille introduced another maid, Francine.

"Francine will look after you," said Sybille.

Francine first removed Arabella's boots, then the stockings, which revealed blisters on her feet, followed by her jacket, waistcoat, breeches and shirt. Then she carefully removed the binding around her chest. Arabella closed her eyes and breathed in deeply, luxuriating in the sense of relief and freedom.

Sitting on the edge of the bed, looking at the large fire burning in the marble fireplace while the tub was filled, her sore body covered in a soothing silk shift, Arabella thought of her mother in England, isolated and unloved in cold, bleak Meltwater. How she wished her mother could be with her in Paris. After bathing to ease her sore body and the scars of the strap around her wrists, Arabella was overcome by sheer exhaustion. Francine helped her into bed. She fell soundly asleep for the next twelve hours.

Below, over supper, Carl Manfred recounted – selectively – to his sister what had happened in England. He did not mention the execution in Norwich or the circumstances of their brother's death in Paris. That disclosure would have to wait for another time.

"Miss Whitfield is beautiful, Carl, and unattached," said Maria Louisa. "It is evident she has warm feelings towards you. She would make you a fine wife at Herzberg. You should declare your intentions

– if, of course, you have such intentions. I warn you that such a fine woman, with exquisite French, is hardly likely to remain unattached in this city. She will be a prize catch, particularly in court circles."

Carl Manfred paused. "She is indeed beautiful," he replied, looking down at the table as he did so. "I have come to admire her courage greatly. But she is young and high-spirited. She deserves the heart of a worthier, younger man than me."

"Carl, this city is full of young men who either break the hearts of young women or corrupt them. Miss Whitfield may have the courage of a lioness but she will be in grave danger if sucked into the corrupt ways of King Louis and those around him. I cannot be her protector. That should surely be you. You deserve great happiness. Miss Whitfield could help you to enjoy such happiness."

Carl Manfred replied, "Maria Louisa, I will reflect carefully on your advice. But Miss Whitfield deserves a life of untroubled charm and happiness, now she is free of her family. I believe she will be better able to enjoy her new liberty in Paris rather than at Herzberg and in Berlin."

With that he took his leave of Maria Louisa and retired to his room. As he passed Arabella's bedroom, he paused and listened. There was no sound and no trace of light under the door. As he continued along the corridor, he thought of her beauty and youth and his heart stirred. Could it be that he had special feelings for her? Not long after, he too was asleep.

But in the shadows of the city the stranger did not rest. Soon his spies relayed the news that George Whitfield had also arrived in Paris, but alone. Across the street from 76 Rue St Louis, the stranger observed a figure he recognised descend from a carriage and stand momentarily outside the gates that protected the courtyard before returning to the carriage, which then drove off. The stranger decided that this troublesome man should be removed. He followed him to the Hostellerie du Coq d'Or where Whitfield was lodging and in the darkness outside began to consider how best to lure his English opponent to his death.

It was late morning when Arabella awoke from her sleep in the comfortable bedroom at 76 Rue St Louis. As she sat up she became aware of someone else in the room. It was Maria Louisa's maid, Sybille, sitting in a chair with a yellow dress across her lap. Francine stood close by.

Sybille rose to her feet.

"Bonjour, Madame."

"What time is it?" asked Arabella.

"It is almost midday, Madame. I am pleased to see you awake after such a long sleep."

"Good heavens. I must get up."

"Dinner will be at five o'clock," replied Sybille. "Madame de Vervins has asked us to help the seamstress measure you for this dress so that she can make the necessary adjustments in time for you to wear it."

After her toilette, Arabella stood in front of the seamstress to be measured for the gown Maria Louisa had selected for her to wear at dinner, the two maids on hand to hold the tape, or her, as instructed. After the seamstress had left to complete the alterations, and she had assured Sybille there was nothing more she needed, Arabella sat in front of the fire in her silk shift. Her wrists still bore traces of the strap, but beyond that blemish and the blisters on her feet, her complexion had been considerably restored. Her hair, brushed by Francine, hung loose. There was a knock at the door.

"Please come in," said Arabella.

Maria Louisa entered. Arabella stood up and curtsied.

"Good morning, Arabella. I hope you do not mind me calling you by that name. I am pleased to see you awake and trust that you are well-rested. My brother has told me of your dreadful journey across the sea from England. I scolded him for treating you in such a way but he convinced me that it was necessary. He seeks your forgiveness."

"I do forgive him," insisted Arabella. "I will tell him so again. He truly helped to save my life. Without his compassion and the assistance of his companion, I would not be here now. In a few days I promise to relinquish your kind hospitality and to seek alternative refuge in Paris."

"Dearest Arabella, you may stay here as long as you wish. Once upon a time, I left home for the love of a man. It was not easy and I, too, faced hardships, but I persevered and now I am most content with my husband, Captain de Vervins. I hope that one day you will find the same happiness."

The two talked for a while about life in Paris and the court in Versailles.

"I dare say that before too long you will be invited to court. Or at least, General de la Rivière will see to that. Tongues wag in this city and the arrival of a beautiful young English woman will soon cause much curiosity, which only your attendance will satisfy."

"Heaven forbid," said Arabella. "I am from a modest landowning family in England. I am the last person to be invited to court."

"We shall see," said Maria Louisa. "Tonight," she added, "there will be a dinner to welcome the return of my husband, Etienne, and his commanding officer, General de la Rivière, from Versailles, as well as the safe return of my brother and, I may add, your arrival in our house. We will dine at five o'clock, a little later than usual, and after dinner we will gather in the library for music. Do you play?"

"Yes, I do," replied Arabella. "I play the harpsichord, though I am ashamed of my skill at the keyboard after hearing the young Mr Mozart play in London earlier this year."

"Ah, the Mozarts! My husband and I met them when they passed briefly through Paris on their journey back to Salzburg. Excellent, you shall play for us this evening and perhaps you might sing for us too. Is that a music book I see on the table?"

Arabella blushed.

"Perhaps, as I am German, you might sing us one of Mr Handel's arias, which I understand remain popular in London. England was so lucky that he chose to live there for most of his life."

"If you so wish," said Arabella.

"Good, then it is decided. We will look forward to hearing you entertain us later," replied Maria Louisa.

Later in the day, the seamstress returned to fit the dress. Arabella put it on. It was a beautiful yellow gown in the so-called sack-back style, which Maria Louisa said was all the rage at court. Made of silk, probably from Spitalfields in London, it hung lightly from her shoulders, with white silk embroidery on the puffed sleeves and a soft cotton ruff around the neck. With the dress came some yellow heeled shoes and goat-skin gloves. Francine rebrushed Arabella's hair, asking if she would like it pinned up and powdered.

Arabella declined, preferring instead to have her hair loosely tied back with a matching yellow ribbon.

Sybille returned to tell Arabella that Captain de Vervins and the General had returned from Versailles and Madame de Vervins wished her to join them. She added that Herr von Deppe was also keen that she should come quickly, since he had not seen her since their arrival last night.

A few minutes later, Arabella descended the staircase, carrying her music book. Carl Manfred was standing at its foot, looking handsome in a red embroidered jacket, blue waistcoat, white breeches and black buckle shoes. He gazed in amazement as this young and beautiful woman appeared to float down the stairs. He recalled a poem an English soldier had once written down for him. He had always kept it close, reading it many times, indeed memorising it and dreaming of the day when he might say the words to describe a woman he loved.

Whenas in silks my Julia goes,
Then, then, methinks, how sweetly flows
That liquefaction of her clothes!

Next, when I cast mine eyes and see
That brave vibration each way free,
– O how that glittering taketh me!

He could not believe this was the woman upon whom he and the stranger had imposed such terrible hardship in Dover.

"Miss Whitfield, you are an angel descended from heaven," he said as he kissed her gloved hand. "May I have the profound pleasure of escorting you to dinner?"

"It would give me the greatest pleasure if you did so, Herr von Deppe." She placed her hand delicately on his arm.

Dinner lasted two hours. Arabella sat opposite Carl Manfred, as designed by Maria Louisa. There was much laughter and repartee, as well as tales from the King's court, with gossip about those climbing the ladder towards the King's bedroom and those on the way down. The ladies then adjourned, switching to more earnest and intimate conversation, while the men discussed the aftermath of the Seven Years War. Carl Manfred spoke with great discretion, as he knew that any unguarded remark might find its way to the ears of His Majesty King Frederick.

A short while later the dinner guests reassembled in the library. The General's wife, Madame Victoire de la Rivière, asked her daughter, Sophie, to sing some songs popular at court. Arabella turned the pages of the score as Madame de la Rivière played the harpsichord. Then Maria Louisa asked Arabella to play some music from London. She blushed but took her place at the keyboard, opening the music book she and her mother had compiled at Meltwater, and which, with her missal, was the most precious of the few belongings she had brought from England. After Arabella had played two short pieces, Maria Louisa asked her to sing.

"In honour of Madame de Vervins, I would like to sing this aria from Mr Handel's opera *Rinaldo*. It will also serve to remind me of England – his adopted home and my childhood home – which I have just left," said Arabella. "Almira, beloved of the Christian knight, Rinaldo, has been captured by a sorceress, and is subject to unwanted advances from the Saracen King Argante. She sings of her sadness."

Framed by the soft, deep-yellow candlelight, Arabella began to play and then sang, in perfect Italian:

Let me lament
my cruel destiny,
and yearn
for liberty.

May grief,
in its mercy,
shatter the bonds
of my torment.

The room sat in wonder and silence at the delicacy of her fingers on the keyboard and the sweetness of her soprano voice as the notes she sang floated like feathers in the air. Carl Manfred was transfixed by Arabella's beauty and sensuality, which her singing intensified. When she finished, the audience's silence of sheer wonder continued for a moment longer. Then Maria Louisa stood to applaud, followed by her other guests.

"Please sing to us again," was the cry.

"If you would kindly permit me, I should like to sing another aria, which my dear mother used to sing. It is from Mr Handel's *Giulio Cesare*," said Arabella.

She looked down at the keyboard as she played the opening bars. Then, as she uttered the first words, she looked across towards Carl Manfred, standing at the back of the room:

I adore you, eyes, Cupid's darts,
Your sparks are welcome in my breast.
My sad heart craves your mercy,
For ever calling you its dearest love.

Was she singing to him, pondered Carl Manfred? Their eyes momentarily met before she turned again to the music book and then to others in her audience. As she finished, she glanced at Carl Manfred once more and gently smiled.

He realised for the first time that perhaps it was possible he might be in love with her. But how could this be? She was young and beautiful. He was much older, a stiff Prussian ex-soldier, his life full of bloodshed on the battlefield, tarnished values and disappointments. What could he, the owner of a large estate in distant Prussia, offer to such talent and beauty? His life was more than half run. Before long it would be on the ebb, while the tide of her sweet life was rising. He would enjoy being close to her in Paris and kissing her hand in the coming days. But on the first of January he had to leave Paris for Berlin, to discharge his obligation to King Frederick, after which he would return alone to Herzberg. It could not be any other way. Miss Whitfield would surely be summoned to court and follow a life far different from his. As he sat gazing at her receiving the plaudits of Maria Louisa's guests, he heard the General say to Maria Louisa that he would arrange for her to sing to King Louis at Versailles without delay.

The guests lingered but Arabella asked Maria Louisa if she might retire, as she was still tired after her journey from England.

"Yes, of course, my dear. You sang with exquisite beauty and sensitivity. Thank you for reminding me so poignantly of my homeland and its musical creativity, often forgotten in the fog of war. Go and rest. Tomorrow morning we shall go riding while the house is prepared for Christmas. The weather promises to be good. Goodnight."

Arabella replied, "I wish to thank you and Captain de Vervins for your most gracious hospitality and great kindness. It was an evening of pure enchantment, which I will long remember."

After taking her leave of Captain de Vervins, General de la Rivière, Madame de la Rivière and their daughter, Sophie, and Maria Louisa's other guests, Arabella left the room, her hand on Carl Manfred's arm. At the foot of the staircase, he lifted her hand from his sleeve and kissed it, then wished her good night.

"It would give me great pleasure if you would ride with us tomorrow," said Arabella.

He bowed.

"It would be an honour to do so."

He returned to join the remaining guests.

As Carl Manfred was about to retire to bed, he received a note, hand-delivered to the door. It was from the stranger. He put on his coat and slipped quietly out of the house to cross the courtyard.

At the gate was the stranger.

"What are your plans for tomorrow?" he asked Carl Manfred.

"My sister has arranged to ride in the Bois de Boulogne while the house is prepared for Christmas. Miss Whitfield will join her, as she is much refreshed from her ordeal. And I will accompany them," he replied.

"Good," said the stranger. "But be vigilant. That cur, George Whitfield, is in Paris and I have seen him observing this house. I have put a plan in motion to rid us of this man. We will carry it out tomorrow. Be watchful, and ride close to Miss Whitfield. She is in great danger while her brother is at large. And so are we, as he draws unnecessary attention to us. Tomorrow you will need to act with great speed."

"I understand," replied Carl Manfred.

With that the stranger melted into the shadows. Carl Manfred returned to the house and, after assuring Maria Louisa and her husband that he had only been taking the night air, he retired to his room. As he did so, he passed Arabella's room, but as before there was no sound or light. Standing in front of her door, he pledged silently that he would do all he could to protect her from harm.

* * * * *

George Whitfield, newly arrived in Paris, was sitting late in the Hostellerie du Coq d'Or that evening, drinking and playing cards, when he received an anonymous note to say that Arabella Whitfield, his sister, would ride in the Bois de Boulogne the next day around noon, with one of the men he sought, and others. A contact would come to the hostellerie early in the morning to assist him in the abduction of Arabella and her removal to England. The note, which asked for a reply, was signed with initials familiar to Whitfield: those of the man with whom he had travelled to France, and who had finally disclosed his identity to him and his father before they left Dover. George Whitfield scrawled at the foot of the message his glad compliance with the enterprise and handed it back to the runner. He returned to his cards and asked the young buxom girl to bring him more wine. He was keen to bed her. If the writer of the note was now recovered and in Paris, and their business was soon to be concluded, as its contents suggested, he had no time to lose.

The following morning a thin, mean-looking man, known to those who hired his dubious services as Berthould Dressler, arrived at the hostellerie at eleven o'clock to take George Whitfield to the Bois de Boulogne in a red closed carriage. Whitfield asked his name.

"Better you do not know, Mr Whitfield," Dressler replied. "That is the way we like it in our business. But be assured, I am here to help you."

Dressler said that he would take Whitfield to a particular vantage point in the park where, from a concealed spot, he would be able to see the pathway that ladies tended to use on their morning ride. It was a cold morning, and there were still remains of snow on the ground, but visibility would be clear.

"How are we to abduct my sister?" asked Whitfield.

Dressler replied that he intended to place an obstacle on the bridle path to cause the ladies' coach to stop. He and Whitfield, who should fire his pistol to ward off anyone who might be tempted to intervene, would rush forward to seize the young lady, take her to their own coach, drug her and immediately leave for Calais and England. The key to success was speed. He could, of course, kill his sister. But there was a risk that if they were apprehended in such an act they would be arrested and sentenced to death for murder. Whitfield readily agreed to the plan.

Dressler mounted the front of the coach and it moved at a fast pace from the hostellerie towards the Bois. Whitfield sat inside, still recovering from his heavy drinking of the night before and mixed fortunes at cards. The young buxom serving girl had resisted his advances.

Thursday, 5 December, was cold. There were few people riding in the Bois. The red carriage came to a stop in a copse of trees close to the bridle path. The mean-looking man found a heavy fallen branch and dragged it onto the pathway. He told Whitfield to remain in the carriage until he signalled him to come.

George Whitfield sat back and waited. The moment had surely arrived to take his troublesome sister back to England and deliver her to his father for disposal. Despite the allure of Paris, he was anxious to return to his usual habits of cards, drinking and womanising in London, and indeed to see his father in a better temper. In return for satisfying his father's appetite for revenge against Arabella, he would ask for a substantial payment to settle his freshly mounting debts and to pursue a wealthy heiress in Dorset. He also had a score to settle against Herr von Deppe, but he had to pass that opportunity by. Only Arabella was in his sights.

* * * * *

By mid-morning the riding party was assembled in the courtyard of 76 Rue St Louis. General de la Rivière was busy in the library, composing a message to the King seeking permission to present a young English lady at court on New Year's Day, so that His Majesty could listen to her exquisite singing. His aide de camp, Captain Etienne de Vervins, was with him.

The sky was clear and the sun shone. As the ground was slippery from the remaining snow, it was agreed that the ladies would not venture out on horseback; the conditions were judged too hazardous to ride side-saddle. They would take carriages instead. Despite Carl Manfred's earnest advice to use closed coaches, they insisted on riding in open carriages, the better to enjoy the sunshine, with heavy blankets over their knees against the cold.

Arabella wore a dark-blue velvet riding habit from Maria Louisa's wardrobe. It had a large black ribbon tied in a bow at her throat over the white frilled collar of her undershirt. She wore a wide-brimmed black hat, pinned to which was a large white feather. Black gloves and ankle boots completed her outfit. Arabella sat in the second carriage with General de la Rivière's daughter, Sophie, while Maria Louisa rode in the first carriage with Madame de la Rivière. Carl Manfred rode on a black horse alongside. The gates of the courtyard opened and the carriages turned into the Rue St Louis in the direction of the Bois de Boulogne.

The two open carriages entered the Bois shortly after midday. They proceeded at a gentle trot along the pathway. Maria Louisa and Madame de la Rivière were talking excitedly about the prospect of a new year and a hunting trip to the General's country estate. Behind them, Sophie de la Rivière and Arabella compared the prevailing fashions in Paris and England. Carl Manfred was tense as he remembered the words of the stranger the night before. He dropped back until his horse was almost parallel with the second carriage.

Looking about him, he thought he caught the glimpse of movement ahead. As they went further along the bridleway, he suddenly saw a large tree branch blocking their path. He sensed this was a moment of utmost danger.

The driver of the first carriage brought the horses to a stop.

"What is it?" asked Maria Louisa.

"It looks like a branch has fallen, Madame," he replied. "I will have to remove it before we can continue."

"I will do it," said Carl Manfred, as the second carriage drew to a halt.

As he rode to the front, a man with a scarf covering his face and brandishing a pistol suddenly ran out of the trees towards the second carriage, with another man running close behind him. As the first man was about to aim his pistol, the second man pulled him to the ground. They began to struggle. Carl Manfred leapt from his horse and pinned the masked man down, while his pursuer – Dressler – tied his wrists with cord from his pocket, whispering to Carl Manfred that he was an agent of their mutual friend. The man on the ground was struggling violently to free himself and yelled obscenities in English.

At that point the stranger suddenly appeared from the trees to help pull the man to his feet. He struck him a violent blow across the face and, together with Dressler, quickly dragged him towards the red coach concealed in the trees. Turning to Carl Manfred, the stranger said that he would come to the Rue St Louis that evening. Carl Manfred knew that this meant they would at last confront the victim, now slumped in the coach with a damp cloth held to his mouth.

Carl Manfred returned to the pathway. He hurriedly removed the fallen branch, remounted his horse and urged the coachmen to return swiftly to the Rue St Louis. After reassuring Maria Louisa and Madame de la Rivière that all was well and waving away their acclamation of his bravery, he moved back until he was abreast of the second carriage. Sophie de la Rivière was talking excitedly about what had happened and what she would be able to tell her friends. Arabella sat motionless, white as a sheet.

"We must talk at once on our return to the Rue St Louis," she said to Carl Manfred as she evidently struggled to hold back her tears.

At the Rue St Louis the incident in the Bois became the talk of the house. General de la Rivière said that the attempt on the ladies was scandalous. More had to be done to ensure safety in the royal park while its gates were open each day. Captain de Vervins said he would ensure that in future the ladies would have better protection. Both the General and Captain de Vervins thanked Carl Manfred for his timely and courageous action.

A few minutes later Arabella and Carl Manfred were alone together in the library.

"Who was the man in the Bois? And why was your companion there?" she asked.

"It was your brother, Miss Whitfield," he replied. "Yesterday I received reliable information that he was in Paris and that he had been watching this house. My companion, whose honourable role I am not at liberty to describe, decided that it was necessary to set a trap to catch him, because we had reason to believe he intended to abduct you and return you to England."

Arabella gasped in horror.

"I could not allow that to happen," continued Carl Manfred, "but you must understand that I was unable to disclose our intentions to you or, indeed, to anyone in this house for fear of compromising our intervention. So the encounter in the Bois had to take place. I beg your forgiveness for not taking you into my confidence. Miss Whitfield, do not misunderstand me. I place the highest value on your safety, and have already had good cause to admire your courage. But in a house full of soldiers it was imperative to proceed as we did. Our sole aim was to save you from those determined to make you a victim of their malice. I wish no misfortune or injury to befall you. Your liberty and love of life must not be snatched from you."

"Thank you, Herr von Deppe. You are indeed the kindest man I have ever met. I have already shown – on the wretched journey from Dover, when I was bound and sealed in that dreadful box in which I almost suffocated – how much I trust you. Why is it that my father will not let me go? I will live in France for the rest of my life in whatever circumstances necessary so that he can pursue his career with the memory of me erased. But so far it would appear that his obsession with avenging my leaving home has no end, no boundaries. I do not know what is to be done. Why will they not leave me alone?"

As she uttered these words, Arabella seemed utterly lost. Carl Manfred drew her towards him as she began to cry.

"All will be resolved, Miss Whitfield," he said, as he looked into her tear-stained face. "Please continue to place your trust in me."

"I will," said Arabella.

She then left the library to go to her room to compose herself.

"What is the matter, Carl Manfred? I thought I heard Miss Whitfield crying," said Maria Louisa as she entered the library.

"She was indeed," said Carl Manfred. "The incident in the Bois brought back unpleasant memories of England. She will rejoin us later. Before we return to the others, I wish to tell you, Maria Louisa, that I will have to leave the house for a while this evening. It is on King Frederick's business that I do so. I will come back for tonight's festivities as quickly as I can. But I must begin preparations to leave for Berlin immediately after the New Year."

"Carl, that is indeed most regrettable news," said Maria Louisa. "I will be most sad to see you leave. It is all the more reason to complete your business this evening without delay. After all, I am not the only one who wishes your company. Miss Whitfield will also be greatly reassured to have you close by."

Carl Manfred blushed but made no comment. Maria Louisa smiled and squeezed his arm as they walked towards the others, who were standing in the *grande salle* still discussing what had happened in the Bois.

It was about four o'clock in the afternoon when Carl Manfred received a note to say that a coach awaited him at the courtyard gate. He knew the purpose. After asking the footman to inform Madame de Vervins that he was going out for a while, he put on his overcoat and hat. Ensuring that his small pistol was in his pocket, he walked across the courtyard and out to the Rue St Louis, where he climbed inside the waiting coach to sit opposite the stranger. Neither spoke.

After a journey lasting some twenty minutes, the carriage entered a narrow, dingy street. The two got out and went inside a tall, dilapidated building. They descended into a basement. Immediately, the darkness, damp and smell reminded Carl Manfred of the hideous cellar in Norwich. Sitting on a chair and chained to the wall by his left leg was a dishevelled George Whitfield, still recovering from his drugging. Dressler stood guard behind him.

Carl Manfred scrutinised Whitfield. He was well-dressed but unshaven, with heavy dark rings around his eyes. His hair was unkempt. A wig lay on the table in front of him.

The stranger sat down on the other side of the table, facing him.

"Whitfield, I have been looking forward to this meeting for some time. You have been following us. But we have followed you. This morning you did not get what you wanted. But we have got what we wanted – you. I think you like to play cards. I do, too. You and I are going to play pharo. If you win, we will let you go. If you lose, the forfeit will be your life."

The stranger placed a deck of cards and some coins on the table. He then drew his pistol and knife from his coat and laid them out as the intended weapons of execution if Whitfield lost. Carl Manfred placed his own pistol on the table, with the barrel facing Whitfield.

"Let the game begin," the stranger said.

"You cannot do this," protested Whitfield, trying to rise from his chair but restrained by the short chain.

"Sit down," barked the stranger, turning, like Carl Manfred had done, the barrel of his pistol and the point of his knife towards Whitfield.

The stranger dealt the cards and the game of pharo began – a game banned in France under the most severe penalties. Whitfield was a good player and indeed an accomplished card sharp. But however hard he tried that evening he could not win. He lost.

"The cards are marked," he cried out.

"They are. And so, it seems, were the cards you used when you played my brother," interjected Carl Manfred. "He, too, was good, but he lost because you cheated. You then chased him into the streets for money he did not owe and could not pay. With your friends you killed him in cold blood."

"Forgive me," implored Whitfield.

"But that is not all, is it?" said the stranger. "This morning you were armed with a pistol, intending to abduct or kill your sister."

Whitfield pleaded for mercy.

"It is my father who is constantly pressing me."

Carl Manfred spoke. "I cannot forget that you killed my brother in cold blood. You will stop at nothing, not even murder, to get what you want. This morning it was your plan to deliver your sister into the hands of your father, in return, no doubt, for money to pay your debts."

"You are a killer, a wastrel, corrupt in mind and body. You have no future," added the stranger.

Carl Manfred looked intently at Whitfield. He remembered his brother; he remembered Arabella's deep distress earlier in the day; and he remembered his silent promise to protect her at all costs. He felt her hand on his arm. He half turned but she was not there – her presence in the cellar was a figment of his imagination. Though she was only in his mind, he realised that, such were his feelings towards Arabella, he would indeed kill anyone who threatened her. He looked again at the prisoner who would never win his last game of cards. The inescapable facts were that Whitfield had tried to abduct his sister and, according to the stranger, whose word he believed, had killed Carl Manfred's brother in cold blood. And it was possible he was in league with others to betray the mission they had completed by command of

King Frederick. Carl Manfred slowly picked up his pistol and aimed carefully at Whitfield. The stranger took aim with his own. Images of killing on the battlefield and the execution in the cellar in Norwich flashed before Carl Manfred's eyes. But through the images peered the cold, cruel eyes of Whitfield, staring at him.

The shot rang out. Whitfield fell forwards onto the table. The stranger put his pistol down and then picked up the knife, plunging it into Whitfield's right hand, his card-playing hand, uttering the words, "With His Majesty's compliments." Whitfield groaned in agony and fell silent.

The stranger turned to Carl Manfred.

"I had no doubt you would shoot him in revenge for your brother. But because of your high regard for Miss Whitfield – and, I suspect, hers for you – I thought it more appropriate that I should shed his blood and not you. My hands are already so steeped in the blood of others that a few more drops will make no difference."

Carl Manfred replied, "Thank you. But you may rest assured I would have done the deed for the best of motives."

He put his pistol back into his pocket. His brother had been avenged and Miss Whitfield had one less enemy.

The stranger addressed Dressler.

"You have done well today, my friend. You have earned your pay. Dispose of Mr Whitfield without delay somewhere he will not be quickly found. And remove from here all trace of our presence. We will meet later, as we still have important work to do. The King's enemies remain."

The stranger left quietly the way he always did – in the shadows.

Carl Manfred returned to 76 Rue St Louis. He heard much happiness and laughter as he entered. Maria Louisa greeted him.

"Dear Carl, at last you have returned from King Frederick's business. We will now eat. Let us begin to enjoy Advent."

It was an evening of great joy, pleasure and amusement. Arabella wore a blue satin décolleté dress, with the front exposing a deep-yellow petticoat – a style she knew from London, where it also prevailed. After dinner, she sat at the harpsichord to accompany Sophie de la Rivière, who sang more songs fashionable at court. Maria Louisa sang airs from her homeland, and the men joined in the entertainment with military marches. Later in the evening, musicians arrived and there was dancing in the *grande salle*. General de la Rivière and Captain de Vervins danced with Arabella. Carl Manfred danced with Madame de la Rivière, Sophie and Maria Louisa. And then Maria Louisa said to the General, "You must permit Mademoiselle Whitfield to have at least one dance with my brother before you completely exhaust her."

Arabella was delighted to receive Carl Manfred's invitation to dance. First, they danced a bourée and then a minuet.

"Miss Whitfield, there is no end to your accomplishments – the harpsichord, singing and now dancing."

"You flatter me, sir," said Arabella.

"I speak the truth," he replied.

After dancing a third minuet, Carl Manfred suggested that they pause, knowing the dancing was likely to last many hours yet and he could not monopolise Arabella, however much he wished to do so.

"Miss Whitfield, though I have no wish to remind you of this morning's event in the Bois, I wish you to know that the matter of your brother has been resolved. You need no longer have any fear of his actions, though I cannot speak of your father's intentions. Tonight you may sleep in peace and, I hope, tomorrow and the day after."

"What occurred this evening?" Arabella asked.

"That is not a matter for now, Miss Whitfield. Please enjoy the celebrations."

"I do not know what may have happened, sir, but I am even more in your debt for your protection. I will never forget your kindness. May we dance together once more? It would please me greatly."

"Of course," said Carl Manfred.

And so they returned to the dance floor and the festivities, which continued long into the night.

Meanwhile, late that night, the body of George Whitfield was carried quietly, in the shadows, by Dressler and an accomplice, towards a dark and frightening place. The male heir to Meltwater was soon to be no more.

At 76 Rue St Louis the succeeding weeks passed in a flurry of activity and laughter. Carl Manfred and Arabella spent much time together. He even accompanied her to Mass. But the most notable event was the invitation to attend the court at Versailles for the traditional ceremony to mark the New Year, 1766, and the commencement of the formal dancing season. So, on 1 January, General de la Rivière, his wife and daughter, Maria Louisa and her husband, and Arabella and Carl Manfred left in coaches for the royal palace to join the hundreds of other guests.

The occasion was spectacular and breathtaking. His Majesty King Louis made his grand ceremonial entrance into the famed Hall of Mirrors accompanied by Queen Marie Leszczyńska and her amazingly coiffured ladies-in-waiting. There was no official royal mistress in attendance, the position having remained unfilled since the death of the Marquise de Pompadour in 1764; speculation as to who her successor might be provided everyone present with an inexhaustible topic of conversation. The court glittered. Arabella was speechless. She had never seen such wealth, artistry, pomp, glory and sheer egotism. She had read accounts of the Sun King, Louis XIV. The present King might be less extravagant than his predecessor, but the drama and revels being acted out before her left her in wonderment.

The ladies of the court were beautifully adorned and exquisitely powdered, but they were merely accoutrements to the aristocrats and officials executing their roles before the King. For Arabella, this was a world that seemed to bear little relation to the brief glimpses she had seen of ordinary life in France – or England, for that matter. She felt uncomfortable and kept close to Carl Manfred, whom she sensed, from his tense posture, was equally ill at ease. For him, this charade of powder and play-acting was far removed from the stringency and bareness of King Frederick's court in Berlin and Potsdam.

Before the King withdrew, General de la Rivière asked him to grant his earlier request to present Mademoiselle Arabella Whitfield from England. The King agreed with little enthusiasm. He wished to return to his bedchamber for other sport. Arabella suddenly saw General de la Rivière coming quickly towards her.

"His Majesty the King wishes to meet you. Come immediately, as he is about to retire."

Arabella gasped.

"But General de la Rivière," she replied, "there must be some mistake. Why should His Majesty wish to see me?"

"But he does," insisted the General, seizing her by the arm and steering her through the crush of guests.

Arabella looked back at Carl Manfred, seeking the reassurance of his smile, but he was talking to someone nearby.

When Arabella stepped forward in her alluringly low-cut pink satin dress, which Maria Louisa had specially chosen from her wardrobe, the King's attention was no longer diverted by those around him or pleasures to come. Arabella shook with nerves as she curtsied deeply.

"I hear you play and sing," said the King, eyeing her cleavage.

"Your Majesty, I am only good enough to play privately to my friends."

"I am your friend. After all, you are, I am told, a citizen of France, courtesy of your mother, and if that is the case, should you not obey your King? And we are in private," retorted the monarch, laughing. "So sing to me. Please bring forward a harpsichord immediately."

And so it was that Arabella Whitfield sang to the King of France and his court on New Year's Day, 1766. As she did so, the King looked at the young, slender, dark-haired beauty, her exquisite breasts almost completely exposed in keeping with the prevailing fashion, and thought that perhaps he should invite her to reside at court so she would be available to share his bed as one of his many mistresses.

"De la Rivière," he whispered to the General, "please see to it that she is given lodgings at court without delay."

After two songs from Arabella, the King rose, the court bowed and the royal entourage left. Later, the coaches returned to Paris. Arabella and Sophie talked and giggled about what they had seen. Carl Manfred sat opposite them, only half listening as he thought of his imminent departure for Berlin. In the preceding coach, the General told Maria Louisa what the King had whispered into his ear. Arabella was, as she feared, about to be recruited to the royal stable for possible bed duties.

It was the early hours of the next morning when the inhabitants of 76 Rue St Louis returned home. Shortly after everyone had retired to rest, Carl Manfred once again received a message that he had a visitor at the gate. He crossed the courtyard and joined the stranger in his coach.

"His Majesty King Frederick has asked when he might expect you in Berlin. I have already replied that it is your intention to leave Paris imminently. The appearance, however innocent, of close fraternisation with the French would displease him. Whatever may be your intentions towards Miss Whitfield, you must leave quickly."

"I had already resolved to leave without further delay. Miss Whitfield must now find her own future in France."

"I am pleased to hear of your intentions. You have made a wise decision," replied the stranger.

Carl Manfred looked sharply at him but said nothing.

"But before you leave there is something more you should know," the stranger continued as they sat in the closed carriage. "I have received reliable information that the elusive Bolton will shortly arrive in Paris to seek an early audience at Versailles. It would appear from unimpeachable evidence now in my hands that my earlier suspicions have been confirmed. He is serving the French while masquerading as an agent of King Frederick. That being so, it is likely that he plans to embarrass His Majesty by disclosing to the French that the execution in England was on the King's personal instructions. Bolton will no doubt say that, in ordering such a deed, our King was interfering in the affairs of England through committing cold-blooded murder. And now that your sister has been involved in the introduction of a young and attractive English girl to the French court, Bolton may allege that it is with the express design of introducing her to Louis's bed to spy for us. Then there is the Whitfield family, already known to Bolton. It appears that he and they did have contact in England, as we had reason to suspect on the return journey to London and in Dover. Sir Robert Whitfield may wish to have a part to play in such an exposure, so as to retrieve his waning political ambitions in England.

"Such allegations and revelations would cause His Majesty great discomfort and anger, and it would bring grave danger of French charges of treason for Madame de Vervins, her husband and indeed the General. His Majesty in Berlin would find it difficult to counter such charges, if published, particularly concerning what might be claimed to have happened in England. We have a problem to solve. I will find Bolton and interrogate him. If he has committed treason, he must pay the price for his treachery. His fate is my responsibility. What you must do is go to Berlin quickly to assuage any doubts that the King may have of your loyalty as a result of rumours from other sources. "It was Machiavelli who said, 'For when you are on the spot, disorders are detected in their beginning and remedies can be readily applied; but when you are at a distance, they are not heard of until they have gathered strength and the case is past cure.'

"Make sure you say nothing to your sister or to the girl about this matter. A coach will come for you at midday to take you to the border, where others will meet you. I will stay in Paris to intercept Bolton and so stop him reaching King Louis. Once that business is done, I will follow you."

Carl Manfred sat dazed by what the stranger had revealed. He said he had many questions but only one was uppermost in his mind.

"Is Arabella Whitfield a spy? Has she duped us or is she an innocent pawn, unaware of the game now being played?"

The stranger thought carefully before replying. He had first seen Arabella in London, used – at John Bolton's instigation – in the role of a prostitute to deter Carl Manfred from the streets of London. Until the encounter with her father in Norwich, he would not have put his mission at risk to save her. But from close observation he believed that, while she may have begun a new life in London as a courtesan, it was indeed probably caused by circumstances beyond her control. London was a seedy and corrupt city where the innocent were easily fooled. His overriding concern was to get Colonel von Deppe back to Prussia as fast as possible to speak to the King, while he secured the capture of another traitor to His Majesty. He dismissed from his immediate preoccupations the involvement of a woman who was clearly in love with the Colonel and most likely he with her. Affairs of the heart could not be allowed to interfere with completing the secret fulfilment of the King's wishes.

"Well, what is the answer?" pressed Carl Manfred.

The stranger turned to Carl Manfred and replied, "I believe Miss Whitfield is entirely innocent, but her involvement in our affairs must end."

But this was not to be, as he already suspected.

As he stepped down from the carriage, Carl Manfred turned to the dark profile inside.

"Just who are you? You have never told me. I wish to know."

"I have said before," replied the stranger, "you do not need to know. To quote Mr Machiavelli again, 'it is necessary to be a fox to discover the snares and a lion to terrify the wolves.' Like a fox, discovering snares is what I do from the shadows, and in the shadows the least known the better. Now be gone."

Carl Manfred returned to the house, going straight to his room to prepare for his imminent departure from Paris. Then he spoke to his sister, who was giving instructions to Sybille for the day ahead.

"Maria Louisa, I must leave today for Berlin. A coach will come for me at noon. I wish I could stay longer with you, your husband and Marie-Aurore, but that is not possible. King Frederick has become impatient for my return and monarchs must not be kept waiting."

"Dear Carl, that is indeed sad news. Please come back to Paris as soon as you can. We still have much to talk about after our long time apart."

Carl Manfred replied that it was unlikely he would return soon. After his audience with the King, he would have to go immediately to Herzberg, from which he had been absent for over four months. He hoped that before too long Maria Louisa would visit him there.

He then said to Maria Louisa, "It is likely that I will be gone before Miss Whitfield awakes. Please tell her that I was called away to Berlin at short notice and, as it is unlikely I will see her again, I wish her well in her new life in France, where I hope she will find much personal happiness. I know you will do all you can to see her safely settled."

"Carl," Maria Louisa replied, "she will be deeply sorry to see you go. I believe – it is a woman's intuition, you might say – that you hold a special place in her affection. I have seen how lively and engaged she is in your presence. Please put in writing to her what you have asked me to say. I will do my best to assuage her sorrow at your departure and to delay her inevitable summons to the palace to join the bevy of mistresses King Louis is sampling to replace La Pompadour. Arabella and the others may be chosen but they will have no lasting future there. The Marquise's successor will see to that. And then Mademoiselle Whitfield will be on the royal scrapheap, discarded into the hands of some minor title either to produce endless children or to sit at home and sew while her husband keeps the beds of other women warm. With beauty, a sharp mind and such brilliant musical talents, Arabella does not deserve that. Carl, have you considered whether she might share your life at Herzberg?"

"I thank you for your concern," said Carl Manfred, "but I believe she is only twenty-two and I am twice her age. I am a retired soldier, now trying to maintain a large estate in Prussia. The road of my life has been a long and hard one and is more than half-travelled. I cannot offer her the life befitting such a beautiful young woman full of vigour and brimming with hope for long and enduring love. Now that she is free of her past, she should follow your example and marry a handsome, rich young Frenchman. If I marry – and I doubt I shall – it will no doubt be to a dull middle-aged Prussian lady who will help me keep the Herzberg accounts in good shape."

"Carl, you deprecate yourself too much," said Maria Louisa. "Self-deprecation and loneliness have characterised you since you were a boy. You lived for too long in your brother's shadow. But you are strong, handsome, determined and kind, and few men have won the King's confidence and trust to the extent you have clearly done. You would be a fine catch for any young lady, including Arabella Whitfield. Please remember that as you travel east. That is the least you can do for me."

"I promise I will," said Carl Manfred. "And, Maria Louisa, please do all you can to prevent Miss Whitfield returning to the palace. I cannot explain now but it would be better for you, your husband and, indeed, the General if she stayed quietly in Paris at least for the next month, until I have reached Berlin. I cannot say more, other than to remind you that we live in a nest of vipers. I would prefer no harm to befall any of you, particularly you, my dearest sister."

"What are you saying, Carl?" asked Maria Louisa.

"I cannot explain. Please do as I ask. And be vigilant. Difficult times may lie ahead."

Maria Louisa nodded, though deeply troubled.

He went upstairs to finish packing and to write his letter to Arabella.

Dear Miss Whitfield,

It is with profound sadness that I must leave immediately for Berlin, to attend upon His Majesty King Frederick in respect of some most urgent matters, and thereafter depart for my estate at Herzberg, from which I have been absent for many months. It is unlikely that I will return to Paris in the foreseeable future. I much regret that I did not have the opportunity to say farewell to you in person.

I wish you to know that I have come greatly to admire you, your talents, your courage and your determination to succeed in life against all odds. You are a truly remarkable young woman. You should know that you have brought me great warmth and happiness in the short time we have been together. I hope that before too long you will be able to share your life and ideals with someone who will show you the kindness, respect and love you so richly deserve. You will always be amongst my most cherished memories. My sister will do all she can to ensure that, after the past dark months, 1766 will bring you great peace and fulfilment in France.

Your most obedient servant,
Carl Manfred von Deppe

He then went downstairs, placed the sealed letter on the table in the *grande salle* and said a fond farewell to Maria Louisa, her husband and Marie-Aurore. At the stroke of noon he climbed into the coach arranged by the stranger and began his return to Berlin.

As the carriage moved away from 76 Rue St Louis, Arabella awoke. An hour later she went downstairs. Maria Louisa asked her to join her in the library. She handed Arabella the letter from Carl Manfred. Arabella opened the letter and read it. Deeply upset by its contents, she said, "He never found the time to say goodbye. I had so much that I wanted to say to him."

Maria Louisa leaned across and took her hand.

"Arabella, I wish you to be frank with me. Do you love him?"

"I do. I love him deeply," she replied.

"But," asked Maria Louisa, "why should you love him? You are young and attractive and with many gifts – exquisite French, great musical skills and a pleasing humour. If you are invited to court, as

I believe you will be, you will be surrounded by many young and charming French nobles looking for someone to bed and perhaps to marry, enabling you to live a titled life of some luxury within sight of the Palace of Versailles. Carl is older, less vivacious than those who surround the King, and preoccupied with maintaining a large estate in faraway Prussia. I am sure you will soon forget him."

"Madame de Vervins, I lived as a child in a comfortable house in England. I love my mother. She taught me so many ways to enjoy life, to seek liberty and equality between a man and a woman, and to pursue one's destiny, hard though that might prove to be. I miss her so much. My father's brutality, driven by an out-of-date attitude and cruel temperament, separated me from my mother and my home. I will never forgive him nor ever bend to what he wants me to do. For that reason I went to London to fend for myself and witnessed a life I have no desire to emulate and which has left me stained. I do not wish to become the wife of a man who lies and who has mistresses in the evening. If he will take me, I wish to love a man with all my heart and for him to love me as his equal – a love that is based on a bond of trust. Your brother showed me great kindness. He protected me from my father's wrath. Herr von Deppe is in my soul, in my heart. Before him I saw only darkness. Now he has brought light. I truly love him," said Arabella.

"Arabella," replied Maria Louisa, "if you are truly sure, then you must fight hard for what you want, as you say your mother taught you. If when you wake tomorrow morning you are still convinced that you love my brother, and you are prepared to put your love to the test, then I will gladly arrange for you to travel to the border. From there, with further help, you should travel to Berlin and declare your love to him. Remove his silly and stubborn blindness and convince him that in his heart he loves you."

"I will do so," replied Arabella.

She then asked if she might go to the nearby Church of St Laurent to pray.

"Of course, I will arrange for you to be taken there within the hour," replied Maria Louisa.

Arabella went to make her first confession since leaving Meltwater and to pray that she might travel safely the next day to begin her search for Carl Manfred.

That evening, Arabella sat with the de Vervins family in the library. They were joined by Sophie de la Rivière, who entertained them at the harpsichord. When Sophie suggested to her that she might sing, Arabella opened once again her treasured music book and sang Handel's air *The Triumph of Time and Truth*:

Guardian angels, oh, protect me,
And in Virtue's path direct me,
While resign'd to Heav'n above.
Let no more this world deceive me,
Nor let idle passions grieve me,
Strong in faith, in hope, in love.

The following morning, after Maria Louisa had explained with great difficulty to her husband, ensconced with General de la Rivière, their guest's sudden decision to depart Paris for Prussia, Arabella climbed into a coach paid for by Maria Louisa. She was accompanied by Maria Louisa's trusted confidant, Father Johann Enders, a German-born priest from the nearby Church of St Laurent in the Rue St Louis, whom Maria Louisa had persuaded to act as escort. Arabella did not know that it was Father Johann who had heard her confession the night before. Dressed in the blue riding habit she had worn in the Bois de Boulogne, but with the clothes she had worn in her escape from London to Paris in her bag, she faced a daunting journey across France and Germany in pursuit of a man with whom she was deeply in love.

As the coach headed out of Paris towards the north east, she recalled a poem by the Ancient Greek poetess Sappho. Her mother had read it to her many times, as woman to woman, in their more recent private moments at Meltwater:

He looks to me to be in heaven,
That man who sits across from you
And listens near you to your soft speaking,

Your laughing lovely: that, I vow,
Makes the heart leap in my breast;
For, watching you a moment, speech fails me,

My tongue is paralysed, at once
A light fire runs beneath my skin,
My eyes are blinded, and my ears drumming,

The sweat pours down me, and I shake
All over, sallower than grass:
I feel as if I'm not far off dying.

The stranger watched from an entrance across the street, forewarned by the priest – one of his network of spies. He wished the girl had not left. She was in a comfortable place. Why could she not stay there? But affairs of the heart had once again intervened in what was about to unfold. Upon reflection, however, the stranger concluded that her journey to Berlin might, after all, serve as bait to catch his traitor. Bolton would recognise Miss Whitfield if brought face to face. If Bolton were to find out that the woman he had put to use in London was on her way to join Carl Manfred von Deppe in Berlin, to help denounce his treachery to the King, he might urgently defer his request to see King Louis. He might reason that it would be better to dispose of them both as quickly as possible, rather than simply expose von Deppe in front of the French king. And if Bolton did reason his predicament in this way, thought the stranger, he would fall into the trap he now intended to set. He would then have his traitor in his grasp and His Majesty King Frederick would be rid of another enemy.

And so the stranger sprang the trap.

CHAPTER 15

Traps Sprung and Foiled

By the time Arabella left the Rue St Louis early on Friday, 3 January 1766, in the company of Father Johann, the weather had turned. The cold but clear, bright days of the last week of December had vanished. The sky was now leaden and low, and it was miserably bitter and wet. With the bad roads, the coach took four days to reach the border at Maastricht, by which time the weather had worsened. The rain had turned to snow and the temperature was falling steadily.

In the event of pursuit by her father, Arabella had decided, on the advice of Maria Louisa, to travel under an assumed name. So she carried in her possession a laissez-passer in the name of Antoinette Badeau, quickly prepared and signed by Captain Etienne de Vervins on behalf of General de la Rivière. Arabella had sought to erase Antoinette from her mind, but her recent familiarity with the role might make it easier to convince anyone who questioned her identity at a border crossing on the long journey to Berlin. After all, why would she, a young, unmarried English woman, be travelling alone towards Germany? She also carried a second laissez-passer in the name of Monsieur Aristide Badeau, to use if she was obliged, for her own safety, to resort to her previous male impersonation.

The Captain initially resisted his wife's request for the two documents. He had already been faced with explaining – with considerable difficulty – to an angry customs official from Calais why two foreign citizens had, in his name, removed without permission a large wooden crate brought from Dover and assaulted one of his guards in the process. As aide de camp to General de la Rivière he had no wish to compromise his career in the King's Guard. Besides, he was deeply suspicious of why Arabella Whitfield should want to masquerade as a man under an assumed name. Why should such a beautiful young woman wish to do such a thing? Maria Louisa had not given him a convincing answer. But his wife's persuasion had prevailed. In the end he shrugged his shoulders, signed both documents and hoped that no ill would come of what he had done, adding that he would not assist again in such matters.

Arabella was obliged to stay three nights in a convent near to Maastricht, in the care of the Mother Superior, while Father Johann sought a suitable coach and escort for her onward journey to Prussia. Finding a safe conveyance for a young woman travelling alone was not easy, particularly as the weather continued to deteriorate.

While at the convent, Arabella once again reflected on what had happened to her in the past months, especially her remarkable and perilous journey from Norwich to Dover and from there to Paris, and now to the French border. She prayed alone in her small, unheated room and with the sisters in the chapel, asking for forgiveness and the strength to complete the task ahead of her. She ate little at the communal meals. When she was not at prayer in her room, Arabella would leaf through her music book, humming the notes and recalling the happier memories of life at Meltwater. She also looked again and again at the map that Maria Louisa had given her. Arabella had marked in ink the progress already made, but she could see that many days' travel were ahead of her.

She added to her earlier written entries at the back of the music book the following:

> *I am deeply in love with a man but I fear he does not know I love him. I have held him; I have shared his bed; he has given me great joy. I must continue to pursue him, whatever the cost, so that I can declare my love, whatever his response may be.*

She thought of her grieving mother, her unloving father and her despicable brother, whose fate in Paris was unclear. Several times she undid the box containing her mask, removed the mask slowly and gazed at it. It reminded her painfully of Mrs Hallam and Mrs Rathbone and the seedy world of the London demi-monde which she had inhabited for a dark while. These were events in her life that she wished to bury deeply for ever. But the mask also evoked memories of the two nights she had shared with Carl Manfred von Deppe, two nights of profound physical pleasure in which she had not felt used or soiled. He must never know of the mask as it would link her to the woman – a woman of the night – who had visited him. She knew she should destroy it but could not bring herself to do so. Besides, it was a reminder of how her lithe and supple body had attracted men. If her attempt to win Carl Manfred failed and all other doors closed, the mask would enable her to return to her alter ego, Antoinette Badeau, who seemed to be smiling behind the mask in her hands.

By Friday, 10 January, the weather had sufficiently cleared for Father Johann to return to the convent to tell Arabella that the time had come for her to resume her journey. He said he would go with her for a while beyond the border, in the direction of Cologne on the River Rhine, to help find suitable means for her onward travel on the other side. He would then have to take his leave and return to Paris.

The Mother Superior, who had been deeply impressed by Arabella's poise, strength of character and, of course, her singing at Mass, had often thought during the past days of persuading Arabella to extend her stay, in the hope that perhaps she might make a longer commitment to the convent. But over the many years of her life the Mother Superior had become a good judge of human nature. She knew that Arabella was a restless spirit, anxious to move on towards the east.

When the time came to board the coach, Arabella thanked her warmly for her protection, hospitality and support at a time of personal soul-searching and anguish. Her stay had enabled her to reflect on all that had happened to her. She was resolved to continue her journey. Nothing could deflect her from her aim of seeing it through to the end.

"Please pray for me, Reverend Mother," said Arabella. "I do not know whether I will be strong enough to complete my journey. But I have prayed hard to the Mother of Christ to intercede for me, even though I am profoundly unworthy of her intercession. I hope that out of the kindness of your heart you will add your prayers to mine."

"Of course, my child. We will pray for you," said the Mother Superior. "We will pray to Hildegard of Bingen. She was a brave advocate for us, the weaker sex, and throughout her life she never gave in."

Taking Arabella's hand, the Mother Superior reminded her of what Hildegard had once written:

> *There was once a king sitting on his throne. Around him stood great and wonderfully beautiful columns ornamented with ivory, bearing the banners of the king with great honour. Then it pleased the king to raise a small feather from the ground, and he commanded it to fly. The feather flew, not because of anything in itself but because the air bore it along. Thus am I, a feather on the breath of God.*

"Arabella, may you have a safe journey to the east, and as you travel may you be a feather on the breath of God."

"Thank you, Reverend Mother. I will never forget you, your kindness and your generosity of heart," said Arabella, deeply moved by the Mother Superior's words.

The Mother Superior placed a letter in Arabella's hand and then gave her one last hug. Arabella climbed into the coach with Father Johann. It pulled away. A few minutes later, Arabella opened the letter and began to read the Latin words of a song by Hildegard:

Columba aspexit
per cancellos fenestre
ubi ante faciem eius
sudando sudavit balsamum
de lucido Maximino.

The dove peered in
through the latticed window,
where before her face

raining, a balm rained down
from the brightness of Maximinus.

After the last verse, the Mother Superior had written:

> *Remember, Arabella, that the dove is the Holy Spirit and the light penetrating through the window is Christ's mercy. There is nothing that can be hidden from His sight. So share with Christ all your hopes and fears on the road ahead and put your faith in Him. Adieu*

Arabella read the words several times before finally placing the letter in her music book, lying beside her on the seat.

And so it was that on the afternoon of Friday, 10 January 1766, Arabella left France and by so doing became, unknown to her, a chess piece in the stranger's game to trap a traitor. Ahead of her, Carl Manfred was pressing on towards Berlin, not knowing that Arabella was about to risk her safety because of her love for him.

After further travel, her coach arrived at a small village where, because of the difficult weather, it was decided she would stay the night before resuming her onward journey the following morning. That evening she bolted the door of her room, deeply apprehensive at what lay ahead – a long and arduous journey by coach, travelling without companions towards an unknown outcome in Prussia. Below, Father Johann sat with an old man staying at the inn who said he was travelling alone in his own coach in the direction of the Prussian border and would welcome a young lady's company. The stranger's web was further spun around Arabella.

* * * * *

John Bolton had finally arrived in Paris after a slow journey from the coast due to his deteriorating health.

Born and educated in Edinburgh, he had subsequently travelled to France where he became part of the circle around James Keith, a man who was to play a major role in his life – as Peter Keith, to whom James was unrelated, did in the life of the stranger. James Keith, second son of William Keith, the 9th Earl Marischal, had fought under the Pretender's standard against the English at the

Battle of Sheriffmuir in 1715. Fleeing Scotland following the Jacobites' defeat, Keith had settled in Paris, studying mathematics and military tactics and becoming a member of the Académie des Sciences. He left France to obtain a military command first in the Spanish then in the Russian army, where, under the Czarina Elizabeth, he distinguished himself in campaigns against the Turks and Swedes. Subsequently, in 1747, transferring his services to Prussia, Keith became a field marshal, governor of Berlin, and a companion and confidential adviser to King Frederick. He died on the battlefield at Hochkirch in 1758.

Bolton had decided to remain in Paris when Keith left France, following from a distance the fortunes of the man he much admired for his great talent, bravery and rigid honesty. Then, seeing an opportunity to exercise his own skills and strengths, he had left Paris and its comforts in 1749 to join Keith in Prussia as one of his assistants and confidants, notably in the acquisition of information to help ensure that King Frederick was always well-informed about the policies, plans and plots of other governments seeking to promote their own influence in Europe.

A particular preoccupation at that time was the employment of agents to serve the King and help thwart his enemies. Amongst those recruited, though not by Bolton, was a young man named Waldemar Drescher. He was rumoured to be a skilled swordsman with a knack of uncovering men's secrets, weaknesses and indiscretions, a consummate manipulator. By all accounts he was a worthy recruit and the King was evidently pleased to make use of his talent for intrigue and the acquisition of information, through which he was often able to trap his enemies. Word had it that he was ruthless in his methods, worthy of the Borgias, some said. Soon Drescher disappeared into the shadows and Bolton saw and heard little of him.

By 1753 it was evident from the rupture of the King's friendship with the French philosopher, Voltaire, and with others in the once glittering circle he had formed around him, that Frederick had become irascible, ungrateful and disloyal to his friends, often criticising them behind their back. Though Bolton still admired the Prussian monarch, he too had become profoundly disaffected because of the bickering at court in Berlin and the King's increasing ill temper. On a visit to Paris to spy for the King, he had met old friends and, following an approach from the French King's own agents, with the prospect of rich rewards for his loyalty, he turned to spy for the French King. And so it was as a double agent, residing in Berlin but travelling frequently to France and occasionally to London, that Bolton plied his trade in treachery towards Prussia. So far, no one at King Frederick's court had unmasked him.

It was while he was in England in 1765, to ascertain (more for his clients in France than in Prussia) England's policy towards Europe at the end of the Seven Years War, that he had received written instructions – brought to him by Carl Manfred von Deppe – to kill a man who had betrayed Frederick a long time ago. He believed this bizarre order displayed a temperamental monarch steadily losing his grip – and perhaps his sanity. He realised that the perpetration of this crime could, if skilfully disclosed, embarrass King Frederick in front of King Louis and, indeed, King George of England. But his problem now was that King Frederick had mysteriously sent Drescher, who had suddenly appeared after years of obscurity, to ensure that Carl Manfred von Deppe, a close military confidant of the King, witnessed the killing of the man who had betrayed the young Crown Prince Frederick to his father all those years ago. The instructions effectively made all three accessories to judicial murder. As long as Bolton made his French masters aware of what King Frederick had ordered, he would be safe. As for the other two, he was confident he could deal with von Deppe, but he knew from his knowledge of Drescher's early years that he should not be underestimated. If Drescher really was as good as he was once said to be, he could be a deadly opponent. While exposing two agents of the King would therefore require skill and all of Bolton's wits, success in unmasking and apprehending Drescher and von Deppe would be a major coup for him and his French paymasters. Moreover, he had King Frederick's personally signed documents to prove royal guilt.

Timing was paramount. If news of the murder became known to the French and English too soon, Bolton would have to explain his own role in the affair. He did not wish to compromise his position with his French paymasters by causing them to think that he was still in league with Frederick; they might then fear that he was really spying for Prussia and therefore that he had previously passed incriminating French intelligence to Berlin. Moreover, since being turned by the French, he had received substantial financial benefits and other favours, and he did not wish to jeopardise them, not least the prospect of comfortable retirement in Paris. So, if he were to succeed with this plan, both von Deppe and Drescher would have to be betrayed as the perpetrators of the crime when they were already under lock and key in England.

Though Bolton was confident his stratagem would work, he was acutely aware of the risk involved; he would be playing for high stakes in denouncing two Prussians for treason. And once his treachery had been exposed, his own life would be in danger, requiring him to travel immediately to France to seek royal protection. But he concluded, after much careful thought, that, despite the risk of having to explain his role as a spy for Prussia, he should still reveal the killing to his French paymasters, encouraging them to use the information he had provided to disgrace the Prussian king. That would surely not be a problem for King Louis.

His mind made up, Bolton had secretly planted a note, wrapped in some oilcloth, on the man executed that night in Norwich, revealing the culpability of Carl Manfred von Deppe and Waldemar Drescher. And the day before the planned execution, he had put it about amongst the town's rivermen that he had heard there might be an interesting body to fish from the River Wensum in a day or two, for which there could be a reward.

Following the execution, and relieved that he had prevented Drescher from checking the body for the contents of its pockets, he had subsequently worked hard to recruit Sir Robert Whitfield, whom he had met in Norwich by accident at that time and who was fortuitously trying to get hold of his daughter. That helpful fact, he had reasoned, together with Sir Robert's money and political influence (which Bolton had overestimated), would surely be of great assistance in apprehending von Deppe and Drescher and handing them to the English authorities – to be tried for murder and other associated crimes, including abduction of the Whitfield daughter. The appearance of the two men in an English dock would, he had surmised, heap even more embarrassment on the Prussian king, while protecting Bolton's position as a double agent working secretly for the French. But the failure to stop Carl Manfred von Deppe and Drescher from leaving England along with Sir Robert's daughter, and the mistake of George Whitfield's friend, James Danford, being seen near Ashford in collusion with Arabella's family, meant that unless the fugitives were stopped from reaching Berlin, his treachery to Prussia might be revealed and his life and fortune placed at risk.

And so it was that, following his arrival in Paris on Sunday, 5 January 1766, John Bolton received a note from George Whitfield – the note written under duress while he was chained in the Paris cellar, the writer now a month dead and his body disposed of, neither fact known to Bolton – informing him that Carl Manfred von Deppe had already left Paris for Berlin to report the recent events in England and what had happened subsequently. The note added that the writer's sister, Arabella, was following close behind von Deppe. Finally, it stated that he had been wounded in a fight over cards and was now under arrest for playing pharo. He could therefore no longer assist, but urged Bolton to intervene.

Bolton decided it was now paramount to chase his quarry and to delay his report to his French masters. If he did not do so, his plan could easily and quickly unravel. And there was no knowing what Whitfield might say in custody. He himself might become the hunted quarry.

On Tuesday, 7 January, Bolton left his small but comfortable house on the Place Royale for the French border. The journey towards Maastricht was agonisingly slow in the poor weather and Bolton's deteriorating health made the road even more uncomfortable to bear. He eventually arrived near the French border late in the afternoon of Friday, 10 January, shortly after Arabella had crossed it earlier in the day.

Resting at the inn that night, he asked the innkeeper which guests had recently stayed at the inn before leaving France for the east. The innkeeper revealed – with the incentive of some money on the table – that on Sunday, 5 January, a well-dressed German gentleman of military bearing had stayed one night before moving eastwards the next day, despite the worsening weather. The description fitted von Deppe.

His host then revealed that a priest had arrived on Tuesday, 7 January, in a private coach from Paris. He had stayed three nights because the snow had made onward travel almost impossible. He remembered that the priest had been accompanied by an attractive young woman, whom he had later escorted to a nearby convent, where she stayed until returning to the inn with the priest to eat breakfast before both set out for the border that very morning. The innkeeper thought he had heard the priest mention to another traveller also intending to cross the border that their destination was Berlin.

Bolton smiled. His judgement to leave Paris without delay had been right. His quarry was not far ahead and the bad weather was now a factor in his favour. Von Deppe and the young woman would be moving slowly. He decided he would press ahead the next morning regardless of the snow and conditions on the road. Within a handful of days he would have resolved his problem: von Deppe and the woman would be dead. Then his secret would be safe. Or would it? He worried about the whereabouts of Drescher. Was he still in France? Or on his way back to the safety of Prussia? It was more likely that he would return quickly to Berlin. If that were the case, perhaps he too was on the road, either with von Deppe or with the girl. Or was he the other traveller the innkeeper had mentioned? He should have asked for a description. Perhaps he would find all three. To capture one would be good; two would be a bonus; three a windfall.

But what the scheming Bolton did not know was that someone else would be waiting to intercept him in the forests ahead.

* * * * *

At Meltwater the lack of any news from either George Whitfield or John Bolton (as weak as his wife at keeping secrets, Sir Robert had soon revealed to her the name of the man who had helped their son get to Paris) was of increasing concern to Sir Robert and Lady Whitfield. Not only did their daughter remain missing following her escape – or abduction – from England to France, there was no up-to-date message from George, other than his first hurried communication to say that he had arrived in Paris and, after initial enquiries, believed that his sister might be alive and staying in the vicinity of the Place Royale. He had added that he would await further instructions from his father and the arrival of Mr Bolton, who, he said, was as anxious as ever to see the French authorities arrest quickly those who had travelled to France with Arabella. Sir

Robert had replied immediately – that is, as immediately as the serpentine line of communication would allow – to tell George that he had received his message and that he was indeed right to take no further action without his or Bolton's advice.

At the end of December, Sir Robert decided that he and Lady Whitfield should travel to London. He encountered considerable difficulty in persuading his wife to do so, not least because she was reluctant to stay at their London town house, where she had good reason to think – prompted by the gossip of some of her friends – that Lady Ward had recently been a very frequent guest. But Sir Robert persevered, finally succeeding on the grounds that it would enable her to travel more quickly to France to be reunited with her daughter, if she were found there safe and well.

By Monday, 6 January, there was still no further news from George and, unknown to Sir Robert, Bolton had only arrived in Paris the day before. With her husband clearly indecisive as to what to do next, Lady Whitfield suddenly announced that she would travel immediately to Paris to meet George and Mr Bolton, if he were there, and to try to find her daughter herself. Sir Robert was greatly taken aback by his wife's decisiveness. He offered to go with her. But Lady Whitfield refused his offer, preferring to be accompanied by one of her few friends in London, Lady Pamela Hartley. Lady Pamela travelled frequently to Paris to see her sister who had married a French nobleman, the Comte de Caullery, now in his dotage on the family estate near Tours. Lady Whitfield believed that she and Lady Pamela would be best able to find the answers to Arabella's continued disappearance. All Sir Robert had to do was to pay for the journey. He did so without question. His wife had become formidable overnight.

Four days later, on Friday, 10 January, Lady Whitfield and Lady Hartley boarded a boat at Dover for Calais. With a favourable wind they were in France without undue delay and early the next morning they left Calais for Paris and the Hostellerie du Coq d'Or from which George Whitfield had written his note to his father.

* * * * *

On the same morning that her mother left Calais, Arabella rose early, unaware that her mother was on her way to Paris to look for her.

After breakfast, Father Johann introduced her to an elderly, stooped man with a heavy, unkempt grey beard. He said his name was Herr Kempe and that he was going towards Magdeburg. He would be pleased to have the company of the young lady on the long and lonely journey ahead. At Magdeburg he would help her to find suitable conveyance to Berlin and someone to accompany her. Kempe was somewhat dishevelled and slightly odd in behaviour, but Father Johann assured Arabella that he was a well-read man and that she should have no fear of travelling with him. It would be better to share a private carriage than travel on a public coach. Such coaches were slow and often overcrowded. All would be well, he insisted. And so she took her leave of Father Johann and climbed into the carriage occupied by Herr Kempe. The next stage of her long journey had begun.

The roads were better than those in France. Indeed, the further east they travelled the more they improved, and in the hands of a skilful coachman the coach made rapid progress, despite the bad weather. On two occasions Arabella thought the coach would overturn it was going so fast. Kempe sat opposite her and rarely spoke. Though his eyes were often closed, she sensed that he was still looking at her. This unnerved her. The landscape was bleak and it was bitterly cold. Plain gave way to patches of dark and eerie forest, only to give way to yet more plain. Day after day of interminable winter landscape passed.

At nightfall on 16 January, Arabella and her companion arrived at a small inn on the edge of some forest. As Arabella descended from the coach, supported by the gnarled gloved hand of Herr Kempe, she felt she had become lost in a bleak and soulless wilderness. She was frightened, but she could not turn back. She had to go forward and fight for what she wanted; she remembered her mother's words, which she had quoted to Maria Louisa. But if anything was to befall her, she would surely vanish without trace, becoming a nameless ghost trapped and forlorn in a vast empty wasteland. Later that evening, as the wind blew strongly outside, Arabella sat in front of the fire. She felt deeply alone. At Kempe's urging and his forewarning of more long and difficult days ahead, she went to bed and slept fitfully as dark dreams beset her.

Meanwhile, the trap was being laid for a killing in the forest.

* * * * *

On arrival in Paris Lady Whitfield and her friend, Lady Pamela Hartley, went directly to the Hostellerie du Coq d'Or to find George, only to be told that he was no longer there. The staff had last seen him on 5 December, when he left mid-morning by coach for an undisclosed appointment in the Bois de Boulogne. He had announced as he left that he would not be coming back, since it was his intention to return without delay to England. They added that following his departure several people had come to look for him to settle some outstanding gambling debts. He had not been heard of since.

An angry Lady Whitfield returned to the home of the Comtesse de Caullery. With no George, only unsettled gambling debts, she had to decide what to do next. Why had George disobeyed his father's instruction to remain in Paris until he received further orders? She and her son had obviously passed each other en route. And now that George had gone, how could she establish contact with the mysterious John Bolton? Should she return immediately to England or should she remain in Paris for a while? Lady Pamela and her sister, the Comtesse, decided that Lady Whitfield should stay in Paris for at least a few days while they made enquiries of their own about Arabella. After all, if Arabella were alive and free, someone would surely know her whereabouts. She was a beautiful, high-spirited and accomplished young woman who would turn the head of any man in French society. The Comtesse said she would start asking her friends straightaway.

A day or so later the Comtesse reported to Lady Whitfield that an acquaintance of hers had been to a soirée with her husband where they had heard a most charming, elegant and attractive young English girl sing. She had performed beautifully two arias by Mr Handel and had referred to her love of England and her beloved mother. The soirée had taken place at the residence of Captain and Madame de Vervins in the Rue St Louis, where the young lady was staying at the time. If they remembered correctly, she was called Mademoiselle Arabella. She had become the talk of aristocratic circles in Paris and it seemed she had even been to Versailles on New Year's Day to sing to King Louis himself.

Lady Whitfield cried at this news. Was it real or was it a cruel hoax? Lady Pamela and the Comtesse said that this could be the information for which she had long been waiting, though they warned her that it might not mean Arabella was still in the Rue St Louis.

The Comtesse suggested that Lady Whitfield should write to Madame de Vervins immediately, to ask if it would be possible to call on her without delay in order to establish the truth of the report and if she knew where Arabella might be now. Lady Whitfield sat down to compose the note straightaway. She decided not to write to her husband at the same time. She would only do so if she had positive news to give him.

It was in the evening that Maria Louisa de Vervins received a most unexpected letter from Lady Thérèse Whitfield, currently with her friends Lady Pamela Hartley and the Comtesse de Caullery in Paris. Was it true that her daughter, Arabella, had stayed with her? Was she still there and, if not, where was she now?

For Maria Louisa the question was whether she should reply in writing or invite Lady Whitfield to call. Not entirely sure of Arabella's true feelings for her mother (though she knew plainly her opinion of her father, as Carl Manfred had explained), or of Lady Whitfield's for her daughter – or even whether the writer was who she claimed to be – Maria Louisa decided on a letter in the first instance. She wrote:

> *Dear Lady Whitfield,*
>
> *I am deeply honoured to receive your letter and welcome you to Paris.*
>
> *It is indeed true that Mademoiselle Arabella Whitfield came to stay with us recently, following her arrival from England, and that while here she sang to my friends. She was a most charming guest and became our good friend. Sadly, she is no longer with us.*
>
> *If I may be of further assistance you are most welcome to call on me at a mutually convenient time.*
>
> *Yours most cordially,*
> *Maria Louisa de Vervins*

The next morning Maria Louisa received the reply that Lady Whitfield very much wished to call on her. Maria Louisa invited her to come alone at three o'clock that day. She would be able to judge from Lady Whitfield's demeanour and responses whether she was indeed Arabella's mother and the strength of the bond between mother and daughter. She would then decide how much she should disclose about Arabella's onward journey.

That afternoon, Maria Louisa and Lady Whitfield sat down in the library at 76 Rue St Louis. Maria Louisa asked her visitor to describe Arabella and to explain more precisely why she had come to Paris.

Lady Whitfield recounted Arabella's childhood at Meltwater and how, under her mother's guidance, she had grown up to become an accomplished dancer, musician and singer. Perhaps it was because of her mother's French blood that she was single-minded and sometimes stubborn. Her relationship with her father had deteriorated as she grew older. Lady Whitfield blamed herself profoundly for not intervening earlier to stop her husband bullying his daughter to marry a person of his choosing rather than a man Arabella truly loved and respected. The dispute over whom Arabella should marry had reached such a pitch that one day her father was physically cruel to her and she had consequently run away to London. Arabella had been out of touch for several months but had returned unexpectedly to see Lady Whitfield in Norwich at the end of the previous year. Her father, who happened to arrive during her visit, had attempted to bring Arabella home against her will. Once more, Arabella had run away, this time in the company of two men, who were believed not to be English.

Lady Whitfield confessed it was a deeply sad story. She was pleased to have this chance to admit to a complete stranger her culpability in her daughter's profound distress. She loved her daughter devotedly, and it was not until these recent dreadful events that she had realised how much joy Arabella brought to her life. For the present there appeared to be no prospect of a happy ending. Instead she feared a tragedy. Be that as it may, it was now time, if it were not too late, for her to try to make amends.

Lady Whitfield finished by saying that, if Arabella were alive and well, it would be best for her not to return to England and face possible renewed misery, but to stay in France and perhaps find happiness there. She would now do anything to protect her daughter. She added that all she had revealed to Maria Louisa had never been disclosed to others, only her husband.

Maria Louisa sat in rapt silence listening to Lady Whitfield's account. She had revealed information about Arabella that an imposter would not know – indeed, much information that Maria Louisa herself did not know. Lady Whitfield had clearly spoken from her heart as a mother. Some of what she had heard reminded Maria Louisa of her own circumstances following her decision to leave Herzberg in order to follow her future husband to Paris. She replied with great sensitivity, as Lady Whitfield was clearly distraught at losing contact with her daughter.

"Lady Whitfield, I am most grateful to you for speaking so openly about your daughter. We had sincere pleasure in meeting her on her arrival in Paris after her unpleasant crossing from England to France, the details of which I need not disclose now. She came in the company of my brother, who treated Arabella, in her own words, with profound care and gentleness. He is now on his way back to Berlin, on business of His Majesty King Frederick, which is why he cannot himself vouch for what I am telling you now.

"While she was in Paris, Arabella won many hearts with her grace, beauty and many talents, particularly her singing, often from the music book that she kept close to her heart throughout her stay here. I should also tell you that Arabella even sang to His Majesty King Louis at Versailles on New Year's Day.

"I may add that Arabella said many times how much she missed you. She clearly wanted you to be by her side. And she was deeply troubled that you did not know where she was."

Lady Whitfield, her eyes full of tears of joy, asked where she could find Arabella and so begin to show her the renewed affection she was rightly due.

Maria Louisa replied, "Sadly for all of us, Arabella has left Paris in search of the man she says she truly loves. She departed a few days ago and is en route to the east as we speak."

"Who is this man?" Lady Whitfield asked urgently.

"It is my brother," Maria Louisa replied, "though he is unaware of the depth of her feelings. She is following him to Berlin to reveal her love for him."

"Is she travelling alone?" cried Lady Whitfield.

"No, she is not," replied Maria Louisa. "I have arranged for her to be accompanied."

"I must follow her," declared Lady Whitfield.

"I urge you not to do so," replied Maria Louisa sharply. "After all that she has suffered, it is best for her to find her destiny on her own. As you have yourself admitted, this is not something she has so far been allowed to do. If Arabella does indeed find the happiness she so desperately seeks, whether it is with my brother or someone else, then you should go to her. Until then I beg you to wait here in Paris, as I will do, for news from my brother, a distinguished officer and much-trusted friend of His Majesty King Frederick. I am sure we will hear before too long the outcome of her journey."

"Madame de Vervins, please forgive me," replied Lady Whitfield. "You are right. We must trust Arabella's judgement."

It was therefore agreed that Lady Whitfield would remain in Paris. She promised not to disclose to her husband the content of her conversation with Madame de Vervins. That night, she wrote to her husband to say simply that their son was not in Paris but she intended to remain in the city for the time being. Several days later she received a letter from Sir Robert agreeing to her decision, but reporting that there was no sign of their son, George, in England.

Neither knew that a badly decomposed body had risen to the surface of the River Seine at about that time. Its identity was unknown. There was speculation that it might be that of an Englishman, judging by the style of dress. The body was removed to the morgue, like so many others fished from the waters each day. A cursory examination uncovered no trace of who it might be, concluding only that it was indeed probably a foreigner who had been robbed, killed and thrown to the fish. The body was subsequently buried in an unmarked grave in the city cemetery.

* * * * *

John Bolton awoke on the morning of 11 January. He felt unwell and the deep cold was numbing his bones. He was tempted to linger for an extra day in front of the fire but he knew he had to summon the strength to dispose of the young woman and, if possible, to intercept Carl Manfred von Deppe before he reached King Frederick. After breakfast he climbed into his coach and set out in rapid pursuit.

But there was someone following behind him. Bolton stopped later in the day for refreshment. Within an hour he was dead, murdered not far from the inn by someone he knew well. His assailant hastily buried his body.

* * * * *

Early on Friday, 17 January, Arabella and her companion, Herr Kempe, set out on the next stage of their journey. Two days later they arrived at a small village not far from Helmstadt and about a day's ride from Magdeburg. It was already evening but, after a further change of horses and refreshment, Kempe insisted that they travel on through the night, so ensuring an earlier arrival at their next destination where, he said, he had important business once he had made arrangements for his young companion's onward journey. Arabella, much travel-stained, was too fatigued after so many hours in a small coach to dispute the wishes of an old man who said little and who appeared to be asleep most of the time.

It was after midnight on the 20th, following another change of horses in a hamlet, that the coach jolted and came to a sudden stop. The driver called out that he thought there was a problem with a wheel. Kempe slowly climbed down. The driver reported that one of the wheels had cracked and it was necessary to seek the assistance of a blacksmith from the hamlet they had just left. Kempe agreed and at once ordered the driver to walk back to the hamlet for help. Arabella sat alone in the coach while Kempe attended to the horses. Her only illumination was the candle in the small lantern beside her. The driver had taken one of the exterior lanterns to light his way to the hamlet. Kempe had the other.

In the silence of the surrounding trees, Arabella became aware several minutes later that she was alone. She stepped down from the carriage. The horses were still within their traces but there was no sign of her companion. She called his name three or four times but there was no reply. Arabella was completely alone. It seemed she had been abandoned. Her trust in Herr Kempe had been misplaced. Verging on tears, Arabella assessed her predicament. She had nowhere to go. She could detach one of the horses and ride on through the rest of the night towards Magdeburg but, if she reached there in the early hours of the morning, who would believe her? So, she decided to stay in the coach in the forlorn hope that the driver might return. If neither he nor Herr Kempe reappeared by daybreak, she would seek the help of a passing carriage, trusting she would not have to wait too long. Arabella climbed back inside, wrapped a blanket tightly around her, and prayed. She held firmly in her hand a piece of broken branch she had found by the roadside. If anyone attempted to harm her, she would use it to defend herself. She would resist to the end. She fell into a restless sleep.

Arabella was suddenly awakened by the sound of galloping horses in the distance. Her prayers had been answered. She got out of the carriage, holding the small lantern which she had detached from inside, and stood beside the track. A large coach, heading towards the hamlet, loomed out of the night. It swerved to avoid her but rushed on into the darkness. The driver must have thought she was a robber.

Arabella fought back her tears, telling herself she had to stay composed. She was about to step back into the coach to try to get warm again when she thought she heard the sound of more horses in the distance, this time coming from the opposite direction. She listened intently. The noise got louder. Arabella once more stood by the side of the track and called out as loudly as she could, "*Aidez-moi!*" again and again. It seemed the coach was not going to stop, but a short distance past her it halted.

The driver shouted out, "Who's there? What is the matter?"

"Please help me," Arabella called back. "Our coach is broken. The coachman has gone for help and my companion has left me. I would like to continue my journey towards Magdeburg."

Then she heard another man's voice, calling out to the driver. A dark figure descended from the coach and, taking one of its lights, walked back towards her, the driver following not far behind with another lantern.

The man, his face partially hidden by a thick scarf, held up his lantern to see Arabella's face. She thought she saw his eyes widen, as if in surprise.

"How can I help you, Madame?" he said.

Arabella, gripping her makeshift club, repeated what she had called out to the driver.

"Where have you come from?" the man asked.

"I have come from Paris. I am travelling eastwards, towards Berlin," Arabella replied.

"And, Madame, may I have the pleasure of knowing your name?" he asked.

Arabella paused. Which name should she give, her true name or the name on her laissez-passer? She answered, "Madame Antoinette Badeau."

He turned and told the driver, now almost beside him, to return to the carriage and prepare for an additional person to join them. The driver grumbled and walked off.

The man stood in front of Arabella.

"Now we are alone, whore," he said. "You are the girl from Mrs Rathbone's house in London, the girl with the elaborate mask, the girl Mrs Rathbone sent to von Deppe's room at Mr Bolton's request to stop him from making a fool of himself on the streets of the city. I did not realise von Deppe and his accomplice had recruited you as an agent of King Frederick. Now you are on your way to Berlin to join von Deppe to report to His Majesty. I can give you a ride to Magdeburg but that is as far as you will ever go. I will see to it that on arrival you will be kept under lock and key until either my friends in Paris come to take you to the Bastille or your beloved father comes to fetch you. I am not sure which you will find worse. Or I might perhaps arrange for your disposal in these parts. Come with me."

He tried to grab her arm to drag her towards his coach. Arabella stood her ground, lashing at the man with her club. Then two men – Kempe and their coachman – suddenly sprang from behind the nearby trees, yelling at her assailant. He turned to confront them. An intense struggle began. Lanterns fell. The driver from the attacker's carriage joined the fray. He was big and strong. In the darkness, bodies wrestled on the ground.

A pistol shot was fired and Kempe slumped back, gripping his shoulder. While the two coachmen continued to struggle, Arabella's assailant reloaded his pistol and took aim at the injured Kempe. Arabella ran forward, half stumbling in her long skirt on the rutted road, and struck him as hard as she could on the back of his head with her club. He was momentarily stunned but, recovering, he turned to face her, his pistol now pointing at her. He took unsteady aim, screaming, "You damned whore!"

Arabella, staring at death, fell to her knees, praying, "Lord Jesus Christ, have mercy on my soul." Eyes fixed on the pistol, waiting for the shot, she saw Kempe get to his feet, draw a sword from his belt and plunge it into the man as he fired. The shot went into the trees. The wounded man sank to his knees, clutching his side. Kempe withdrew the sword and then sliced it across the back of the burly coachman who had pinned the other driver to the ground with his hand around his neck. The driver fell back, mortally injured.

Kempe then drew a pistol from his belt and stood in front of Arabella's attacker, who was lying on the ground, hands clamped to his wound.

"You are an arch traitor to His Majesty," he said, his voice icily calm. "You pledged loyalty. You took his money. But you sold his secrets to the French. You were on your way to Berlin to protect your cover, to accuse others of treason. You will not live another day, John Bolton. On behalf of His Majesty, I find you guilty of corruption and betrayal. Your sentence is death. What do you have to say?"

He pulled the scarf from the man's face. It was not Bolton but Auguste Gaillard.

Kempe showed little emotion. Arabella, still stunned, rose to her feet.

"I have nothing to say to you," replied a defiant Gaillard.

Arabella looked in horror at Gaillard's contorted face. This was the man she had remembered from her childhood, telling her stories of France. This was the man who had made her mother happy. This was the man who had befriended her in London after her flight from Meltwater.

"Go back to your dungheap," snarled Gaillard. "And you, too, whore. I sent Bolton to his fate with my own hand. Let your royal master rot in hell. Long live His Majesty King Louis of France."

Kempe raised his pistol at Gaillard's forehead, slowly squeezed the trigger and fired. Gaillard cried out and fell back. His body shook for a moment and then ceased to move. He was dead, would never know that he had tried to kill his own daughter. Kempe turned to the fallen coachman, reloaded his pistol and fired.

Arabella watched the killings, stupefied and unable to control her violently shaking body. Then Kempe came towards her, his left shoulder bleeding, the pistol in his right hand. She fell to her knees, pleading for mercy between her sobs. Kempe raised his left hand painfully to his face and tugged at his long unkempt beard. It came away. He then reached behind his head and pulled. Long hair fell about his face. He straightened his stooped back. Replacing the pistol in his belt, he used his right hand to raise Arabella from her knees.

"It is I," he whispered.

Arabella gasped. It was the stranger she had first met in Norwich – in that darkened room at Mrs Willoughby's; the stranger who had smuggled her out of England.

"I assure you, Miss Whitfield, you are now truly safe," said the stranger. "Let us resume our journey. But for once it is I who needs your help." As he said this, he winced in pain. "Go back to the coach. The coachman and I will bury these bodies and dispose of Gaillard's carriage. Then we will ride quickly to Magdeburg and thereafter on towards Prussia, where I intend to make arrangements for your safety."

He put his right arm around Arabella and tenderly guided her back to the coach.

As she climbed inside, she asked why he had killed the two men.

"Miss Whitfield, Auguste Gaillard, the man who called you a whore, was, like John Bolton, an enemy of King Frederick, in the pay of the French. He turned informant out of sheer unprincipled greed, and it is my belief that he had done so even before he met and charmed your mother and entertained you both. For years it was worthless gossip gleaned from the coffee house that he passed on, but then he met John Bolton and became more dangerous. The King had trusted Bolton for many years. But he betrayed him to His Majesty King Louis for money. Moreover, during Herr von Deppe's and my business in England, he encountered your father and together they plotted to seize you and us in order to send us all to the gallows. Bolton feared that Herr von Deppe would reveal his treason and, because of your link with him in London, thought that you too had become an agent of King Frederick. He therefore determined to kill you both. I set a trap. He fell into it and had been following you from Paris. But Gaillard intervened – because, I believe, he and Bolton had fallen out over who should receive the French King's reward for publicly exposing Prussia. His presence here tonight surprised even me.

"I must admit that your decision to follow Herr von Deppe to Berlin complicated my plan. I could not tell you in advance what I had devised. Tonight was the best chance for the action I had in mind. Traitors always struggle for life, fearful of the retribution that awaits them. But your brave decision to go alone to Berlin in pursuit of Herr von Deppe and your extraordinary courage tonight saved my life and my coachman's. More than that, tonight you helped His Majesty maintain the protection of Prussia. You are a truly remarkable young woman." He kissed her hand. "Now, into the coach. There is much to be done."

Her face tear-stained, Arabella turned to the stranger.

"Sir, I am not a whore. To escape from my father, I had to survive in London and I was betrayed and misused. But I beseech you to believe me, sir, I am not a whore. I wish a better life than that."

The stranger whispered in reply, "Miss Whitfield, no one, including Herr von Deppe, will ever hear that word from my lips. I judge people by their actions. Tonight you have helped to save His Majesty from two vipers. You are not a whore, nor will you ever be. I believe you were betrayed in London by the very man I have just killed. No, you are not a whore. You are a most kind and loyal friend of the King."

"Thank you, sir," she replied.

Arabella sat back in the coach, her head swirling with the bloody events she had just witnessed and unable to stop her tears. She had reached the point of death. But she had been saved from the precipice. Now the next peril awaited her: crossing Prussia. Within the hour the coach was on its way, leaving behind a burning empty coach, its horses in flight, and two new mounds amongst the silent trees. The stranger, huddled in a blanket, lay against her, in deep pain from his wound.

As the coach disappeared, a shadow emerged from the darkness. It was Philippe Robinet, the man who had looked after Sir Robert

Whitfield, his son and John Bolton in Dover and who had been travelling in the same coach as Gaillard. He had seen all that had happened. He vowed that he would follow those in front of him to Magdeburg and Berlin to seek revenge for Auguste's death, however long it would take. He began to walk through the forest.

The coach arrived in Magdeburg shortly after eight o'clock on the morning of Tuesday, 21 January. As they entered the ancient town, the stranger awoke and, though in obvious pain, calmly directed the driver to a house in a narrow street not far from the cathedral square. As Arabella stepped down from the coach she noticed there were blood stains on the thick blue riding habit she had worn all the way from Paris to keep warm in the cold winter weather. A stout, jovial woman, Frau Kirschner, opened the door and showed them into the large, warm kitchen where she invited them to sit down in front of the blazing fire. It took several minutes for Arabella to overcome the numbing cold she had endured since her ordeal in the forest. She looked around her.

The floor was stone. In the middle was a long butcher-block table, with two enormous wooden legs set into a crude and substantial timber rectangle stretcher matching the length of the block. On the table rested an axe that, judging from the bloody blade, had just been used to cut meat. To one end of the table were some copper plates and tankards. Carcases hung from hooks set into a thick wooden frame suspended from the ceiling. In between the carcases hung iron pans for cooking. On the floor beyond the table were various large, deep copper pots containing water. There were assorted wooden chairs and stools of different sizes, some of which had vegetables on them. A straw bonnet rested on another. The plaster walls were mainly bare and cracked in places. At the far end of the kitchen some smocks were hanging from a clothes line strung diagonally from one wall to another. The fireplace was the centrepiece of the room. It blazed fiercely. There was a large amount of ash beneath it, sprinkled with cascading glowing embers of wood. A big kettle hung above the flames. To the left of the fireplace was a large wicker basket of logs. The air was strong with different smells, some more pungent than others. No one spoke.

Arabella looked into the flames of the fire. Their warmth and brightness contrasted with her bleak and bare surroundings. Her arrival in Magdeburg with a wounded man after nearly being murdered the night before by Auguste Gaillard, her mother's friend, underscored even more graphically the never-ending repercussions of her spur-of-the-moment decision to turn her back on Meltwater. Its wealth, elegance and comfort – and indeed the more recently enjoyed grandeur of 76 Rue St Louis – were now distant memories of a remote and unreachable world. She had run away from home because of her father. But now she was penetrating ever deeper into a German wilderness in pursuit of a possible mirage. Perhaps she should have stayed in Paris. But she had not.

The outcome of her journey, if completed, would be either to find and secure the personal happiness and fulfilment for which she longed or to endure rejection. If the latter, there would be no going back. Her survival in a provincial German town would ultimately depend on resorting to the use of her only asset – her body. Its sale would bring short-term gain but lead eventually to degradation. All that would then remain in her extreme vulnerability would be the choice to live – however squalid her conditions might be – or to die. If death, it would be at her own hand by her own decision; the decision to lie down and not to wake up. Yet though Arabella feared she was once again balanced precariously on the narrow ledge overlooking the dark and bottomless pit into which she had peered before her departure from Mayfair, she still clung to the belief that her survival so far on her perilous journey eastwards was a sign from her Catholic faith that she should hold on, however hard it may be to do so. If that were true, then she had to keep her nerve and survive in order to resolve her fate. She opened her bag and took out the music book and began to hum a melody from one of the sheets of music.

A few minutes later the coachman joined them. Frau Kirschner poured some wine from a pitcher she took from the hearth. It was warm and comforting to drink. She cut thick squares of rather stale bread from a large loaf on the table and slices of pork. The conversation around the table was in German. Though Arabella did not understand most of it, she thought she caught the words "von Deppe". She asked the stranger whether she had heard the name correctly.

"Yes, you did. Herr von Deppe stayed here two nights ago before travelling on towards Berlin. He should be making good progress by now."

Arabella blushed as the stranger half smiled at her.

Frau Kirschner lowered the kettle of water hanging over the fire closer to the flames. Once it had boiled she poured some water into a small copper bowl. She helped the stranger to remove his long overcoat and his jacket. Then, cutting the left sleeve of his blood-stained shirt beneath, she proceeded to tend his wounded shoulder. He grimaced with pain as she used a needle to prise some pistol shot from his flesh. She cleaned the wound and bound his arm. Next, Frau Kirschner tended the bruises and cuts that the coachman had sustained. Afterwards the three sat silently before the fire, saying little, while Frau Kirschner busied herself at the table.

After a few minutes, Arabella felt faint. The sudden consumption of wine, the lack of food, the heat of the kitchen, the exhaustion from the long journey and the delayed shock from the night before suddenly took their toll. She asked the stranger if Frau Kirschner would allow her to lie down. As she attempted to rise to her feet, she swayed and grabbed the edge of the table to support herself. The coachman sprang forwards and with Frau Kirschner's help caught her as she fell to the floor. The two helped the barely conscious Arabella up the narrow stairs to a small bedroom at the back of the house. They laid her on the bed. On it was a straw mattress, draped with various blankets of different sizes, half covered by a thick, red counterpane. There was a roughly made headboard with an attractive carved fleur de lys atop a floral wooden edging.

The coachman left the room but Frau Kirschner stayed to remove Arabella's hat and outer coat and then wrap her in blankets. She took a small cloth from the bedside table, dipped it in a ewer of water and gently dabbed Arabella's forehead and lips. Arabella stirred but Frau Kirschner placed yet another blanket tightly around her to restrain her from moving. By the time the tireless Frau Kirschner had made sure she was well covered, Arabella had fallen deeply asleep. She slept until the late evening, rousing only when Frau Kirschner returned with a candle and some broth. Arabella half sat up and sipped the broth from the large copper mug. She then lay down again, once more quickly falling asleep. Frau Kirschner smiled, remembering her daughter sleeping many years ago in the same bed. She extinguished the candle and closed the door.

Later that night Frau Kirschner was tending the wounded stranger in the kitchen below when she heard a scream. She rushed upstairs. Arabella was awake. She was pale and frightened, awoken by a nightmare of her impending death. Her hot forehead and damp hair showed she was feverish. Frau Kirschner rearranged the two pillows on the bed and encouraged her to sleep once more. She sat at Arabella's bedside for a while, holding her hand and mopping her forehead. Arabella asked her to pass her music book, lying by her bag on the floor. Frau Kirschner did so. Arabella clutched it closely as the blankets were pulled tightly over her. When she was sure Arabella was once again asleep, Frau Kirschner returned downstairs leaving the candle burning by the young woman's bedside.

It was not until the middle of the next day that Arabella awoke. A strong white light penetrated through the rough sacking used for curtains. She left the bed on unsteady legs to peer through the window. Though her room looked towards the back of another house across the yard, it appeared there had been a further heavy fall of snow.

Wrapped in a blanket, Arabella sat at the plain table and opened her music book. Using a half-broken quill, which she dipped into the almost empty inkpot, she quickly wrote on the back of a small sheet of unused paper in her music book:

> *I am in a bleak place. Although those around me are kind and protective, I feel deeply alone. I cannot see what will become of me in this eastern land of snow, darkness and bitter cold if the outcome of my endless journey is not as I would wish it.*
>
> *I cannot go back to England or to Paris. If my efforts to secure what I seek fail, perhaps the time has come to end my existence in a tomb of snow and ice. But I still hold out, in hope that I may avoid such a fate.*
>
> *Holy and Immaculate Mary, I beg your love, understanding and protection. Have mercy on me.*

She quietly cried.

Hearing movement above, Frau Kirschner went up to the room, bringing hot water and some clothes. She helped to wash Arabella, to brush her hair and to dress her in local peasant style.

Then still with a heavy blanket around her shoulders, Arabella went downstairs to the warm kitchen. The stranger was lying on a truckle bed. He looked gaunt and in obvious pain. The coachman was not there. The stranger said he was out tending to the horses and making sure the carriage was in safe hands, away from prying eyes. Its interior was stained with blood.

* * * * *

While Arabella and the stranger rested in Magdeburg, Carl Manfred had persevered with his journey. He had followed the stranger's instruction to return to Berlin by a different route, wherever possible, from the one he had taken from Berlin to Paris to avoid any interception or being followed. But the bleak weather and deteriorating travelling conditions had somewhat slowed his speed, making his progress arduous. By the time he had reached Frau Kirschner's house in Magdeburg he was exhausted, not only from the journey but, with the possibility of enemies on his heels, from the pressure to secure an audience with the King as quickly as possible. King Frederick could be impatient, irascible and, as he knew from what he had witnessed in England, vengeful if he thought his wishes had not been carried out with the speed and effectiveness he demanded. Carl Manfred prized his liberty and his neck.

After Magdeburg, he decided that, with aching bones and filthy clothes, he would briefly divert to Herzberg, a hard day's ride from Berlin, for a short rest and the comfort of his own bed. From there he would ride the next day to Potsdam to see if King Frederick were there. If he were not, he would ride on to the royal palace in Berlin.

And so it was that, nearly four months after his departure for England, Carl Manfred returned to Herzberg on the evening of Friday, 24 January 1766.

The house was dark and cold. In the grey, empty winter landscape its exterior appeared forbidding. But within an hour of his arrival the servants had lit fires in the main rooms and the pulse of life began to beat again – faintly at first and then more strongly as each hour passed. Later that evening, as more snow fell, he sat in the library in front of the fire and thought of all that he had done and witnessed. With great joy he had found his sister, Maria Louisa, in Paris and spent many hours in her company, and that of her child, recalling their childhood at Herzberg. In England he had witnessed a bustling London, shared his bed with an unknown girl in a mask and seen a rich rural landscape. But in between memories of light and pleasure there were darker ones. He had seen the brutal beheading of a man, personally ordered by King Frederick. He had become a fugitive but had managed to elude capture. On his return to Paris he had been presented to His Majesty King Louis at the lavish Palace of Versailles, a world beyond imagination and far removed from the poverty of the ordinary people of France he had seen so vividly in his travel across its lands. He had seen the stranger avenge the murder of his brother. He had learnt of John Bolton's possible treachery.

But then there was the beautiful and captivating Arabella Whitfield. He saw her face in the flames of the fire – sometimes sad but often alight with joy and laughter. He recalled her voice as she sang Handel arias from her music book. He knew now that he loved her. Falling in love had been an unforeseen accident. It had happened. But because of his stubborn refusal to comprehend and accept the depth of his feelings towards her he had let her slip through his fingers. Now she was gone. He would never see her again. He would only have his memories of her. Filled with sadness, he fell asleep.

He awoke some hours later. He went to his desk and late into the night he wrote a short account of his journey to hand to the King. By nine o'clock the next day, he had mounted his horse and set off for Potsdam.

* * * * *

The coachman returned to the kitchen to report rumours that there had been an ambush and murder on the road to Magdeburg. A postal coach had apparently seen the burnt remains of a black coach in the French style and four horses had been seen wandering nearby. A search party had left the town to look for survivors. The discovery of French bodies would lead to suspicion that locals or Prussians had been involved in their killing.

That evening the stranger, still weak from his wound, decided that it was unwise to stay longer in the town. It would not be long before nosey citizens knocked on Frau Kirschner's door enquiring about the identity of her visitors. He decided that he and Arabella should leave at first light for Berlin. It was essential to report to the King what had happened, so that he was well prepared before he received any complaint from the Magdeburg authorities about a murder possibly involving his agents and a young foreign woman. It was well known that the Duchy of Magdeburg had a fragile relationship with Brandenburg-Prussia, its administrator. The local nobility still suspected King Frederick's regional ambitions – and the Duchy's place in those ambitions – following earlier attempts by Prussia to interfere with their local rights. It was highly desirable not to make matters worse.

In the early hours of the next morning, Thursday, 23 January, the stranger and Arabella prepared to leave Magdeburg. The stranger warned there would be various checkpoints on the way and great care would be required to see that their intentions were not compromised. Arabella knew of the risks that lay ahead but, though weak and still feverish, she also knew that the final stage of the journey ahead would bring her closer to Carl Manfred.

Arabella looked at her clothes. She could not travel in her peasant attire and her blue riding habit was deeply stained with blood from the stranger's wound.

"I have with me the clothes in which I escaped from England and a laissez-passer in the name of Aristide Badeau. I propose that I dress again as a man and with those papers help you to reach Berlin."

The stranger looked closely at Arabella. She was young and clearly exhausted but her courage and fortitude were remarkable. Throughout his life he had had no need of women. His physical needs were met in the company of men in seedy backstreets. Besides, women often got in the way, risking his plans. But he was wounded and, if caught in Magdeburg, he could be arrested, convicted and put to death. He could not reveal his identity. To survive, he required support. This young woman could be the key to his survival.

"Madame, please do so. Much depends on us reaching Berlin safely."

Arabella went upstairs, removed her peasant clothes and with

Frau Kirschner's help dressed once again as a man. Frau Kirschner bound her chest so tightly she could hardly breathe. She put on the white shirt, the leather breeches, the waistcoat and her stockings and then pulled on the boots. Frau Kirschner tied her hair back with the black ribbon at the nape of her neck, and helped her into the jacket. And then Arabella went downstairs. The stranger was all ready to leave but looked ill and moved with great pain. He and Arabella sat before the fire in the kitchen and drank mugs of broth and ate some bread. After a brief respite, the coachman knocked on the door to say that the coach was ready.

The three said goodbye to Frau Kirschner and stepped out into the darkness, snow and bitter wind. Arabella went in front, carrying a lantern. The stranger moved slowly, supported by the coachman. They walked to the end of the narrow street. The snow muffled their steps and they did not speak. At the corner they paused to look back to see if they were being followed. There was no sign. They then turned right and after a short distance turned right again, down an alley to the stables. The coachman tipped the night watchmen, loaded the bags onto the coach and lit the lanterns. He then beckoned the stranger and Arabella to climb inside. It took a while for the stranger to do so, followed by Arabella. Once aboard, the coach moved forward, heading north.

The road was difficult. Deep snow hindered progress. At Burgstall they stopped to change the horses but by early afternoon they had pressed on. In great discomfort, breathing heavily and with blood beginning to show through his bandage, the stranger was relieved to arrive at the final customs checkpoint before Potsdam. Though unwell, he insisted that the coachman continue before nightfall rather than find accommodation nearby. He wanted to stay overnight closer to Berlin, where there would be greater safety, and, of course, closer to the King.

The coach took its place in the queue waiting for authorisation to proceed. The checking was slow and by dusk it began to snow again and the wind had got up. At last the coach reached the front of the queue. The customs official opened the door.

"And who do we have here? Papers, please," he demanded.

As Arabella handed her laissez-passer to the official, the stranger replied, "Beside me is Monsieur Aristide Badeau, en route to His Majesty King Frederick with a message from General de la

Rivière, commander of King Louis of France's Guard."

The man turned to the stranger.

"And you, who are you?"

The stranger, clinging tightly to his overcoat so that the official would not see his injured arm, pulled a piece of paper from his pocket and handed it to him. The official scrutinised both papers.

"I want you both out of the coach – now. I need to ask you more questions and to inspect your baggage. There are rumours of murder on the road near Magdeburg and the perpetrators are said to be on the loose. Coachman, pull over."

The stranger called out to the coachman not to move. He then leaned towards the official, who now had one foot inside the coach and the other on the footplate, and seized him by the lapel.

"If you do not open the gate ahead, I will personally tell His Majesty King Frederick that you have interfered in state business. We are trying to avert further war between France and Prussia. You may not like it but you are under Prussian authority and if you do not stand back I will return with a warrant for your arrest and make sure that you are in the front line when French forces move against His Majesty. And when there is war, what will your local nobles say? They will bellyache that more war means more taxes on them and they will squeal. I will have great pleasure in pointing the finger at you. Now give me those papers back and get out of our way and let us pass."

"No. We are closed for the night," said the official, fingering his pistol.

As he did so, the stranger drew his pistol and took aim.

"I never miss," he said.

The man stood his ground, smarting from the torrent of abuse from the stranger.

"Damned Prussians, you are all the same, throwing your weight around. You bring us nothing but trouble."

Other border guards gathered behind him. The stand-off continued. The stranger flicked the pistol into firing position.

Arabella, who had been sitting motionless, now intervened, speaking in French though not knowing whether the guards would understand her.

"I have left my country to come this far in the interest of harmony between Prussia-Brandenburg and France. His Majesty

King Louis seeks the continuation of peace after many years of war and a lost generation. Please allow us to proceed without further delay, so you and your children, indeed all of us, can live in safety rather than die on the battlefield. I beg you, please let us through. There is no time to waste." She smiled at the official.

The stranger repeated her words in German.

After a pause, a voice from the back barked out, "Let them pass. It is time to go home rather than be stuck here in the cold. We don't want to freeze to death in this wind. We will get them another day."

The official withdrew his foot from inside the coach, swore and threw the papers back at the stranger and Arabella.

"I'll watch out for you. Next time you'll get your come uppance, you damned Prussian."

He kicked the coach door shut, such was his anger at being humiliated. The border gate opened and the coach moved closer to the capital of Prussia. The stranger, in evident agony from the physical effort of the altercation at the border, opened the window and called out to the coach driver. "Stop at Grosskreuz for the night. We will go to Berlin in the morning."

The following morning, Friday, 24 January, the stranger and Arabella awoke at Grosskreuz on the final stage of their journey. Later that same day, Carl Manfred reached Herzberg to refresh himself before setting off on the last leg of his own journey to Potsdam.

The stranger told Arabella that he would now travel alone to find the King, who could be at Potsdam, or at the royal palace in Berlin, or at Schloss Charlottenburg. She should remain at the inn in the care of the innkeeper and his wife. He assured Arabella he knew them well and that she would be safe. But she should remain in her disguise as her riding habit was soaked in blood and that might arouse unnecessary attention even at this late stage. He would arrange for an escort to come for her the next day.

The coach left Grosskreuz with the injured stranger. Arabella was now alone in Prussia. She sat before the fire to keep warm. Travellers came and went. After dusk she ate some food and then retired to the tiny room she had been given. It was cold and damp. She bolted the door and without undressing pulled the musty-smelling blankets over her. She looked at the shadow cast by the candlelight on the ceiling. The wind blew outside. What would be the outcome of her perilous journey?

The following morning, Arabella woke early, went downstairs and once again sat by the fire. She ate a little bread and meat and sipped some beer. Her breasts were sore beneath the rough linen binding Frau Kirschner had tightly wrapped around her and her boots and breeches were damp and uncomfortable.

It was mid-morning when a smartly dressed young officer entered the inn and asked, in perfect French, for Monsieur Aristide Badeau. Arabella hesitated. Was she going to be arrested for illegal entry into Prussia? But placing her faith in the stranger, whose life she had saved, she stood and said, "I am Monsieur Badeau." The officer stepped forward and bowed as he would to a fellow officer. "I am Lieutenant Hartmann of His Majesty's Life Hussars. I have been asked to accompany you to Potsdam, where we await further instructions. Please come with me, if you will." He gestured to the doorway. Seeing Arabella was deeply apprehensive, he assured her she was not being arrested.

Outside was a light-blue coach with the Prussian black, spread-winged eagle coat of arms on the door. Lieutenant Hartmann invited her to step inside. He followed and sat beside her. Facing Arabella sat a delicate and fine-featured woman, dressed in an elegant red riding habit.

"Monsieur Badeau, or perhaps I should say Mademoiselle Whitfield," he said with a smile. "I wish to introduce Countess von Schlegel. On arrival at Potsdam she will take you to Schloss Richemont and there you will be able to change, refresh and rest."

Arabella replied, "I am honoured to meet you, Madame, and you, Lieutenant Hartmann. I am so sorry to cause you such inconvenience."

"We are most honoured to meet you," replied the Countess. "We have heard much about you."

Some two hours later the coach drew up outside Schloss Richemont, a large and elegant house in extensive grounds on the outskirts of Potsdam, not far from the King's summer palace of Sanssouci. The Countess showed Arabella to a spacious bedchamber on the first floor. There was a welcoming fire burning in the grate.

"My ladies will help you to undress and offer you some fresh clothes. You may then wish to rest. We will see each other later in the day."

Arabella detected a possible Russian accent in the way the Countess spoke French. She had never met a Russian before but she had heard Herr Kunzl mimic the accent one evening at Meltwater. Arabella was not to know then that she and the Countess would later find themselves on opposing sides in a battle of state affairs.

It was early evening when Arabella went downstairs. Though still exhausted from her long and perilous journey, she looked striking as she entered the library to join the Countess and her husband, Count Ernst von Schlegel. They asked her about her journey and about Paris, wanting in particular to hear how the New Year was celebrated at Versailles. They then ate supper, for which they were joined by Lieutenant Hartmann. As the meal came to an end, a footman brought a message to the Count.

He read it, passed it to the Countess and said, "Mademoiselle Whitfield, we have received a message that His Majesty wishes us to go immediately to see him at his palace nearby. You are to accompany us."

Arabella gasped.

"Come, we must hurry," said the Count.

On arrival at the Sanssouci palace, which King Frederick often insisted on using in the winter even though he regarded it as his summer residence, the Count, the Countess and Arabella waited in an elegant ante-room furnished in the French style. No one spoke. A few minutes later, the door opened and a footman appeared. He motioned the Count and Countess to follow him. Arabella was left alone. There was no sound other than the sparking of freshly burning wood in the elaborate fireplace and the ticking of the clock on the mantelpiece above, reminding her for a moment of the ticking clock at Meltwater. A few minutes later the Count and Countess returned. They sat down, smiling at Arabella. The door opened again and the footman reappeared. He asked Arabella to accompany him. She looked at the Count and Countess for reassurance. They gestured her to go as directed.

She entered a much smaller room. The footman said that in a few moments he would open the door in front of her. She should enter and walk slowly to the far end of the room, where His

Majesty the King would be standing. Arabella should curtsey and respond to his questions. She should relax, not be afraid. The King always looked stern but he had a warm sense of humour.

The footman stepped forward to open the door. Arabella entered a long, elegant room with black and white lozenge-shaped tiles on the floor, large windows to the right, half covered by strongly patterned curtains, and floor-to-ceiling French-style mirrors on the opposite wall. Three chandeliers of burning candles hung from the ceiling, their light reflected in the mirrors. Arabella noticed a harpsichord and a music stand near one window. At the far end of the room were finely carved rococo-style chairs either side of the fireplace in which great logs burned.

Standing in front of the fire was the King, in the traditional military uniform he wore every day in public and in which he was often painted in profile. Beside him, on a rug near the fire, was a large dog. Arabella stopped, unsure whether to go further. The King gestured to her to come nearer. Here, before her, was the man so often vilified in Europe as a warmonger. Here was the man who had become known even in his lifetime as Frederick the Great. He resembled the engraved picture she had once seen of him in a book in the library at Meltwater. But he looked older and stooped. After witnessing the elaborate ritual of the court at Versailles and the distance maintained between King Louis and his courtiers, Arabella was uncertain how far to walk before she should curtsey. She walked further forwards and again stopped. The King motioned her to come even closer. She did so until she was within touching distance. Arabella, nervously, curtsied deeply. He reached out and took her right hand and raised her. He spoke in fluent French.

"Mademoiselle Whitfield, it is not often that I am able to see such a beautiful and charming young woman at Sanssouci. I have heard much about you, in particular of your courage and determination. I admire people with these qualities, people with steel who overcome profound setbacks to achieve their goal. That is how I believe military campaigns should be won. Now, I hear you play the harpsichord well and sing exquisitely. I hope that one day you will sing for me."

"Of course, Your Majesty, it would be an honour to do so," replied Arabella, as she curtsied again.

There was a moment or two of silence as the King gazed at her intently. He suddenly pointed to the harpsichord.

"Mademoiselle, though it is late, perhaps you would be kind enough to play me a little tune now? It might help me to sleep."

"But Your Majesty I do not have my music book."

The King turned to the mantelpiece and picked up a brown leather-bound book. Arabella suddenly recognised it was hers.

"I believe this is yours. The Countess sensibly thought we might have need of it." The King handed it to her. "Please, choose something suitable for me." He gestured once again towards the harpsichord. "Judging by its thickness there is much for you to choose from. Or you may wish to show me your talent by playing me something from memory. This aged King is much in need of music."

Arabella hesitated. "I am unprepared, Your Majesty."

"I understand you played – and, indeed, sang – unprepared late one evening at Versailles for the King of France, did you not? I would like the same immediate pleasure as he had. Surely you would not wish to discriminate in favour of France? Surely you cannot deny me reciprocity?"

Arabella blushed. Again, he jabbed his finger towards the harpsichord.

There was clearly no escape. Arabella had to play. She could not offend the King, particularly as he seemed to be remarkably well informed about her visit to Versailles. Moreover, she suddenly realised to her horror that he may have looked inside her music book. She sat down at the keyboard. Though she would play for the King as he insisted, in her heart she would do so for Carl Manfred, for whom she longed. But what could she play from memory? She could hardly ask the King to turn the pages of her music.

She then recalled a composition that her music teacher, Herr Kunzl, had brought her – straight from the English royal court. Kunzl said he had met Johann Sebastian Bach's youngest son, Johann Christian, in London when he was music master to Queen Charlotte. Johann Christian and Kunzl had enjoyed a musical evening together. Earlier in the day, at the Queen's request, Bach had instantly composed a keyboard sonata for her. The Queen had liked it greatly and Bach proudly played it to Kunzl. Kunzl, in turn, was so impressed by a piece played only hours earlier in the Queen's private apartments that he had written down the score that very evening, and Bach had kindly corrected it. On a subsequent visit to Meltwater, Kunzl produced the score from his bag with a great flourish. He played it through and then set Arabella the test of learning the first movement, ready to perform it from memory on his next visit. Arabella had played the music often to her mother.

Trembling with apprehension at the thought of playing for the King of Prussia in his fabled summer palace, Arabella closed her eyes and played the spirited allegro first movement. Her fingers flew across the keyboard. She felt carried along by a wave of emotion at reaching the end of her epic journey. She paused at the end of the first movement but the King urged her to continue.

Playing the second, adagio movement, Arabella recalled Carl Manfred's face as she had sung Handel's aria in the library at the Rue St Louis in Paris. If only she had told him then that she had sung it for him in gratitude for saving her from a life she wished to forget. Then, without looking at the King, Arabella played the final prestissimo movement. She hoped that soon she would be able to see the man she truly loved, to play this piece to him. But, she asked herself, did she love him as the kind of father figure she had always wanted but had never had? As she played the final notes of the movement, she knew she loved him for who he was.

Arabella stood up and curtsied to the King.

"Your Majesty, my fingers fail me at this late hour."

"Brava," replied the King. "Now, who was the composer?"

"Monsieur Johann Christian Bach," Arabella replied.

"Of course," he said as he slapped his thigh. "Where would we be without the Bachs? Dozens of them – they bewitch us all. The father once came here. I thought I could outwit the old boy but I should have known that would be impossible. Clearly, Mademoiselle Whitfield, you are an accomplished keyboard player. You must come back again. When you do, I should like you to sing – something to celebrate the anticipated arrival of spring after this accursed long winter. Your beauty personifies warmth and light."

Arabella replied, "I would be deeply honoured to do so, Your Majesty."

"And Mademoiselle Whitfield," said the King, "I wish to thank you for saving the life of a dear friend. You are indeed a true citizen of Prussia."

Arabella blushed and her mouth became dry. She was momentarily lost for words. Then she became conscious of someone behind, moving closer to her.

"I think someone else would like to thank you, too." The King gestured to the person behind her to step forward. "I wish to introduce my loyal and lifelong servant, Herr Drescher. He is my eyes and ears, my spy in the shadows, a fearsome spider who traps many in his web."

Arabella turned. She gasped. There was the stranger, but freshly shaven and elegantly dressed, his long hair tied back by a large black ribbon and his arm in a silk sling under a blue frock coat with silver buttons. Drescher smiled and slightly bowed. Arabella curtsied.

"It seems, Mademoiselle Whitfield," continued the King, "that, notwithstanding the weather, the many tribulations you have faced and the fact that you departed Paris after him, you and Herr Drescher have reached me before my other loyal servant, Colonel von Deppe. I understand that he has now arrived and intends to come to see me tomorrow. I hope that in the coming days you and he may have the opportunity to meet again. Now, Mademoiselle Whitfield, you should go and rest. You will be safe in Potsdam."

Arabella curtsied to the King once more. Drescher offered her his uninjured arm and both left the room.

In the ante-room he thanked Arabella again for saving his life and hoped that one day their paths might cross, though in happier ways. She curtsied to him, which he acknowledged with a deep bow. He then whispered to her, "Be careful what you say to the Countess. She is of Russian birth and, though it appears she is happily married and His Majesty enjoys her company, she still has many friends at the Czarina's court. The Czarina Catherine, though of German birth, is a canny adversary of His Majesty. He has not yet outwitted her and so far she has not outwitted him. We need to make sure that she does not gain the advantage."

"Herr Drescher," replied Arabella, "I have learnt this past year that there are few people in this world in whom one can place one's trust. There are only two people in whom I would place mine – you and Herr von Deppe."

He placed his hand on her arm and said, "I agree, Mademoiselle Whitfield. Never trust anyone. Everyone has their price, unless a bond of deep love provides a barricade that disloyalty has no chance to penetrate. But let me say, Mademoiselle Whitfield, you should add His Majesty to your list of those you can trust. Though many may disagree, you will come to see that I am right in that respect."

After leaving him in the ante room, Arabella returned to Schloss Richemont with the Count and Countess. She went to bed that night thinking of whether she might see Carl Manfred again and, if she did, what she might say to him.

CHAPTER 16

Confession and Salvation

Carl Manfred reached Potsdam late on the evening of 25 January at the end of his long and eventful journey to England on the King's business. He arrived at the Golden Eagle Inn where he had stayed so often in the past as a soldier. He enquired of the innkeeper whether the King was in residence at his summer palace of Sanssouci or in Berlin, perhaps at Schloss Charlottenburg. The innkeeper replied that he had seen military activity in the town to indicate that His Majesty was indeed at Sanssouci.

Carl Manfred called for paper, ink and pen to write to the King's chamberlain seeking an audience with His Majesty at the earliest opportunity. A messenger took the request immediately to the head of the palace guard. Afterwards Carl Manfred ate a meal, then sat in front of the fire, again reflecting on the past four months. A kaleidoscope of images, many dark and oppressive but some lighter and, of course, one that constantly recurred – Arabella Whitfield, the woman he now knew he loved but whom he had left behind in Paris – crowded his mind. He wondered what she would be doing in Paris. Was she still with his sister or already at the Palace of Versailles waiting to be bedded by King Louis? He cursed himself for not declaring his affections for her as Maria Louisa had urged him to do. There were so many missed opportunities and regrets in his life. Now there was another.

When he woke the next morning, he found a note had been pushed under his door while he slept. He was expected at the Palace of Sanssouci that afternoon at two o'clock. In preparation, Carl Manfred re-read his short account of his journey to England and the execution. He decided to amend what he had written.

The coach arrived in good time to take him to Sanssouci. Shortly after the appointed time, the King received him in his study.

"Colonel von Deppe, I wish to thank you for completing the task I asked you to do. I wanted a trusted witness to be in attendance and to ensure that my order was carried out. You discharged your role with great discretion. I expected nothing less from you, which is why I chose you above all others. While I have long valued your loyalty, it was necessary to put you to the test once again. You prevailed, as I hoped and indeed expected you to do."

Carl Manfred replied that he had been honoured to serve him but that he had not been alone. He wished to pay tribute to the man who had accompanied him but whose name he did not know. The King smiled but said nothing. Carl Manfred handed the King the leather case he had received from him so many months before.

"Your Majesty, here is my short report of what happened."

The King took the case and put it to one side unopened. Turning to Carl Manfred, he said, "Thank you for your great loyalty. The matter is resolved and we shall not speak of it again."

Carl Manfred wanted to ask why the King had sent him to England when his network of spies and assassins could have executed the condemned man without the need for his presence. But he knew that, even if he asked the question, he would not receive a satisfactory answer. He would have to be content with the explanation the King had given: that he had wanted him to be present to ensure that those he had asked to do his bidding had truly done so. Not even a king – perhaps least of all a king – can trust his servants. But more likely there was another, unfathomable reason in the inscrutable King's mind. He was unlikely ever to know his real motive.

The King was a puzzle. There was his deliberate and skilful public portrayal of himself to Prussians as the valiant, ascetic soldier king, defending their country from its adversaries, overcoming all odds to win decisive battles and crushing the ambitions of his foes. Beneath this persona was the very private Frederick, which only the close circle around him ever saw: enjoying the company of his dogs, eating good food, shedding his uniform – and being suddenly vindictive to his friends and close advisers by playing cruel practical jokes on them. It was this unpredictable behaviour that had lost him many friends in recent years, not least Voltaire. And then there were the impenetrable dark recesses of his mind into which no one could peer. Here amongst complicated wheels and cogs lay his deepest secrets and the demons that drove him forward.

Despite the King's increasingly vindictive behaviour, Carl Manfred continued to admire him for his still dazzling charm and brilliant mind, and for the warm personal friendship and trust he had shown Carl Manfred in the past. His loyalty to the King was of greater value than any sum of money. But that loyalty had now exacted a higher cost. He would never be able to forget that dreadful scene in the cellar in Norwich. Whether the killing in England, the settling of an old and bitter score that the King had obliged him to witness, would at last give King Frederick peace of mind Carl Manfred would never know. The matter was closed in their conversation on that day.

Although the King did not wish to speak of it again, Carl Manfred was indelibly stained with a man's cold-blooded murder. He would have to live with that for the rest of his life. And he would never forget the cellar in Paris and the staring eyes of George Whitfield before the pistol shot. But it had been necessary to protect the woman he now knew he deeply loved but had foolishly lost. She would be free in France to pursue a fresh life and would never know that she had become part of his inner being. Her image haunted him every moment of his day. It too would remain with him for the rest of his life, wherever he went.

Though it was a cold and overcast day, the King invited Carl Manfred to walk with him on the terrace, as he had on their last fateful meeting. He talked about what the season ahead held for the palace garden, about the further progress in the construction of the Neues Palais nearby, and he asked about the estate at Herzberg.

"One day," the King said, "I would like to return to Herzberg, to see for myself what more you have done to improve it. I enjoyed my last visit there. But before then there will be other matters for us to discuss. Your loyalty has proved how close I should have you at my side. But let us talk about that on another occasion."

After several more minutes walking side by side back and forth along the terrace, the King turned to Carl Manfred, indicating that their conversation was at an end. He drew a small, soft-leather pouch from his pocket and, handing it to Carl Manfred, said, "This is a small token from me to you in remembrance of our time together over many years and perhaps in recognition of times yet to come. It is fully deserved and I hope that you will wear it with pride."

The King smiled and turned. As he walked away, he called out, "I hope that she will come to sing for me soon."

Puzzled by this remark, Carl Manfred looked back. He saw that the King, hunched in his overcoat, had been joined at the far end of the terrace by a younger, well-dressed figure with hair tied back and wearing a fine tricorne. He thought for a moment he recognised the profile of the man beside the King. Could it be the stranger? Then the two disappeared from view.

Carl Manfred walked to the end of the terrace, and from there followed a footman to the front of the palace, where his carriage would be waiting. He looked back towards the palace once more, wondering whether he would indeed ever see the King again. Then he walked towards the waiting coach.

But it was not the one that had brought him to Sanssouci. The coach door bore the King's crest; the window blinds were drawn. His baggage, which he had left at the inn, was already in place at the back. The coachman said that he had received instructions to take him to his estate at Herzberg.

Carl Manfred opened the coach door and stepped inside. It was hard to see in the interior gloom. Instead of the stranger who had dogged his heels over the past months, there sat a veiled woman. His heart stopped.

"It is I," said Arabella softly, as she raised her veil.

He sat beside her.

"My dearest Miss Whitfield, how is it that you are here?" he said in joy and astonishment.

"That is a long story, Herr von Deppe," she replied. "Let us speak of it later." She placed her hand in his and whispered, "I love you with all my being."

As the coach slowly turned away from the palace he kissed her hand.

"I love you, Miss Whitfield. I have done so since I first saw you. And then I let you go. But now you are with me. I wish you to stay at my side."

"I will never leave you, never let you go," she replied.

She put her arm through his and he held her hand tightly. His loneliness was at an end. Her face was radiant with joy.

Sitting back, Carl Manfred remembered the small pouch the King had given him. He pulled it from his coat pocket and opened it. There inside was the insignia of the rank of Count. He showed it to Arabella.

"Richly deserved, my dearest Count von Deppe," Arabella replied, as once again she and he tightly clasped hands.

They sat back as the coach sped on its way to Herzberg.

The next day – cold but sunlit – Carl Manfred took Arabella round the garden at Herzberg. She had passed a sleepless night in her bedroom. Now, as they walked together, side by side, she decided that, however painful the truth, it was necessary for her to confess to Carl Manfred what she had done in London and to reveal the identity of the woman behind the mask. She had to tell him because he would discover on their wedding night that she was blemished. Arabella asked Carl Manfred to sit with her for a few minutes on a bench in a shaft of winter sunlight. He looked at her and noticed how pale she had become.

"Miss Whitfield, if you are cold, we should go back to the house without delay."

"Please, Herr von Deppe, I would prefer to sit here and share with you a secret that may destroy your love for me."

"Dear Miss Whitfield, what are you saying? Nothing could come between us!"

"Herr von Deppe, please let me explain. A year ago I ran away from my home because my father demanded I should marry a man I knew I could not love. I refused many times. He would not desist and one day early last year he struck me."

"How cruel of your father!" Carl Manfred interjected.

"You must let me finish," insisted Arabella. "I ran away to London to seek help from friends. But one particular woman – I do not know her name – in the house of the second person I turned to for help, betrayed me by giving me the address of a lady whom she said would give me refuge. I soon realised that the house where I had sought shelter was one that provided comfort to men. Rather than return home and compromise my belief that I should be free to marry a man of my own choosing, I compromised my self-respect and principles. I allowed myself to become used. To hide my identity – and my shame – the lady of the house gave me a mask to conceal my face and the pseudonym of Antoinette Badeau. The weeks and months that followed were the saddest of my life so far. My father was searching for me, I could not seek refuge in my mother's arms, but I needed shelter in London. I deluded myself that I had taken the right decision. It was only when I went to hear the music of the young Mr Mozart that I realised I had to escape and rediscover my moral principles.

"As I was planning how to find the means to do so, I was passed from the house in Mayfair where I had first found shelter to another. That was the house in which you came to stay. I was instructed, when you arrived, to go to your room and comfort you. I confess that it was me, posing as Antoinette Badeau, who came to your room on the first night. But it was me, Arabella Whitfield, whom you held in your arms on that second night.

"I was obliged to be with other men for many months. I am not chaste. I am soiled. By definition I am a whore and therefore deeply unworthy of you. Those who came to my bed were men I found repulsive. But the night I first came to you I experienced an inner release, a joy, I had not experienced before. That same feeling of joy overwhelmed me even more greatly the next night. I had never loved a man before you. When we travelled from Norwich I could not stop recalling the physical comfort and security you had given me. It was your kindness, the way you held my hand and the protection you gave me in the face of great danger, that made me realise I was falling in love with you. My love for you intensified during the time we were together in Paris. And when you left I was heartbroken. I had to find you by whatever means and whatever the danger to declare my profound love for you. I do so again without reservation.

"But I realised last night that it was foolish to hide the truth of my past from you, to delude myself that we can be together. I realised I could not deceive you. I had to disclose the innermost secrets of my life. I have now revealed all to you. I do not seek your mercy, but your understanding of the predicament in which I stupidly put myself. I wanted to find true happiness in my life. I have done so, but at great cost. But we cannot unpick the decisions we make in life.

"I have concluded that, as a whore, I have no right to share your life here at Herzberg. To think I could do so was a grave mistake. You deserve better. My past deserves worse. I have therefore decided that I must leave you. I do not know what will become of me. But I will leave this place of tranquillity with the knowledge of your profound love. I will never forget you."

With that Arabella withdrew her hand from his and stood up to leave. Carl Manfred seized her arm and asked her to sit beside him once more.

"Dearest Arabella – and I insist on abandoning all formality to use that name – I will not let you leave Herzberg. I do not mean that I intend to keep you here by force but to do all within my power to persuade you to stay of your own free will.

"We are what we are in life. We are all beset by profound difficulties and impossible situations not of our making. We see things in life that we could never have imagined. We are sometimes forced to undertake appalling and unjust actions against our will. You spoke of betrayal in London and of actions you were forced to take because of the cruelty of others. I have been a soldier and there are many deeds I have committed in my life that I have come deeply to regret and indeed abhor. There are some things I have done of which I am deeply ashamed. I have also witnessed deeds of gross inhumanity by others where I did not intervene as perhaps I should have done. But however much we may be overwhelmed by what we have seen and by our guilt, we must try hard not to allow the past to stand in the way of our future happiness. The past must become the past. The agonies of life are painful enough. We must not make them worse by unending remorse. We have to look to the future.

"I love you deeply. That moment when you looked at me across the room in Paris as you were singing made me realise how much you had entered my heart. The way you sang seduced me. But I stubbornly rejected any notion that we could be happy together.

You are young, beautiful and magical. I admire your beliefs and your commitment to personal liberty and your willingness to suffer for them. I saw that when you allowed us to bind and seal you in that dreadful box. In Paris I considered myself too old to give you the life I believed you deserved and to reward your faith in me to keep you alive. I ran away, frightened of the future and locked in the past.

"Dearest Arabella, you are no whore, nor could you ever be. You are the purest angel from heaven, as I first saw when you descended the staircase in Maria Louisa's house. You are truly an incarnation of all that is unstained. So you see, you cannot leave me or Herzberg. You must stay. I wish us to be joined together and to enjoy our love in all of its manifestations, including the renewed coming together of our bodies."

He stood up and took Arabella's hands in his. She rose, grasping his hands tightly.

Looking searchingly into her eyes Carl Manfred said, "Dearest Arabella, I am deeply in love with you. Under this proud tree on my estate and in this shaft of winter sunlight, I pledge the rest of my life to your honour and happiness. I therefore ask you to marry me, to be at my side until the end of time. If you were to leave I would only follow you."

Arabella, tearful but her face full of happiness, paused and then replied, "I will, Carl Manfred von Deppe. And I thank you with all my heart for your forgiveness."

"There is nothing to forgive," he replied.

They kissed in the sunlight and embraced each other. Then they slowly walked back towards the house, arm in arm, so that Carl Manfred could announce with great pleasure that Herzberg would shortly have a new mistress.

A month later Arabella returned, with Carl Manfred, to Potsdam, where she sang about spring to His Majesty King Frederick in the Sanssouci palace. They travelled on to Berlin to be married on Tuesday, 18 March 1766, in the chapel of the Royal Palace in the presence of Protestant and Catholic priests. Bringing her daughter, Marie-Aurore, with her, Maria Louisa travelled from Paris to be present. She was overjoyed to see her brother so happy. Beside her was Arabella's mother, Lady Whitfield, who had also come from

Paris, with the Comtesse de Caullery, proud that her daughter had found the happiness she sought in an illustrious marriage.

At Arabella's strong insistence, Waldemar Drescher emerged briefly from the shadows to present her at the altar, though few knew who he was. Arabella thus became Arabella, Countess von Deppe, and mistress of the Herzberg estate.

EPILOGUE

Some weeks after their return home, Carl Manfred and Arabella hosted a glittering musical evening, of which the high point was the performance of Georg Philipp Telemann's *Saget der Tochter Zion: Siehe dein Heil*, in which Arabella sang to her husband and her other guests alongside her music teacher, Herr Kunzl, specially invited for the occasion.

She and Carl Manfred then took to the floor for a Polish dance and a galliard by the German composer, Christoph Demantius. As a student, Carl Manfred had heard his music performed at Freiberg and subsequently received a copy of the score of several secular pieces. He had accepted Arabella's challenge to learn the steps and thus lead his guests as they danced in celebration.

Much later that evening, Carl Manfred and Arabella took leave of their guests and retired to the master bedroom, turning the key to exclude the world outside. As she looked round the room, Arabella thought it impossible she could feel happier, safer or more loved.

In pride of place was a seventeenth-century four-poster bed, complete with heavy, blue and gold brocade curtains. It was a gift from Maria Louisa and her husband. Above the bed was a large, sixteenth-century tapestry of the Triumph of Charity, depicting her surrounded by biblical episodes and holding a heart in one hand while pointing with the other to the sun. Across the top were the words: "He who shows strength of heart in the face of danger receives Salvation as a reward." On the wall facing the bed, between the two large windows overlooking the garden, was a smaller, late sixteenth-century tapestry showing the Triumph of a barely clothed Dawn over darkness. Both tapestries were the gift of Lady Whitfield and, of course, her husband.

Opposite the fireplace was a large, baroque wall mirror supported by amorini, with smaller amorini holding candles. Beneath was a small but elaborate dressing table, given to them by General and Madame de la Rivière. Both were gifts to remind Arabella of Paris.

Over the fireplace was a portrait of Arabella, which Carl Manfred had quickly commissioned. On the mantelpiece was a medieval painted figure of St Florian, bought by Carl Manfred for Arabella to remind her of the one she said she had so admired at Meltwater and to protect her new home.

Arabella's gaze lingered on the crest of the von Deppe family, fixed above the end of the bed and borne by two large, magnificently carved wooden amorini. Then her eyes fell to the bedside table, on which lay her music book, tied in new ribbon.

They were now alone, standing in front of the fire, not speaking, just listening to the crackling of the wood. Carl Manfred sipped a glass of wine as he pondered all that had happened to him. He wore a rich-red dressing gown over his simple white nightshirt. Arabella wore a white silk nightgown beneath a deep-blue velvet cloak, held across her shoulders by a gold clasp, her face encompassed by its hood.

The moment had come. Arabella reached beneath the bed for the elaborate box to which she had clung over the past months. She opened it, removed Antoinette Badeau's mask and asked Carl Manfred to cast it into the flames. For a moment he let it lie in his hands. It brought back the memory of the masked woman. He then slowly placed it on the fire. The mask burned with intensity. Its gilded decoration melted in the heat and rivulets of liquid gold trickled and hissed between the glowing logs below. Then it became merely an ember. Antoinette had gone; only Arabella remained.

She then thrust the box that had contained the mask into the fire. At first it burned slowly and for a brief moment an intense smell of rich perfume hung in the air. Carl Manfred silently recalled the fragrance the masked woman had left on his pillow in London. Suddenly the box burst into flame. The lid began to shrivel in the intense heat of the fire. Then there was another burst as the pages of her intermittent diary, which she had removed from her music book and put in the box, caught alight. Her secret thoughts – of her despair and her hopes – vanished into ash. All that was left was the sheet of paper on which she had written the words in her bedroom shortly before her departure from Meltwater. So were erased Arabella's painful memories of Mayfair and of her long and perilous journey.

Carl Manfred drew close to him the woman who had made love to him so sensuously in London and kissed her tenderly as she placed her hands in his.

"I am a soldier and not good with words. I have learnt, because of what I have seen on the battlefield, to disguise my emotions. But I want you to know that, before I left for England, I was resigned to living alone for the rest of my life. Then I saw you for the first time – on that cold early morning we left London. Even through your veil, I glimpsed your sad but beautiful face, and I was touched by the way you briefly glanced at me. Later, the more we spoke the more it became clear to me that you were different from any other woman I had ever met. In Paris I knew I had fallen in love with you, but decided you were beyond my reach. By becoming my wife you have made me deeply happy – at ease, untroubled for the first time in my life. I dedicate what is left of it to you. My darling wife, my darling Arabella, I place my very being into your hands."

He drew her more tightly against him.

"My dearest loving Carl, you embody all that I believe love to be. I lost my way after leaving Meltwater. I travelled through a deep dark valley. Were it not for you I would still be there. I am at last safe. You have my life and my love in your hands. Carl, possess me."

He kissed her.

"*Déshabille-moi*," Arabella whispered. "Undress me."

She lowered the hood of her cloak, kissed him again and then untied the ribbon to let her hair fall onto her shoulders.

Carl Manfred tenderly unfastened the clasp at her neck holding the deep-blue cloak in place. It slid slowly down her body to the floor. He then began to undo the delicate white ribbons down the front of her gown. Arabella began to tremble, not from fear but expectation. This intense moment was what she had always imagined.

"*Vite*, my darling, quickly," she urged him.

When the last ribbon was loosened Carl Manfred opened the gown, gently removed it from her shoulders and let it cascade in folds around her feet. She stood before him unclothed, her slim body illuminated only by the firelight.

She then undressed him. He kissed her breasts before taking her in his arms and carrying her to their marriage bed. He laid her gently down and after drawing the brocaded curtain around them to seal their private world of profound and lasting pleasure, he tightly embraced the lithe, warm, sensuous and sculpted body of his beautiful young wife. They took each other to become one.

* * * * *

Maria Louisa returned to Paris with her child to be reunited with her husband, Etienne. She was deeply sorry to leave her "Dearest Arabella" but pleased that Herzberg had been reborn. She pledged to return in the summer months with her husband and Marie-Aurore. Herzberg would later become Marie-Aurore's refuge during the French Revolution's Terror.

* * * * *

Lady Whitfield returned to England several weeks later.

In a letter sent from Paris in advance of her arrival at Meltwater, she told her husband that she had witnessed, in Berlin, the marriage of their daughter to a tall and gracious former soldier and now a much-trusted adviser to His Majesty King Frederick. She had great pleasure in telling him that Arabella had become the Countess von Deppe and mistress of the large estate of Herzberg. She reminded Sir Robert that, if George did not reappear, Arabella would become heir to his title and lands.

On her return, Lady Whitfield became an invigorated mistress of Meltwater and a renowned social figure in the county of Norfolk until her sudden death seven years later. During those seven years Meltwater continued to witness the changing seasons and to prosper, but the house greatly missed its young spirit. The staff still hoped that Arabella would one day return.

Sir Robert paid a heavy price for what he had done to Arabella. He had lost his daughter's love and her presence at Meltwater. His son had disappeared without trace. He made no more than three visits a year to Meltwater. They were solely designed to ensure that those who managed the estate continued to produce the income needed to sustain his and Lady Whitfield's elegant, expensive – and separate – lifestyles. When he visited he slept alone at the far end of the corridor from his wife's bedroom. He did not become the Member of Parliament for Freshchester. Instead he divided his time between his Westminster town house and Lady Barbara Ward's large house in Chelsea, where in the summer of 1766 she gave birth to an illegitimate son, who received the name George Robert Whitfield. Divorce for the Whitfields remained a distant prospect. Lady Whitfield saw to that. But the birth of the illegitimate Whitfield boy had sown fresh seeds of disharmony that would come to undermine Meltwater. After Lady Whitfield's death, Sir Robert married Lady Barbara.

The whereabouts of the first George Whitfield remained a mystery. The body in the River Seine turned out not to be his. Missing, presumed dead, he was mourned by his father and began to fade from his mother's memory.

* * * * *

Waldemar Drescher returned to the shadows. He burnt the two documents that Carl Manfred had conveyed to London, having recovered them from Bolton's pouch, which he had found on Gaillard's body. He returned the precious lock of von Katte's hair to the King. His Majesty continued to plot to extend Prussia's borders.

* * * * *

The head of Thomas Wolff was not found for another two hundred years, when the grounds of that brooding edifice in Norwich were dug up to make way for new houses. It was put in store at Norwich Museum. The headless body fished from the

River Wensum was buried in an unmarked grave of which there is now no trace. The identity of the body was never established, as despite the oilcloth wrapping the note John Bolton left in the pocket was too sodden to read.

* * * * *

Auguste Gaillard's body remained undisturbed in its unmarked grave – amongst the trees half a day's ride from Magdeburg – until after the Second World War.

An unsung agent of the French King, he had overreached himself through greed and lack of moral principle. When it became clear to his coffee-house patrons in London that he would not be returning, they took their custom elsewhere and the premises became instead a purveyor of books. When Lady Whitfield heard from Arabella of his demise, she smiled. The secret of the identity of Arabella's real father would go with her to the grave.

* * * * *

Philippe Robinet eventually reached Herzberg to seek employment in charge of the stable. But no sooner had he arrived than he was arrested for entering Prussia on forged papers and placed in the custody of the King's spymaster for further examination.

* * * * *

John Bolton's body remained undisturbed until 1935 when it was disinterred by the building of an autobahn.

* * * * *

Mrs Rathbone continued to search for Antoinette Badeau and sought a summons at Bow Street Magistrates Court for her arrest on the grounds of the theft of clothes that belonged to her. But Antoinette Badeau had disappeared, presumably returned to France, and the arrest warrant was never served.

Mrs Hallam died of consumption.

*****

As for the portrait of Carl Manfred, after its brief appearance in the drawing room at Meltwater it was returned later by mysterious means to the gallery at Herzberg. Alongside it would soon hang a painting of the new Count and Countess.

*****

Before her departure from Herzberg, Lady Whitfield promised Arabella that on her way back to Paris she would stop at the convent to inform the Mother Superior that her daughter had safely reached her destination, and to make a generous offering. Arabella asked her mother to give the Mother Superior an envelope bearing the von Deppe crest in which she had placed a small white feather she had found in the garden at Herzberg, and a letter.

> *Dear Mother Superior,*
>
> *I send you my warmest greetings.*
>
> *I wish to thank you and the sisters for your great kindness during my short stay in your protection as I contemplated the next stage of an unknown road to the east. You cared for me at a time of great personal anguish in my life as a consequence of painful and degrading experiences I would never wish to repeat. You encouraged me not to give up but to press on regardless of what might lie ahead and at whatever cost. I followed your advice. With your intercessions and God's mercies, I arrived safely at the end of a long and sometimes difficult journey.*
>
> *I found this small and outwardly insignificant feather while walking in the garden at Herzberg this spring, following my marriage to Count von Deppe. Its discovery was for me a deeply personal reminder of your words on the day I left your care. You said you would pray to our Lord that I should, in the words of Hildegard, be carried to my destination like a feather on the breath of God. I earnestly believe that this small feather was a gentle reminder from Him to me that, despite my unworthiness, He did in his supreme charity convey me safely to my destiny. I have expressed my gratitude to the Lord and Our Lady daily*

ever since. I wish you to have this feather as a reminder of my stay and of me.

You and the sisters will always be in my prayers. If I am ever blessed with a daughter she will be called Hildegard, in honour of a unique and special woman. You encouraged me to admire her because, as a woman, she struggled against adversity and, with great determination, overcame the many obstacles placed in her way to become a beacon of hope for the weaker sex. Though we may be less strong than others, are often ignored and occasionally sorely abused, it is my strong belief that we still have the right to be treated as equal to men and to be respected as such.

I have found deep happiness with a man who regards me as his loving equal. But my happiness will never cause me to close my eyes to the continuing disadvantage of others. Nor will it stop me doing what I can during the remainder of my life to achieve greater understanding of the contribution women can make to the freeing of the human spirit.

Your most devoted servant,
Arabella von Deppe

* * * * *

In 1792 Mary Wollstonecraft published *A Vindication of the Rights of Woman.* Its strong advocacy that women deserved the same fundamental rights as men conveyed eloquently the very sentiments that Arabella had expressed passionately to her mother at Mrs Willoughby's lodgings in Norwich in December 1765; sentiments that had caused her to pursue the fulfilment of her ideals despite much pain and degradation.

* * * * *

Although summer arrived early, it was not long before dark and ominous shadows were cast over Prussia. As they grew darker, a letter from the King arrived at Herzberg. There was no escape from its disturbing contents. But this time Carl Manfred von Deppe was able to share them with his beloved and trusted Arabella.

* * * * *

And what happened to Arabella's music book, you might ask?

King Frederick, generally regarded by those around him as a spiteful old curmudgeon, was so moved by Arabella's singing at his beloved Sanssouci Palace that he presented her with a new, rich-blue, leather-bound music book, bearing the gold embossed arms of the Prussian kingdom, in which were transcriptions of some of his own flute compositions and several original sheets of music that Johann Sebastian Bach had presented to him all those years ago in 1747 at the same palace.

Inside the cover of the book the King had written in his distinctive scrawled handwriting:

> *To the Countess von Deppe, in admiration and deep appreciation for cheering an old man's heart at the end of a long winter.*
> *Frederick*
> *King of Prussia*

On receipt of this unique gift, Arabella decided that she would hand to her mother as a keepsake the music book she had brought from Meltwater all the way to Herzberg. The book had been such a comfort during her long and often painful journey from Norfolk to London to Paris and then to Potsdam. It was difficult to let it go but Arabella knew that her future now lay with her husband's in Prussia. Her old music book belonged to the past, while the King's music book represented a new beginning. Besides, her mother was deeply upset to leave her daughter with whom she had shared so much of her life. It was therefore important that she should have a reminder of their time together at Meltwater.

So on the morning of Lady Whitfield's departure from Herzberg, Arabella handed the brown leather music book to her mother. But before doing so she removed the sheet of paper that the Mother Superior had given her and placed it in her new book. Arabella wanted Hildegard's song to be a constant daily reminder of what she had achieved and what more she wished to do. She also removed the crumpled, stained map, given to her by Maria Louisa before she left Paris earlier in the year, on which she had traced her long, arduous and dangerous journey. She wished to keep it as a reminder of what she had done to find the genuine love and respect she had sought so keenly. She had found it not at Meltwater but at Herzberg.

"Dearest Mama," she said, her eyes filling with tears, "it is sad that we have to part. But my destiny is with my husband in the plains and forests of Prussia. I love him deeply and together we will ensure that Herzberg flourishes. You must return to Meltwater to ensure that its future is safe in your hands. I am certain that one day we will meet again – here or in England – but until then I wish you to have my music book as a personal and special reminder of the many happy moments we had together at the keyboard. When you play the harpsichord at Meltwater please think of me. You will be much in my daily thoughts here at Herzberg."

She handed the book to her mother. Lady Whitfield took it but was overcome by tears. She hugged her daughter one last time and then, holding the book tightly to her breast, walked to the coach to begin her journey back to Paris and England. Lady Whitfield waved as the coach turned away from the house. Arabella waved in return. Mother and daughter were never to see each other again.

Lady Whitfield kept the music book close to her throughout the rest of her life. On her unexpected death in 1773, after catching a severe chill during a bitter winter in Norfolk, Sir Robert gathered up his late wife's most personal belongings and correspondence. He put them into two large wooden trunks, which he asked the staff to place in a locked room in the attic at Meltwater, the key to which he kept in his desk drawer. In the second of the two trunks lay Arabella's treasured music book, which Sir Robert had found it too painful to open. The wound he still believed his daughter had unjustly inflicted on him remained too sore.

Much later in Meltwater's ownership, Robert Whitfield – who was the son of George Whitfield, Sir Robert's son by Lady Barbara Ward – went into the attic and discovered the locked room. Eventually finding the key in a cloth drawstring bag of displaced oddments, he opened the door and broke the padlocks on the two trunks. He soon found the music book and took it downstairs. That evening and the evening after, he and his wife, Emily, carefully leafed through the pages of music written out nearly a hundred years before. Emily played some of the melodies on the piano, which had replaced the harpsichord in the drawing room.

A month later Robert Whitfield sat down at his club in London and wrote to the Secretary of State at the Foreign Office, Lord Clarendon, asking for a passport as soon as possible to enable him and his family to travel on the Continent to retrace the steps of a member of the Whitfield family two generations before. The passport was granted and so Robert Whitfield and his family left Dover on that October morning in 1853 in search of the story of Arabella Whitfield.

It was 159 years later that the auctioneer banged his gavel twice to record that the music book had been sold for a record price to an anonymous bidder, together with the passport.

The End

AFTERWORD

Since completing *The Music Book*, I have established, with the help of experts in Berlin, the real identity of the man in the picture that I described at the start of the novel and to whom I gave the fictional name of Carl Manfred von Deppe – the man who married Arabella Whitfield and who helped to found an equally fictional Anglo-Prussian family.

The sitter's real name is Wilhelm Rudolf Daniel Ludwig Philipp von Gall, born in 1734 near Kirchhain, the third of eight children. In 1768, at the age of thirty-four, he married Albertine Juliane von Curti, ten years younger.

Wilhelm von Gall was an army officer: first a colonel and later a brigadier general. He fought first in the Seven Years War and later – from 1776 until 1781 – led his Hesse regiment, with various controversial ups and downs, alongside British forces firstly in Canada and then during the American War of Independence. On his return to Hesse, he had an equally controversial career, culminating in his appointment as Marshal of the Court of the Elector William the First. The painting in my possession shows him in a red coat, the uniform of Marshal of the Elector's Court. On von Gall's death the Elector described him, perhaps unjustly, as "the most stupid of all men".

The emergence of the sitter's real name presented me with a dilemma. Should I rewrite the story to fit – in a more biographical way – the facts that had come to light? But to do so would mean losing the fictional connection with Frederick the Great and expunging the character of the feisty and beautiful Arabella Whitfield, replacing her with Albertine Juliane, about whom little is known. Or should I leave the story as I had written it?

After careful reflection, I decided on the latter course. Having "lived" with them for over two years, I would have found it too painful to lose Arabella, Carl Manfred and King Frederick from the narrative. Nonetheless, von Gall's military career and his evident character flaws have provided a rich vein of material and ideas for the sequel to *The Music Book*. This will address what happened to Carl Manfred and Arabella after their marriage. Could he have gone to America as von Gall did or did King Frederick have other plans in mind – such as in the east to which Prussia always looked? There has been much to ponder.

Finally, just a few weeks ago, a German art expert living in Potsdam wrote to tell me that he believed the painter of the picture of Wilhelm von Gall to be Anton Wilhelm Tischbein. He was born in 1730 in Haina, the youngest of five sons of a master baker. Each son became a painter, including the important and most well-known Johann Heinrich Tischbein the Elder. Taught by another brother, Johann Valentin, Anton Wilhelm eventually moved to Hanau where he remained until his death in 1804, as painter to the Court of Prince William. Known as the Hanauer Tischbein, he painted not only the family members of his royal masters but also other wealthy patrons, including in Frankfurt.

If you have enjoyed *The Music Book*, I invite you to read the subsequent story. It will stretch through the remainder of the eighteenth century, through the Napoleonic Wars to the First World War, when the pressure of divided loyalties will finally tear apart the two families created by Carl Manfred von Deppe and Arabella Whitfield. The story will be told in two further volumes, with planned publication dates of 2016 and 2018.

Edward Glover
Norfolk
March 2014

ABOUT THE AUTHOR

Edward Glover was born in London in 1943. After gaining a history degree followed by an MPhil at Birkbeck College, London University, he embarked on a career in the British diplomatic service, during which his overseas postings included Washington DC, Berlin, Brussels and the Caribbean. He subsequently advised on foreign ministry reform in post-invasion Iraq, Kosovo and Sierra Leone. For seven years he headed a one-million-acre rainforest-conservation project in South America, on behalf of the Commonwealth Secretariat and the Guyana Government.

With an interest in 16th- and 18th-century history, baroque music and 18th-century art, Edward was encouraged by the purchase of two paintings and a passport to try his hand at writing historical fiction.

Edward and his wife, former Foreign & Commonwealth Office lawyer and leading international human rights adviser Dame Audrey Glover, now live in Norfolk, a place that gives him further inspiration for his writing. Edward sits on the board of trustees for Size of Wales and is a director of the Foreign & Commonwealth Office Association, an associate fellow of the University of Warwick's Yesu Persaud Centre for Caribbean Studies and a board member of The King's Lynn Preservation Trust.

When he isn't writing, Edward is an avid tennis player and – at the age of 71 – completed the 2014 London Marathon, raising almost £7,000 for Ambitious about Autism.